MISS GATHERCOLE'S GIRLS

A captivating historical family saga

JUDY GARDINER

JOFFE BOOKS

Joffe Books, London
www.joffebooks.com

First published in Great Britain in 1984

This paperback edition was first published in
Great Britain in 2023

Cover art by Jarmila Takač

ISBN: 978-1-80405-982-1

CHAPTER ONE

Because the birth of Jessica Marlow's child had been a strenuous and protracted affair, it seemed pleasingly appropriate that the cessation of suffering should coincide with the ringing of London's church bells in celebration of the relief of Mafeking. The year was 1900, Victoria was on the throne and the Marlows had been married for ten years.

'I want her christened Cassandra,' Jessica said, gazing at the crumpled hobgoblin face lying upturned in the crook of her arm. The eyes were no more than thin slits and the hair was still slightly damp. 'I like it because it's from the classics.'

'Oh, my.' The nurse fussed about with the small garments hung to warm on the bedroom fireguard. She had been on her feet for many hours, inciting, cajoling, running up and down stairs, and she felt very tired. More tired and with more justification, it seemed to her, than the woman in the bed.

'And I want her to be somebody in life. Not just ordinary like the rest of us.'

'Nobody's ordinary if you look underneath, dearie.'

'Yes, I know, but just because my daughter's a girl I don't want everybody taking it for granted that she'll simply get married and do housework like the rest of us while the men have all the fun.'

'Lord Roberts is a wonderful man, dearie, and I don't expect he's having much fun fighting all them wicked Boers.'

'But he's winning, isn't he? And that's what matters.' Jessica traced the faint outline of the baby's eyebrows with her forefinger. 'If there's another war after this one, I don't see why girls shouldn't go off and fight in it too, if they want to.'

The nurse looked shocked. 'Fancy saying that when you've just received a precious gift of life from your Maker!'

'I know, but . . . Do you think she's going to look like me, nurse?'

'Hard to say. But I don't doubt she'll turn out a nice mixture of you and your hubby.'

With a crackle of starched apron she approached the bed and scooped the baby from Jessica's arms. She visualised herself lying back on the pillows with legs outstretched and ankles crossed; with a cup of tea on the bedside table and the small of her back cosseted by a feather cushion; they could do what they liked with the baby. Nevertheless she laid it with practised hands in the muslin-draped cot and tucked the covers in securely.

'And you must take a nap too, madam, after all that hard work.'

Madam now, not dearie. The sweaty drama that had made them more intimate even than husband and wife had ended, leaving them with nothing deeper than the old prosaic relationship between employer and employee.

As the Marlows were not well off the nurse was only a daily one, and at six o'clock she was waiting downstairs in the parlour for Mr Marlow to return from his office so that she could officially hand over responsibility for the night. Weariness throbbed in her like toothache and she sat with her buttoned boots propped defiantly on the horsehair couch. The parlour was small and overcrowded, with a patch of damp coming through the wallpaper and moth holes in the carpet, but the pleated fan of red paper in the empty grate gave a splash of colour and elderly relations stared at her from silver frames. Lugubriously the nurse stared back.

Lulled by the creaking of her stays she drifted on the edge of sleep until the rattle of a key in the front door lock announced the arrival of Mr Marlow. Gliding swiftly to her feet she straightened her bonnet and went out to meet him in the hall.

'A little girl, sir,' she said. 'A dear little girl, and her and her mama are doing nicely.'

She waited, half-anticipating some sign of disappointment at the lack of a son. Most men preferred sons, particularly when it was the first and had only been achieved after years of waiting. But Gilbert Marlow hung up his bowler hat, smiled and said: 'Capital. And Mrs Marlow will be very pleased.'

'And you, sir?' The nurse hovered. 'Are you pleased it's a girl instead of a boy?'

'To be perfectly honest I don't anticipate being able to tell the difference at this stage. But whatever it is, I'm sure it will be very jolly to have.' He stood with his hand on the banister.

'That's nice to hear anyway, sir. I always like my fathers to be pleased.'

But the nurse went home puzzled by his reaction and made uneasy by some strange quality in his smile.

Gilbert went up to the front bedroom to meet his offspring and to congratulate his wife.

Having slept for several hours she was now sitting alert and poised on a rubber air-ring and seemed to be possessed of a new and remarkable vigour. Her eyes were sparkling, her plait of hair was coiled tidily on top of her head and her nightgown smelt of Sunlight soap and lavender water. Having associated childbirth with a lingering aftermath of weakness and wanness, her husband was relieved and gratified. He bent to kiss her brow.

'It's a girl and I want us to call her Cassandra,' she said. 'Go and look at her.'

He tiptoed over to the cot and gazed for a moment at the little creature muffled in flannel and lace, ribbon and rabbit wool.

'How very jolly,' he said.

'Cassandra's from the classics and I've been lying here making plans for her. I don't really mind which of them she chooses so long as she does something with her life. I want her to *be* somebody.'

'Yes, of course,' agreed Gilbert. 'It's very important.' He left the cot and stood staring down into the street.

'She'll probably be clever because you are—'

'So are you, dear.'

'No, I'm only practical. I hope she'll be nice-looking although looks aren't as important as brains, but most of all I want her to achieve something special. And I don't just mean a rich husband — what's all that noise going on?'

'People going up to the West End to celebrate Mafeking. They say Baden-Powell's safe and that the Queen will make a triumphal drive.'

'That's nice. As I was saying, if she gets rich — which would be something, wouldn't it? — I want her to do it through her own ability. Not through anybody else's.'

'Yes.'

He remained with his back to her, fiddling with his watch chain and looking down at the group of young men and girls giggling and shoving and waving Union Jacks. The Walham Green bells had stopped ringing but the joyful sound was still floating on the early summer air from neighbouring parishes: Fulham Road, Parsons Green, West Brompton and even Earls Court. The mood of excitement, like a crackling in the atmosphere, seemed to be increasing with the approach of nightfall.

'Gilbert—' There was a slight edge to Jessica's voice. 'Can you stop standing there wool-gathering for a minute and talk about your little girl?'

'I'm so sorry, dear.' He turned immediately, contrition in his smile.

'First of all, do you really like her name?'

'Yes, I like it very much.'

'It's from the classics.'

'I know. Cassandra was loved by Apollo and had the gift of prophecy.'

'Yes, well. But do you think it'll *suit* her?'

'Well, I suppose it isn't easy to tell at this stage, but I daresay it will.'

'And are you really pleased with her? I mean, are you *proud* that we've got a baby?' She shifted impatiently, and under the blankets the air-ring made a farting sound.

'It stands to reason that I'm pleased and proud,' he said. Then added: 'Do you want the chamber-pot?'

'That wasn't me. You see, I can't help being ambitious for her, Gilbert, but before we start expecting things from her, she's every right to expect a certain amount from us, hasn't she?'

'Naturally. Of course.'

'So I was wondering whether we couldn't . . . Well, whether it wouldn't be possible for you to . . .'

'To what, dear?'

His light blue eyes met hers, smiled, flickered, then went politely blank.

'To make it up with your father. Or if not that, to — to find better employment.'

'Clerking suits me very well.'

'But it doesn't pay much.'

'I think we manage quite nicely.'

'I do my best, I'm sure. But for all the hours you spend — you even bring work home in the evenings now — I think they could pay you a little more.'

'I'll raise the matter with them at the end of the month,' he promised.

'Because now we've got little Cassandra to think of—'

His eyes were still blank. Almost as if he didn't see her. Yet he smiled at her with the utmost sweetness.

'Oh, Gilbert . . .' she said, and the trailing silence which followed was heavy with yearnings unexpressed. Yearnings which were mostly pointing in Gilbert's direction.

Younger son of a north country spice merchant, he was intelligent, well educated, charming, good-looking and totally ineffectual. His first job after graduating was at his father's request in the family firm, but incompetence coupled with hay fever brought about by floating particles of nutmeg and cinnamon caused a swift retirement from the scene. He then tried teaching, switched to banking, then opened a domestic employment agency which lost money so disastrously that he and his young bride had to leave their four-bedroomed house in South Kensington and rent a cheap terraced one near the Smallpox Hospital in Walham Green. Wildly in love, Jessica was anxious but not dismayed. As a shop assistant's daughter (they met on top of a horse-drawn omnibus when Jessica's twopenny ticket blew away), she was well accustomed to the rigours of genteel poverty, but in those early wide-eyed days there was something beautiful about walking two miles to buy a leg of mutton at a knock-down price, and about turning shirt cuffs and darning socks and scrubbing the scullery floor because a charwoman had become an unnecessary expense. But it went on for such a long time. Quietly and with little sign of enthusiasm Gilbert tried stockbroking like his brother Harry, commercial travelling, importing ostrich feathers for the débutante market and managing a restaurant.

He abandoned them all, his explanations for doing so becoming a little more perfunctory on each occasion. It was when he left the restaurant — 'I don't care for the smell of cooking unless I feel hungry' — that the newly pregnant Jessica suddenly became exasperated. For the first time she called him a rotter and a blighter, a bad egg and a ne'er-do-well, then collapsed in a flood of tears and refused to be pacified. He went for a walk, and because the evening was mild kept on walking and spent the night on the Chelsea Embankment, thinking and watching the river, oblivious to the poor human wrecks who lay around him dead drunk on three penn'orth of gin.

He did a lot of intelligent, analytical thinking, but none of it solved the problem of how to earn a living in a way that was congenial. Everything he had tried so far seemed extraordinarily unreal; buying and selling, keeping records and accounts, teaching Euclid to the young or sneezing through a cloud of powdered cloves, all seemed of so little importance. And the people he worked with, whether waiters or ostrich feather packers, seemed equally inessential. It was as if he were seeing life through a dust-covered window.

Then three months before the birth of his daughter something strange happened. Unbidden and unsought, a name suddenly dropped into his mind like a letter through a letterbox. Captain Shovel. It was a name he thought he had never heard before. He dismissed it, but it refused to go away. Captain Shovel, Captain Shovel. Irritated, he sought to rid himself of it by tracing its probable origin. A boys' adventure story read many years ago, perhaps? A name from a newspaper column that had become inadvertently hooked to his mind like a burr on a sleeve, or a brand of horse liniment seen on an advertising hoarding? He asked Jessica if she had ever mentioned a Captain Shovel to him but she shook her head, equally mystified.

Instead of fading the name seemed to grow, pressing itself urgently on to his mind until he found himself writing it down on scraps of paper and then staring at them as if mesmerised. His present job in a solicitor's office was laborious but not arduous and he began to amuse himself by inventing a personality to fit the name.

Captain Gerald Shovel, dashing man-about-town and hero of the Peninsular War, or what about Captain Zachariah Shovel, sturdy patriarch and pillar of the Salvation Army? But like a seed fallen on unexpectedly fertile ground Captain Shovel began to grow of his own accord, and Gilbert discovered that Captain Sam Shovel, master of a coal-carrying tramp-steamer was his true designation. He began to see him more and more clearly, a broad-chested, big-bellied man balanced on neat haunches and hard strutting legs. He had a robust beard and strong yellow teeth, and when he was ashore lived next to a public house in Wapping High Street. He smoked black shag and drank ale laced with bootleg brandy and in spite of a roaring temper was unexpectedly kind to small animals.

His vividness increased, bringing with it a strengthening desire on the part of Gilbert to know more about him, to flesh out the details as it were. Captain Shovel was aged forty-five, was born of a Grimsby fisherman and a window-cleaner's daughter and at the age of twelve ran away from the snug stone cottage to sail before the mast. Cape Town, Montevideo and the screaming winds of Tierra del Fuego, then into the South Pacific where he came to manhood among Polynesian belles with flowers in their hair. He left behind him a brown-skinned son called Oho.

The story expanded, unrolling an endless length of picturesque narrative through Gilbert's head, and although in the early stages he made several determined attempts to suppress it and to substitute reality in its place he met with only partial success; so he gave up trying to ration the adventures of Captain Shovel to the twenty-five minutes' walk to and from his place of work and started jotting them down in a notebook hidden furtively among the wills and affidavits on his desk. He continued jotting at home, crouching up in the back bedroom while Jessica, sewing baby clothes down in the parlour, thought he was working on papers brought home from the office. Sometimes when he joined her for their bedtime cocoa he almost wondered who she was, and, although he meant to bring home a bunch of flowers for her on the day the baby was born, when the time came he clean forgot.

'Gilbert,' she repeated as he continued to stand motionless, seeing and yet not seeing, by the side of the bed. 'You're not keeping anything from me, are you?'

'Good gracious, dear,' he said. 'Why ever should you think that?'

If he had entertained the hope that the arrival of the baby would take precedence over the affairs of the imaginary Captain Shovel, the hope was not fulfilled. Captain Shovel had chosen that particular time to become involved in the illicit shipment of Stephen's ink to a small country not far from New Guinea where the inhabitants, ignorant of its correct use, mixed it with betel nut juice and became ecstatically drunk on the result. An English missionary of impeccable dreariness rumbled what was going on and denounced Captain Shovel to the appropriate authorities, and in planning the captain's escape from incarceration Gilbert forgot to register the baby's birth.

He also forgot it the next day, and on the day after that arrived panting at the registrar's office to find that it had already closed. On the fourth day he was successful. Or at least partly so, for, although he arrived home bearing the appropriate document, Jessica gave a piercing scream when she read it that brought the nurse running.

'Cassandra! Oh, my God, I told you Cassandra!'

'What have they put, then?'

'Cassica! They've gone and put *Cassica*!'

'Well, I expect we can soon put it right, dear . . .'

'No, you can't — I don't think you can!'

She sobbed, in fury at his incompetence and in pain at his sweet indifference, and the nurse drew the curtains and made her lie down flat because of upsetting her milk.

And Jessica was right. The registrar said that to make any alteration on a birth certificate was totally beyond his jurisdiction, even beyond that of the Senior Registrar at Somerset House, and added that if wrong names were issued to people on account of airy-fairiness on the part of those doing the naming it was nothing to do with him. So Cassica it was and Cassica it had to remain, but if in time Jessica grew to quite like her daughter's unusual praenomen she refused to admit it.

* * *

The little girl grew, passing from cherub chubbiness to live-wire leanness, and promised to be tall like her father. She played hopscotch, and bowled a hoop along Seagrave Road, and with Jessica's encouragement had learned to read the easier advertisements on the sides of omnibuses by the time she was five.

She had dark brown hair, but a fair skin like her father, and although her eyes were sometimes filled with a dreamy look they were hazel rather than light blue in colour. Jessica dressed her very neatly; blue serge in winter and Madras cotton in summer, and suspicious of the dreamy look started her on multiplication tables. She was a bright child who learned with pleasure as well as facility and Jessica mourned the lack of her company when she started school.

For by this time life had settled into a very dull rut in the Walham Green house. Gilbert had left the solicitor's office and gone to work as an accountant in a small brewery. The money was about the same, and so was his air of gentle absentmindedness; he treated both wife and daughter with the same affectionate courtesy but was as nonplussed when Jessica suggested a week's holiday at Broadstairs as he was when little Cassie asked him to play at being a wild bear.

And the liveliness was fading in Jessica and becoming replaced by a sharp asperity. In the early days love had made her struggle hard to emulate Gilbert in speech and manners so that he would never have cause to be ashamed supposing his family should ever express the desire to become better acquainted with her, and now refinement had become second nature. Strangely enough she seemed to cling to it with added fervour as her illusions regarding Gilbert finally faded, and she refused to allow Cassie to mix with the other children in the street because they dropped their aitches; as for their mothers, she passed them by with no more than a distant nod.

Occasionally the vicar called, and once a gratifyingly genteel lady asked if she would care to join a society devoted to the rescue of fallen women, but she declined. If women fell by the wayside it was their own lookout, and in any case it would cost money.

And money was by now the other preoccupation in Jessica's life. Driven to desperation by Gilbert's ineptitude both in the making and the managing of it, she had long ago suggested that he turn his weekly wage packet over to her, a suggestion received with equanimity on his part. So she gave him his lunch money plus a weekly half-sovereign for fares and expenses and kept the rest, hoarding it in her purse to pay the rent and the gas, the coal and the grocer, and striving to put a little on one side for clothes and boot repairs. There was never anything to spare, but they were never in debt, and the time came when she could pass the milliner's shop window without even being aware of the joyous flower-trimmed boaters on display.

By the time Cassie was ten Jessica had reached the age of forty, with pepper and salt hair and a brisk, disparaging sniff, and her expression only appeared to soften when her daughter entered the room. It softened, yet became mingled with a fierceness, a stern watchful pride that once prompted even Gilbert to enquire whether she wasn't perhaps being just a shade critical of the child.

'Critical?' She repeated the word so sharply that Gilbert flinched. 'Sometimes we have to be critical to be kind.'

'But she only said "what?"—'

'When she should have said 'beg your pardon'.'

'At least, she didn't say "eh?"' Gilbert said, attempting a joke. Which fell flat.

'It's all very well to make light of good manners when you were brought up in ignorance of there being any other sort,' Jessica said in a low, bitter voice. 'But here, where we have to live because it's all that our income allows, there are lots of other examples, most of them very bad ones, and if Cassie's to make anything of herself she's got to be taught what's right and what isn't. Starting with manners.'

'There are other things, too.'

'Yes. But they all start with saying 'beg your pardon' and not 'what'.'

Gilbert smiled, got up from his chair and walked out.

He returned in time for supper; poached eggs on toast followed by soda bread and pound cake, and Jessica passed him a cup of tea and said: 'By the way, I've made up my mind that I want her to go to St Etheldreda's.'

'St Etheldreda's, dear?'

'The High School for Girls.'

'Can we afford it on my pitiful wages?'

'No. But with the help of your family we can.'

Gilbert ate in silence and Jessica told Cassie to eat with her mouth closed.

'I can't. It isn't big enough.'

'Nonsense. Do as you're told.'

'She's going to have a proper education and a proper career,' Jessica continued. 'Sacrifices will have to be made because the most we can expect from your family is that they might pay the bare fees. We'll have to manage the books and the uniform and the train fares, and Cassie's going to repay us by working hard and getting a scholarship to a university. By the time she's ready to go they'll be letting more and more women in, and she'll get qualified like you did.'

'And it is to be hoped put it to better use?'

'You said that, not me.'

'Would you like that, Cassie?' Gilbert asked. 'Is that what you want?'

'Of course it's what she wants.'

'I was asking Cassie,' he said mildly.

'Yes, Father,' Cassie said.

So confronted by writing pad, pen and ink, and urged by Jessica to be polite but firm in his demand, Gilbert wrote to his father for the first time since marrying a girl beneath his station in life. He was not surprised when there was no reply, but some six months later he was informed by a solicitor's letter that the late John Harold Marlow of The Limes, Brindley Walk, Scarborough had bequeathed the sum of one thousand pounds to be used for his granddaughter's education.

Jessica cried. Then wiped her eyes and said that the money had got to be put in a savings bank where it would earn a little bit of interest until Cassie was ready to start at St Etheldreda's. Prodded by his wife, Gilbert wrote a filial note of condolence to his mother but received no acknowledgement.

Thus, at the age of twelve young Cassie became a High School girl, setting off each morning on the Metropolitan

& District Railway from Walham Green to Putney Bridge Station. To begin with Jessica accompanied her, and repeated the journey in the late afternoon, but as it was a ride of only three stops and Cassie showed every sign of being a level-headed and responsible child, she was eventually allowed to travel on her own. The uniform was dark grey flannel, with a wide-brimmed hat encompassed by a green-and-white striped hat band. They wore high-necked shirt blouses and men's ties and thick woollen stockings that itched, but unlike her first schoolfellows nobody laughed at her name.

It was a school which took the education of young women very seriously, and, with a quick mind now coupled to dutiful diligence, the young Cassie saw no reason why she should not fulfil her mother's dreams of success.

* * *

She was learning Latin and chemistry and playing lacrosse for the Junior School when the assassination of some obscure archduke somewhere precipitated the First World War. No one in Walham Green took it very seriously to begin with, but war fever quickened at the sight of brave young Tommies marching towards Victoria Station and hardened into hatred of the despicable Hun when the first casualty lists appeared.

'Will you have to go?' Jessica asked Gilbert.

'At forty-six I doubt whether I'd be much use to them.'

'No, I suppose not.'

Their relationship had now reached a point when it was difficult for her to judge whether she was relieved or disappointed. Having long been accustomed to his habitual vagueness she was no longer troubled by it. She expected little from him in either a material or an emotive sense and had reached a sort of contentment. At least he was unfailingly good-tempered, and the knowledge that his good temper resulted largely from the fact that he scarcely seemed to notice her, or his daughter or his home, wounded her no more. They had become equally insubstantial to one another, and when she and Cassie inadvertently witnessed a drunken man hitting his wife in the street, and Cassie said: 'Doesn't it make you realise what a *good* man Father is?', she agreed without reservation. He had been working at the brewery for longer than he had ever worked anywhere else, and in a sudden spirit of magnanimity she allowed him to take control of his own wage packet again and was quite touched when he continued to retain only his lunch money and a half-sovereign for contingencies. She became fond of him again because she didn't really need him. Now, it was Cassie who filled her life with hope.

As for Gilbert, he was happier than he had ever been in his life. Like someone in the continual grip of a fatal passion he had long since surrendered to the extraordinary compulsion of Captain Shovel. The random jottings on bits of paper had done nothing to assuage the irresistible obligation to explore the captain's world in greater and more meticulous detail and so he bought a threepenny exercise book, and after supper that evening told Jessica he had brought some urgent work home from the office. In the privacy of the back bedroom, he removed the exercise book from his attaché case, opened it at the first blank page and then unscrewed the cap from his fountain pen. He began to write without hesitation or premeditation, just letting the words that had for so long filled his head stream out on to the paper.

Samuel Augustus Shovel was born at twenty minutes to three on the morning of Friday 13 August 1889 . . .

He continued rapidly and without correction, and when the threepenny exercise book was filled, he bought another one. Then another, and another. And although the act of writing seemed in one way to restrain his preoccupation with the imaginary Captain Shovel, in other ways it merely stimulated it the more. He began to realise that Captain Shovel's birth was not the real beginning; the beginning began with the coming together of his parents, their childhoods, their own births. Then what about the parents' parents? The characters tumbled out of him, warm, rich and vivid, and all he had to do was to write them down and describe what they did in plain and simple English because there was no time to ponder the choice of words. He was at the heart of a huge and teeming new world, and the reason why he had always found work and family, and now even the war, so blankly unreal at last became clear. The only reality for him was that which was unreal.

It never occurred to him that he might be a novelist. Neither did it once cross his mind that it might be possible to make capital out of this strangely powerful and enduring daydream. He never once mentioned it to Jessica, much less asked her to read any of the exercise books but kept them hidden in the attaché case until there were so many that the lid wouldn't close any more.

Then he did an extraordinary thing. He gave his notice in at the brewery and rented a room off the Wandsworth Bridge Road for five shillings a week and there he continued to write between the hours of 9 a.m. and 5 p.m. from Monday to Friday, and on Saturdays from 9 a.m. until midday. The room was far enough from home for him to be sure of anonymity, yet not so far distant that he had to waste too much precious time in travelling. Other than the need for paper and pens and a hot meat pie at lunchtime, his requirements were practically nil, and every Friday night he continued to give Jessica a kindly little kiss on the cheek as he handed her the housekeeping money which he was now drawing from the sum set aside for Cassie's education.

And in the world outside people were queuing to see *Chu Chin Chow* while the boys in khaki were preparing to face the first battle of the Somme.

CHAPTER TWO

If Gilbert Marlow had a secret life, so at the age of sixteen had his daughter.

Hers began like a pain, a quietly yearning ache coupled with a feeling of lassitude that made her yawn over school textbooks and take elaborate precautions against being called upon to wipe the supper dishes while Jessica washed them.

'Cassie?'

No reply.

'Cassie, will you come and wipe up, please? *Cassie!*'

The quick pounding of feet that signifies the hunter determined to run its quarry to earth.

'I can't. I'm in the w.c.'

'What, *still?*'

'I've got a pain.'

'In that case you'd better come out and have a dose of cascara.'

Sitting on the cold lavatory seat Cassie brooded over her ghastly name. No one else was called Cassica, so why should she have to be? *(I didn't choose it,* her mother had said. *It was your father's doing.)* Cassica, cascara, cassock, casket — all the words associated with it were as boringly ghastly as Cassica itself. Cassica, Cassica, massacres brassica . . .

'Cassie, I'm waiting for you to come out and wipe up.'

'Why can't Father do it?'

'Your father's had a hard day. In any case, men don't wipe up.'

'I don't see why not,' muttered Cassie.

Neither do I, thought her mother. But there you are.

She waited at the foot of the stairs where the gaslight hissed and popped and after a moment or two Cassie slowly descended, one hand trailing down the banister rail.

'Have you really got a pain?'

'No, thank you. It's gone now.'

'Good. And I don't expect it'll come back again before this time tomorrow night.'

'Perhaps it's the wartime diet,' Cassie said plaintively, and drifted out to the scullery to find the tea towel.

'Done your homework?' The flash of work-reddened hands in hot water and soda crystals.

'Yes.'

'That's a good girl. What was it?'

'The failure of Pitt's constitutional reform.'

'Oh.' Jessica had heard of Pitt but couldn't exactly place him. Pride in the difficult things Cassie was learning eased the tired ache in her shoulders.

'Won't it be nice when you've finished all your exams and you've been to university like Father?'

'Ummm.'

'Don't forget that education's something nobody can ever take away from you. Having letters after your name will make all the hard work seem worthwhile and your father and I will be very proud of you.'

'Are you proud of me now?' Cassie shoved the balled tea towel into the interior of a jug and ground it round and round.

'Yes,' said Jessica. 'As far as you've gone.'

'Sometimes it feels as if it's been a jolly long way.'

'Never mind, only two more years at school,' encouraged Jessica, scrubbing at a saucepan.

Then Cassie placed the jug on the table, leaned back against the wall and said: 'Mother, I want to go into a munitions factory.'

'You want to *what*?' Aghast, Jessica stood with the dripping saucepan poised. 'What in heaven's name for?'

'To make munitions. I want to help the war effort. Oh, Mother, I've always dreamed about doing something practical and useful — after the war's over I could always go back to studying — but now's the time when—'

'Now's the time when you leave running the war to people who are older and wiser than you are—'

'You don't have to be old and wise to make bullets and things! You just stand there pulling levers and pressing knobs — Mrs Packer's daughter does it and she says it's ever so easy. And you get paid a lot of money.'

'I know Mrs Packer's daughter,' Jessica said grimly. 'She paints.'

'She does no such thing!'

'If you'll excuse me, she does. She puts red stuff on her lips.'

'Well, maybe — but, Mother, can I?'

Jessica rinsed the saucepan under the single brass tap that stood above the chipped earthenware sink. 'No,' she said. 'Your duty to your King and country is to finish your education. After that, we'll see.'

'But the war'll be over by then!'

'The way it's going,' retorted Jessica, 'you'll be a grandma before that happens.'

They said no more but remained tight-lipped with one another for the rest of the evening while, benevolent but oblivious, Gilbert sat cracking cobnuts and throwing the shells into the bright heart of the fire.

Although her daughter's request had shocked and alarmed the Jessica who had once declared that girls should be allowed to fight in wars if they wanted to, its overall effect had almost faded after a week, soothed by the knowledge that daughters of sixteen could do nothing without parental permission. But what for Cassie had begun as a mere spur-of-the-moment idea refused to be dismissed. *Oh, Mother, I've always dreamed about doing something practical and useful*, she had said, but this wasn't strictly true because she only started dreaming as she heard herself uttering the words.

She discovered that her simmering discontent at school was entirely due to frustrated patriotism. She loved good old England with an ardour that stung her eyes, and during her country's life-or-death struggle with the common foe it was monstrously unfair that she should be prevented by a mulish mother from doing her bit. She wrote to Lloyd George asking whether Jessica's refusal to let her work in a munition factory could be overruled by the National Coalition Government but the answer, via a secretary, was in the negative. She then wrote a long letter to the family of the late Lord Kitchener saying how deeply sorry she was that he had drowned, and one Wednesday morning played truant from school in order to gloat over the remains of a Zeppelin brought down over Barnes Common. Cheered by the knowledge that she had done something illicit, she spent the journey back to Walham Green picturing herself as a dangerous spy like Mata Hari.

Dreams of valour proliferated. Most of them involved Cassie as heroine, but a nasty situation arose when she told a particularly gullible girl at school that her mother, Lady Marlow, had earned a decoration during her tour of duty with the Artists' Rifles on the Western Front. The tale spread with fatal rapidity and one afternoon the school secretary, a little surprised at the modesty of her surroundings, knocked on the Marlows' front door and asked Jessica if her mistress was at home.

Blankly Jessica replied that she hadn't got one and became increasingly hot and bothered at being invited to lecture to the sixth form of St Etheldreda's on her experiences at the third battle of Ypres.

'How *could* you tell such awful, wicked lies?' she stormed at Cassie. 'I've always brought you up to know that telling lies is wrong and not only have you been doing that but you've been telling them about *me*! When that woman stood in here and went on about me taking secret messages between the lines and something about Auntie's trifles—'

'Artists' Rifles . . .'

'Don't interrupt. I didn't know where to look. I just wanted to hide my head in shame. And when she kept calling me Your Ladyship—'

'I'm sorry—'

'Sorry! That's a fine word and no mistake for all the damage you've done. I feel I'll never look the world in the face again—'

'Well, things are so jolly boring as they are—'

'*Boring*? Is that all you've got to complain about? And is that supposed to be a good excuse for telling lies? For making stupid stories up? Suppose we all did that? What then? Suppose your father spent all his time inventing things about other people instead of getting on with his proper work? We'd be in a fine old state then, wouldn't we?'

The questions came thick and fast and it was obvious that Cassie was not required to answer. So she stood in an attitude of humility, hands clasped behind her back, head bowed and lower lip caught between her teeth, and waited for the storm to subside.

She had another unpleasant interview to endure, this time with the headmistress of St Etheldreda's, which ended with a scathing comment on the quality of her term's work and the question of whether she could ever be regarded as potential university material.

'If we wish to place ourselves on the same footing as men, Cassica, we must be prepared to prove that we are not merely equal in ability, we are superior. Academic doors do not yield easily in the face of womanhood and it is only by proving ourselves worthy, not only in the scholarly but in the *mature* sense, that we may hope to be admitted to the groves of Academe.'

'Yes, Miss Higgins.'

'And taking all this into account I have instructed your form mistress to set you an hour's extra preparation each evening for the remainder of the term, with the emphasis on your weakest subjects. She has suggested that Latin is one of them, so you will prepare a translation of Book Three of Virgil's *Aeneid* and bring it to my study on the last morning of school.'

'Yes, Miss Higgins.'

Moaning came out of the cauldron and a voice fell on our ears: O Trojans, you men in endurance, this land that gave birth to your sires welcomes you back to her nourishing bust . . . The dry smell of old second-hand textbooks, the slow crunch of cartwheels outside the window and the voice of a rag-and-bone man raised in melancholy entreaty.

Yet the dreams of personal glory refused to fade, and it occurred to Cassie that only a ninny would ask permission to do something that was forbidden. The mature thing (if they had to harp on about maturity) was to do first and ask afterwards.

With this in mind she told Jessica that she was going to the public library and went instead to the branch of the British Red Cross that had been set up in the Fulham Road, and said that she had come to enrol as a VAD.

They eyed her suspiciously, white butterfly caps emblazoned with the blood-red cross tied down low over their foreheads.

'How old are you?'

'Eighteen.'

She looked it, standing very tall and erect in a grey flannel skirt, long woollen cardigan and her schoolgirl's pigtail tucked up beneath a floppy velvet tam-o'-shanter.

'Know anything about nursing?'

'Oh, yes.'

'Certificates?'

'Well, no. Not yet . . .'

They asked her what experience she had had and Cassie replied that she knew how to stop a nosebleed.

'How?'

'A cold key dropped down the back.'

'Down the back of what?' They kept very straight faces, but the gauzy butterfly caps seemed to quiver slightly.

'Down the back of the patient.'

'And what else?'

Cassie thought. Then thought some more.

'Ever dealt with a case of mustard gas?'

'No. As a matter of fact—'

'How about removing a shell splinter?'

'Well . . .'

'Sewing up a flesh wound, dressing an amputation, dealing with shell shock?'

'I take it,' the senior-looking one of them said, 'that you know how to administer last offices?'

It was the wet fag-end of yet another wartime summer and all of them had been bitterly marked by the work of patching broken bodies in field hospitals behind the lines, in readiness, as it happened, for the supreme horrors of Passchendaele. So there was irony, even a hint of malice in the fun they were having with this silly schoolgirl, and when they had finally wrung from her the admission that familiarity with the respiratory system of the earthworm was about all she had to offer in the technical sense, they let her go.

* * *

She then tried her father.

He was alone in the parlour, turning over the pages of the *Daily Mail* in a desultory fashion when she sat down opposite him, propped her chin in her cupped hand and said: 'Father, do I get my sense of urgency from you?'

He lowered the paper and gazed at her thoughtfully. 'I think it probably comes more from your mother.'

'Oh, Mother's the absolute opposite of urgent! Whenever I want to do anything, she says no I can't.'

'What sort of things do you want to do?'

'Well, for one thing I want to join the war. I want to help in some way.'

'Do you mean that you want to fight?'

'I wouldn't mind. I wouldn't mind anything so long as I wasn't just sitting messing about with learning.'

He continued to gaze at her with his strange light blue eyes while out of the clouds of vagueness came a memory of Jessica sitting very upright on a rubber air-ring and repeating what she had said to the nurse: *If there's another war I don't see why girls shouldn't go off and fight in it too, if they want to.*

It had struck him as strange at the time that any real-life people — let alone women — should wish deliberately to expose themselves to violence, and he realised now with a little sigh of relief that Jessica seemed to have lost any desire for family prestige. She had certainly stopped complaining about his lack of ambition years ago and seemed, so far as he could judge, relatively content with her lot.

'Your mother's a very sensible woman,' he said finally. 'And I think it's best to do what she says. I generally do.'

'Yes, but she doesn't make you wipe up all the time, or stop you going out whenever you want to, or—' She paused, then said with a hint of wonderment: 'But you don't generally seem to want to do a lot, do you, Father?'

His eyes smiled at her before looking away. He began to fold the *Daily Mail,* stroking it into neat creases with his pale hands.

'I'm very content to live as I do.'

'What I mean is — you haven't got any hobbies, have you?' She was gazing at him now as if she had only just met him.

He shifted evasively and said: 'What with work and everything, there doesn't seem to be time.'

'People make time.'

'Yes, I suppose they do.' He laid the paper aside and then took out his pocket watch. 'Soon be time for supper.'

'It's cod,' Cassie said dolefully. 'And I suppose I'm expected to go and lay the table.'

He made no effort to detain her, and she left the room thinking that there was something almost ghostly about him.

In a way, it was as if he wasn't really there, and she had never noticed it before. The idea startled her.

At suppertime he helped himself to a little more parsley sauce, then broke the conversational void by saying: 'It must be rather jolly to have a sense of urgency.'

The months crept by, leaden-footed and loaded with war. America joined in and sent her doughboys to Europe in time for the second battle of the Somme. The slaughter had become an endless routine, and the eldest son of the family next door to the Marlows came home with both lungs rotted by gas. He had a silver tube in his throat and breathed with a whistling sound that on bad days could be heard through the bedroom wall.

Food became rationed, people became glummer, and in a sudden mood of revulsion young Cassie turned her head away from it all and went back to her schoolbooks. At the beginning of the 1918 spring term she had a new form mistress, a Miss Dillingham, who had a gift for making her study for pleasure and not merely for profit. She was a quiet, gracious woman with a lot of wavy hair secured by a black velvet ribbon and had a subtle way of treating Cassie as if she were a contemporary without ever encouraging intimacy.

She broached the subject of university entrance, and her lightness of touch almost immediately fired the perverse adolescent mind with a fierce determination to work for it. As Gilbert had used the back bedroom as a refuge in which to fill the first secret notebooks about Captain Shovel, so Cassie now worked with equal assiduity at the little bamboo table in her own room. Miss Dillingham was also teaching her a lot about the art of work itself, and with the steady decline of childish resentment came a very real satisfaction in organizing and collating the large amount of knowledge she was absorbing.

Sometimes Jessica would tiptoe in with a cup of cocoa, then cock her head at the wall with a sigh.

'That poor chap's at it again.'

'Umm? Oh, yes.'

'I hope it doesn't get on your nerves.'

'I don't really hear it anymore.'

She no longer followed the war news, and most of those who still did took the sudden collapse of Bulgaria with no more than a weary shrug. It was September, and at St Etheldreda's they were planning the new season's lacrosse fixtures with the Prendergast Grammar School at Catford and St Angela's at Forest Gate.

'They say the Kaiser's not sleeping a wink these days.'

'Uh-huh.'

'Did you hear that Turkey's given in?'

'What, for good?'

'Well, I don't suppose anyone'll feel like starting all over again once they've stopped.'

'No . . .'

One hand on the door and a secret, loving little smile directed at her daughter's bent head. 'You're growing out of your uniform again. You'll have to have another skirt, at least.'

'No, I won't.' Cassie looked up then. 'It's not worth it because I'll be going up to Cambridge next year.'

'You hope you will.' Now it was Jessica's turn to be cautious.

'I'll be at Girton.'

'Where's that?'

'Cambridge, Mother. There are two women's colleges there and Girton's the one I've decided on.'

'Oh, well, there you are then. But, Cassie, that skirt's got ever so short.'

'No it hasn't,' Cassie said patiently. 'I've got ever so tall.'

'Have it your own way, Miss Clever.'

The Armistice bells rang out on 11 November, drowning the laboured whistling of the boy in the bedroom next door and frightening the butcher's horse, so that it bolted down Farm Lane leaving a trail of wreckage before being caught grazing the sacred turf of the West London Athletic Club.

Everyone was glad it was over, and the more exuberant went up to the West End to shin up lamp posts and ride on the roofs of motorcars and taxis. When night came it was lovely to see the gleam of lights once more, and a group of rejoicing shopgirls lit a bonfire on Eel Brook Common, and when a policeman remonstrated, they knocked his helmet off. The pubs filled; people cried, and a man jumped off Putney Bridge waving a Union Jack. He drowned, and most of the onlookers, by now aflame with beer and exultation, thought the whole incident a scream.

But on the morning after, the streets were messy with vomit and bits of dirty red, white and blue bunting, and the sight of a pair of women's pink drawers impudently attached to the gates of Fulham Union Workhouse was no longer funny. Sobered, people began taking stock of what victory had brought them and discovered that it wasn't all that much.

By the summer of 1919 Cassie and another girl had been up to Cambridge chaperoned by Miss Dillingham in order to sit for a Girton College entrance award, and Gilbert Marlow's Captain Shovel had reached the age of seventy-eight, but showed no signs of dying. With ruddy countenance topped by hair like a fresh fall of snow he was living at the heart of a now vast family of children, grandchildren and first and second cousins. As far back as 1916 it had become expedient to draw up a family tree, although Gilbert rarely needed to refer to it for practical purposes. Unerring as a tunnelling mole he was able to find his way through the complex maze of relationships that surrounded the captain, adding a little subterfuge here, a little machination there, and all of it dictated by the mysterious impulse that had first knocked on the door of his brain all those years ago.

Oho Shovel, the captain's eldest son, had left his birthplace in the South Pacific and had become keeper of the Sub-Tropical Gardens in Battersea Park. He was getting on for sixty now, and thinking of retirement, but the Royal Botanical Society had recently sent him a collection of flora from a previously uncharted island in the Indian Ocean with the request that he use his, by now legendary, skill in order to classify it. His compliance, it was hinted, would be rewarded with a knighthood.

A trifle wearily, Oho set to work. In the privacy of his laboratory, he opened the box containing the specimens and began to lift them out one by one. Berries, catkins, and strangely shaped leaves; lichens and straggling lianes, and — Oho started backwards with a muttered exclamation. A sharp pain had stabbed at his finger ends and involuntarily he pressed them to his lips. There was little left in the box now save what looked like a small purplish mushroom. Cautiously Oho removed it with a pair of pincers, still holding his stinging fingers to his lips. The mushroom gave off a sweetish scent and was quite unlike any of the more familiar fungi with which he had dealt in the past.

The pain in his fingers had subsided and he began the long careful work of examination and analysis which would lead to identification. Two hours later he pushed his microscope aside and stood up, holding his head in his hands. He swayed, overcome by a sensation of intense nausea. His head was hot, his eyes burned and his throat was rough and dry. He staggered to the door to summon his assistant but before he could do so, darkness encompassed the laboratory and he fell senseless to the ground.

Gilbert paused, then laid down his pen and took out his watch. Ten to five. Time to pack up. Without glancing at what he had written he blotted the page, closed the notebook and placed it in the drawer of the dreary little dressing-table that served as a desk. He put on his hat and coat and, locking the door behind him, left the lodging house off the Wandsworth Bridge Road.

Going home on the tram to Walham Green he realised that his head was aching and his throat was dry, and came to the conclusion that it must be in sympathy with poor Oho.

* * *

The Spanish 'flu epidemic raged throughout Europe as if the declaration of peace had finally prompted long-abused nature into opening hostilities on her own account. People in varying stages of ill-health and under-nourishment died in their thousands. Medicines were scarce, food stocks were exhausted, and the virus ran riot among the remnants of both Allied and enemy troops with strict impartiality.

Drifting in lurid fever Gilbert tried to focus his eyes on the face of Jessica suspended somewhere above him like a pale and anxious moon. Slipping her hand beneath his head she kept trying to raise him from the pillows in order to sip a little gruel; then weak tea, and then, finally and despairingly, just plain water.

He wanted to comply, but the liquid ran out of his mouth on to his nightshirt and she bent closer, wiping him with a damp cloth and trying to catch what he was saying about a shovel.

Cassie shared the long hours of sitting by his bedside, and on the third day Jessica wrote to Mr Willis, the head bookkeeper at the brewery, apologising for her husband's absence from his place of work due to a fever, and hoping that he wouldn't be unduly inconvenienced, yours faithfully. The letter came back unopened, and enclosed in another envelope which contained a note saying that Mr Willis had retired eighteen months ago.

Then Gilbert appeared to rally. The high temperature dropped and he lay looking about him with eyes no longer clouded by delirium. The doctor said that if he maintained progress he would be allowed to sit up, and perhaps take a spoonful of coddled egg. He seemed to sleep then, breathing so quietly that Jessica, dozing by the bedside, was startled when he cried out.

'Mopsy — Mopsy, where are you?'

It was the nickname he had used during their courting days. She bent over him, feeling relief and fear and a sudden anguished return of the old love for him. His hand was groping urgently and she took it in both of hers, wetting it with hot, painful tears.

'I'm awfully sorry, old girl,' he said. 'So awfully sorry . . .'

It took her several minutes to realise that he had died. She stood rubbing his hand and then blowing her warm breath on to the palm before folding the fingers shut on it in a dazed and desperate effort to keep the final coldness at bay. The ticking of the bedroom clock seemed very loud when she finally stumbled from the room.

Without telling Cassie what had happened she sent her to fetch the doctor, and when it was all over and the death certificate had been signed the doctor turned to Jessica and asked what steps she was taking.

She looked at him blindly.

'We must realise that we are in the middle of an epidemic as virulent as the Black Death, Mrs Marlow,' he said. 'And we must take all steps to ensure that we too do not succumb. After all, someone has got to carry on.' He made it sound as if dying of influenza was an act of deliberate selfishness.

'Yes. I suppose so.'

'Inhalation is the answer. Deep inhalation six times a day with a thick towel enclosing both head and basin, the face to be held no more than two inches above the surface of the preparation, which must be at boiling point initially. Eucalyptus, Mrs Marlow, alternated with Friar's Balsam, taken deep into the lungs and then expelled slowly and positively through an aperture made ready in the towel.'

He demonstrated, nostrils flaring, face reddening and mouth gaping in uncanny portrayal of a goldfish. Cassie gave a convulsive hiccough and bolted from the room.

But they obeyed his injunction, even coming home after the funeral and sitting down in their black clothes on either side of the kitchen table, each shrouded in her own towel, her own steam, and her own melancholy.

The next dreadful blow fell four days afterwards when Jessica went round to the brewery in person to tell them that her husband, Mr Marlow, had passed away.

'Mr Marlow?' they said blankly, and it became revealed that he had left their employment some three years ago.

She didn't know what to say, what to do or what to think. She could only mumble some stupid and confused apology and hurry away from their curious glances. She walked home, unable to bear the stifling confines of a tram, while her mind tried to assimilate the shock of Gilbert's deceitfulness. Why had he not told her? Had he left under a cloud? She wished that she had the resolve to go back to the brewery to ask. But most of all she wondered where he had really been working during the past three years. Was it somewhere that he had felt would shock her? A public house, perhaps, or a pawnbrokers, or, worst of all, a music-hall? Tears filled her eyes at the thought of his consideration, and at the almost unendurable strain the duplicity must have imposed on him. Gilbert had never been strong, and she realised now how much her impatience and outbursts of temper must have hurt him. The tears overflowed, but no one in the street took any notice because weeping women in black had become a common enough sight during the past five years.

The final shock was delivered by afternoon post.

As the capital sum deposited by you has now been withdrawn save for an amount of seven shillings we write to enquire whether you wish us to close the account. Your early instructions will be appreciated.

The letter was signed by the local branch manager of the London Provident & Mutual Benefit Society.

And so it became clear; bitterly, bitterly clear. Gilbert had left the brewery and instead of working had been spending his time on a fancy woman.

Jessica screwed the letter into a ball and flung it on the floor. With clenched hands and closed eyes she stood in the narrow little hallway and gave a long hoarse scream. It was an unrefined, unladylike sound, and her own family, had they been living, would have been as shocked by it as Gilbert's.

She opened her eyes and her gaze alighted on the row of clothes pegs on the wall, and on the black bowler hat which still hung there. She took it down and carried it into the kitchen. She laid it on the table, and then seizing the heavy steel poker raised it above her head in both hands and brought it crashing down in the centre of the hard velour crown.

It buckled into a trilby shape. She brought the poker down again and again; the bowler hat sprang off the table and fell on to the floor. Panting, she pursued it, bashing it, smashing it, mashing it, chasing it in and out of the furniture as a terrier would chase a rat. The crown parted from the brim. The lining waved loose like a helpless little flag of surrender but she kept on hitting biffing and killing — killing the hated symbol of male respectability, the horrible embodiment of suburban dignity, of tinpot pride, the prim outer covering of a mind seething with filthiness and beastliness and cynical disregard for everything that was decent and honest, clean and truthful. Savagely she drove the poker through the battered remains of the crown, skewered it through the broken brim and then thrust them both into the fire, and at that moment Cassie walked in.

Dropping her old leather satchel down she said in a voice that strove to sound suitable to a house of mourning: 'Mother, they've just told me I've got a place at Girton!'

* * *

She had to tell Cassie, of course. She broke the news that there would be no Girton, no nothing, in a flat dry little voice with the words falling like pebbles on the listless parlour air.

Cassie's face went very pale. She gave an incredulous sob.

'But I've worked — I've worked so hard—'

'I know you have—'

'And I did it because of you—'

'Yes. And now it's all come to nothing.'

'But what's Father been *doing*?'

'I'd rather not say. But I'm certainly not the first woman it's happened to.'

'Mother, what do you *mean*?'

'You're too young to know. Let's just say that one wife isn't enough for some men and they decide to look for their pleasure elsewhere. Not that I ever suspected your father of being one of them.' She choked.

So Father had had a mistress. Dutiful indignation mingled with a shamefaced sense of gratification. He had always seemed so dull, and now here was proof that beneath a conventional exterior had raged the tormented passions of illicit love. A Marie Corelli novel heavily disguised as a copy of Hazlitt's *Lectures on the English Poets* had recently passed round the sixth form leaving an afterglow of purple prose and turgid emotion, and Cassie was not the only one who now felt better equipped to understand the wilder emotions of the human heart. But common sense told her that to air such knowledge now would be ill advised; in any case, her own situation needed very careful consideration.

'Well, what are we going to do?'

'We'll both have to go out to work, I suppose. It's the only thing we can do.'

'Didn't Father leave *anything*?'

'Seventeen and six in his trousers pocket, two pounds ten in the bureau drawer, nothing in the tin we used for the rent and rates, and two threepenny bits on the bedroom mantelpiece. Oh, and we mustn't forget the seven shillings left in the savings bank.'

'If we told them at Girton, do you think they'd understand?'

'Only enough to give your place to somebody else,' Jessica said.

She lay awake that night staring into the darkness, and worry about the future took precedence over the bitterness she felt towards Gilbert. Going out to work was easier said than done with the men coming back from the war and wanting their old jobs back. She supposed she could always get a job as a daily domestic and perhaps Cassie would be lucky enough to become a shop assistant up in the West End.

In the meantime, she would have to try selling a few things. Perhaps the man in the second-hand shop might buy the Worcester tea-set that had been their best wedding present, or what about the silver frames that still encompassed the unsmiling ranks of elder Marlows? Her mind reviewed the sepia faces, so remote and yet so familiar after all the years of dutiful dusting, and came to the conclusion that they must all be dead by now except for Gilbert's brother Harold up in Liverpool.

Then her thoughts returned to Gilbert. To his light blue eyes, sweetly vague smile and gentleness of manner. *I'm awfully sorry, old girl . . . awfully sorry* . . . he had said just before he died, and now of course she understood the reason for his sorrow. Tossing restlessly she wondered about his fancy woman; what she looked like, where she lived, what her name was. Somewhere, perhaps only a few streets away, she too was lying sleepless in the bed they had shared — and the idea of being in bed with another woman's husband during the actual hours of daylight was an additional source of horror to Jessica.

She thought with sickened fascination about the rumoured accoutrements of a sinful union; presents of scent and knickers with frills, bunches of red roses and bottles of champagne, all presumably provided by the brazen barefaced woman who had stolen from another. Unless, and this was an equally painful thought, Gilbert had inherited a lot of money unexpectedly and had been lavishing it where it didn't belong while still paying the old paltry sum each week to his legal wife and daughter. But whatever his financial jiggery-pokery he had cheated Cassie out of going to university.

She got out of bed and went over to the window. Pushing the lace curtain aside she saw the dawn coming up over the roofs of Walham Green and wondered if there was any point in going on anymore. The future would hold nothing more than continual work, continued struggle to survive, let alone make ends meet. She was getting old, with grey hair and a varicose vein, and she felt like chucking it all. But of course, there was Cassie. And Cassie needed her more now than she had ever needed anyone before.

Her head ached with worry and her throat felt sore. She supposed she ought to go down and inhale some Friar's Balsam — neither she nor Cassie had inhaled once that day — but now she couldn't be bothered.

She went back to bed shivering and tucking her cold toes in the hem of her nightgown and when Cassie came in with a cup of tea next morning her temperature was 102.

'Don't trust men,' was all she would say, over and over again like a parched gramophone record. 'Don't trust men because they're all heartless and horrible . . .'

On the following day she roused herself sufficiently to dictate a telegram to Gilbert's brother in Liverpool.

'Don't make me go there, Mother — I don't want to go there—'

'You've got to go somewhere—'

'No, I haven't! I'm staying here with you — you're going to get better!'

'You're going to Liverpool. Your Uncle Harold will give you a nice home. They've got money up there, and they'll see you take your place at Girton.'

'I've already given it up! I told Miss Dillingham after prayers this morning—'

'In that case you'd better go and untell her.' Jessica's gaunt face softened a little. 'Now go and send that telegram like a good girl, so Uncle Harold can get in touch with us. He's supposed to be a nice enough chap and he'll do what's right.'

'I thought all men were horrible—'

'Do as I say, or I'll get cross . . .'

She went. And on the way home picked a couple of red roses that were hanging over someone's gateway and laid them on her mother's pillow.

* * *

'It seems no time at all since the day I delivered her in child-birth,' the nurse said. 'And now here I am laying her out.'

'What am I supposed to do about undertakers and everything? Mother saw to the last lot.'

'It's all been taken care of, dearie. You don't have to do anything except look your best for the funeral. She'd have wanted that.'

'I won't have to go and look at her, will I?'

'Not if you don't want to. Some people like to say a last goodbye, others prefer to remember their loved ones as they were.'

'That's how I feel.'

Cassie and the nurse were drinking tea and eating ginger biscuits in the kitchen, while Jessica, small and waxen, lay upstairs. In a way it seemed callous to be eating ginger biscuits, but no meals had been cooked for the past four days and, despite almost constant weeping, Cassie was hungry.

'She made a lovely little mother,' recalled the nurse. 'Sitting up there proud as punch with her baby in her arms, and so pleased and excited when her hubby come home.'

'Yes.'

'They made a lovely couple, your ma and pa. And if you ask my honest opinion, she didn't want to go on without him. She just turned her face to the wall and gave up.'

'She had Spanish 'flu.'

'Yes, dearie, but I've seen a lot of deaths in my time, and I know when somebody just gives up. When they just want to slip quietly away.'

'Yes.'

'Without being any trouble to anybody.'

Cassie's eyes filled, and the nurse helped herself to another biscuit. During the years she had grown very stout and now she had some curly grey whiskers sprouting on her chin. Cassie didn't like her very much.

'So what are you going to do now, dearie?'

'My uncle in Liverpool has arranged for some auctioneers to deal with everything here, and then I'm going to live with him and his wife. At least, I'll just be staying with them when I'm not at Cambridge. I've been offered a place at Girton.' She was clinging to the idea of Cambridge now as if it were her only hope of survival.

'So everything's going to be sold?'

'Yes, I'm afraid so.'

The nurse refilled their cups. 'In that case, can I have that dinky little jug as a memento?'

'Yes, if you want it,' said Cassie. Then added: 'Let's say one and sixpence.'

The nurse recoiled. 'Oh my word, I can't help thinking your poor ma would have been shocked to hear you say that.'

'My father might have been,' Cassie said, 'but not my mother. She understood the value of things.'

But in the end she gave the jug to the nurse, and the nurse insisted on giving her ninepence for it, poking about in a worn leather purse that opened like a concertina. She kissed Cassie goodbye, and the action dislodged a biscuit crumb suspended between two whiskers.

'A beautiful baby you were,' she said. 'Eight pounds or more, and I never heard a lustier first cry in all my life.'

The next two weeks were like a dream. Like shadows on a wall people came and went, sticking labels on furniture and counting the knives and forks. The gasman emptied the meter and the rent collector took the last twelve and sixpence, drew a red line through the remaining two pages of the old dog-eared rent book and handed it back to her.

'I don't want it.'

'It's yours by law.'

So she took it, and sat counting all the columns of twelve and sixpences that went back to before she was born. Unbelievably, there were one thousand, one hundred and forty-seven, and each one represented seven days of cleaning and polishing, washing and ironing for her mother with only dreams and aspirations to sustain her, while her father had frittered them all away on a fancy woman. The Corelli influence had faded, and Cassie could only contemplate the unknown woman with Jessica's bitterness.

A few neighbours called in to see if they could do anything and went away content when she said no thank you. The most painful visit was the one made by Miss Dillingham, with her quiet solicitude and mute reminder of the old carefree days. In the same way that she had the gift for making difficult subjects intelligible, so her mere presence seemed to bring all the loneliness and uncertainty of Cassie's future into sharp unwavering focus, and instead of asking her to come in she just stood in the front doorway wearing her mother's pinafore and grinding her knuckles in her eyes like a small, abandoned child.

In a way, Cassie's age was an additional source of confusion to her because it seemed to mean different things to different sorts of people. Better class ones like Miss Dillingham regarded a girl of nineteen as still perilously young and in need of wise support, while others like the woman next door with five kids besides the whistling boy upstairs considered her quite old enough to fend for herself.

She dreaded the contents of the house going up for auction, and the day before they were due to be taken to the sale-yard an old man with a horse and cart knocked on the door and said he had heard she was selling up. After taking a quick look round he offered her ten quid for the lot.

It seemed a lot of money to Cassie and impulsively she accepted, and once they got started it seemed as if she couldn't get rid of the things quickly enough. The old man had a boy to help him, and between the three of them they lugged everything out — beds, carpets, rolls of lino, tables and chairs and the mahogany chiffonier, all of them already marked with the auctioneer's serial number. They wrapped the china up in the sheets and blankets and balanced the old iron mangle on the tailboard. It took only two hours from start to finish, and she went back into the echoing little house with its faded patches of wallpaper, clasping the grimy one pound notes and saying to herself: 'This isn't the end, you stupid, it's the beginning.'

The suitcase for Liverpool was already packed so she left the house, and in this new mood of adult optimism booked herself into the Bluebell Temperance Hotel in the North End Road for the night, and on the following morning sent a telegram to Uncle Harold and his wife to say that she would be arriving three days earlier than previously arranged.

She left Walham Green on 7 August, at about the same time that a mystified landlady was chucking armfuls of exercise books filled with a lot of scribble on to a bonfire in her Wandsworth backyard.

CHAPTER THREE

The train arrived at Lime Street during the late afternoon and a grey-haired man stepped from behind the ticket barrier, raised his hat and said: 'Am I addressing Cassica Marlow?'

She said that he was, and shook hands, and he summoned a porter with a small authoritative movement of the eyebrows and then led her across the station to where a car stood waiting. It was a chauffeur-driven Daimler and at first Cassie assumed that it was a taxi.

The suitcase was disposed of, the porter tipped, and Cassie and her Uncle Harold sank side by side on to the dove-grey rear seat which was separated from the chauffeur by a wall of plate glass. Dove-grey dingle-dangles of great complexity hung at the windows, cut-glass ashtrays and what looked like a scent bottle twinkled in gold fittings. Tearing her gaze from it all Cassie glanced cautiously at her companion.

He was of a heavier build than Father had been, with a neatly placed little nose that reminded her of a hen's beak and an iron-grey moustache poised above firm red lips. His collar was very high and very starched, and he wore an old-fashioned stock secured in place by a ruby pin. He had an aura of wealth and unassailability, and as she watched he removed the scent bottle from its holder, poured a little of its golden contents into its gleaming gold cap and drank it at one noiseless swallow. He then turned to Cassie and smiled, and although he had the same unusually pale blue eyes as Father, they were crisply alert instead of dreamily elusive.

'Now, my dear,' he said, taking her hand. 'I must begin by offering you my sincere condolences in your tragic loss. To lose one parent is gross hardship, to lose both is a shattering blow.'

'Yes.' There was little else she could say.

'But my wife and our two boys intend to do everything within our power to support you and help you on your way. You stand on the threshold of life and the next few years are of paramount importance.'

'Yes, I know,' she said gratefully. 'I've won a place at Girton and I want to go terribly, but—' It was difficult to say more without implicating her father and this she was not prepared to do, particularly as he had only just died.

'I daresay it can all be arranged,' he promised, and the smile he gave her bore the sharp scent of whisky. She smiled back, and thought I'm in Liverpool . . . isn't it funny . . .

Once they had passed the wide streets and large formal buildings it began to look very poor. Even poorer than the poor parts of Walham Green. Small blackened houses and small women enveloped in black woollen shawls which made them look as if they had suffered the same incrustation of soot. Some of them stopped to stare after Uncle Harold's Daimler with pale faces devoid of expression.

'The boys are both up at Oxford,' he said. 'Lionel at Balliol and Desmond at Oriel, so you'll have something in common with them. Lionel comes down next year.'

'Oh.' There was so much she wanted to know but couldn't very well ask.

Then quite abruptly the poor streets were left behind and turning in between two small ornamental lodges they were bowling through what seemed like the country. Deserted roads bounded by smooth grass and stately trees, and every now and then large gate posts and railings which hinted at the presence of a house hidden from view.

'This is Sefton Park,' Uncle Harold said.

The Mount stood at the end of a long drive, surveying its croquet lawn and ornamental lake from a point of elevation that had been artificially created. The house was neo-classical red brick with a conservatory on one side and a stable block on the other. A stone terrace surrounded it, then the ground fell away in a series of rockeries with little artfully created rivers trickling tunefully between the boulders and beneath little white wrought iron bridges. Flower beds blazed with geraniums and standard roses stood fiercely to attention, and Cassie had never seen anything so amazing or so beautiful in all her life.

A maid in starched uniform opened the door.

'Good afternoon, Hannah,' said Uncle Harold. 'This is Miss Cassica.'

The maid bobbed, quick eyes taking in the quality of Cassie's mourning wear.

'Is your mistress at home?'

'Yes, sir. Mistress is in the library.' Another bob, and a quick, covert smirk.

Uncle Harold led the way, and a woman rose from one of the large club sofas and came towards them with head thrown back and arms outstretched.

'This must be poor little Cassica!'

'Cassica,' began Uncle Harold, 'this is Aunt Barbara—' Then he stopped, took a hurried step backwards and said: 'Merciful heaven, Babs, what on earth have you done?'

Aunt Barbara left off embracing Cassie and performed an airy little pirouette.

'I've had it cut off.'

'But why — in God's name why?'

'Don't you like it? Everyone else thinks it's charming.'

She stood still again, and pouted, and Cassie found herself taking stock of a petite and extremely pretty woman with large expressive eyes set in a heart-shaped face, and short fair hair cut skilfully into the nape of her delicate little neck. She was wearing a loosely fitting chenille skirt and tunic and Cassie's awed amazement overflowed at the sight of her patent leather slippers adorned with silver buckles.

'You had no right to tamper with it without consulting me. A woman's crowning glory is her hair, and your hair, Babs, was of exceptionally fine quality—'

'Oh, Harry darling, don't be such an old bear—' She put her arms round his neck and kissed his cheek, and Cassie's amazement increased. It seemed to be increasing all the time.

'You should have consulted me—'

'Oh, no I shouldn't!' She laughed over his shoulder at Cassie. 'Because you would never have given me permission.'

'I'm very angry, Babs,' he said, removing her arms. 'Really very angry and disappointed . . .'

'But it's much nicer now, Harry — look, you can run your fingers through it . . .'

She seized his hand and brushed it over the shining bob of hair, shaking it over her forehead and then tilting her head back and closing her eyes as his fingers began to move over her scalp.

'It's all very well,' Uncle Harold said, then removed his hand and briskly cleared his throat. 'But in the meantime I suggest we show this young lady to her room and try to make her feel at home.'

'Yes, Harry, of course.' Aunt Barbara turned away from him and gave Cassie a brief conspiratorial wink. 'Now, Cassica — such an interesting name — let me show you round the house and explain things to you, and then it'll be time for a teensy glass of sherry before dinner.'

She was as good as her word, showing her the drawing-room, the morning-room, the dining room and the billiard-room before leading the way up the wide shallow staircase. Cassie's room overlooked the tennis court at the back of the house and was furnished expensively by Waring & Gillow. Her suitcase had been placed at the foot of the bed.

'Can you unpack for yourself? Hannah is really my personal maid, but if you want anything just ring the bell and either she or Dora will come. We gave you this room because it's one of the prettiest' — she smiled gaily from the doorway — 'and I should warn you that it's next to Lionel's but no flirting with my big handsome son because he's still only a baby at heart!'

She tripped away, and very slowly Cassie set about the business of unpacking. Her wooden-backed whalebone hairbrush looked very incongruous on the dressing-table and it occurred to her for the first time that out of all the family photographs displayed in the Walham Green parlour, not one of them had been of her own mother and father. She sat down on the edge of the bed and tears filled her eyes because she was so far away from where they were buried and because the dressing-table would have looked so much more homely with their photo standing on it.

Lionel was apparently staying with friends for a few days, but she met Desmond at dinner. He was a large youth who moved his big feet carelessly and banged into things. He made a token show of shaking hands with her.

'Awfully sorry to hear about your people.'

That said, he ignored her, and spent most of the meal discussing cricket with his father.

Dora waited at table in a long black dress and white cap and apron, and Cassie, who had never encountered lobster before, didn't know which implement to use.

'We had some marvellous meals in Le Touquet this year,' Aunt Barbara recalled, 'but Uncle Harry got dreadfully scoldy with me when I lost twenty pounds in the casino.'

'Oh dear, did you drop it somewhere?'

Aunt Barbara laughed merrily. 'No, darling, playing *chemin-defer*—'

'It wasn't the money,' put in Uncle Harold, 'it was the fact of your being there. A casino is no place for a woman, even when she's accompanied by a man.'

'But you were so horribly scoldy that anyone would think you didn't trust me.'

'Of course I trust you.'

'Then you must behave as if you do, and not always be so *cross*, Harry.'

He didn't look cross now. He was smiling at her fondly, as one might smile at a beautiful wayward child.

'It's so lovely being able to go back to France again for one's hols, after the grisly old war,' she said. 'Do you know France, Cassie?'

Cassie said that she didn't.

Uncle Harold wiped his red lips on his white napkin and asked where they had usually taken their holidays.

'We didn't usually go on any.'

'Ah.'

But in between talk of cricket and holidays they asked her other courteous little questions about herself, trying to bring her into the conversation without actually mentioning the sensitive subject of her parents. And Cassie didn't mention them either, out of deference to their tactfulness.

When the meal was over Uncle Harold leaned back in his chair and lit a cigar while Dora came in with a decanter of port. She poured some for Uncle Harold and some for Desmond, but didn't include Aunt Barbara or Cassie. They hadn't even been provided with a glass in case they did fancy some, Cassie noted.

Then Aunt Barbara stood up and said: 'Come along, Cassica, let's leave our menfolk to their boring old talk,' and Cassie suddenly remembered that in novels about rich people the ladies always left the table before the gentlemen.

She followed Aunt Barbara into the drawing-room where the lamps glowed and a small bright fire burned in the hearth. A silver tray containing coffee things stood waiting nearby.

'You know, I've got a feeling that you and I are going to be tremendous chums,' confided Aunt Babs, pouring. 'It's going to be such a nice change for me to have another girl in the house instead of being all alone with these three silly big men. So listen to me, my dear' — she turned her attention from the coffee and gazed very earnestly into Cassie's eyes — 'try to think of me as a chum, too. Not just a stuffy old aunt — we all know how stuffy and boring aunts are — but as a friend of your own age you can confide in and have fun with. Don't call me Aunt Barbara, call me Babs, and I'll call you . . . let me see, I'll call you Coco. How's that?'

Mesmerised, Cassie said it would be nice.

'So listen, Coco dear, there's something you must promise me. You must promise me on your honour that if there's anything worrying you or troubling you, anything you're not certain of, or anything you want to know about — about *anything* — promise you'll come to me.'

Cassie promised.

'Nothing's too big or too small or too intimate. We're just a pair of girl chums together, and anything you want to tell me I promise not to split. You do understand, don't you?' The little soft hand she laid on Cassie's knee twinkled with three diamond rings.

Relieved that she wasn't offering to be a mother to her, Cassie said she understood.

'This is your home now — now that things have changed,' Babs continued, skirting delicately round the subject again, 'and so anything you want to *do*, anything you want to *have*, Coco dear, just tell me. Is that clearly understood between us?'

Cassie said it was, then, tearing her hypnotised gaze from her aunt's lovely little face, asked in a hoarse whisper whether she could have a bath. 'I've brought my own towel . . .'

* * *

Unlike Father, Uncle Harold (Uncle Harry now) was a stockbroker who had always been content to remain one, and he set off each morning in the Daimler with Nibbs the chauffeur behind the wheel. After depositing the master at his office

Nibbs would return, so that the motor was always ready should madam require it. Desmond's mode of transport was a motorbike with which he tinkered ceaselessly, and when he came in to luncheon covered in grease his mother would back away crying, 'Oh go away — you *horrid*, smelly boy!', at which Desmond would grin complacently.

'But I do so love masculine men,' Babs would confide, and help herself to a little more sherry.

It all took a lot of getting used to; not only the opulence but also the new leisurely pace at which the day unrolled. Breakfast in the morning-room at nine, with Babs in a negligée opening letters and giving orders for luncheon and dinner. Then wandering round the garden, arranging a few flowers, telephoning friends and wondering what clothes to buy for the coming season. True to her word she did treat Cassie as a close friend and confidante, and spent hours gossiping to her on subjects about which Cassie had only read in the papers. She was as amusing as a kitten, as blithely animated as a canary hopping on its perch, and as different from Jessica as any woman could ever hope to be.

She and Jessica had never met, never corresponded beyond the occasional Christmas card, and although Cassie sometimes felt a considerable yearning to talk about her own parents, her old home and her past life, the subject was always adroitly sidestepped.

'Let's talk about *happy* things, Coco!' Babs would cry, and Cassie never had sufficient resolve to argue that her past life had in fact been very happy. Like most lives seen in retrospect, it seemed to be growing happier all the time.

Sometimes during the afternoon the odd friend would drop in for tea at The Mount. They were mostly youngish men who came by car, who were playful with Desmond, very courteous to Babs and, perhaps because of her black clothes, a little formal with Cassie. They had always gone by the time Uncle Harry came home from the office because Uncle Harry, so Babs confided, was a bit of an old bear until he had had a whisky and soda and had finished reading his evening paper.

'He works dreadfully hard, the old silly, and so we all have to suffer . . .'

Then Lionel came back from staying with his friends and proved to be a slightly larger version of Desmond. He too had clumsy limbs, big feet, and banged into things, and he too, tended to dismiss his cousin after shaking hands and saying, 'Awfully sorry to hear about your people.'

As a lowly schoolgirl Cassie had always visualised undergraduates as people standing at the high peak of adulthood and thus embodying all that was wise, mature and judicial, and was therefore surprised and a little disappointed by the large, curiously unformed faces, the bullock-like stare and the silly bits of swank (like calling their parents Mater and Pater) which alternated with even sillier jokes like setting a mouse loose in the path of Dora who was carrying a tureen full of hot soup, or seeing who could spit plum stones the furthest.

They played tennis with great violence and sometimes used to go swimming in the lake, churning up the water and roaring in loud voices while Babs on the marble seat nearby would laugh and exclaim in mock horror at such rough horseplay on the part of her boys, and it was extraordinary to realise that two such galumphing creatures had come out of such a dainty little woman's body. Then they would emerge from the water gasping and snorting and scattering drips everywhere and Cassie would look covertly at the lumps swinging in front of their cotton bathing drawers and wonder what men were like.

But sometimes they were quiet; very quiet, lying sprawled in the library smoking pipes and reading textbooks, bits of which they sometimes underlined portentously in pencil. At first it seemed as if they were more approachable in these moods and the studious atmosphere rekindled Cassie's yearning for Girton to begin, but if ever she spoke to them, or even sat down on one of the window seats, their silent supercilious disdain, their air of awful swanky uppishness excluded her just as brutally as their noisy masculinity.

Then on the first of September, Babs in her negligée and lace boudoir cap looked critically at Cassie's black frock and black stockings and said, 'Coco darling, you've been in mourning quite long enough, and this afternoon we're going to see Madame Louise about some decent clothes for you.'

Nibbs drove them down into the city and waited with folded arms outside the Bold Street shop where the window was furnished with one frock, a vase of tiger lilies and an air of quiet exorbitance.

Madame Louise was a genuine Frenchwoman, the first Cassie had ever met, and she made them both sit down on little gold chairs while she brought out coats and costumes, frocks and blouses and skirts, and Cassie had never felt more shabby or despairingly gauche in all her life.

'*Mais la pauvre mademoiselle est très haute*,' commented Madame Louise, frowning at the hemlines.

'Yes, it's a nuisance she's so tall,' agreed Babs. 'She's even taller than a lot of men I know.'

They looked at her sympathetically but critically, and Cassie standing gawky in green velvet became aware for the first time that for a woman to be tall was a grave misfortune. Certainly, her mother had often sighed when she grew out of her clothes so rapidly, but that was because of the expense involved. Here in Madame Louise's salon they were sighing because being five foot ten was a social stigma like bad breath or sweaty feet. She stood with her knees slightly bent but they caught her at it and jerked her upright again.

But while Madame Louise's assistant refreshed them with tiny cups of camomile tea they chose two frocks, a coat, two skirts and matching tunics which only needed letting down in order for the poor mademoiselle to look really quite *mignonne*.

They then drove to another shop for shoes, another for stockings and underwear ('*lingerie*, Coco darling, it has so much more *mystique* . . .') and in the window of the Bon Marche they saw a sweet little felt hat with a bunch of cherries on the brim that matched the coat exactly.

They swept home in triumph, and that evening when they showed the hat and shoes to Uncle Harry and told him about the other things that would be arriving in a day or two he nodded approval and then asked Cassie to accompany him to the study.

Puzzled but not particularly alarmed she did so, and Uncle Harry poured himself a whisky and soda, indicated that she should seat herself opposite him, and then said: 'Well, Cassica, you're out of mourning now and I think it's time we had a serious talk about your future. What exactly have you in mind, my dear?'

'I've got a place at Girton, Uncle Harry. I do want to go very much.'

Rather to her surprise he asked her to explain why.

'Why? Well, because I want to earn my own living.'

'You could do that without the aid of a degree.'

'Oh yes, I know, but education's very important, isn't it?'

'Not so much the education as the application of it.'

'Well yes, but I want to do something special.'

'Such as?'

She floundered, then said well, something she could make a real success of.

He asked her what she intended reading up at Girton, and when she said that she was taking the English Tripos he sighed.

'Now listen to me, my dear,' he said, 'while I make one or two things clear. The first one is that due to unfortunate circumstances within your immediate family you are not at liberty to choose precisely what you want to do. You say that you want to earn your own living, a laudable desire with which I concur, but I see a slight difference of opinion when it comes to the method involved. I have been happy to assist you over the first and most critical stage of your bereavement — this was a duty which I undertook gladly. The next duty I have is to make certain that you go out into the world equipped with the ability to support yourself, and this I also undertake to do. But it does not' — Uncle Harry broke off to take a mouthful of whisky — 'it does not include the quite unjustified expense of supporting you during three years at university when you have not even taken the trouble to investigate the choice of possible careers it could lead to.'

Cassie opened her mouth to speak, then closed it again.

'You say that you want to do something special. Something that you could make a success of. In that case I suggest running a small market garden, or making toffee, or perhaps helping in an orphanage. All these things could prove worthwhile and could be made a success of in the long run, and quite honestly I see very little more in terms of either self-esteem or financial profit arising from three years' study of Chaucer and Shakespeare and the long-winded maunderings of John Milton.'

Shocked and confused, Cassie's mind swam with a series of disconnected images, all of which pointed accusingly at the monumental unfairness of his words. She grabbed at one of them.

'But it's not fair — Lionel and Desmond are at Oxford so why can't—'

'For the simple reason that one day they will both marry and have wives and children to support. And when you marry, it is to be hoped that the man of your choice will be prepared to do the same for you.'

'But I've already got my place and everything! I worked hard for it, and Mother said—' Tears threatened and she groped for a handkerchief.

'Your poor mother was scarcely in a position to sum up the true pros and cons of the matter, Cassica—'

'Oh, yes she was!' Fury leaped. 'My mother had always believed in education for women as well as for men, and if only she'd been able to go to college and things like that she wouldn't have been stuck all those years with a — with a—'

Rage against Uncle Harry transferred itself to the memory of Father spending all the savings bank money because of wasting his time on a fancy woman instead of going to work, yet even now family loyalty choked the words back. She sobbed uncontrollably. 'I think you're mean and horrible and deceitful—'

'Upon the subject of deceit,' Uncle Harry swallowed the last of the whisky and set down the glass with a bang, 'I have yet to receive an explanation for your conduct regarding the firm of auctioneers employed to act on my behalf during the sale of the Walham Green furniture and effects. They spent a great deal of time listing every item, then on the morning they were due to remove everything to the sale-yard they found the house not only empty but also vacated by you. I can only assume that you decided to take matters into your own hands at that late date, and that without bothering to consult me you sold the furniture elsewhere. In which case, where is the money you received?'

'I only got ten pounds, and I—'

'As I had already telegraphed a money order to you for ten pounds to cover immediate contingencies, and have had to pay the auctioneers for their time and trouble, I consider that the ten pounds of which you speak belongs to me.'

'Well, I haven't got it—' Defiance was drying her tears.

'What have you done with it?'

'I spent it on staying in an hotel for the night, and on having a steak and kidney pie. Then I bought some tooth powder and a new sponge, and a ticket from Euston to Liverpool.'

'Which still leaves the other ten pounds to be accounted for.'

'I had to use it for a week's rent that was owing, for paying the milkman and for buying some more black stockings and — and . . .'

She couldn't remember how she had spent the rest of it. Misery, and the trancelike state of the last days at Walham Green, had helped it to trickle away on dozens of little items, some necessary and some not, and it hadn't occurred to her that later she would be expected to account for every penny. Heatedly she told him so.

Uncle Harry held up his hand for silence and it was obvious that he was controlling his temper with difficulty.

'Money,' he said, 'may seem vulgar, and to talk about it may seem in bad taste to some people, but no amount of coyness or patrician disregard will ever alter the fact that money is what counts. Without it we are sunk. I well remember Father trying to instil this fact into us as boys; I learned, but Gilbert didn't.'

'My father is — was—'

'I know, I know. Your father was a dear fellow; nevertheless one could scarcely admire his mode of life, and at times his irresponsibility towards you and your mother was little short of criminal.'

This time she didn't try to argue. The fight had gone out of her and she could only wonder how much Uncle Harry really knew about her past family life. He was looking at her now, thoughtfully pinching a pleat in his lower lip between two fingers.

'Cheer up,' he said.

She made a wry face. 'So if I can't go to university, what's the alternative?'

'A year at a commercial college,' he said quickly and very smoothly. 'There is one in Liverpool with a distinguished reputation for training first-class secretaries and book-keepers. The fees are high, which ensures that they only take girls from a decent background, and take it from me as an undisputed fact that the door to a woman's freedom lies in the typewriter. More and more intelligent young women are being allowed to take their place by the side of men in the world of commerce, the arts, the sciences, and armed with accurate shorthand and typewriting—'

'But I don't want—'

'Young women have been helping to shape history at the Paris Peace Conference, did you know that? Young women skilled at Pitman shorthand were present at the signing of the Treaty of Versailles; they have been fully conversant with the aims and ideals of the League of Nations long before we ordinary mortals—'

'Supposing I don't want to be a secretary,' she said in a chill voice. 'What happens then?'

'I have already entered your name for the autumn term. Not to have done so would have meant a delay of twelve months.'

'Oh.'

She didn't feel like thanking him. She didn't quite know how she did feel. Cheated, fed up, disappointed, jealous, all of those things, yet she didn't argue any more. She just sat looking at him in silence; at his high starched collar and ruby pin, his rich little bulge of stomach beneath the gold watch chain, his elegant grey spats and manicured nails, and there wasn't a morsel of him that didn't seem to be purring with quiet success.

'All right,' she said, getting up from the chair. She even managed to add: 'Thank you.'

She had reached the door when he called her name.

'If it's any consolation, I always insist that both Lionel and Desmond account to me for every penny of their allowances while they're up at Oxford.'

'Goodnight, Uncle Harry,' she said.

CHAPTER FOUR

Emilia Gathercole woke slowly, her mental faculties returning before the power of physical movement. With closed eyes she listened to the quiet fretting of the sea at the end of the garden and wondered if she had remembered to replace the blue folder in her briefcase.

Everything else was ready. Without opening her eyes she could see the plum-coloured marocain frock hanging outside the wardrobe, the petticoat, stockings, corsets, knickers and bust bodice waiting on the chair, and the polished low-heeled court shoes standing to attention beneath it. Her beads were placed ready on the dressing-table together with a clean handkerchief and a swansdown powderpuff enclosed in its own square of beige georgette. Only the blue folder eluded her sense of calm certainty; she had been checking its contents shortly before going to bed and it was possible that she had left it on the arm of the sofa instead of including it with the other books, papers and folders in the leather briefcase that Wilfred had given her four Christmases ago.

She could hear him breathing beside her; quiet, regular intakes of air held for a second and then expelled like a sigh. His body lay still and peaceful, and although they were not touching his warmth seemed to enfold her. She unsealed her lips from the night's silence and said: 'First day of term, loved one. Do you want bacon or boiled eggs?'

He stirred, snuffled, and then fumbled sleepily for her hand. It lay within his own, small, smooth and placid.

'Eggs, I think. What's the time?'

'I haven't looked, but the alarm has not yet gone.'

'Another five minutes . . .'

'Perhaps . . .'

They lay holding hands, faces upturned, eyes closed.

'Looking forward to going back?'

'Not at the moment,' he said. 'I feel rather timid and incompetent.'

'Think how the new students must be feeling. It is not unusual to have tears on the first day.'

'You're never nervous of anything, are you, Emilia?'

'Mice?'

'That's different. I mean, people don't intimidate you.'

'Not now. I'm too old.'

'Old?' he said, turning towards her. 'What are you talking about? You're not old.'

'Fifty-two.'

'Well, I'm forty-nine.'

'There is a surprising amount of difference between forties and fifties. However, I am in splendid health.'

'And I love you.' The sheet rustled as he turned to nuzzle at her ear. 'Ours is a wonderful love, isn't it?'

'Yes, my heart.'

'And it'll never end, will it?'

'Only when we die.'

As if to emphasise life's transience the alarm clock began to clang. It danced irritably across the surface of the bedside table but Emilia stifled its antics with a brief flick of her free hand.

'Be nice if we could wake up to Galli Curci, wouldn't it?'

'I suppose we could bring the gramophone in here. Wind it up in readiness and leave it down by the side of the bed.'

'I might fall over it if I got up in the night.'

'Yes . . .'

'Don't go off to sleep again.'

'I never do, once I have awoken.'

They lay in comfortable silence for a few minutes before throwing back the covers, then Emilia went across the landing to the bathroom while Wilfred in silk dressing-gown and slippers pottered downstairs to fill the kettle for breakfast.

They lived at Hoylake, a small and reticent seaside town on the Wirral Peninsula where rambling houses lay concealed within meandering gardens. The roads, tree-lined and high-walled, were equally secluded, and apart from a small off-shore island reached at low tide by a hired pony and trap, and an excellent teashop in Market Street, there was nothing organized for the enticement of trippers.

Emilia and Wilfred's house stood with its back to the sea, its long garden planted with tamarisk and sheltering evergreens ending at a high brick wall pierced by a narrow archway. The solid wooden door admitted no glimpse of the interior, and although it was used daily by both of them they always made a point of locking it behind them. The real entrance to the house was in the quiet road that ran parallel to the sea, but was used only by tradespeople. The house itself had walls of grey stone and Gothic windows peering cautiously through dangling curls of wisteria. The sound of the sea was always present and in all the rooms there was a slightly damp, salty smell. They had lived there for almost fifteen years and had made no friends. They needed none.

It was eight o'clock when they sat down to breakfast, Emilia in the plum-coloured frock and beads and Wilfred wearing a suit of black-and-white spongebag check. He was a slenderly built man with hair and moustache of a soft uniform yellow, and with a late summer rosebud set in his buttonhole looked like a man going off to the races rather than to work.

He cracked the top of his first egg with a flourish while Emilia, seated opposite, drank coffee and perused the contents of the blue folder which had, as suspected, been left on the arm of the sofa.

'Four Barbaras, two Rhodas, the usual sprinkling of Joans and Jeans, an Edith and an Alfreda . . .'

'Do Alfredas get called Alf at home?'

'A distinct possibility, if I remember the last one correctly. She must have weighed twelve stone, poor child.'

'I remember. Went into insurance, didn't she?'

'No, the Civil Service. We also have two Paulines and a Paula, but not a single Margaret or Mildred. We seemed to have dozens of them last year. Strange how names go in annual fashions, like hats . . .'

Wilfred buttered more toast. 'I remember a girl called Desiderata. God knows how she came to be saddled with a name like that.'

'This year we have a Cassica.'

'A what?'

'A Cassica.'

'Parents must have been off their heads.'

'When I was a child,' Emilia said, 'I planned to have twins called Fungus and Mildew.'

'Thank God that plan never matured.' Then quickly he touched her cheek. 'Sorry, was that an unkind thing to say?'

'Good heavens, no.' She poured more coffee.

'Would you have liked children, Emilia?' He glanced at her cautiously.

'Yours. But I settled for the next best thing years ago.'

'All the Joans and Jeans and Ediths?'

'Not to mention the Desideratas and Cassicas—'

'*Cassica* — poor little devil!'

'I have a feeling,' Emilia said meditatively, 'that this Cassica will prove to be something of an oddity quite apart from her name.'

'What was she like at the interview?'

'Very tall and rather sulky. Probably been pushed into secretarial training against her will, like a good many of them.'

'Oh really, all these ill-treated little ex-schoolgirls! What on earth *do* they want, if it's not the chance to earn a decent wage in congenial surroundings—'

'They'd like to be princesses,' she said mildly, 'or actresses or nuns. The only decent thing about being seventeen is the certainty that heaven is round the next corner.'

'And you love them all, don't you, my darling?'

'Love is a powerful word,' she replied. 'And I don't care to use it with impunity.'

Leaving the breakfast things for the daily woman to clear away they put on their hats and coats and set off down the long path that wound through the tamarisks and evergreens to the outside world. Just before stepping through the door on to the sea front Emilia slipped her wedding ring from her finger, and with a face devoid of expression dropped it into a little chamois leather drawstring bag as Wilfred locked the door behind them.

They walked to the railway station in silence; at peace, and yet as if some kind of painless metamorphosis was already taking place. For when the Liverpool train drew in to the platform they lightly touched hands before seeking separate carriages.

* * *

The only child of a loveless union between retired Indian Army major and grizzling hypochondriac, Emilia Gathercole spent her formative years on the Irish estate that had been her mother's dowry. Wild hills, sullen seas, weeping rain and watery sunlight; an old ramshackle house and the sound of her father's hunting crop smacking the sides of his riding boots. He brought to Ireland the same choleric thunder that had carved his reputation in India, and the Irish peasants responded to his bullying with the same stealthy malevolence as his subordinates in Bengal. Under the impression that the family was in residence they burned the house down, and the fifteen-year-old Emilia was the first to notice the smoke drifting above the treetops on their return from a weekend in Dublin. The shock of it killed her mother, and her father emigrated to Canada and left his daughter in the care of his sister who hunted, drank port, and sometimes dissolved into long bouts of harsh and inexplicable weeping. She lived in Cheshire with her best friend, a foxhound called Deathwatch.

Thankfully Emilia met the local vicar's family, a jolly, bouncy, affectionate brood who read books and played charades and joked about Father's sermons. (Father sometimes joked about them, too.) They endeavoured to teach Emilia the difference between living and existing, and this led to the sudden realisation that she could, if she chose, be mistress of her own fate. Unsophisticated, and ill-educated beyond reading, writing and arithmetic, she removed herself from Cheshire at the age of twenty-two and with the aid of a small allowance from her father set herself up in two rooms in Liverpool.

And it seemed as if she and Liverpool had need of one another from the very start. A brash bustling seaport that had reaped a fortune from the slave trade, and more recently from cotton and shipping, Liverpool was as eager for self-improvement as Emilia Gathercole. Penny readings in cold temperance halls were no longer sufficient for the parents of children now receiving compulsory education, and Emilia began teaching her landlady to read the *Daily Post* as a jest which very quickly became serious. She also taught her how to add up without recourse to her fingers, and her landlady, pleased and incredulous, asked Emilia if she would mind teaching her two sisters and also her friend who kept the shop next door. Emilia obliged, and the small charge she made was put towards her own night school fees.

For it was becoming increasingly clear that the future lay in commerce; Liverpool was leading the way for her by building larger and ever more stately temples to the great gods of banking and insurance, merchant shipping and municipal management, and feeling herself to be more and more a part of the zestful scene Emilia saw no reason why she shouldn't help to provide these holy shrines with young lady clerks trained by herself to a fitting degree of competence and responsibility.

Consumed by the brilliance of the idea she laboured assiduously at night school to master Sir Isaac Pitman's system of shorthand-writing, and then went on to learn book-keeping and the art of office procedure. From the very beginning she was well aware of the importance of providing young *lady* clerks, and, although her first establishment consisted of five pupils of humble calibre grouped together in her landlady's threadbare front parlour, she stressed the need for personal fastidiousness and hammered anyone who said 'yer wot?' She was happier than she had ever known it possible to be and had no intention of ever jeopardising the future by getting married.

Aided by two ex-pupils she opened the Gathercole Commercial Academy in the late summer of 1891. She chose the premises because they were cheap and in the vicinity of Dale Street and the heart of commercial Liverpool.

Number 3 Hockenhall Street was a strange old building, random and disorientated, and possibly part of a once splendid town house. It had voluminous basements and an entrance hall impressive in size and portentous in gloom. The panelled walls had been painted garden-seat green and the main source of illumination was a vast stained-glass window portraying draped Grecian women with jugs on their heads. A very fine carved staircase led to the first floor, only part of which was included in Emilia's premises, the remainder of it being sealed off and rumoured to contain the furniture and effects belonging to a baronet who had died at sea many years ago. The occasional mouse could be heard on the other side of the wainscot.

But the first-floor room included in Emilia's territory, she at once decided to make her own office sanctum. The panelled walls had escaped the green paint and were tinted a soft ivory. There was a marble chimneypiece, and the Georgian window looked down on to a little paved garden in which grew a fig tree of remarkable beauty. High walls of sooty brick surrounded the garden, and into the corner opposite the old iron seat spiralled the fire escape from the top floor of the building, which had been converted into a small pillbox factory. A group of girls in drab overalls spent ten hours a day gluing the little white cardboard shapes together, and sometimes on fine days they would sit out on the fire escape to eat their bread and cheese; but they never went down into the garden because it was part of the Gathercole Commercial Academy.

Through an archway in the hall were three big rooms highly suitable for the teaching of pupils, and Emilia filled them with second-hand desks, tables and chairs and, to begin with, four typewriters, which were all she could afford. It was all rather bare and shabby (but so, she had heard, were the interiors of both Eton and Harrow), and it was also the first establishment of its kind in Liverpool. Within a gratifyingly short time genteel young ladies who needed to earn their own living began to arrive at her door, all of them carefully escorted by parents or elder brothers. Some were her juniors by no more than a few months, but at twenty-four Emilia's features seemed to have set in a preternatural maturity.

Short of stature, she had a nice little figure set on slightly bulbous legs, and she dressed with a view to the academy's reputation rather than the prevailing fashions for young women. Fawn, grey, and teapot brown in worsted, serge and union flannel. Her dark hair she wore pulled back from her wide intelligent forehead and tightly plaited in a bun, and her features were unremarkable: rather small, rounded eyes, a nose with neatly chiselled nostrils and a wide pale mouth clamped firmly over good teeth and a smile of surprising charm. Very speedily the role of headmistress became second nature, and a kind of equable asperity her most familiar characteristic.

She met Wilfred Sissley in 1907 when he applied for the post of replacement Pitman shorthand instructor, and she interviewed him from behind her large oak desk in the ivory-panelled study.

'To be perfectly frank, I had not envisaged a male person,' she said.

'Male persons are in plentiful supply at the moment, and your advertisement didn't stipulate either sex,' Wilfred replied, and Emilia, now a virgin of forty, visibly recoiled from the three-letter word beginning with s.

'Perhaps not. But now, since you are here—'

'Oh, I can easily go away again,' he said cheerfully. 'I already have two other offers to consider. One in a bank and another connected with duties in the Lord Mayor's Parlour.'

'As you wish. But you may as well leave your name and address, in case I should have anything to offer.'

He did so, and she engaged him after an unsatisfactory trial period with a lady instructor who suffered from gallstones.

They got on surprisingly well from the very beginning, Mr Sissley treating both Miss Gathercole and her academy with seriousness tempered with genial good humour. He taught well, leading his pupils rather than driving them, and occasionally one of them would develop a crush on him; Emilia always noticed whenever it happened, but could never be certain whether or not Mr Sissley had done so. She concluded, approvingly, that he was too much of a gentleman to be aware of such foolishness.

Strangely enough, the first intimation she had of her own feelings towards him was on the morning he mentioned quite casually that he was married. Although as prospective employer she had demanded to know his age, his religion, and whether he drank spirits, it never occurred to her to probe his marital status. The news that he had a wife filled her with inexplicable depression, and she remained very tart with him for several weeks. He became aware of her change in manner, and one morning when the classes had finished and Emilia was about to start marking a typing test he asked if he had done anything to annoy her. No, of course not, she said with her back turned. In that case, he replied, may I have the pleasure of escorting you to lunch?

She was frankly astounded, first that he should defy the proprieties by asking her, and secondly by the wicked little surge of joy she experienced. So she prevaricated, trying to refuse him gently while making it quite clear that she was not accustomed to being escorted to lunch or anywhere else by married men.

'Please,' he said. 'It would be such fun.'

The words took her back to the Cheshire clergyman's family, and she realised that once again she had become a stranger to the idea of doing anything for fun. She prevaricated a little more and then capitulated, sternly rattling the keys of the Gathercole Academy and saying that a poached egg on toast was all she normally required.

Instead, she had steak and kidney pie and cabinet pudding at Rigbys, an ancient hostelry nearby, and insisted that they sat screened from view behind a potted plant. They talked about work, scrupulously avoiding all topics of a more personal nature, and by the time he had escorted her back to the door of the academy she had almost succeeded in persuading herself that there was nothing wrong with liking a married male person purely as a friend. She began taking him into her confidence over business matters, and when he had been at the academy for two years she allowed him to assume some of the administrative chores and raised his salary by five shillings a week. He never betrayed her trust, and her feelings for him were now under control sufficiently for her to be able to cope with his physical nearness. She still had no intention of acknowledging even to herself that should he go away her life would be cold as a graveyard slab.

Then one morning his wife arrived. She was shown into Emilia's office on the assumption that she was a parent of one of the girls. Emilia rose from her desk and held out her hand, and the woman, youngish and prettyish and with a straw hat balanced on a lot of curly black hair, said without preamble: 'I've come to tell you that I'm Mrs Wilfred Sissley and that my husband has deserted me and that I want to know why.'

Shock held Emilia rigid for a moment, then despite the confusion of emotion she managed to speak very calmly. 'I am afraid it is no use coming to me. I am not in the habit of discussing my employees' private affairs either with them or with anyone else.'

Replacing her unshaken hand in her grey cardigan pocket she sat down again and pretended to look through some correspondence.

'No, I daresay not,' the woman retorted. 'There's no smoke without fire.'

'I am afraid I do not quite grasp your meaning.'

The first astonishment at finding herself confronted by Mr Sissley's wife had given way to astonishment that he had left her, and now the desire to protect him from possible embarrassment was only slightly surpassed by the desire to protect the Gathercole Commercial Academy from any hint of scandal, whether merited or not.

'My meaning is that my husband's interests have strayed. They've strayed from me and from his home ever since he took employment here, and I want to know *why*—'

'In that case, I can only suggest that you should ask him, but not during his hours of business. And now, if you will kindly excuse me—' Emilia rose to her feet and, brushing past Mr Sissley's wife, opened the door. 'I bid you good day.'

'I want him back. He belongs to me and I want him. I want him to tell me when he's coming back.'

'My dear good woman.' Emilia gritted her teeth. 'I do not employ people on the understanding that they may conduct their marital bickerings in my time and on my premises. I have no proof that you are Mr Sissley's wife and I have no intention of interrupting his class in order to find out. So have the goodness to leave my establishment before I have you ejected as a common nuisance!'

Taking the woman's arm she attempted to heave her through the doorway. The woman resisted. There was a brief and undignified little scuffle, during which a feather became detached from the woman's straw hat, and when it floated close to Emilia's face she blew it haughtily away.

'All right,' Mr Sissley's wife said, and stopped struggling. 'All right then. I'll go now because I've found out one thing I wanted to know and that is that it isn't *you* who's made him stray away.' Removing her arm from Emilia's grasp she stood looking at her for a long moment. 'You're much too old,' she said, 'and much too beastly stuck up!'

She turned then and began to scuttle rapidly downstairs. Emilia stood motionless, listening to the tap-tap of her feet across the hall followed by the bang of the front door. Then she went back into her office and closed the door and wept for the first time since childhood.

Drying her eyes she pondered the problem of whether or not to tell Mr Sissley about his wife's visit. The thought of causing him pain and mortification filled her with repugnance, and a deep selfish dread that his reaction might be to immediately give in his notice and leave the district in an effort to escape. Supposing he went all the way to London, or even abroad? But if she didn't tell him and he found out from whoever had let his wife in, could her silence be construed as cold indifference, or, even worse, as prim disapproval of a situation which must already have caused him a great deal of unhappiness? She couldn't bear to risk that. Pacing the office she strove to consider the position dispassionately, and to suppress the ignominious little bubble of hope caused by the knowledge that he no longer loved his wife.

She was still undecided about her best course of action when there was a tap on the door and Mr Sissley came in. He sat down on the chair facing her desk and said: 'That was my wife, wasn't it?'

'Yes.'

'What did she want?'

'You.'

'I see.'

'I told her you were busy.'

'Thank you.'

They sat listening to the rhythmical sound of machinery stamping out little bits of cardboard up in the pillbox factory. It only stamped them out on Mondays and Thursdays.

'I'm very sorry,' Emilia said finally.

'It's I who should apologise, Miss Gathercole. Very bad form, bringing one's personal problems to—'

'It was your wife, not you.'

'Well, makes no odds really, does it?'

'Yes,' said Emilia. 'It makes me sympathetic towards you but not her.'

They said no more, but were not surprised when Mrs Sissley called again. She was not admitted, and appeared rather pathetically resigned to the politely worded message that Mr Sissley could accept no visitors during business hours, and it was on her third visit that the shocking thing happened.

As luck (or ill-luck) would have it, her arrival coincided with the departure of Emilia and Wilfred, to go their separate ways. It was half past four, both students and staff had left, and only the caretaker remained on the premises.

Opening the heavy front door Wilfred all but collided with his wife, who gave a hoarse cry and raised both her arms, and for the remainder of his life he was never to be sure whether she intended to strike or embrace him.

He sidestepped, then turned towards Emilia who was coming through the doorway behind him. Seeing Mr Sissley's wife, Emilia halted abruptly, then took a quick backward pace as if she intended to retreat inside the building and close the door. The woman rushed at her, and, sensing that she was about to attack Emilia, Wilfred seized her arm and pushed her away. She clung to him, swaying and panting, and the embarrassing tussle only ended when the woman suddenly let go and dashed away down the steps.

'I won't — I won't!' they both heard her cry, and Emilia screamed as the woman seemed to ricochet across the pavement before abruptly disappearing from view beneath the front wheels of a passing motor van.

In the seconds which followed, everything seemed very still and very quiet. Panting and ashen-faced, Emilia and Wilfred rushed down the steps and the driver of the motor van leaned out of the window crying uselessly: 'What was it? — oh, God, just tell me what was it?' and then a crowd began to collect. Even a little dog appeared and started sniffing at one of the motionless black shoes lying in the shadow of the running-board. The driver got down, peered queasily about him and then sat down in the road with his head in his hands.

A policeman arrived, and it took a long time to get her out. Sick and shaking, Emilia averted her eyes, but there was very little blood and nothing terrible to see. The woman's curly black hair was tumbled and dusty and there was a long smear of dirt down her cheek. They laid her on the pavement, waiting for a stretcher to arrive, and she opened her eyes for a moment, wide and vacant as two empty saucers.

'She's still alive . . .' someone whispered.

Wilfred accompanied his wife to the infirmary; two more policemen arrived to question the driver of the motor van and then to ask Emilia if she could give an account of the accident. She did her best to comply without revealing the woman's identity, but when pressed had to admit that she was the wife of her employee, Mr Sissley. Then the crowd dispersed, and Emilia was walking slowly up the front steps of the academy when one of the policemen touched her shoulder.

'Perhaps you could take care of this for the gentleman's wife, madam,' he said, and handed her the woman's straw hat. The brim was crushed, but the bunch of feathers remained cheerfully intact. Emilia took it without speaking.

Upstairs in the office she unlocked the first aid box that was kept in the cupboard, and discarding the iodine and bandages, the sal volatile and waxen coils of Aspro, poured herself a tot of brandy. She sat at her desk, holding the glass in both hands and trying to regain composure by breathing slowly, and comfort by looking round at all the familiar objects in the room. The red and blue Turkey carpet, the glass-fronted bookcase, the chairs, the cupboard, and the big important desk with its telephone and folders and papers, but all she could see was the woman's straw hat sitting like some poor little unclaimed animal on the chair by the door. She wanted to cry, but no tears would come.

* * *

The woman didn't die, at least not in the technical sense.

A fractured skull and dislocated spine were diagnosed, and, although she appeared to regain lucidity for a short while, it was feared that little could be done for her. Speechless and motionless, she lay supine on the infirmary bed, staring with expressionless and unblinking eyes at the ceiling.

And although life seemed to proceed as usual at the Gathercole Academy — fortunately there had been no report of the accident in the press and the other staff appeared unaware of the drama that had involved Mr Sissley's wife — both Wilfred and Emilia were infected by a growing tension. To Emilia in particular it seemed as if a huge and unscalable wall had been formed out of all their unspoken words, leaving her on one side and Wilfred on the other. She still found it difficult to confess even to herself that she loved him, and the genteel reticence of the times prevented her from hinting her concern for him in even the most tenuous fashion. She considered giving him a bunch of flowers for his wife as a mute token of her feelings, then dismissed the idea as both craven and dishonest. The principal of the Gathercole Commercial Academy pursued no one, any more than she would pretend pity for a woman who had been impertinent to her. The charge of being old and bossy had cut deeply with Emilia, and despite the woman's melancholy situation she felt no inclination to forgive. So she did nothing, said nothing, but her tendency to upbraid her pupils and bark at her teaching staff caused a certain amount of aggrieved comment, and her restless nights were spent pondering and probing the possible motive for Mr Sissley's conduct towards the woman in the infirmary. Gentlemen rarely deserted their wives without very good reason. Did she drink? Fritter money? Or, worst of all, was she faithless? The questions seethed, her appetite waned and she lost several pounds in weight.

And Wilfred was equally tormented. Spending half an hour each lunchtime and another half-hour each evening in dutiful vigil by his wife's bedside, he too pondered the situation, but, unlike Emilia, saw no harm in comforting himself with thoughts and dreams and desires. He loved Emilia with a wonderful, entranced delight, and it was impossible to believe that any emotion that brought such warmth into his life could be touched by such words as shameful or immoral. Yet the very nature of his love recoiled from involving her, from indicating his feelings by the slightest glance or touching of hands because he was not at liberty to do so. There were odd moments when he fancied that she was aware of his miserable predicament, but her attitude towards him was one of consistent unapproachability. So far as he could envisage, the terrible deadlock could only be broken by either the death of his wife or by her complete recovery, for in the latter case he was now determined to divorce her. But although divorce would bring him freedom, he doubted very much whether it would bring him Emilia; apart from the question of whether or not she loved him, he was fairly certain that she would never risk jeopardising either her own or the academy's reputation by marrying a divorcee.

But as so often happens, the impasse was resolved in quite another way; in this case, by the unwitting intervention of an extremely small brown mouse which darted with terrified speed across Emilia's office carpet. Gasping, she leaped in the direction of the desk, then turned in a frenzied half-circle and, catapulting herself in the direction of the door, found herself in the arms of Mr Sissley.

'Under the desk! — it's under the desk!'

'It's all gone — all gone now—'

'It was *huge*!'

'You're quite safe now . . . quite safe—'

'I simply can't bear any *more*—'

'There's no need to. I've got you safely, my darling, and I'll never, *never* let you go . . .'

* * *

They talked and talked. As if they had at last found the key to some precious casket, the words poured out bright, revealing and beautiful as jewels. To begin with, the discovery of their reciprocal feelings took precedence over every other consideration, and the sheer wonder of it banished all constraint in speaking honestly and frankly about Wilfred's wife.

'Why did you leave her?'

'I didn't. We were living under the same roof until the time of the accident, but for some reason she seemed to take pleasure in telling people that I'd deserted her. She told many extraordinary tales about me in her time, preferably wherever it would cause maximum embarrassment—'

'Is she deranged — I mean, *was* she, before the accident?'

'Not certifiably. I think she just lived in some imaginary world of her own—'

'But how cruel of her—'

'It doesn't matter . . . Oh, Emilia, nothing matters now . . . you'll never know what these last few weeks have been—'

'Yes, I do. It has been exactly the same for me — wondering, and not knowing anything for sure . . .'

They went on talking long after the academy had closed. Emilia made tea on the little spirit stove and they sat on either side of the fire, taking an almost perverse pleasure now in the fact of not touching, while their loving eyes all but devoured one another. Unobserved, the mouse discovered a loose thread from the carpet which took its fancy and carried it back to its nest behind the wainscot.

During the weeks that followed Wilfred and Emilia became lovers, and shortly after his wife's transfer to a small private home for incurables at Seaforth they set up house together, first in a ground-floor flat overlooking Princes Park, and then in the secluded seashore house at Hoylake.

To local tradespeople they were known as Mr and Mrs, and, having once taken the immense step of exchanging a life of unblemished virtue for that of married man's mistress, Emilia adapted with surprising ease to being Miss Gathercole during business hours and Mrs Sissley at all other times.

It seemed as if love filled her with even more calm self-certainty, and when at Wilfred's instigation she had her front hair cut and frizzed in a fringe the effect was not one of frivolity but of added dignity.

After the first two or three years together they seldom spoke of Wilfred's wife, but when they did so it was with scrupulous courtesy, as if she were some mutual acquaintance who had emigrated to far-off shores. The nurses who ran the home for incurables advised Wilfred to regard her as one of our Lord's everlasting flowers, and this he agreed to do; she still lay motionless and open-eyed, but with the passing of time she became increasingly blanched and shrunken, with strange little hollows appearing in her hands and face, and her once lively black curls were sparse and dry, like the hair of something on display in a museum. For a long while he called to see her once a week, but by 1919 he had limited his visits to Christmas and her birthday, with a few random telephone enquiries in between. Emilia always bought flowers for him to take, and immediately on his return poured him a small glass of Madeira, serving it on a little silver salver with a Bath Oliver biscuit.

And sitting on her own in the train bound for Liverpool on that September morning in 1919, Emilia reminded herself that today was not merely the first day of term at the Gathercole Commercial Academy, it was also the poor unfortunate's birthday. The two had never coincided before, and by the time they reached Central Station she had discarded the idea of pompon dahlias and in a sudden spirit of magnanimity decided to buy carnations instead.

CHAPTER FIVE

Ten minutes to nine on the first morning of September term at the Gathercole Commercial Academy in Hockenhall Street. Dark rooms lit by hissing gaslight, the smell of chalk and paper and newly oiled typewriters, the clatter of feet on stone basement floors and a cloakroom crowded with lost, nervous, giggly girls trying to establish kinship among the clothes pegs. There were more than fifty of them, long-haired and long-skirted, pink-faced with bashfulness or white-faced with worry.

'Were we supposed to bring our own pencils?'

'Where are we supposed to go?'

'Oh, doesn't it feel like school again?'

'Is it all right if we change our shoes?'

'Can anyone lend me a hairpin?'

Bobbing, jostling, fussing and fidgeting. Sharp elbows nudging at young ribs already encased in whalebone corsets, in spencers and berthas and new winter vests that tickled and tormented. Girls with acne, girls with pince-nez, and over by the small foggy mirror a girl openly powdering her nose.

A woman wearing a dark blue smock with a bow at the collar clapped her hands in the doorway and asked everyone to accompany her. They did so, shuffling up a flight of stone steps into what looked depressingly like a big school hall.

'Oh help, are we going to have prayers?'

'People don't have to pray in *offices*, do they?'

They waited, having automatically formed themselves into orderly ranks that faced the staircase, with the woman in the smock standing a little to one side in an attitude of meek servitude, head bowed and hands folded in front of her crotch.

Unhurriedly and very grandly Emilia Gathercole descended the staircase from her office and then stood, four steps from the bottom, with one hand on the banister while she surveyed the first half of the new year's intake. Fifty-seven young faces, anxious, earnest, resolute; timid, awed, uncertain; and all of them striving with varying degrees of success to pass from child to adult in the one swift and decorous step that was all convention allowed.

'Good morning,' she said.

'Good morning,' they replied in a polite buzz of voices.

'The name is Gathercole,' Emilia said graciously. 'I am Miss Gathercole, and my first duty is to welcome you to the Gathercole Commercial Academy.'

They murmured a constrained and wordless thank you.

'And here at Gathercoles we are proud of our reputation for training secretaries and book-keepers to a very high standard,' she continued. 'It is a reputation which has been built up little by little over the years, and each time I greet a new set of pupils I find myself wondering which of them will achieve eminence in her own particular field. For I wish to make one thing clear: the pupils we enrol here at my academy are of university entrance standards in intelligence, in education and general comportment, and they are all imbued with a desire for success in their chosen career. This is a desire which I applaud, and will seek to encourage whenever I can, but I warn you' — Emilia held up her unadorned left hand — 'I warn you that you will be expected to work hard. Learning Sir Isaac Pitman's system of shorthand is no parlour game, no aimless occupation for a wet afternoon. It is difficult and intricate, and demands the same level of concentration as the learning of, let us say, a classical language. There are no short cuts. Each step must be mastered in its turn, each outline must be practised and practised until, by the time you leave here with your final certificate of proficiency, you will be capable of writing Pitman shorthand even in your sleep!'

She made it sound amusing so that most of them laughed politely; only a few dared to shudder.

'And the same thing applies to your typewriting. Here at Gathercoles we teach the art of touch-typing, which means that you will learn to use your machine with unerring precision and at high speed, without ever needing to glance at your keyboard. This is a very modern accomplishment eagerly sought by discriminating employers, and it is also, I might add, an accomplishment which you will find yourselves cherishing with pride. You will be *proud* to be able to tell people that you are touch-typists. But hand in hand with the skills of fast and accurate Pitman shorthand and touch-typing, we seek to turn out secretaries of a very high *general* standard. And this includes appearance. Here at my Commercial Academy we produce a quiet, well-spoken, pleasant and unobtrusive personality dressed in a neat dark frock or blouse and skirt. Tidy hair in earphones or a bun — we regard the shingle as unpleasantly strident — fingernails short and of course scrubbed very clean, shoes brightly polished and plain stockings without — I repeat, without — clocks. For the perfect secretary is modest and self-effacing; her demeanour at all times unassuming, unpretentious, unimposing. She is there to assist, to show loyalty and allegiance, and to leave decision-making and all other matters of vital importance to her employer.'

There was a short, impressed silence, during the course of which Emilia gazed out over the upturned faces, and when her eyes encountered those of a tall girl standing in the second row her well-trained memory instantly supplied the name. *Cassica.* (Oh, foolish, foolish parents.)

She began speaking again, aware that for some reason she was addressing Cassica on behalf of all the others.

'And now to practicalities. You will be divided into two classes, the only difference between you being that Class A will study shorthand from nine o'clock until eleven, followed by typewriting instruction from eleven fifteen until one, the procedure being reversed for Class B. And although neither class has afternoon tuition, please do not assume that half a day's work is all that will be required of you. While we are engaged upon instructing our afternoon pupils you will have been given sufficient material for a further three hours' study to take home with you. Homework will be marked and your progress monitored with the most scrupulous care, but apart from that you will be treated as responsible adults. It now only remains for me to introduce you to my staff. First we have Miss Whittaker, whom I believe you have already met—' The woman in the smock bobbed her head in acknowledgement. 'Miss Whittaker will teach you touch-typing, together with Miss Williamson, whom I see over by the door . . . forward please, Miss Williamson . . . and book-keeping will be taken by Miss Sturgeon in her class at the far end of the corridor . . .' A stout, cheerful woman acknowledged the heads turned dutifully in her direction. 'And finally we have Mr Sissley, who, together with occasional tuition by myself, will be instructing you in the art of Pitman shorthand.'

They looked round the hall with slightly quickened interest but there was no sign of him. Instead, he came down the staircase as Miss Gathercole had done, but in his case running lightly and smilingly, a man with golden yellow hair and moustache and a rose in his buttonhole.

'This,' said Miss Gathercole impressively, 'this is Mr Sissley, who has toiled longer and more ardently at the academy than anyone, save possibly myself.'

She stood gravely aside, one hand on her beads, while Mr Sissley began to address them breezily.

'How jolly to see you all here . . . hope you'll take note of what Miss Gathercole has said and end by covering the dear old academy in glory and being a real credit to her, and to every one of us who will be working jolly hard to turn you all into the perfect ideal of the modern post-war secretary!'

With a wave of the hand he skipped down the last three steps and began to push his way through the now disintegrating ranks of girls. They saw him talking to the woman called Miss Whittaker and noted how she blushed with gratification.

'He's rather swish, isn't he?' whispered the girl next to Cassie Marlow.

'But I don't think much of *her*,' Cassie hissed back. 'She looks a real old gorgon.'

The wheels of the Gathercole Academy began to turn. With a smoothness born of long practice the classes were organized, the pupils sorted, tabulated, marshalled and then finally seated, each in her designated place. In the big room filled with typists' tables Miss Williamson, also dressed in blue smock and bow, began to enumerate the principal parts of the typewriter ('This is the platen which lies in the bed of the carriage around which the paper is designed to roll once it has been inserted in the correct manner'), while across the hall in the room filled with desks and a blackboard the genial Mr Sissley was demonstrating in chalk the first letters of the Pitman alphabet. ('Excellent. Now say after me, pee-bee, tee-dee, chay-jay, kay-gay . . .')

They did so, their voices rising in a rhythmic drone to the office upstairs, where Miss Gathercole sat, pen poised, already checking the names of the girls who would be arriving for the academy's afternoon session. Contentment filled her, seeming to spread its warmth into her furthermost extremities, and she paused for a moment to look with fond eyes at the room which had become so intimately a part of her. In some ways it meant even more to her than the house in Hoylake.

During her nineteen years' occupancy the walls had gradually passed from ivory to a richly shaded golden brown. Soot streaks had smudged pleasing shadows in the corners and accentuated the plaster acanthus leaves round the ceiling. The red and blue of the Turkey carpet had faded to more subtle hues, and her desk now faced the two portraits, one of herself and one of Wilfred, which hung from their long cords so close together that their frames almost touched. They had been commissioned, and executed in oils by a Liverpool artist of comfortable repute, to celebrate the academy's Silver Jubilee.

They had long decided to mark the occasion by the expenditure of a fixed sum of money, but as the time drew nearer the choice became more difficult. A new boiler to replace the ailing monster down in the basement? Too costly. New desks for the book-keeping room? Too prosaic. They toyed with the idea of taking the entire establishment, staff and pupils, on a day trip to New Brighton, renting a private steamer and booking a three-course luncheon in a restaurant, but the idea was finally abandoned as not quite in keeping with the dignity of Gathercoles.

What they really wanted was something novel; a hint of grandeur well within the bounds of propriety and good taste as Emilia herself put it, and that was how they arrived at the idea of the portraits. To begin with there was to be only one, of Emilia herself, then she insisted that there ought to be one of Wilfred as well.

'I don't really see why. After all, I'm only an employee.'

'For the moment, yes. But I have plans.'

'I mean, if I were a partner or something, it would be different, wouldn't it?'

'You are more than a partner, loved one, you are the mainstay of my life. In any case, two portraits would look more *balanced*.'

So he capitulated, and Emilia made a note to see her solicitor about drawing up a partnership; she had been meaning to do it for a number of years, but it was one of those little chores that always seem to get overlooked in the busy hurly-burly of everyday matters.

Originally the two portraits had been intended to embellish the hall, but when the completed articles finally arrived in their heavy gold frames, doubt made them reconsider.

'Might it not seem a little pompous of us?' Emilia wondered.

'I suppose it's too late to have Miss Whittaker, Miss Williamson and Miss Sturgeon done as well. But it would have put paid to any suspicion of pomposity.'

'Too late and too expensive. For the price of three more portraits we could have had a new boiler *and* new wash-hand basins in the pupils' cloakroom.'

In the end they decided that the portraits should only be hung in the hall when they were dead, and in the meantime they were to adorn the study wall opposite Emilia's desk. They looked very nice there, and after the first few months Emilia stopped wondering whether the artist had made her chin too prominent and came to accept them as part of the room's furnishing. She remained forgetful about Wilfred's proposed partnership.

'. . . pee-bee, tee-dee, chay-jay, kay-gay, eff-vee, ith-thee . . .' droned the new pupils, and from overhead came the intermittent murmur of gossiping voices from the pillbox factory.

Then the fifteen-year-old called Mavis, whom Emilia employed in starched cap and apron as parlour maid, tapped on the door and said: 'Ooh, a young gentleman's called to see you, madam.'

'Has he an appointment?'

'I don't think so, madam.'

'Did you ask him?'

'Ooh well, I was just going to, but—'

'What is his name?'

Mavis looked harassed. 'Ooh, I didn't really catch it, madam, but he wants to see you about shorthand and typing.'

'You had better show him in.' Emilia sighed, and wondered whether time and perseverance would obliterate Mavis's Liverpool accent and her tendency to begin every utterance with 'Ooh'.

The young man who entered was pale and nondescript, with short-clipped hair and small round spectacles hooked behind prominent ears. He appeared to be still in the process of growing, for his trouser turn-ups were several inches above his stout, well-polished brogues, and his wrists, big-boned and very pink, hung well below his cuffs.

'Good morning, Miss Gathercole. Pardon me for calling without an appointment, but I wondered whether I might enrol in one of your classes if you have a place to spare.'

The quiet self-confidence in his voice was curiously at odds with his gangling appearance. Surprised and a little intrigued, Emilia said: 'I would have to consult with my Miss Sturgeon, who is in charge of the book-keeping department. You have left it rather late, apart from—'

'I came as soon as I could, but I've been indisposed.'

'Quite apart from the fact that the academy does not normally—'

'And I wish to study shorthand and typewriting, not book-keeping, Miss Gathercole.'

'Shorthand and typewriting?' Emilia shifted her blotter a little to one side, then studied it intently. 'Is that not rather an unusual choice for a young man?'

'I'm afraid I don't know. Is it?'

'I would have thought so.'

'You see, I've decided to become a male secretary.'

'A *male* secretary?' Emilia raised her eyes from the blotter and regarded him with growing distrust. 'I see.'

'There are such things as male secretaries, I believe?' He spoke with deference.

'Possibly so. I may have heard of one or two isolated instances where men have—'

'So might I enrol — Miss Gathercole?'

'I may not have room,' Emilia said. 'Apart from which, I have my other pupils to — to consider.

'Oh? But if they have already started their course I think I can promise that I will soon catch up with them. My lagging behind would be no problem.'

'I daresay not.' Emilia folded her hands majestically. 'The problem I envisage is that all my pupils are female.'

'And I'm male — you mean?'

Emilia stared at him without blinking.

'Must that be regarded as an obstacle?' His deference increased.

'It is difficult to regard it as anything else.'

'But I'm quite sure that I would find it no—'

'Probably not. But I repeat, I must consider the feelings and the general welfare of my other pupils. Here at the academy—'

'I promise not to interfere with their welfare in any way, Miss Gathercole. I just want to learn the knack of shorthand and typing in the shortest possible time, so that—'

'Shorthand and typewriting can hardly be described as a *knack*, Mr er—'

'I beg your pardon, Miss Gathercole.' Instant contrition. 'The art—'

'As I was saying before you interrupted, here at the academy, where Pitman shorthand and touch-typewriting are regarded as two of the exact sciences and cannot be scrambled through with one eye on the clock — here at the academy we are only accustomed to dealing with pupils of the feminine gender. Never having been called upon to enrol a male pupil during the whole course of our twenty-eight years, you will appreciate that to do so now would call for a certain amount of realignment, not to mention reorganization of a structural nature within the building itself.'

'Oh, but surely—'

'There is no "Oh, but surely" about it. This establishment has always been noted for its high regard for the proprieties and I do not, to be perfectly frank, envisage a sudden high expenditure of capital on things which are not essential to the general well-being—'

'I'm sorry Miss Gathercole, I'm afraid I don't quite follow—'

'You would have to have your own w.c.!' cried Emilia with mounting impatience. 'Good heavens, man, have you no imagination at all?'

'Oh dear.' He thought for a moment, then said meekly: 'I believe there's a public urinal on the corner of Cumberland Street—'

'Oh, don't be ridiculous! No, no, I'm afraid the whole thing is quite untenable. We have never pursued a policy of taking male pupils and I see no point in starting now, Mr er. The drawbacks far outweigh the advantages — in fact, I find it quite impossible to envisage one single advantage of any sort—'

The door opened and Wilfred came in.

'This young man wishes to study shorthand and type-writing,' Emilia said repressively, 'in order that he may become a male secretary.'

'He could hardly become a female one, could he?' Wilfred gave a jolly laugh, shook the young man's hand and said: 'Well, I don't see why not. There's room in my mid-morning class for another person, and I daresay Miss Whittaker could fit him in for typing. Yes. Splendid. So consult with Miss Gathercole about the fees and start tomorrow morning.'

'Mr Sissley,' said Emilia warningly. She tried to catch his eye.

'I suddenly remembered about the flowers,' Wilfred said. 'You know what today is, don't you?'

'The matter of which you speak will be attended to in the usual way. But referring to this young man's—'

'Perhaps I could use this gentleman's—'

'This gentleman,' said Emilia very slowly and very painstakingly, 'is a senior member of my staff, and, as such, is entitled to a special arrangement.'

'What are we talking about?' Wilfred looked blank.

'Never mind now, Mr Sissley. But in the meantime, there are one or two obstacles of a practical nature standing in the way of this young man's admittance—'

'Really? I'm quite sure they can be disposed of—'

'Apart from which, I still think it rather strange that a young man — apart from yourself — should wish to learn Pitman shorthand and—'

'Shaw has written some of his plays in shorthand, and I wouldn't call him strange—'

'I would,' retorted Emilia. 'I would call him very strange indeed.'

'I expect there's also one on Central Station,' said the young man. 'But it's not as near as Cumberland Street—'

'What isn't?' Wilfred asked.

'The gentlemen's convenience.'

'Who's talking about gentlemen's conveniences?'

'Miss Gathercole and I were.'

'I give him ten marks for sheer persistence,' Emilia said wearily. 'And since I appear to be in a minority in more senses than one, I will enrol him as a pupil in my academy. This, I would point out, is against my better judgement, and I can only pray that no ill will come to it. The fees' — she turned to the young man — 'are three guineas per term, payable in advance. And now, may I have your name?'

'Arnold Beckworth Openshaw,' said the young man, and gave her a smile of sudden and extraordinary sweetness.

'Be nice to have another chap about the place,' Wilfred said from the doorway, and winked at Emilia. She failed to respond.

* * *

To begin with Cassie drove to the city with Uncle Harry each morning and Nibbs would call for her at 1 p.m., but after the first couple of weeks she insisted that she was quite capable of going on her own.

For one thing, she was in the process of discovering that her fellow students' attitude towards her was less cordial than it might have been. Although they chatted freely among themselves, whenever Cassie ventured a remark, it seemed to be greeted with disparagement. Rather to her surprise she learned that it wasn't what she said, but how she said it. To pronounce path and bath as *parth* and *barth* was apparently a ludicrous affectation, and the two girls she overheard discussing her were torn between indignation at her stuckupness and laughter at her ignorance.

She discovered that London itself was stuck up: that it hated and disparaged the entire north of England — and Liverpool in particular — as being unsophisticated, unrefined and unreservedly second-rate. In fact everyone south of Birmingham gave themselves airs which fair-minded Liverpudlians found hard to tolerate.

Never one to submit to injustice, Cassie informed them that she liked what she had seen of Liverpool and its citizens, but when they pressed her to tell them what people in London really thought of people in Liverpool she had to admit that, so far as she knew, Londoners didn't generally think about Liverpudlians one way or another, which brought about a fresh charge of arrogance.

And so of course the sight of the uniformed Nibbs standing with folded arms beside the Daimler every lunchtime increased their hostility, and sensing that it would be useless to protest that the Daimler's owner was a Liverpudlian and not a Londoner (in any case, why *should* she?) she contented herself with asking Nibbs if he would mind waiting round the corner and then, finally, deciding that she would rather travel by public transport.

Which was when she started getting to know Liverpool on her own terms. The smell of soot and turgid river water, the blackened buildings and the singsong Liverpool voices blending with the high wail of tramcars. Sometimes she walked part of the way home, carrying her shorthand notebooks in the attaché case that had once belonged to her father, seeing and yet not seeing the abrupt changes from affluence to dire poverty; silk-shaded lamps gleaming through the windows of the mammoth North Western Hotel, a woman swathed in fur and velvet and peacock feathers being escorted up the steps of the Adelphi as if she were a treasure of the most awesome fragility, and round the corner in the narrow back streets the barefoot slimy-nosed children huddled on doorsteps. Once she passed a row of silent, black-shawled women queuing with jugs and basins outside a dilapidated shack without realising that it was a soup kitchen for the destitute. And street after street echoed with the sad hoarse wail of voices upraised in bitter travesty of song as mutilated ex-servicemen tried to earn a copper or two. They sang, they played musical instruments, and sometimes formed themselves into ghastly little jazz bands, those with hands to hold them playing cornets and saxophones, and those on crutches singing and trying to importune the hurrying passers-by. No one took much notice of them, and, after the first sharp pangs of compassion, neither did Cassie.

Uncle Harry invited her to lunch with him so that he might show her some of the splendours of the city, and she was instructed to present herself at his offices in the State Insurance Buildings at 1.25 precisely. She did so and sat waiting on a black leather couch with sphinxes' heads carved on the armrests, and watched rather dolefully Uncle Harry's row of prim lady typists sitting with heads bent and ankles crossed before their chattering machines.

Over lunch at the Conservative Club he told her that he was a committee member of the Liverpool stock exchange. 'And one day I shall be president.'

'That'll be nice,' she said encouragingly.

'I think it will mean something to your Aunt Babs.'

'Yes, I'm sure.'

'I only do these things for her.'

'Do you, really?' Cassie looked at him with sudden new interest, but Uncle Harry raised the menu between them and asked rather abruptly whether she would prefer cauliflower or broccoli.

After lunch he showed her the Town Hall, the Dock Board Building, the glorious mass of the Cunard headquarters, and then took her up to the seventh floor of the Royal Liver and she looked down on the crowded overhead railway, at the tramcars and stubby black steam engines weaving bustling, complex patterns on the landing-stage. He recited the names of the great shipping lines — Cunard, White Star, Bibby Brothers, Elder-Dempster, C. T. Bowring . . . and she peered obediently through the bristling cranes to catch a glimpse of the appropriate funnels.

'Atlantic liners must wait to dock until the tide approaches flood, and it's impossible to over-estimate the skill of the pilots who guide these great ships through the Mersey channels.'

'Yes. I'm sure.'

They walked across the Strand and sat for a while in the gardens of the old Liverpool Parish Church that overlooked the river. The afternoon was mild and damp and silvery-grey, and over on the far bank they could hear the rhythmic clang of hammers coming from the Cammel Laird shipyards.

'The clock on the Liver Building is far larger than that of Big Ben,' Uncle Harry said presently. 'And it only needs winding once in every thirty years. It is a masterpiece of horological art.'

'Yes.'

'Liverpool is the second city of the Empire. She was granted her charter by King John.'

'London got hers before that,' Cassie muttered.

'Still missing your parents, are you?' He gave her hand a sudden kindly little pat.

'Yes. Well, just a bit.'

'It's bound to take time.'

They remained staring out across the Mersey. A ferry-boat was arriving at the landing-stage, the gulls screaming a raucous welcome.

'I'm not really sure I'm going to like Liverpool,' Cassie said in a voice that was barely audible.

'That also needs time. Getting to know a place is the same as getting to know friends, and you'll find that Liverpool has a great heart to offer.'

'Has it?'

'She,' said Uncle Harry. 'We always think of her as a she.'

Abruptly she felt the need to tell him about the other girls at the academy but didn't because she realised that he too was imbued with some of their prickly defensiveness. It had surprised her that an elderly and very important man like

Uncle Harry should think it worthwhile knowing that the clock on the Liver Building was bigger than Big Ben.

Nibbs was waiting on the corner of Water Street, and they drove home in almost unbroken silence.

In a lot of ways Aunt Babs seemed ideally suited for the role of confidante; the only snag was that she had obviously earmarked Cassie for the same role and being older and quicker she always got in first.

'Now, Coco darling, tell me all about your morning and how you're getting on with your squiggles. My morning's been unutterable hell. First of all Hannah's in a perfectly foul mood and behaves as if it's all my fault. She's lost my crepe-de-chine blouse — you know, the one with the fringe — and she upset my breakfast tray all *over* my bed, drenching the eiderdown and incidentally scalding poor innocent me with a *cascade* of Earl Grey . . .' She would rattle on, beautiful, elegant, amusing and tirelessly egocentric.

Now that the boys were back at Oxford she and Cassie quite often had a late lunch in the small gold and white room that had been designated Babs's boudoir; omelettes, or perhaps a *sole bonne femme*, accompanied by a glass of Uncle Harry's Sauterne, with fruit and coffee to follow and then Babs leaning back in her chair smoking a pink cigarette.

'Willie might call this afternoon,' she would say casually. Or it might be Frank or Cyril or Jack. And the throaty little cars would come snorting up the drive while Cassie sat in her own room studying the correct placing of vowel-signs, and, as before, Frank, Cyril or Jack would always depart before Uncle Harry arrived home.

'Willie's such a nice pal to have,' she would tell Cassie. 'We have a million larky things in common and he never wants to be *horrid*.'

Never wanting to be horrid appeared to be the greatest accolade Babs could ever bestow upon anyone of the male gender; neither Frank nor Cyril nor Jack ever felt the urge to be horrid either, and one Sunday morning when Babs appeared looking unusually pale and heavy-eyed, she whispered crossly that it was all because of Uncle Harry, who had insisted upon being horrid for what seemed like all night.

She tended to treat Cassie as if she were sexually experienced and, loath to disillusion her, Cassie made the most out of not very much.

'A man sits next to me at Gathercoles,' she said offhandedly.

'You mean to say they've let a *man* in there, darling? I thought it was a heavily female establishment!'

'It is, except for just this one. And Mr Sissley, of course.'

'But Coco, what's he like? Do tell!'

'Oh — not much to write home about, really. I mean, when you've seen one you've seen them all.'

'Oh, you weary little cynic!'

'Well, I'm getting on for twenty, you know.'

'And he sits next to you *always?'*

'I can't get rid of him.'

'Coco darling — what enormous fun! Why don't you bring him out to lunch one day?'

'I think I'd rather not encourage him,' Cassie said smugly.

It was true that Arnold Openshaw sat next to her in Mr Sissley's shorthand class. He had done so from his very first morning, sliding deftly along the bench towards her while remaining careful to maintain a discreet distance of some four or five inches from her actual person. But sometimes the sides of their knuckles inadvertently touched because Arnold was left-handed.

As the autumn progressed and the weather became colder and wetter he began to snuffle, and after being away for several days with a chest cold returned smelling strongly of camphorated oil. Cassie remained unenthusiastic, but hesitated to actively discourage his gentle overtures because of the other girls. Several of them had made it clear by coy glances and little simperings that they would more than welcome his attentions, but because of their attitude towards her Cassie saw no reason why she should do anything to further their little dreams and schemes. So she let her hair brush against his cheek when she asked if she might borrow his spare pencil and sometimes allowed him to carry her attaché case to the tramcar stop, but that was all. She had given up trying to make friends with any of the other pupils, and now cultivated an air of supercilious indifference which, together with her expensive clothes and fancy accent, combined to make them dislike her even more.

She was lonely and lost, and an increasing nostalgia for the old days in Walham Green awakened a new fierce longing to be at Girton instead of Gathercoles. She felt cheated, angry and resentful, and one morning alighted from the tramcar before it reached Dale Street and found her way to Brownlow Hill. It was a narrow street filled with musty little bookshops, and at the top of it stood Liverpool University. She looked at it for a long time from the opposite pavement, taking in the pompous sandstone architecture and the big, tightly closed excluding doors, then turned and strode back to the city, savagely swinging her father's little brown attaché case full of shorthand books.

She went into one of the big stores where it was warm and bright and full of assistants standing to attention in meek black frocks. She rambled moodily through the haberdashery department, through millinery and ladies' mantles until she found herself in the Pagoda Rendezvous where there were tissue paper flowers on the tables and sallow waitresses serving morning coffee in willow-patterned china. She sat there for a long time drinking coffee and crunching lumps of sugar, and no one took any notice of her. Certainly no one guessed that she was playing truant.

She went for another walk, and this time discovered Princes Park. The bare trees stood cold and black, and a man in a dirty white muffler scavenged for fag-ends in a litter basket. He caught her eye.

'Spare us a copper, chook?'

She gave him a threepenny bit.

'Ta, chook. I fought at Gallipoli, y'know.'

Nasal, whiney, singsong voice; thin cheeks, stubbly chin and a runny nose. Averting her eyes, Cassie gave a brief nod and walked away.

She arrived home in time for lunch. Babs was out, and the house was silent and opulent and disinterested. Dora served her a lamb cutlet followed by raspberry blancmange and Cassie ate with a volume of Edgar Wallace propped up against the silver cruet.

Up in her bedroom the little Waring & Gillow writing desk stood waiting in the window. She went over to it and opened the attaché case with the idea of redemption through additional study of Compound Consonants and Aspirated Ws, then abruptly hurled the Pitman shorthand instructor across the room. It landed on top of the wardrobe with a thud. She flung herself on the bed and lay staring at the ceiling, but all she saw was the row of drab, self-effacing lady typists in Uncle Harry's office.

She didn't want to become one of them. Neither, after due consideration, did she want to be another Babs, whose life of pampered ease had to be paid for by allowing Uncle Harry to be horrid. She wanted something quite different; something splendid, challenging and bravely independent. For the first time she considered the possibility of running away and starting on her own somewhere. But starting what? And what with? She remembered the importance her mother had attached to success. How her eyes had glowed when she said, *I want you to be a success. Work hard and you'll be very successful in life and then everyone will be proud of you* . . . How remote it all was now. Her mother and father in Walham Green, the war, the school, and the childish certainty that she could achieve anything she set her mind to.

In a half-hearted attempt to recapture some of the old determination she got off the bed and went to retrieve the textbook from where she had thrown it. The top of the wardrobe was recessed, and she could only reach by standing on tiptoe. Instead of encountering the book, her groping fingers met something soft. She lifted it down and stood staring at it in surprise.

It was a child's doll.

CHAPTER SIX

Babs arrived home with Cyril, her hair concealed beneath a snakeskin flying helmet, her long sable coat gathered tightly round her. Her cheeks had been stung pink in the open car and her eyes sparkled.

'Any messages, Hannah?'

'A telephone call from the master, madam. He will be home a little earlier because of the celebration.'

'Celebration?' She pulled off the helmet and shook out her hair.

'Your wedding anniversary, madam.'

'Oh, yes. We'll take tea in the library, please, Hannah.'

She led the way across the hall and the door closed behind them.

'Darling Babsie — Oh, my darling—'

'Take your muffler off, you stupid boy—'

'Oh, Babsie, if only you knew—'

'I *do* know, for the simple reason that you won't stop *telling* me—'

'But you still don't realise — Oh, my angel girl . . .'

'Be careful, Cyril, someone might come in—'

'But I love you . . . I adore you . . .'

'Which doesn't automatically give you *carte blanche,*' said Babs, sidestepping, 'to kiss me and squeeze me just whenever you think you will. So now.'

'Just kiss me once, properly, and then I promise I'll be a good boy—'

'Really promise?'

'Really promise. God's honour . . .'

She gave a sensuous little shrug and the sable coat slipped in a gleaming pool round her feet. Beneath it she was wearing a pleated yellow silk dress. She closed her eyes.

'That's enough. Hannah will be in with the tea.'

'The kettle can't have boiled yet . . . Oh, God, Babs, you're so lovely—'

'It's not just Hannah, I've got to think about my niece—'

'Oh, Babsie — Babsie—' He began kissing her again, nibbling hungrily at her nose, her lips, her chin, her throat. Once more she closed her eyes, and then reopening them gave a shrill little scream and pushed him away.

'Where's that come from? Who put it there?'

'Who put what—?'

The doll was sitting on a cushion on one of the sofas, propped up as if it were an invalid. It had one bright blue eye while the other socket was a blank hole, and its white lace dress was torn and grubby.

'That thing on the sofa! — where's it come from?' She darted towards it, stretching out her hand, then backed away as if it were something harmful. Her face was very pale.

'It's only a doll — look . . .'

'*Put it down*!' She rushed across as he dropped it back on the sofa, then she picked up the cushion and threw it on top of the doll as if to hide it as Hannah came in carrying the big silver tea tray.

'Will that be all, madam?' Poker-faced, eyes averted.

'Yes, thank you, Hannah. Mr Cyril is just staying for a quick cup of tea, and then he—'

'Very good, madam.'

Still panting slightly, Babs sat down by the tray and began to pour out the tea. Her hand was shaking, and a little of the golden liquid splashed into the saucers.

'Babsie, why were you so upset?'

'I wasn't. Do you take sugar? I've forgotten—'

'But you were, darling. You looked as if you'd seen the proverbial ghost—'

'I said, do you take sugar?'

'Yes, two. But if anything frightens or upsets you, *ever*, you *must* tell me—'

'It was just a surprise, that's all. As if I'd seen a stray cat, or something—'

'But it was only a doll—'

'I hate dolls,' she said. 'I always hated them when I was a little girl. They're cold and creepy, like dead people.'

'Funny little soul . . .' He put his cup and saucer down.

'Now, Cyril, for God's sake don't start again. I've had enough. I'm very tired—'

'But I was only—'

'In fact, I think you'd better go now. I'm tired and upset and Harry will be home soon and I've got to dress and go out to dinner with him.'

'But, Babsie, let me just—'

'Will you *go*! Just go, before I lose my temper and say things I don't mean.'

He did so, smiling at her ruefully as he rewound the muffler round his neck.

'Can I just—'

'Oh, buzz *off*, can't you?'

He went, leaving his cup of tea untouched. A few minutes later Cassie walked in.

'Did you put that doll on the sofa?'

'Did I—?' Then she smiled. 'Oh, yes. I meant to tell you, I found it yesterday.'

'Where did you find it?'

'On top of my bedroom wardrobe.'

'What on earth were you doing up there?' The edgy, irritated voice was not like the usual Babs. Slightly disconcerted, Cassie murmured that she had been looking for a lost book.

'Well, it was rather a beastly sort of joke, putting it on the cushion like that, Coco—'

'I'm sorry.' Cassie poured herself a cup of tea. 'I thought it looked rather funny — so homely among all these beautiful rich things.'

Babs sat staring into the fire without speaking.

'Where did it really come from?' Cassie asked. 'Whose was it, I mean?'

'The doll?' Babs shrugged. 'Oh, it belonged to one of the boys.'

'You mean, to Lionel or Desmond?' Cassie looked amazed.

'I can't remember. No, I think some other child must have left it here — oh, possibly years ago.'

'On top of my wardrobe?'

'It wasn't your wardrobe then. You probably weren't even born.'

'I didn't mean to sound proprietorial . . .'

'Oh, shut up, Coco,' Babs said with something like the old ease of manner. 'I'll get Hannah to throw it away—'

'Oh no, don't do that!'

'Why not?' A new tension seemed to be developing. Cassie felt mystified and slightly upset.

'Oh, no special reason. Just that — that some little girl long ago probably loved it. Even though it's only got one eye.'

'I *hate* things like that,' Babs said in a low voice. 'Things that aren't beautiful and normal and perfect. The only thing to do is to throw them away — get rid of them—'

'Is that how it ended up on top of my wardrobe?'

'Very probably. In the meantime I must go and bath and change. Harry and I are dining out tonight, but I expect the maids will have arranged something nice for you to eat. Cheery-bye, if I don't see you until tomorrow.'

'Have a nice time,' Cassie said. She flopped down on the sofa, then immediately sprang up again. Pushing aside the cushion she saw the doll lying with its legs in the air. She picked it up, and its one eye opened with a faint click. It was not a very big doll, no more than nine inches in length, with a soft body and china head and limbs. The tip of its nose was chipped and its hair stuck out in nightmare ringlets. She tried to imagine Lionel and Desmond playing mothers and fathers with it but couldn't.

Then the door opened.

'Look, Hannah, what I found on top of my wardrobe.'

The maid looked at the doll in silence. 'Someone must have put it up there since last spring-cleaning. Everything in this house is moved and dusted at least once a year,' she said defensively.

'Yes, but whose was it?'

'I couldn't say, I'm sure, miss.'

Oh yes you could, thought Cassie. But you're jolly well not going to.

'Can I take the tray now, miss?'

'Yes, of course. Thank you, Hannah.'

She waited until Hannah had left the room, then went upstairs, taking the doll with her. Sitting on the side of her bed she scrutinised its features as if hoping to glean additional information from them, then laid it gently face down in her underwear drawer and covered it over with a petticoat.

* * *

Oh, Cassica, thought Arnold Openshaw, standing in the doorway of the cloakroom. The place was deserted, the clothes pegs bare except for one which held a navy blue alpaca coat and a hat with a bunch of cherries on the brim. No one else had a hat like that in Gathercoles, and with little eye for fashion Arnold assumed that it must be either ultra-smart or outlandishly frumpish. Whichever it was, it was inexpressibly dear to him.

Oh, Cassica Marlow, oh, Cassica, oh, Cassie, where are you? Why are you so late?

Leaning back against the door frame he rehearsed what he was going to say when finally she did appear. I was wondering whether, Miss Marlow, you would care to come with me to St Ezekiel's Hall on Friday evening to a very interesting lecture. I already have the tickets . . .

Her coat and hat were hanging quite near. Three paces inside the room and he would be able to touch them. To gently caress the sleeve, touch the collar, slip his hand inside the pocket and imagine her own fingers nestling in there, but of course it was impossible. Unthinkable. Although the place was deserted it was still imbued with the dangerous presence of young womanhood, of the opposite sex, the feminine gender, and was thus out of bounds. A cupboard had been cleared out and converted into a cloakroom for his own use next to the boilerman's cubbyhole, and a lavatory of great antiquity found for him in a little brick outbuilding concealed by ivy. Spiders abounded, but, as Miss Gathercole had said, at least it is your own.

Are you likely to be engaged this coming Friday evening, Cassica? I have two tickets for a most interesting lecture, and I wondered whether you would care to accompany me? I would of course be pleased to accompany you home afterwards . . .

He had never been in love before, and it was astonishing how it impelled him to share all his interests, his hopes and ideals with her. I have little to offer in the material sense, Cassica dear, but a wealth of exciting aspirations and the promise of a marvellous new world that we can help create . . .

Happy optimism charged through his bloodstream; to calm himself he took off his small round spectacles and began to polish them vigorously on his sleeve.

* * *

'Your commencement was highly satisfactory — both Mr Sissley and Miss Whittaker drew my attention to it — but now you seem to have petered out. May I ask why?'

Cassie stood before Miss Gathercole's desk, feet at ten to two, hands clasped behind her back. Politely but unwinkingly, she stared down at the Queen Alexandra frizz above the wide forehead and shrewd eyes glinting behind gold pince-nez.

'I don't know.'

'And you seem quite often to be poorly. Five absences, and still three weeks before the end of term. Hardly an impressive record, is it?'

'No. I get headaches.'

'In that case you must consult an oculist.'

'They're not that sort.'

'Then I take it that you are referring to the monthly cycle. Headaches and a general feeling of debility are common before the onset of the flow but we all have to learn to rise above it.'

'Yes, Miss Gathercole.'

Emilia removed a sheet of paper from a pile of others on her desk and studied it intently. Gloomily Cassie recognised it.

'Your last week's test was very bad. In fact it was so bad that Mr Sissley was forced to mark you bottom, which grieved him considerably. And it grieved him because he too knows that you are capable of far better work. Just look at those Shun hooks. A child of five could have done better. And imagine writing the word Shakespeare with a downward *r*; a downward *r* never follows a stroke with a similar slope, and well you know it.'

'Yes, Miss Gathercole.'

'So why *do* it?'

'I suppose I forgot.'

Emilia laid the paper aside and took up another sheet. 'Your typewriting is equally disappointing. Seventeen mistakes, uneven touch — far too heavy on the commas and full stops — and at least two examples of over-typing. Now I am quite sure that Miss Whittaker has impressed upon all of you time and again the evils of over-typing. To backspace and then deliberately to superimpose one letter upon another in the hope that the error will thus be disguised is a mark of the second-rate, the slipshod, the self-taught. Here at Gathercoles we despise this sort of thing, Cassica. We pride ourselves on learning to do things correctly, and hence we never need stoop to subterfuge.'

'No, Miss Gathercole.'

'So I suggest that you go away and pull up your socks, remembering as you do so that the world of commerce into which you are proposing to enter has no time for a slacker.'

'No, Miss Gathercole.'

Dismissed by a regal nod, Cassie left the room. From the floor above came the sound of a girl's voice singing 'My Bonnie Lies Over the Ocean'. She wished that she was a pillbox girl too, even though they didn't knock off until six.

She walked downstairs and across the empty hall, and by the stone steps that led down to the cloakroom Arnold Openshaw suddenly darted out and said in a breathless babble: 'Miss Marlow would you do me the honour of coming to a lecture with me—'

'No thanks,' Cassie said, shoving him aside, 'I've just been to one.'

* * *

'Is she really ill?'

Wilfred and Emilia were walking home arm in arm from Hoylake station that evening. Gas lamps shone a soft light down through the bare trees and gleamed in the puddles. The air was cold and very still, and they could hear the roar of the sea far out in the darkness.

'No, of course she isn't. She's playing truant,' replied Emilia.

'How can you be sure?'

'Difficult to explain. But a lot of girls start well and then seem to lose interest, then they go on again better than ever. And they are nearly always the clever ones. The more mediocre girls proceed at a steady plod.'

'Much less exasperating than girls who proceed in ungainly leaps.'

'I daresay, but also less interesting. Do you remember Ursula Brewer?'

'I try not to, but the memory still returns.'

'She is now confidential secretary to the chief consultant at the consumption hospital. Her position carries enormous responsibility and a very high emolument.'

'Fancy . . .'

Although his sunny demeanour and sprightly appearance made him far more approachable than Emilia, Wilfred had less understanding and in consequence less patience with their pupils. He worked hard and derived pleasure from teaching, but one girl was very like another and he had little interest in, or curiosity about, those who tended not to conform. If a girl cried he would lend her his handkerchief and pat her shoulder (which generally made her cry more), but he seldom enquired the reason for her tears. All girls cried, as all girls got fits of giggles, and sooner or later they would grow out of it.

Emilia was different, and beneath the regal asperity was a mind that brooded and examined, watched and analysed. Boring girls irritated her but she never let it show, any more than she displayed the slightest hint of affection for those of a more mercurial temperament. And if she seemed almost to have been born with a gift for understanding the complexities of the female psyche, years of experience had deepened it and developed it into a profoundly rich and loving wisdom.

'They say consumption is on the increase,' Wilfred said, 'and that they're going to build a large new sanatorium at Broad Green, or somewhere.'

'I would not be surprised if Arnold had a tendency in that direction.'

'Our young Lochinvar? Consumptive?'

'He has the pallor.'

'Poor lad,' said Wilfred, and skipped with her merrily across the road. 'What's for supper?'

'Mulligatawny soup followed by ham on the bone.'

'Oh, Emilia, you are my soul's delight . . .'

Down on the deserted sea front Wilfred groped in his pocket for the key to the door in the wall while Emilia stood close by, slipping her wedding ring back on to her finger.

* * *

'Coco, there's a surprise in your room!'

'What is it?'

'Not telling. Go and see—'

A big white box on the bed tied with gold ribbon. A snowdrift of tissue paper, and rising from it a pale blue chiffon evening frock, sleeveless, with a low draped neckline and a little train at the back.

'That's for the New Year's Ball at the Adelphi, darling. We're going to make up a party, won't it be fun?'

The frock fitted perfectly, and she stood before the mirror like a tall blue flame, smoothing her hair and twirling this way and that.

'You must have shoes dyed the same colour and they must be low-heeled because of your height, but really, Coco, your neck and arms are quite lovely—'

'Are they?' Cassie studied them bemusedly.

Uncle Harry came in, wearing a smoking jacket and black slippers with little flat bows on them.

'Aha — what's this, what's this?'

'Look, Harry, doesn't Coco look simply spiffing?'

'Yes indeed.' He took a step backwards and pretended to examine her with critical severity, but his light blue eyes — so like Father's and yet so different — were smiling and full of affection. 'I have to admit to possessing a niece of quite remarkable splendour, and I hope that I may be granted the honour of the first waltz.'

'You'll have to be careful with the train, Coco,' Babs said. 'Remember not to walk backwards, and when you want to turn, give a little sideways kick, like that . . .' She demonstrated.

'And what will you be wearing, Babs?' Uncle Harry's eyes had left Cassie. He was now looking at his wife with tender indulgence.

'Oh, Madame Louise is making something. I expect it will look all right.'

'You'll be the belle of the ball, as always.' He touched her hair and she gave a brief smile before jerking her head away.

'You must buzz off now, Harry, because Coco wants to change—'

'Thank you, Uncle Harry,' Cassie said. 'Thank you very much indeed for buying me all this.'

'It is my pleasure, Cassica,' he said very sincerely. But his eyes were still on Babs.

The blue evening frock had a profound effect on Cassie. Hanging on the outside of her wardrobe in soft classical folds it seemed to represent the final achieving of adulthood. More than leaving school had done, or putting her hair up, or even disposing of her parents' home. And it also represented very powerfully her new social status, her right to admittance to the glittering enclaves of rich Liverpool. Being rich and grown up simultaneously was suddenly very exciting and she re-examined herself in the dressing-table mirror with joyfulness tinged with reverence.

She graced Gathercoles with her presence on the following morning, and worked dutifully if unenthusiastically at Vowel Indication and the Halving Principle, then after lunching with Babs in her boudoir went along to her room and tried on the blue evening frock again. She practised walking without stepping on the train, then wondered if she would look even more beautiful with her hair cut off. More and more of the fashionable women were wearing semi-shingles — Babs had been among the very first in Liverpool — and it would be rather fun to be the first student at Gathercoles to take the plunge. She could just imagine the Old Girl's face.

Holding her hair up with one hand and the train of her skirt with the other, Cassie sped in noiseless stockinged feet along to Babs's boudoir. It was deserted. At the dead hour of three in the afternoon the maids were off duty and the house silent. She went downstairs and pushed open the door of the library, and heard Babs's muffled voice saying, 'Faster, Willie — faster — *faster—*'

With a suddenly pounding heart she looked over the back of the sofa and saw that a man was lying face down on it and that Babs, buried beneath him, had her legs clasped round him, her ankles crossed above the small of his back. Her shoes were off, and her suspenders were jingling in time to the terrible rhythm.

Still gripping her hair and her skirt, Cassie rushed dry-mouthed and ashen-faced back to her room and slammed the door.

* * *

St Ezekiel's Hall had a corrugated iron roof upon which the rain was drumming a savage tattoo, and in the gaslit murk the wooden seats had the pearly bloom of perpetual damp. Men with thin jackets buttoned close to the neck and a handful of women in black woollen shawls were slinking through the door, their breath clouding the cold air.

Arnold Openshaw sat gazing straight ahead of him to the platform adorned by an embroidered banner (The King of Glory Shall Come In) and furnished with a deal table and chair and a carafe of water topped by a glass tumbler, and he thought, I can't believe it. She seemed so adamant, so horribly aloof, and now here she is. He looked down and saw her gloved fingers twiddling restlessly in her lap.

'Bit draughty in here, isn't it?'

'Shall I help you turn your collar up?'

'No, it's blowing round my ankles.'

'Prop them up on the rung of the seat in front.' He thought how nice it would be to take her naked feet between his hands and chafe the warmth back into them.

'When is it going to start?'

'Eight o'clock.'

'It's nearly five past, now.'

'Perhaps his train's been delayed. He's coming all the way from Macclesfield. But he's an excellent speaker and I'm sure you'll find what he's got to say of tremendous interest.'

'What did you say his name was?'

'Adolphus Beckett. He works in close conjunction with the Webbs.'

'Who are they?'

'I'll explain later . . .

A small disturbance at the back of the hall heralded the speaker's arrival. He mounted the platform and stood behind the table while a man in a clerical collar introduced him with fulsome phrases and a toothy smile. Adolphus Beckett was a gaunt, black-bearded man wearing a green tweed suit and thick country boots, and, having arranged his notes carefully on the table, began to address his audience in an unexpectedly high piping voice.

'I have called my talk Social Reconstruction and the Redistribution of Wealth, and during the course of it I hope to make clear the way in which these two subjects are inextricably entwined, one with the other. Social reconstruction cannot be attempted without the redistribution of wealth on a massive scale, not only in this country but in all countries throughout the world. And what do I mean by social reconstruction?' He placed his two hammer fists on the table and appeared to Cassie to be glaring at her. 'I will tell you. I mean the construction of a society in which men and women will no longer be at the mercy of a harsh and uncaring capitalistic regime. There will be no exploitation of the helpless, no advantage taken of the sick or aged. It will be a society in which love and justice and tolerance will prevail. There will be no greed. There will in fact be no need for greed. And in place of selfishness, jealousy and corruption we will have a sense of loving responsibility towards one another.'

At the back of the hall someone began to cough with a deep barking sound that reverberated round the walls. It was followed by the sound of spitting, then a groan of exhaustion. Mr Beckett waited courteously, and then proceeded.

'Now you may well ask me, how is this earthly paradise, this abode of the blessed, to be achieved? Is it, indeed, even *possible* to achieve? And I will tell you yes, my friends, such a dream is quite within the realms of possibility provided — *provided*,' — and he wagged a finger at them thick as a parsnip — 'we are prepared to undergo a radical change in our thinking. First, we must be prepared to challenge the old concept of one life for the rich and another for the poor; we must challenge the economic injustice that allows some people to amass large fortunes without working, while others must toil for long hours each day in order to earn a miserable pittance. The Bible tells us that the meek shall inherit the earth, but I tell you, my friends, that the meek are not concerned with inheriting the whole earth; all they ask for is what is theirs by right.'

Murmurs of agreement arose from the audience and Cassie noticed Arnold Openshaw's hands clasped together as if about to applaud. She didn't see how anyone could quarrel with Mr Beckett's views, but her mind wandered when he began to explain the Fabian theory of economic radicalisation. She tried mentally transcribing his words into shorthand, then contemplating his strong bushy physiognomy wondered idly what it would be like to be horrid with him.

The discovery of Babs and Willie on the library sofa had had a shattering effect, and for many days she had been unable to banish the picture from her mind; torn between disgust and fascination she thought, one day that will happen to me. It happens to practically everyone except nuns and people like Miss Gathercole, and I suppose it feels much nicer than it looks. But apart from the thing itself, she was upset by Babs's perfidy; by the memory of her whispered confidences about Willie and the others never wanting to be horrid. Having to be horrid, she had led Cassie to think, was something she found boring and extremely distasteful, yet recalling the little panting cries of joy it was no longer possible to believe her.

Cassie was also upset on behalf of Uncle Harry, whose adoration of his wife seemed almost like a palpable presence, and she wondered uneasily what his reaction would be if he found out. She also wondered whether Dora and the poker-faced Hannah knew what went on. The house in Sefton Park was beginning to fill her with a sense of stifling oppression, almost as if she had assumed the mantle of guilt on Babs's behalf, and in an effort to escape from it she told Arnold Openshaw that he could escort her to the lecture after all. The sudden unashamed love in his eyes was gratifying, but she hoped that her acquiescence would not encourage any future dreams, particularly of a horrid nature.

The lecture lasted for a long, long while, the piping voice punctuated by racking coughs and shuffling feet. Now glazed with boredom Cassie tried shorthand again, played anagrams with the King of Glory banner, and when at the conclusion Arnold turned to her it never occurred to him that the tears in her eyes were the immediate aftermath of a huge, stifled yawn.

'Don't cry, Miss Marlow,' he whispered. 'Hard work and determination can banish all the miseries of deprivation.'

'Let's hope so,' she said. 'My feet are frozen.'

Holding her arm he marched her briskly back to the city centre, steering her away from a pub overspilling with wild Irish dockers.

'They're *drunk*!'

'You can't expect much else in an area like Scotland Road.'

'But if they didn't squander their money on drink they could probably afford to live somewhere better.'

'I don't think it's quite as simple as that,' he said deferentially.

He insisted upon taking her home, sitting next to her on the empty, swaying tramcar and then walking through the park with her until they reached the gates of Uncle Harry's house. Lights twinkled through the trees, and although she was aware of silent yearning on his part she made no attempt to ask him in.

'Thank you,' she said, formally shaking his hand, 'for a very pleasant evening. I can find my own way up the drive.'

'Are you going to be very busy all through the Christmas holidays?'

'Oh yes, there's talk of us going to St Moritz. So goodnight, Mr Openshaw, and thank you again.'

'Goodnight, Miss Marlow,' he said wistfully. 'And a very merry Christmas.'

Lionel and Desmond arrived home, Nibbs brought in armfuls of holly and ivy and bowls of orchids, the house glowed with warmth from apple-scented log fires and twinkled with gold and silver baubles and Cassie in a red velvet dress drank three glasses of port after the ritual Christmas dinner and had to go and lie down.

On New Year's Eve, Babs in white chiffon supervised her niece's *toilette* before they set off for the Adelphi.

'Now, Coco, I've bought you this, which I think you'll agree is really *rather* swish . . .'

'What is it?'

'An aigrette.'

'What's that?'

'Bend your head, I can't reach. It's an egret plume, you ignorant old thing. And it goes in the middle . . . just there, like that. And fastens at the back . . . underneath your hair. Darling, it's *divine*!'

The feathery white plume, some six inches long, was lashed to the centre of her forehead by a blue diamante fillet, giving her, Cassie was forced to agree, an air of romantic and exotic mystery.

'Christ — Minnehaha,' Desmond said from the foot of the staircase, and Babs admonished him for being a nasty rude boy. But he danced with Cassie far more than Lionel or anyone else in their party did, and they began to get on rather well together.

'I say, can you do the Mississippi Dip?'

'Gosh no, can you?'

'No.'

'In that case,' he said, seizing her, 'we're bound to make a top-hole success of it!'

He took her in to supper and piled her plate high with Lobster Colbert and all its trimmings, and drank her health in champagne.

'Good old Minnehaha,' he said. 'You're really quite a decent sort, you know.'

'Is it still on straight?'

'What — your badge of office? I think it's listing very slightly to starboard.'

'Oh dear—'

'No, leave it. It makes you look pleasantly rakish . . .'

She danced with Uncle Harry, resplendent in ruby shirt studs, and when twelve o'clock struck hundreds of gaily coloured balloons floated down from the ceiling and a small and almost naked child was drawn into the ballroom in a giant mother-of-pearl shell drawn by four diminutive white ponies. The child wished everyone a happy New Year in a voice set at an even higher pitch than that of Adolphus Beckett, and immediately everyone seemed to go out of their minds with joy. In the opulence of the Adelphi Hotel they laughed and kissed and joined hands and sang and popped balloons and champagne corks. Wet-lipped old gentlemen kissed the child that represented 1920 and dowagers clasped it to their lacy bosoms and pressed the imprint of their — diamonds into its tender skin.

A waiter became noisily drunk and had to be removed, and when Uncle Harry kissed Babs with open mouth and fervent tongue she submitted under the impression that he was someone else.

The bells rang out all over Liverpool, and down on the Mersey the tugs hooted a hoarse greeting. 1920, that wide-eyed little child, was the hope of the future, the herald of a new decade in which the last grey rags of war would be cast off and replaced by lovelier, lighter things. The pursed lips of Victorian prudery would relax, finally and completely, into loving smiles and happy laughter. Long life, short skirts, and cocktails for all!

Then Babs, Lionel and Desmond went off to St Moritz for two weeks. There had been some talk of Cassie's going too, but it would have entailed missing the beginning of the new term at Gathercoles, and this Uncle Harry was not prepared to sanction. Piqued, Cassie remained at home with him, and they met each evening at dinner. Conversation would be courteous but desultory, and although he taught her to play bezique, and one evening took her to the theatre, she knew that he was silently counting the days until Babs's return.

The boys had been back at Oxford for more than a week when Cassie met the woman standing down by the front gates. A raw January mist was creeping over the park, threatening to thicken with the dusk, and Cassie's urge to go for a brisk walk before tea began to falter. She passed the woman who seemed to be approaching the gates, and strode on down the road with ringing footsteps. Ten minutes later she marched back again, chin deep in collar, hands hidden in pockets, and the woman was still there. She was wearing a long coat and skirt and a felt hat with a wide brim, and there was something so strange about her that Cassie paused.

'Can I help you?'

The woman seemed to shrink into herself. She lowered her head, and her voice was muffled.

'No, thank you. I was just . . .'

'Are you looking for someone?'

'Not really. I just . . .'

'My uncle and aunt live here,' Cassie said, rather grandly. 'Their name is Mr and Mrs Harold Marlow.'

'I know,' the woman said. 'They are my parents.'

CHAPTER SEVEN

'I don't think they can be,' Cassie said after a slight pause. 'They just have two sons.'

'Yes, I know. Lionel and Desmond.'

It was difficult to know what to think. Briefly Cassie considered walking back to the house and banishing the woman from her mind as a harmless eccentric. Yet she didn't look particularly like an eccentric, harmless or otherwise. Her clothes were neat, her shoes brightly polished and her voice perfectly normal, if a little timid. Her face was still shadowed by the hat brim and Cassie sensed that it would be the sensitive but rather homely sort.

'Do you want to see your parents, then?'

'Yes, I always want to see them. But they don't always think it best to see me.'

'Why don't they?'

The woman shook her head, and began stirring a fallen twig with the toe of her shoe.

'Where have you come from?'

'The home.'

'What home?'

'The home for incurables, where I live.'

So the poor woman *was* mad. And yet, what was she doing here, and how did she come to know Lionel and Desmond by name? She must have had some form of contact with the family, however fleeting.

Intrigued, and not altogether averse to the idea of injecting a little drama into a boring afternoon, Cassie took the woman's arm and began to lead her through the gates and up the drive.

'Come along then, they're both in. By the way, my name's Cassie and I live with them now. Uncle Harry and my father were brothers, which would make us cousins — if you're who you say you are. Have you ever heard of me?'

The woman shook her head again but allowed herself to be steered towards the house.

'What's your name, by the way?'

'Mona.'

That settles it, thought Cassie. If they'd ever had a daughter, the last thing they'd ever have called it would be Mona. Of all the dreary, undistinguished, old-fashioned names in the world, that's just about the worst. *Moaner* . . . heavens no, Babs would have called it Venetia or Candida or something.

The situation began to appeal to her more and more, and when they reached the porch she propelled the woman inside, then opened the door into the hall. They were both in the drawing-room, Uncle Harry astride the hearthrug with his back to the fire, and Babs curled up in a chair reading a magazine.

'I found this lady down by the gates, and you'll be gratified to know that she thinks she's your daughter. Had we better telephone the police or someone . . .'

The words died as she saw their faces. The magazine slithered from Babs's fingers on to the floor. She gave a little cry, and her mouth remained open as if the effort of closing it were quite beyond her.

'Mona! What in God's name are you doing here?' Uncle Harry spoke first. He took a step forward, but it was in the direction of his wife, not his daughter. 'How did you get here?'

'By train, Papa. Don't be angry, I just wanted to come for the day—'

'For the day? From Llandudno?'

'I had to change at Chester, but I managed . . .'

'It's taken you all this time to get here, yet you propose going back tonight?'

'Oh, *Mona* . . .' Babs gave a long, trembling sigh, and the woman went over to her and gave her a fumbling little kiss.

'Now don't start upsetting your mother,' Uncle Harry began. Then his eye fell on Cassie, standing motionless and appalled over by the door.

'Cassica,' he said, 'this is our daughter Mona. You won't have met before because Mona lives in Wales. Mona, this is your cousin Cassica. Say how do you do.'

'We've already met,' Cassie said.

Babs swung her legs down from the chair and rang the bell for Hannah.

'Take your hat and coat off, Mona, and we'll see about something to eat. You must be ravenous.'

Timidly the woman did as she was told. With her coat laid tidily on the back of a chair she raised both hands to remove her hat and Cassie flinched visibly, for the beauty that was so like her mother's — huge expressive eyes, delicate little nose — was ruined by a hare lip.

The thick seam of flesh began beneath the nostrils and seemed to divide the top lip almost into two. Seen without the sheltering hat brim her timid smile was uncannily like an animal's snarl, and in those first stricken moments it seemed to Cassie as if she were looking at a lovely portrait that had been slashed by a madman.

But she smiled back, and after a second's hesitation went over to the woman and shook her firmly by the hand.

'We'd better start again,' she said in a voice that sounded much too hearty. 'How do you do, Mona? It's nice to meet you.'

The maid Dora tapped on the door and came in. Seeing Mona she drew a sharp audible breath.

'Did you ring, madam?'

'Yes, Dora. Miss Mona has arrived home unexpectedly and would like something to eat. Has cook left anything suitable in the larder?'

'I think there's some cold chicken, madam.'

'Good. Put some on a tray, with some bread and butter and a glass of milk, and Miss Mona will have it in here.'

Nursery food, noted Cassie. She also noticed how Babs had changed; the sparkling vivacity had been extinguished and she looked suddenly ill and tired and years older. Even her voice had changed.

'Did you notify matron about your proposed trip?' Uncle Harry asked.

He too looked different, with his pale icy stare and little hen's beak of a nose thrust forward as if he intended to peck someone with it.

'No, Papa.' The woman pulled at a button on her frock.

'Come over here by the fire. Sit down, you must be tired and cold.'

He stretched out his hand to her, and with the other one indicated a vacant chair. Unobtrusively Cassie sank down on to the sofa.

'Now then, Mona.' Uncle Harry spoke very gently, very quietly. 'What made you suddenly decide to visit us, eh? Was it something very important? Something that couldn't wait to be put in a letter?'

'I just wanted to see you and Mama and Desmond and Lionel because — because of . . .'

'Yes, Mona?'

Cassie stared down into her lap and at the blanched white of her knuckles.

'I can't sleep because of . . .'

'You couldn't sleep. That's a great pity, Mona. There are times when business worries prevent me from sleeping too, so I know what a miserable trial it can be. Even so, I never allow it to impair my judgement, or to precipitate me into unpremeditated action for which I might be very sorry afterwards.'

'It's the horses, Papa. I can't sleep because of the horses.'

'In that case you must tell matron, and she will issue a sleeping draught. I feel very sad because of your insomnia, Mona, but I also feel very sad because of poor matron. Can't you imagine how she must be suffering, what agony of mind she must be enduring, wondering where you are? Think of the agony of all her staff, Mona. All those kind nurses and attendants who try so hard to look after you and make you happy — why, they're probably scouring the countryside for you right now at this very minute. As you sit here in warmth and comfort, they are in all probability out in the dark and the cold risking pneumonia while they look for their poor lost lamb who they fear may have fallen into the sea . . .'

Mona began to cry, hiding her face in her hands. Very gently Uncle Harry prised one of them away and imprisoned it lovingly within both his own. With the ruins of her face left partially exposed, she bent her head even lower and the tears fell on her knees.

'It's the horses, the horses. I can't sleep for thinking of all the poor horses out there who were hurt and wounded and killed. They used to rescue the soldiers and take them to hospitals but the poor horses just had to lie out there in the cold until they died. They screamed with the pain and no one listened, no one cared—'

'Mona my *dear,* the war is over—'

'But it's too late. All those thousands and thousands of lovely horses have died and they'll never come back — no matter what happens, the air will always be full of their screams and they'll never come back—'

'Neither will the poor brave fellows who died with them—'

'But they made the war — the horses didn't!'

'Hush, hush now, Mona, and dry your eyes.' Uncle Harry let go of her hand and produced a crisp white handkerchief. 'Dry your eyes now, there's a good girl. It's very sad about the horses but we must console ourselves with the knowledge that they all died for a cause in which we believe. There's no point in dwelling on sad things that have happened, we must just forget them and pass on to pleasanter things. Now blow your nose and dry your eyes because I hear Dora coming with your supper, and we don't want her to see you crying, do we?'

'I've only come for the day . . .'

'Yes, yes, of course. And we'll make a telephone call to matron to tell her that you're quite safe, and that as it's rather late Nibbs will drive you back tomorrow morning after a good night's rest, eh? After all, we can't have you roaming round the countryside all on your own, can we? Especially after dark.'

Dora came in bearing a tray, and unable to stand any more Cassie muttered an incoherent excuse and escaped to her bedroom.

The curtains were already drawn and a small clear fire burned in the grate. Fleetingly her mind returned to the old days at Walham Green, when fires in bedrooms were only permitted during times of illness. Here, they were a matter of routine from October onwards.

She sat thinking about the woman Mona, trying to adjust herself to the fact that there was such a person, and that she was her cousin. Aware that nice people made a social grace out of ignoring the unseemly, she was nevertheless very shocked that Babs and Uncle Harry — and, of course, Desmond and Lionel — could ignore a close member of the family. It must be awful to have a daughter who was not only disfigured but potty as well, yet to keep her existence shrouded in total secrecy was somehow very chilling.

She remained staring into the fire until the gong sounded for dinner, then went over to the chest of drawers and took out the poor battered little doll. Its one eye clicked open, and with its chipped nose and neglected curls exhibited the same bitter poignancy as the woman who had once loved it.

* * *

Mona didn't return to the home for incurables in Llandudno for the simple reason that matron told Uncle Harry on the telephone that she would rather she didn't. Her inability to conform and her incessant ramblings about horses were very upsetting for the other patients, and now that she had begun running away it was obvious that she would need more closely confining, facilities for which were regrettably not available. So until alternative arrangements could be made for her, Mona slept in a small guest room at the far end of the corridor and tried, with touching eagerness, to fit in with the rest of the household.

She dressed herself with exemplary neatness very early each morning and spent a lot of time working on a large jigsaw puzzle set out in the library. Her demeanour was meek, and the only source of irritation seemed to be the way she persistently tried to help the maids by jumping up to open doors for them or relieving them of heavy trays and coal scuttles.

'Leave Hannah *alone,* Mona,' Babs would cry. 'She's far more capable than you are at *everything*!'

So Mona would subside with a crushed little smile that twisted her top lip, and Cassie found herself covertly winking at her in sympathy.

'I suppose it all started badly,' Babs admitted one afternoon when they were alone. 'Harry let me conceive on my wedding night, such a horrid, ungentlemanly thing to do because after all I was only just eighteen and a perfect *child* — and when it actually arrived I was just too utterly shattered. Well, I'd been buoying myself up with images of little pink and white angels all dimples and curls and of course I don't mind admitting, Coco, all *boys* — and when I looked at what I'd actually *got* — well, I just screamed and cried and refused to have anything to do with it and in the end they had to give me morphia. Harry was nearly out of his mind with worry, and jolly well serve him right, it was all his horrid fault. So you see, it didn't actually start very well.'

'No,' Cassie said thoughtfully. 'It obviously didn't.'

'I wouldn't have minded so much about the lip if only she'd been all there *mentally*. No, that's not true. I simply hated having a baby that looked like a sort of furless rabbit — I've never been able to bear things around me that aren't beautiful or at the very least *amusing*, Coco, and quite honestly the poor thing was neither. Luckily nanny adored her, but you can imagine how absolutely petrified I was when I discovered that I was *enceinte* again. I spent the whole time picturing the most ghoulish things with two heads and webbed feet and everything because I was just utterly convinced that I wasn't capable of producing what *ordinary* women produce so beastly *casually*, so when darling old Lionel turned up all pink and cherubic and utterly *unblemished* I was wild with delight.

'Both the boys were adorable — they said such funny things and made me laugh so much, but Mona never said anything at all, let alone anything funny. Sometimes I'd come upon her sitting all on her own and talking in a funny sort of mutter, but as soon as she saw me she stopped, as if she'd been doing something naughty. But on the odd occasions when she did talk to us it was all a lot of hopeless piffle like don't the trees ever feel lonely and why can't we make little roofs to go over the tops of birds' nests . . . it was almost as if she felt more at ease with animals and plants than she did with the human race. Anyway, when the boys went away to prep school nanny retired, and Mona cried so much that we asked her if she would like to go and live with her. She said she would, so nanny had her until she died. Mona was about fifteen then.'

'So then she went into homes and things?'

'The poor child was quite useless at schoolwork and Harry and I searched madly to find somewhere where they could give her the sort of attention she needed — we found a perfectly lovely sort of historical old place down in Devonshire but she kicked up hell's delight because there were bars on the windows, and then she went to another place in Malmesbury and then — oh, dozens of places, Coco, all costing the earth, but sooner or later she always ran away and came back here where we can't *possibly* manage, what with one thing and another . . .'

'I like her,' Cassie said.

'But, darling, we *all* like her! I mean, it's an utter tragedy the way she looks and the way she's not normal mentally, but other than that I agree! She *is* terribly nice and we *are* all terribly fond of the poor old thing, but as I say—'

'So what'll happen to her now?'

'Well, Harry's interviewing the matron of another home, a sort of convent at a place called Huyton, which isn't far from here and that in itself could prove a bit of a snag.'

'I'd go and see her.'

'Coco, what a brick you are. But I'm not absolutely sure that it would be allowed because the staff always seem to think that having visitors unsettles them. We'll just have to see. In the meantime I must dress because I promised to meet a friend for lunch.'

'Do I know him?'

'*Him*?' Babs paused with her hand on the door. 'Well really, what a naughty suspicious old thing you are! It may interest you to know that I'm lunching with Maud Russell — terrible old bore she is too, but as she's also the wife of one of Harry's big clients, one has to do one's poor little best . . .'

She floated away, trilling 'Tea for Two'.

* * *

Spring sunshine illuminated the dusty classroom and touched the bowed heads with friendly yellow fingers.

'Dear Sir comma,' dictated Mr Sissley, textbook in one hand, stopwatch in the other, 'we beg to acknowledge receipt of your esteemed order of the 15th instant for six dozen boxes of double-hinged brackets comma which will receive our immediate attention full stop We would respectfully point out comma however comma that we have in stock at this present moment more than one variety of double-hinged bracket full stop There is our Excelsior bracket comma measuring four inches by two inches comma which has found great favour with our customers in the past comma but for those of less conservative taste we also recommend the Hotspur bracket comma which comma although of the same dimension as the Excelsior comma has the additional advantage of a small swivel flange in the centre . . .'

Since the beginning of the new term Cassie had been sitting next to a red-haired girl called Alfreda Morris, but although she ignored Arnold's reproachful looks, she remained friends with him; in fact she had now become rather attached to him in the way that one might become attached to an undemanding dog. They often walked part of the way home together, conversing easily and using Christian names, but she never invited him to the house in Sefton Park. With increased understanding of his Fabian outlook, she sensed that its opulence would embarrass him, and also (less commendably) that his lack of sophistication would make Babs laugh.

He told her that both his parents had passed away, his father when he was a baby and his mother two years ago. He lived with a landlady in a little house opposite the pawnshop in Jasmine Street and studied shorthand and typewriting because he was determined to become the secretary of a Labour member of Parliament. She asked why he didn't aspire to become a Labour MP himself, and he told her that he hadn't a sufficient abundance of personality. It was sad to hear him say that, and in a sudden burst of confidence she told him that when she was young, she had always dreamed of being a great success, but didn't suppose that she ever would be, now. He asked what form of success she had had in mind, and when she confessed that she was still not sure he urged her, not for the first time, to think in political terms and to consider the satisfaction of succeeding in helping to reshape the world to a socialist pattern. She repeated that she would think about it.

It was during that same agreeable meander to the next tramcar stop, and then the next, that she told him about

Mona, and the indignation in her own voice rather surprised her.

'They keep saying she's mentally deficient and all that, but I honestly don't think she is! We went for walks together and I found that she was jolly nice to talk to. Not exactly bubbling over, but gentle and quaint, and not a bit *mad* . . .'

'Where is she now?'

'In another home. This one's at Huyton and I go and see her sometimes. I haven't told my aunt and uncle, but I'm sure it helps her to talk to someone about the things that worry her. She minds dreadfully for instance about all the horses that were killed in the war, and although it sounds silly in a way I can quite see her point. But my uncle and aunt only regard it as one more sign of mental deficiency.'

'When are you going to see her again?'

'Visiting is on Sunday afternoons between three and four.'

'If you're going next Sunday, can I go with you?'

'Well, I don't know,' Cassie said doubtfully. 'I suppose you can if you really want to.'

'I do really want to.'

They went by train, Cassie armed with some chocolate and a tin of tooth powder because Mona hated having to share with the woman in the next cubicle. The home was down a country lane, a gaunt Victorian place with an overgrown garden, and they found Mona in the dayroom, sitting next to a woman who twitched and leered and occasionally snorted.

Cassie introduced Arnold as 'a friend' and was surprised at how easily and gently he talked to Mona. He didn't seem to notice the hare lip, or the way it made her appear like an apprehensive rodent, and she talked back to him with obvious pleasure and then asked if they would both like to go for a walk in the garden. They said yes and followed her in single file along the winding weedy little paths and she showed them a blackbird's nest and the bird remained on her eggs as if she trusted Mona not to overstep the bounds of propriety. They sat on a seat by the dank remains of an ornamental lake and Mona insisted upon sharing the chocolate with them.

Cassie was making her laugh with an impromptu imitation of Miss Gathercole when a nun burst through the bushes behind them and cried: 'Here you are! What do you mean by leaving the house without permission? You know you're not supposed to, you naughty girl, and if Mother Superior gets to hear about it, she'll be very, very angry!'

Mona crumpled and put her hands over her face, but before Cassie could begin to expostulate Arnold stood up and apologised for persuading Mona to show them the gardens. 'I'm afraid it was all my fault, I should have realised . . .'

The nun marched Mona back to the house by the arm and returning to Liverpool in the train Cassie burst into tears when she found that she had forgotten to give Mona the tin of tooth powder. She sat looking out of the window red-eyed and sniffling while Arnold sat opposite, once again paralysed into ineffectuality by love.

The ripening of spring into summer tempted the girls from the pillbox factory out on to the fire escape to eat their midday bread and cheese. Crowding together like a flock of jostling chirking starlings they sang, screamed with laughter at rude jokes, and one of them hit Arnold on the ear with a pickled onion as he ventured across the little garden to his w.c. They were rather a nuisance, but as such behaviour was a foregone conclusion among people of their class, they were more to be pitied than blamed.

One of the few Gathercole girls prepared to exchange banter with them was the red-haired girl Alfreda, known now as Effie. Originally one of those most hostile towards the stuck-up London ways of Cassica Marlow, she had come to realise that some people preferred to say *parth* and *barth* in the same way that some preferred tea without sugar. Magnanimity warmed into friendship, which in turn became strengthened by the discovery that they could make one another laugh. It was through Effie that Cassie first learned that a certain stratum of Liverpudlians enjoyed being referred to as Scousers; scouse being a local variety of meat and vegetable stew.

'Me mam an' dad's really Scousers, see, but now me dad's left off wairkin' as a riveter at Cammel Laird's yard an' got isself a job wairkin' in the gate-keeper's office checkin' all the other Scousers in an' out, see?' The adenoidal singsong delivered with monumental earnestness filled Cassie with schoolgirl mirth.

'Go on — say some more!'

'An' if me dad 'adn't bettered isself, see, well I'd 'ave gone to wairk in a shop or gone into sairvice in a private house like, but I've got to keep oop with me dad now, 'aven't I, an' go an' wairk in an office same as 'im.'

She had a sturdy local patriotism, but beneath the joking Cassie sensed that Effie was hellbent on self-improvement. The Liverpool accent all but disappeared whenever she stood up in class to transcribe her shorthand notes, and Cassie was deeply impressed when she got herself a job as a weekend barmaid in a Birkenhead pub to help pay her tuition fees.

'My God, what would the Old Girl say if she found out?'

'She's not gonna find out, is she? 'Er sort never goes slummin' in Bairken'ead.'

Although she was a year younger, Effie had a steely contempt for girls who relied too heavily on mummies and daddies, and theoretically in sympathy, Cassie realised with despondency that to invite Effie out to The Mount wouldn't work. Any more than it would work to invite poor old Arnold.

In fact, as the summer deepened Cassie was finding herself increasingly out of tune with the world of Uncle Harry and Aunt Babs. The opulence had become tarnished by the knowledge of Babs's numerous infidelities — the little sports-cars still buzzed up the drive and Babs was still insistently grateful that none of the occupants wished to be horrid — but even more than that, there was the fact of Mona. Her presence seemed to cast a ghostly shadow over the lovely rooms and languid gardens, and although Babs was as gaily beautiful as ever Cassie could only see her now as some sort of exquisite flower with a canker at its heart. Arrangements had been made by Uncle Harry for the family, including Cassie, to spend August in Deauville and, although twelve months ago the prospect would have delighted her, now she didn't want to be a part of it. Any more than she wanted to be a part of Uncle Harry's arrangements for her to become a junior lady short-hand-typist in his office in September.

Stifled and increasingly alienated she moved through the last days of June, and her only refuge was Gathercoles. The old power of ferocious concentration returned and she worked hard to achieve the speeds and accuracy that would result in a First Class final certificate.

'Oh honestly, Coco, what a beastly old swot you are!' Babs would cry. 'The boys don't swot nearly as hard and they're going in for proper *professions*.'

'As I hoped to.'

'Darling, you *don't* want a profession! You'd get thin lips and bad eyesight and you'd have no time for the important things—'

'Yes, well. In the meantime could you read this bit out to me at about this speed?' Cassie demonstrated, then handed her the textbook.

'An eminent conveyancer by the name of Sir Bartholomew Mellon has prepared a number of Bills of Sale in connection with the instructions issued by the King's Bench Division of the High Court of Justice — Coco, is this *serious?* I mean, is it what they're really expecting girls to find interesting — let alone amusing?'

'Uh-huh. Go on.'

'Where was I? Oh yes — *in connection with the bankruptcy of Messrs Clarrimore and Beatty late of Waterloo Chambers, Holborn Viaduct* — did I tell you my mother's name was Clarice? I'm really Barbara Clarice, you know, and absolutely loathe it . . .'

Dappled sunlight on the lawn, the purring of white doves on the roof and the soft plash of the fountain. A big straw hat etching cream and gold latticework on Babs's face and Cassie absently flapping away a fly. And then the throaty sound of a car.

'Oh, Coco, it's *Ned*! Oh, how ripping, and just in time for tea!'

* * *

'I told you she would pull her socks up,' Emilia said.

She and Wilfred were lying on their backs side by side, watching the moon-filled curtains billowing gently at the foot of the bed. The window was wide open, letting in the quiet hiss and smack of the sea.

'I think she has changed in more ways than one. She is more friendly, and at the same time more serious, and I believe she has not played truant for months.'

'Miss Whittaker seems to think she'll get a First for typing, at any rate.'

Emilia made a murmuring sound of satisfaction, then said: 'But I hear she is going into her uncle's office.'

'Oh?'

'Which is not a good thing. Personally, I believe in young people striking out for themselves.'

'We place quite a number of our young ladies in situations, darling.'

'That is quite different. Our placings are on a professional level only. We strive to find suitable employment for ex-pupils as part of our service, but we do not use influence, nor do we seek to pull strings, loved one.'

They lay in peaceful silence and the moonlight drove a silver pathway along their bodies which dissolved again in the movement of the curtain.

'I was very perturbed to learn that Alfreda Morris is working during the weekends as a barmaid.'

'Who told you that?'

'I have my spies. All very laudable if it is to help pay her fees, but I hope she will refrain from boasting of it. After all, our reputation rests on our ability to turn out the right sort of girl.'

'I suppose the ability to pull a pint could be regarded as an added virtue?' Wilfred suggested.

'A virtue of dubious value. No, Alfreda is a tough nut, and in my opinion will need very careful placing.'

'I've never seen a girl with such an abundance of hair . . .'

'Remarkable, isn't it? Although personally I have never cared for redheads. Unless they are very careful in their personal habits they can so easily offend . . .'

'Really? Ummm . . .'

Hand in hand, and lulled by the sea's quiet rhythm, they drifted into sleep.

* * *

What had seemed to Cassie like an increasingly fragile calm was abruptly shattered a week before they were due in Deauville. And she was the one who shattered it.

It was late Saturday afternoon and the boys had been swimming in the lake. Babs in a floating dress was lying in a long cane chair and Uncle Harry in a panama sat nearby sipping an early whisky and soda. The sun was just beginning to slip a little lower in the sky, lengthening the shadows that fell through the trees. The day had been very hot, and the gardener's boy plodded obsequiously by, unrolling a coil of hosepipe in the direction of the dahlias.

'This time next week we shall be basking on the seashore,' Uncle Harry said, and without raising her eyes from her book or considering the possible impact of her words, Cassie replied: 'I do think it's a shame that Mona can't come too.'

There was a small silence, broken by the sound of Babs turning the page of her magazine with a sharp rattle.

'Don't upset the mater,' Lionel said in a low voice, and Cassie looked down at him from her chair by the marble seat. He was lying on a rug with his head on his arms and drops of water still glistened on his bare shoulders.

'Upset her?' She felt suddenly irritated. 'Why should mentioning her daughter upset her?'

'Mona cannot come for the simple reason that new places over-stimulate her,' Uncle Harry said. 'Allow us to know what is best, Cassie.'

She should have stopped there: changed the subject, or even got up and walked away. But she didn't.

'I think she'd love to go on holiday with all of us. I think she's lonely and bored and wants more stimulation, not less.'

There was another silence, as if the family was mutely drawing together, preparing to take up defensive positions against a possible attack.

'I don't think Mona's ever been on hols with us.' Desmond sat pulling up bits of grass and throwing them in the lake. 'If she has, I must have been too young to remember.'

'Couldn't she possibly come? If she did, I'd help to take care of her — she likes going for walks and talking to animals — and talking *about* them, but not horses because it upsets her — she could sleep in my room if you like, although she says she'd only ever want to sleep in the same room with someone she really likes—'

'You seem to know a great deal about poor Mona's predilections,' Uncle Harry said from the shadow of his panama.

'How do you know she doesn't share a room with someone she really likes at the Convent Home?' Babs spoke at last.

'She told me about it.'

'When?'

Cassie drew a deep steadying breath and said: 'The first time I went to see her.'

'At Huyton?'

'Yes.'

'You've been to Huyton?'

They were all staring at her now. I've shot my bolt, Cassie thought. I've really done it now, I've shot my bolt. It gave her a sudden sense of exhilaration.

'Yes, I've been lots of times. Once I even took a friend.'

'You took a friend — to see Mona?' It seemed as if they could do nothing but repeat the things she told them.

'I go on Sunday afternoons because that's the only time they're allowed visitors. She doesn't like it there because the nuns are very strict and treat everyone as if they're absolute lunatics — some of them may be, but Mona certainly isn't.

Mona's just a bit nervous and shy and gets filled with dread sometimes, which I personally think is jolly understandable because she's made to live such a funny sad sort of life away from everyone she loves—'

'I think you've said enough,' Lionel murmured. He turned over on his back and stared up at her. 'In other words, dear cousin, shut up.'

'Don't tell me to shut up and pride yourself on being a gentleman.' Exhilaration was turning to indignation. 'It's also very cowardly to think that shutting up about problems will make them go away because it won't.'

'So you admit that we have a problem?'

'If you mean Mona, the only one you've got there is the one you've made. You all pretend that the poor thing's a lunatic when all she is is lonely and fed up, and it's all your fault. She never went to school, so she doesn't *know* much. She never gets taken anywhere or given little treats so she's got nothing nice to *remember*. And I'll tell you something else—' The book fell off her knee and fell with a thud on to Lionel's rug. 'You all keep her buried away because you can't bear the look of her!'

Babs gave an audible gasp.

'This really is gross impertinence,' Uncle Harry began to struggle out of his deckchair, 'and I think you had better apologise—'

'I don't give a fig what you think—' Cassie was also standing up, the powerful temper she had inherited from her mother now bursting into flame. 'I hate the way you treat your daughter, I hate the way I've been tricked out of going to university when I already had my place and everything, and I don't like living here where it's all so rich but nothing interesting ever happens, and most of all I'll be absolutely frank and say that I hate, loathe and abominate the idea of being a damned secretary in my Uncle Harry's damned office!'

No one spoke. They remained immobile, as if they were watching a play.

'I don't belong here. I never did and I never will, and one of the reasons is that I'm a girl. Girls aren't liked in this house — which is one more nail in poor old Mona's coffin — no, only nice big stupid hairy men are wanted who all dote on Aunt Babs' — but even in the heat of the moment she refrained from saying for what particular function they were needed — 'they just dote on her and run round in soppy little circles after her . . .'

Very quietly Desmond got up and dived back into the lake. He began to swim to the other side as if trying to distance himself from them all.

'So I'm going. And I'm not taking anything that doesn't belong to me. I'm just going with the things I arrived with that came from my own parents' home—'

'Cassica, will you sit down and kindly stop making such an utter fool of yourself!' Uncle Harry's features had become suffused beneath the sheltering panama. He took a step towards her as if intending to restrain her but she knocked him away with her elbow and began ripping excitedly at the buttons on her blouse.

'I'm going — and I'm not taking anything that you've given me! I don't want this — or this skirt — or this petticoat—' She wrenched and struggled and the garments whirled through the air and went ballooning into the lake. Babs gave an hysterical little shriek that ended in a sob.

'Stop her, Harry — do something to *stop* her—'

'She's mad, poor creature—' Lionel said.

'Yes, I *am* mad! I'm mad like Mona! Which makes me a very nice person in the eyes of everyone except people like *you*—' Her smart little kid shoes went into the lake — splash — splash — sending up a shower of water that got into Desmond's eyes. He shook his head violently, then retreated with powerful strokes to the far end of the lake.

Clad in corsets, silk knickers and a pink satin bust bodice, Cassie placed her hands on her hips and said pantingly: 'I feel better now. I feel like *me*. Clean and honest and worthy, and that's how I'm going to remain. No more other people's charity—'

'*Be silent!*' roared Uncle Harry. He gripped her bare arm, making white fingerprints in her flesh. Roughly he jerked her backwards towards the marble seat and forced her to a sitting position. She stood up again. He forced her downwards and she all but fell over.

'Oh I say, steady on—' From his place on the rug Lionel held out a warning hand. Cassie lashed out at it with her bare foot, lost her balance and fell heavily on her behind. Snorting with rage Uncle Harry hauled her upright and thrust her back on to the marble bench. From the long cane chair Babs gave a high quivering squeal. Like most family dramas, there was more than an element of farce in the proceedings.

'Now be silent and *listen,*' Uncle Harry commanded, holding Cassie down on the bench by her shoulders. Although the sun's strength was now on the wane the marble was still painfully hot through the seat of her knickers. She squirmed unavailingly.

'Listen,' repeated Uncle Harry. 'You have had your say, and now it is my turn. And I would start by saying that from the moment you entered the doors of my house you have caused nothing but trouble. To begin with we had to endure a lot of flighty nonsense about going to university, and when it is agreed that you will undertake a secretarial training, at, I might add, my expense, you are seen on several occasions by a trusted member of my staff sipping morning coffee in the Kardomah Café when you should have been at your studies. I said nothing of this at the time because I wished to make allowances for a girl recently out of mourning and from the type of background where perhaps the finer points of honourable behaviour were not taught, let alone insisted upon — sit *down,* Cassica, and let me finish — but I now discover that your deceit does not end there. You now confess openly and without shame to consorting with my daughter in a manner not only prejudicial to her well-being, but in the most despicable and underhand manner as if you deliberately intended to sabotage the long and carefully thought-out programme that has been devised by her doctors for her welfare. My daughter is a very sick woman, Cassica, whose only hope of serenity lies in the mode of life prescribed by experts and put into operation by her parents. Then you come along and take it upon yourself to interfere with it; you, an ignorant chit from the schoolroom, see fit to cause intrigue and what can only result in boundless misery—'

'I didn't! All I did was—'

'Hold your tongue. Let me finish. Not content with wreaking your wiles on my helpless daughter, you also decide to amuse yourself by philandering with a series of foolish young men who, I have it from impeccable sources, regularly visit my house during the afternoon hours when your aunt is resting and the servants off duty—'

Cassie's mouth fell open. The furious pink drained from her cheeks, leaving them bone white. She wrenched his hands from her shoulders and stood up. From his glacial blue stare and haughty little beak of a nose she looked across at Babs, and Babs looked back at her and smiled whimsically, deprecatingly, with a soft curl of blonde hair half-encircling one lovely eye.

'It's not *true* . . .'

'It *is* true, Cassica, and your eyes give you away—'

'Lies — lies!'

'And your behaviour has forced me to the conclusion that you are nothing more than a light woman in the making — you have only to look at yourself, standing there in the broad daylight in your underthings in front of two — two vulnerable young fellows who have never . . . let alone my wife and myself—' He appeared almost choleric.

'*Let me go!*' She screamed at him, tears bursting from her screwed-up eyes. 'Leave me alone, and don't ever let me see any of you again!'

She turned and began to run blindly away. Leaping the dahlias she collided violently with the gardener's boy, became briefly entangled in the hosepipe, picked herself up and then fled into the house and up to her room.

Still crying, she hauled her old suitcase from the depths of the wardrobe and flung it on the bed. She still had some, but not all, of the modest collection of clothes with which she had arrived, but struggling into her black mourning dress found that it no longer fitted. Fresh tears of rage filled her eyes as she struggled with hooks and eyes that had no intention of meeting. In the end she put on the new dress that she liked least and left the rest. She took all the old things, sweeping them pell-mell into the suitcase together with her shorthand books and the old whalebone hairbrush, and the last thing to go in was the one-eyed doll that had once belonged to Mona.

'Are you going out, miss?' Hannah eyed her with sly curiosity as she crossed the hall.

'Yes.'

'Will you be in to dinner, miss?'

'No.'

She strode across the terrace and over the lawn, aware that they were watching her, motionless. She saw that some of her clothes had been retrieved and spread out on the grass to dry. Pausing a few feet away she thanked them for their hospitality and then bade them goodbye.

'And where do you imagine you are going?' enquired Uncle Harry, fanning himself with his panama.

'I'm going my own way,' she said. 'I'm quite old enough to live on my own now, and to make my own decisions about what I do and who I do it with. In the meantime, I'm going to stay with a friend who *believes* what I *say.*'

Without waiting for their reaction she turned and headed for the front gates.

CHAPTER EIGHT

'I've come to ask you a favour. Can you put me up for the night?'

'What — here?'

'Yes of course I mean here. Where else?'

'But what's happened? Is something wrong?'

'Yes. No. Look, can you or can't you?'

'Come in.'

After blinking amazedly for a few more seconds Arnold led her silently and rapidly up the staircase. His room was on the first floor, its listless shabbiness in no way relieved by flowered linoleum or the large picture of *Sunrise in the Transvaal* hanging over the single brass bedstead. The bamboo table was covered with books and his nightshirt hung on the back of the door.

'Bit of a mess in here — I wasn't really expecting . . .'

'No, of course not.' Cassie sat down on the bed, then after a moment's consideration removed herself to the chair. 'The thing is, I've left home. Well, not so much home exactly as my aunt and uncle's place.'

'Was it because of Mona?'

'You know, you're much brighter than you look,' Cassie said. 'Yes. I only mentioned how nice it would be if she came to France with us, and it sort of went on from there. I admitted that I'd been going to see her and — well, here I am.'

'Do they know you're here?'

'No. I just said I was going to stay with a friend.'

'Thank you, Cassie.'

'What for?'

'For calling me a friend.'

'So is it all right if I stay here, just for the night? And then tomorrow I'm off.'

'Where to?' He continued to gaze at her with loving incredulity.

'Not telling. Let's just say that it's all been planned very carefully, and that it will all be for the best.'

'You make it sound as if you're going a long way away.'

'Do I? Well, well. In the meantime, I'm quite hideously hungry—'

'Oh, dear. My landlady will be calling me for high tea any minute.'

'Can't I come too?' A certain amount of Babs's bright self-assurance had rubbed off on Cassie during the past year.

'Well, I don't know. It might be a bit difficult, because you see she never—'

'Then why don't we go out somewhere?'

'Because she'll already be cooking, and also because—' Arnold looked wretched. 'Well, because just at the moment I'm what would be called in Pitman jargon pecuniarily embarrassed.'

'Oh. So am I — well, I've got to be a bit *careful* . . .'

'The other thing is,' Arnold said, 'the other thing is that Mrs Handsworth — my landlady — doesn't allow lady visitors, and certainly not in bedrooms.'

'She needn't know I've been in your bedroom, need she?'

'But if I suddenly produced you downstairs in the dining room it wouldn't be unreasonable of her to wonder where you'd sprung from, would it?'

'Why can't you say — Oh, Lord, why does a simple thing have to be made so beastly difficult?'

'Working-class respectability. I'm afraid Mrs Handsworth regards all eligible young ladies with dire foreboding. You'd never ever think she'd been one herself—'

'You mean she'd actually think that you and I would actually . . . ?' Watching Arnold's cheeks turn a slow rosy pink, Cassie became aware that her own were doing the same thing. 'Oh, what utter bilge! As if we *would* . . .'

'I tell you what,' Arnold said. 'You stay here and keep quiet — after all, the damage is done now — and I'll go down to tea as usual and I'll bring you something back. I often bring an extra slice of cake or a few left-over sandwiches back upstairs with me for later on when I make myself a cup of Oxo on the gas ring. I sometimes sit up rather late reading, you see.'

'Fine,' Cassie said without enthusiasm.

'And Cassie—'

'Yes?'

'It's awfully nice, having you here.'

When a piercing soprano voice called 'Tee-eee!' from the foot of the stairs Arnold quickly smoothed his hair with both hands, shunted his spectacles further up his nose with his thumb, then with a warning finger to his lips glided swiftly towards the door.

'Won't be long. Don't forget, keep mum.'

With an enviously rumbling stomach Cassie examined the piles of books on the table. They were all very dull, with titles like *In Defence of Humanity* and *The Insufficiency of the Profit Incentive.* She went over to the window and peered gloomily through the lace curtain to the pawnshop and the prim houses opposite and she still couldn't get over being blamed for Babs's boyfriends. Most of all, she couldn't get over Babs allowing her to be blamed. For the first time since it had happened she began to reconstruct the scene down by the lake, and although she remained satisfied that she had acquitted herself reasonably well, the full consequences were only now beginning to come home to her. She had said some dreadful things (but so had Uncle Harry); she had flung a pure silk blouse and a very expensive new skirt into the lake, together with a pair of shoes that had cost four guineas. She had stood defying them all in her underwear, and finally she had rendered herself homeless.

She began to feel chilly. She sat down on the chair with her hands clasped between her knees and her shoulders bowed, and when Arnold returned with a plate containing two cold sausages, a tomato and a chunk of seed cake she apologised faintly for not feeling hungry anymore.

'What's the matter? Cassie, your teeth are chattering—' He drew her hands from between her knees and began to rub them. 'Aren't you feeling well?'

'Yes, I'm all right. I've just got to get used to something . . .'

'What sort of something? Tell me.'

'No, I can't. It's just somebody's opinion of me . . . and it's not true . . .'

'If it's anything nasty it certainly won't be true,' he said comfortingly. 'Look, have a nice sausage—'

'No, I don't want one—'

'Go on, they're pork—'

'I'm sorry . . .'

'But you were so hungry.'

'I'm not now. Later . . .'

'Oh, my dear Cassie,' he said, still rubbing her hands. 'You're cold and not hungry because you're in some sort of trouble with your family and it's upset you. I know it's something to do with Mona, so why don't you tell me all about it, eh? Just pretend I'm an uncle, or something.'

'I think I've had enough of uncles for the moment.' She raised her head and managed a rueful smile. 'No, it's all right now. It just suddenly hit me, that's all — I mean, that I'm homeless and everything.'

'I thought you said you'd made plans, and that tomorrow you were off somewhere?'

'Yes, I am,' she said swiftly. And immediately began to feel better. 'I'm off first thing tomorrow morning, but I'm not telling you where. I'm not telling anyone until I'm settled. Then I'll write.'

'And you'd rather not talk about what happened?'

'No, thanks. I'll just get angry all over again.'

She removed her hands from his and stood up, smoothing her frock.

'I've never seen you wearing dark grey before.'

'I don't like it much, but it's fashionable. Look, let's talk about something else.'

'What would you like to talk about?'

She shrugged. 'Don't mind — anything. Politics, if you like. I don't know about you, but I'll want to go to bed early.'

Seeing his face turn pink again she began to laugh; a shrill sound with an edge of hysteria. 'Oh, pardon me, I didn't mean . . .'

'Hush,' he said warningly. 'Or Mrs Handsworth'll hear.'

She put her hands over her mouth to stifle the laughter, and then began to cry. Very gently he placed her on the chair and wiped her eyes with a clean handkerchief taken from the drawer. He touched her hair and caressed with his eyes the way little short bits of it curled against her neck. He patted her shoulder, and when her tears had ceased succeeded in tempting her to eat one of the cold sausages.

He talked politics to her because she had asked him to, and she sat saying yes and sometimes no, while all the time her mind ran on ahead to tomorrow, and the certainty that she was going to make a success of her life began to grow strong again.

They arranged themselves for the night with quietness and commendable decorum. Having made sure that the coast was clear, Arnold showed her where the bathroom was, and afterwards resolutely locked himself in there until she had had time to get into his bed. As for Cassie, she wondered briefly whether she should undress or not, then decided to compromise with knickers and bust bodice beneath her nightgown. She was lying with the bedclothes up to her chin and her gaze fixed rigidly on the ceiling when he returned.

'I'll keep my eyes shut while you undress.'

'Don't worry,' he said, spreading a coat down on the rug beside the bed. 'I'll stay as I am.'

'Oh I say, have one of my pillows—'

'No, no. I'm perfectly all right.'

'No, you're not! Arnold, you can't sleep curled up on the floor like a *dog*!'

'Yes, I can. Go on, go to sleep.'

'Well . . . goodnight, Arnold.'

'Goodnight, Cassie.'

The real darkness seemed a long while in coming. Although the curtains were drawn, the lingering summer twilight still crept between them and filled the room with silvery violet shadows. And the place was so quiet that the occasional rustle of bedclothes and the tiny sound of human breathing seemed charged with terrible and overwhelming implication.

I'm in Arnold Openshaw's bedroom, thought Cassie. I'm in his actual bed. It smells of him, smells of *man,* and he's lying on the floor beside me like a big docile animal. I wonder what they'd say at The Mount if they knew I was spending the night with someone of the opposite sex? Sleeping with him, as you might say. I bet they wouldn't half be shocked at Gathercoles. Perhaps Effie wouldn't, but all the staff certainly would. Particularly if they knew it was me and Arnold . . .

As quietly as possible she turned on her side, and the scraping of her eyelashes on the pillow sounded ridiculously loud.

Babs wouldn't be shocked. At least, if she was, she'd be a hypocrite. No, she'd probably say Coco *darling,* how *delicious* — but what on earth is the poor boy doing on the *floor*?

A pleasant little tingle of eroticism filled her and she thought, well, after all, why not? I'm twenty, and I live my own life. Arnold loves me and what's wrong with finding out what it's like? It can't be all that ghastly or Babs wouldn't have devoted so much time to it . . . and then blamed it on me, the two-faced *thing* . . .

The tingling increased and she dangled her hand over the edge of the bed. Her fingers brushed Arnold's hair. She began to imagine him kissing her, touching her, and she imagined for the first time in her life the powerful pleasure involved in the ritual submission to the demands of masculinity after it has been sufficiently teased and tormented.

'Arnold . . .'

'Umm?'

'Come up here.'

No reply.

'Are you asleep?'

'Umm.'

Sensuous woman fingers touching his hair. He wished he had washed it. He lay with his eyes shut, trying to breathe slowly and to quell the involuntary stirrings of his private part. To take crude advantage of a young lady who had asked for his help in the name of friendship would be the action of a callous brute and despite her innocent child's whisperings he must remember that the responsibility for her well-being, both emotional and physical, lay in his hands alone until early next morning when she must slip quietly back through the front door the way she had come.

The fingers found his nose, grasped it and gave it a sharp tug.

'*Arrr-nold . . .*'

He made a stifled, guttural sound.

'Arnold, can't you . . . don't you want to . . . ?'

Oh, the leaping torment. Quietly and despairingly he pressed his hands down hard upon himself and remembered what Lord North had said about all men being corrupted by irresponsible power.

'Go to sleep, Cassica. I'm very tired.'

Cassica, not Cassie. The fingers were removed from his nose. Through squinting eyes he saw the dark outline of them dangling above him. The urge to seize them and kiss them and squeeze them was almost unendurable, so he closed his eyes again and then turned resolutely on his side with his back to her.

Cassie's tingling died, doused by his indifference. The emotional tumult of the day began to take effect and she slept, while Arnold lay listening to her robust snores and waiting with grief mingled with longing for the first signs of dawn.

* * *

It was raining in London, and strange to see different curtains hanging at the window of the house in Walham Green. It was strange too, to think that if she knocked at the front door it would be answered by someone she had never seen before.

She walked to the end of the street, noting the little changes that had taken place during her absence. New paint outside forty-seven, a To Let notice outside twenty-two and a neat little card saying Palms Read by Appointment in the front window of number three.

She walked back again and rang the bell of what had once been the house next door. The same neighbour opened it and didn't seem all that surprised to see her.

'Well, if it isn't you again. Got fed up with the north, have you? Come in and see Norman, he's up today.'

So Cassie went in, and was amazed at how small the rooms were. A new cat lay on the rag rug in front of the iron range and the boy who whistled through a silver tube in his throat was huddled in an old armchair with the stuffing bursting out. Despite the muggy warmth of the day he was wrapped in a blanket.

'Norman, here's the girl who used to live next door to see you. Say hullo to her, duck.'

'Hullo,' he fluted obediently. He smiled at her, and Cassie went over and seized one of his hands and shook it. It lay cold and shockingly inert against her palm and after a moment she gently replaced it in a fold of his blanket.

'He's coming on lovely, aren't you, duck? Nurse is ever so pleased with him, which reminds me she's calling round for a cup of tea this afternoon. Fred's left school now and gone into the iron foundry and Mary's got a nice place in service with a doctor in Wimbledon. Dad was off work with phlebitis in April — or wait a minute, was it May? — but anyhow he's doing nicely now and nurse is *very* pleased . . .'

Cassie signified that she was pleased too, but declined the invitation to stay for a cup of tea on the grounds that she was rather pressed for time. Thankful to escape reunion with the nurse she walked back to the old Metropolitan railway and on impulse took a ticket to Putney Bridge Station and went to look at her old school. It was still there but closed for the summer holidays. She stood in the roadway staring up at its dusty blank windows as if she were searching for a reassuring glimpse of the old Cassie; if it had been term-time she would have called in to see them all, but instead she turned away.

She visited all the old places she had known, and some she hadn't known (like Madame Tussauds) but only heard about. This is London, she kept saying to herself; this is where I belong. But London seemed indifferent. No one spoke to her or smiled at her, and even at the old Bluebell Temperance Hotel, where she had taken a single top-floor room for a week, they were no more than tepidly polite. She thought they would at least have remembered her from the last time. On the third day she began studying the newspapers for secretarial work and called at two employment agencies in the city.

'What type of situation are you seeking?'

'I wish to be a secretary.'

'What experience have you had?'

'None yet. I have only just completed my training at the Gathercole Commercial Academy in—'

'May we see your certificates of proficiency?'

'I haven't any. I left just before the examinations.'

'May we ask why?'

'It was a family matter.'

It was all so eerily reminiscent of the abortive schoolgirl interview with the wartime Red Cross, except that during the interim period she had developed a little more protective haughtiness.

At the first agency they terminated the interview by telling her that it was their policy never to place potential employees on their books unless they were certificated, and left it at that, but at the second they not only reiterated the same silly rule, they also proceeded to tick her off for wasting their time. Being certificateless seemed to fill them with dark suspicion, which deepened immeasurably when she gave them her address at the Bluebell Hotel.

'We only place young ladies on our books who are certificated and who live securely.'

'With the aid of a remunerative situation,' Cassie said, falling in with the correct parlance, 'I also would be in a position to live securely.'

But they wouldn't play; security was a euphemism for respectability, for living safely and inconspicuously at home with mother and father, and after they had pointed this out for the second time they gave her a brief lecture on promotional procedure in the secretarial world.

'You would commence (supposing you were equipped with your final certificates of proficiency) as a junior, where the making of tea, the sticking on of stamps and the filing of letters would be among your duties. Perhaps after two or three years you would be promoted to general shorthand-typist, and only after very considerable experience in office procedure *and* only after acquiring the ability to transcribe anything (absolutely *anything)* into fast and accurate shorthand and thence into an equally fast and accurate typescript — only *then* would you be considered suitable material for the rank of secretary. And just for good measure I would add that nowhere in the whole of London are you likely to find anyone who has attained the position of personal private secretary under the age of forty-five.'

'Thank you for your help,' Cassie said. 'Good afternoon.'

From her cramped little room in the Bluebell she answered three advertisements, but the jobs had already been taken. In a sudden mood of rebellion she went to Harrods and asked if they had any *vacancies* for salesladies. They asked what experience she had had.

'None in an actual shop,' she said. 'But I can offer the advantage of having taken a training in shorthand and typing at the Gathercole Commercial Academy in—'

'In that *case*,' they said, reasonably enough, 'why not go and work in an office?'

'Because I would prefer to work in a shop.'

'I'm afraid,' they said, 'that in the case of our emporium we only engage staff who have had suitable previous experience.'

On the fifth day she succeeded in being offered a job checking washing lists in the Kilburn Model Laundry and Dye works, but one horrified glance at the ghostly downtrodden figures toiling in a billowing cumulus of hot wet steam prompted her to refuse it. Once more she was ticked off for wasting people's time.

London didn't seem to want her. Although she was one of its children it remained stonily indifferent to her talents and monumentally unimpressed by the name of the Gathercole Commercial Academy. Each day it rained, each day her small stock of money dwindled, and on the seventh day she awoke with a streaming cold.

To return to Liverpool was a bitter decision, and before she paid the bill at the Bluebell and set off for Euston she took a last melancholy trip to Walham Green. At the gates of the cemetery she bought a small bunch of Michaelmas daisies from a rain-sodden old flower-seller and laid them on her parents' grave. She whispered goodbye, blew her nose violently and then walked hurriedly away.

She slept for most of the journey back to Liverpool and arrived at Lime Street station cold and hungry and bleary-eyed. There was no point in abasing herself by returning to The Mount because the family would now be in Deauville and the house shut up, so with a resigned sigh she picked up her suitcase and set off on the long walk back to Arnold's place. This, she felt, was going to be quite self-abasing enough.

His landlady opened the door. Mrs Handsworth, Cassie remembered, and did her best to prepare a winning smile.

'Mr Openshaw?' The face was grim, the voice harsh. 'He's gone.'

'Gone? Oh heavens, where?'

'Left.'

'Gone left? I don't quite—'

'He's gone. Which is another way of saying that he's left my premises.' The door slammed so hard that the windows rattled.

Sitting on the edge of a stone horse-trough in Smithdown Lane Cassie realised for the first time that she was both homeless and penniless.

* * *

Emilia Gathercole paused outside the police station and looked up at the ornate soot-encrusted facade for a moment, then began with slow deliberation to mount the front steps.

Although it was early afternoon in late July, the interior was illuminated by gas jets. A policeman with a heavy moustache asked her in what way he could be of assistance.

'I have called,' said Emilia, 'about a young lady called Cassica Marlow. I believe that she is staying here.'

If her manner indicated that she might be interviewing an hotel flunkey, the policeman gave no sign.

'Cassica Marlow,' he said. 'Is that a female name?'

'It is.'

'In that case she will be listed under Women, seemingly.'

'Cassica Marlow is a young woman, yes. And having established that, I should like to see her as soon as possible.'

'Perhaps you would care to sign here.' He pushed a large book towards her, dipped a wooden pen in the inkwell and then handed it to her.

'What am I signing?' Emilia asked sharply.

'The daybook, madam. Every visitor is asked to sign their name and state their business in order to assist with our records.'

Emilia scratched her name with an impatient flourish. Then wrote 'Appertaining to Miss Cassica Marlow' beneath it. The policeman scrutinised what she had written, blotted it, then led her down a long stone corridor into a room furnished with benches and a table and a picture of Queen Mary. He invited her to sit down, then left her, and a few minutes later a tall woman with a large bust compressed beneath a policeman's tunic came in. Her uniform skirt touched her ankles and she wore black boots.

'Miss Gathercole, I gather.'

'You gather correctly.'

'And you are here concerning a Miss Cassica Marlow.'

'Yes. May I see her?'

'I am afraid that is not possible,' the policewoman said. 'She is not at this present moment on our premises.'

'Would you mind telling me where she is? I was after all summoned here in order that I might—'

'Miss Marlow is not in custody, she was merely provided with emergency accommodation for the night. We therefore have no authority over her comings and goings.'

'As she now appears to have gone, are you authorised to tell me whether or not she will be coming back?'

The cheerless room seemed charged with the presence of three powerful women: Emilia, the policewoman, and the queen who hung on the wall.

'I am authorised to tell you that Miss Marlow left a message to say that she would hope to return to collect her suitcase by four o'clock.'

'It is now only two forty-five.'

'You may wait here at your convenience,' the policewoman said. 'There is reading matter on the table but smoking is forbidden.'

Left to her own devices Emilia sat studying the wall opposite, then with a sigh reached for a handful of dog-eared periodicals. They were mostly of a repressive evangelical nature and after a cursory examination she put them back. She looked at her watch and decided that she would wait no longer. Not only was she wasting an afternoon of her summer holiday, she was wasting it in a manner hitherto undreamed of. She had entered a police station on only one previous occasion in her life and that was to enquire about a missing brooch — even the terrible drama concerning Wilfred's wife had merited no more, finally, than a discreet visit to the academy by a sergeant in a tweed suit — and now here she was sitting on a hard wooden bench at the invitation of a hard wooden policewoman waiting for the arrival of one of her own pupils who had been — what was the expression? — *dossing* on the premises.

Cassica Marlow was nothing but a source of trouble. A restless, tiresome girl spoilt by the over-indulgence of a rich family. She had no moral fibre, no grit. She worked no more than spasmodically, was the only girl to have trifled with the affections of the academy's only male pupil, and a succession of quiet little talks had done nothing to alter her approach to life, which was essentially negligent and airy-fairy and quite out of keeping with that of a potential Gathercole secretary. Crossness swelled in Emilia's bosom, and at that moment the waiting-room door burst open and Cassie rushed in.

'Oh, Miss Gathercole,' she cried, 'how nice of you to come! And what d'you think? — I've got a job!'

'A job?' Slowly Emilia rose to her feet.

'I beg your pardon.' Cassie drew a deep breath. 'I have acquired a position.'

'May I ask what as?'

'As general secretary at fifteen shillings a week and one Saturday morning off in four.' Still sparkling, Cassie dropped her suitcase down on the floor. 'I've also found myself a room in a very nice house and I've just come back here to collect my belongings — they've been ever so kind to me here — we even had fried herrings for breakfast — and so thank you very much indeed, Miss Gathercole, for taking the trouble to — to . . .'

'Sit down,' said Emilia. 'It is time that you and I had another of our little talks.'

'But you see, I—'

'I said sit down.'

Cassie did so, pulling her skirt down tightly over her knees. The sparkle began to fade.

'First of all,' said Emilia, 'I am sure that you must be extremely curious to know how I succeeded in discovering your whereabouts; I daresay you are equally curious to know what possible business your whereabouts are of mine. I will tell you. Your uncle got into touch with me the day before he left for France; he told me that during the heat of a family altercation you had removed yourself from his care, and he asked me to act as deputy guardian until his return, supposing your whereabouts could be traced in the meantime. We then lodged an official description of you with the constabulary together with the request that I should be notified of your new address, supposing you had one. They telephoned me at my private address this morning to say that a young woman bearing your name had called at one of their stations last evening to ask for asylum.'

'I just asked for a bed. I didn't say anything about asylum.'

'Be that as it may,' retorted Emilia, 'the fact remains that you have behaved in the most reprehensible fashion, Cassica. You have caused your family a great deal of anguish—'

'Not enough to stop them going on holiday—'

'In heaven's name what do you *expect?*' Emilia brought her handbag down on the table with a crash. 'Are you such an immature child, such a dog in the manger that you expect everyone to cancel their arrangements, to sit at home and wring their hands over your foolishness? Your uncle was pale with worry, I saw it with my own eyes, and although I am not accustomed to having my private life interfered with, I felt bound to advise him to take his holiday as arranged, and to rest in the knowledge that I would deputise for him to the best of my ability.'

'I don't need anyone to look after me. I've just proved that I'm quite capable of looking after myself.'

'Which brings us to the second point. What exactly is this situation of which you speak? What is the firm, and what is their business?'

'It's William Hoskins and Sons Limited.'

'And their function?'

'They travel about and they — they sort of help the bereaved.'

'A charitable concern?'

'Well, no. As a matter of fact they're undertakers, but they prefer people to call them Funeral Furnishers and Monumental Masons and they seem very nice and informal and they said — at least, Mr Hoskins said, and he's the boss — that as I'd be running the office I wouldn't have anything to do with the . . . their clients, who go straight down to the basement apparently where the morticians put them in their coffins and so on, then they go up to the private chapel of rest where their relations can go and say goodbye if they want to before the lids are put on. I think,' Cassie said defiantly, 'that I'm going to find it very interesting.'

'A novelty,' said Emilia. 'No more. And you have overlooked one thing.'

'Oh?'

'You omitted to sit for your final certificate of proficiency.'

'I don't think they care about that.'

'No, but I do. I have the reputation of my establishment to think of.'

'Well, it's too late now, Miss Gathercole,' Cassie said. 'I've left.'

'Arrangements can still be made. For the sake of your future I am prepared to allow access to my academy for the time necessary, and I daresay that Mr Sissley could be persuaded to act as invigilator during the course of the examination.'

'Thank you very much, but there's really no need—'

'There *is* need,' cried Emilia. 'You are cutting off your nose to spite your face, you ridiculous girl. To go out and find a position for yourself may seem very brave and laudable but you are not yet capable of sorting the wheat from the chaff. At your stage in life you cannot be expected to sum up the future possibilities, the chances for promotion, for bettering yourself, for increased increments, for progressing up the commercial ladder. You have intelligence, Cassica, a good appearance and a pleasant enough manner when you choose, therefore do not be so foolhardy as to throw them all away in a stupid fit of defiance. Your shorthand will be wasted on a meagre and obsequious vocabulary, your typewriting will be limited to rendering accounts to the bereaved and you will become utterly bored within the space of six months. But already you will have become imbued with the unfortunate aura of undertaking. Most people are discomfited by the thought of death and all its trappings, Cassica, and you will find yourself shunned socially. And the stigma will follow you. What was your first position? people will ask when you apply for another post, and you will be obliged to say, I worked in an undertaker's parlour; here is the reference with which he furnished me. And make no mistake, Cassica, whether the reference is good, bad, or merely non-committal, it will be signed William Hoskins, Undertaker, and any future employer will shudder with distaste and pass you over. Our references are an integral part of our lives; they are our mainspring for the future, our passport to success. They are documents that should be cherished with pride and displayed, in the right quarters, with triumph. So do not take up a position with an undertaker, Cassica, however reputable he may be; sit for your final certificate of proficiency as I suggest, and then allow me to find you a situation that holds a better future.'

'My uncle arranged for me to go into his office, but I don't want to.'

'I see your point. I also hold the view that the modern young woman should strike out for herself, should regard independence as a virtue, but in the rush to paddle her own canoe she should take care not to paddle herself up the creek, as it were. Now, how would you like a situation with the

Cunard Shipping Company, Cassica? I have already placed several of my best girls there, and one of them is now secretary to a very big man indeed in their accountancy department.'

'But I've already taken this job with Mr Hoskins — I'm due to start tomorrow and I want to go there, I'm looking *forward to* it, and in any case I . . .'

'Yes?'

Emilia studied her carefully, unsmilingly, and Cassie thought oh, my God, why won't she leave me alone? What's it got to do with her? I've left her rotten academy and it's none of her business where I go and work.

Aloud, she said: 'When I explained my circumstances to Mr Hoskins he very kindly gave me an advance on my first week's wages. I need the money to pay for my room and to buy some food.'

'You can return the money from the allowance your uncle has made for you and entrusted to my care until he returns from holiday in September.'

'Oh . . .' Surprised gratification lit Cassie's features for an instant. 'But I hope he doesn't think I'm going back to live with them.'

'He has said nothing to me on the subject, and my own conclusions are that he would be well advised to relinquish the burden of responsibility as soon as possible,' Emilia said dryly.

They continued to stare at one another from opposite sides of the table and Queen Mary appeared to be scrutinising them both with equal disdain. Outside in the corridor they heard the bang of a door and the rattle of keys. Then Emilia opened her handbag and took out a white envelope.

'One week's allowance. The next one will be due next Monday, according to your uncle's instructions.'

'Doesn't he even trust me to—'

'Has he any particular reason to?' Then Emilia added: 'The arrangement is only a temporary one until his return.'

'So I'm supposed to come and collect it and—'

'Give me the address of this room you have taken, and I will see that it is posted to you.'

Cassie did so, and Emilia glanced at it briefly before putting it in her handbag and snapping the clasp shut.

'It's very nice there and I'll be private, with no one bothering me—'

'Now listen, Cassica,' said Emilia. 'Go and see this Mr Hoskins and tell him that you now find yourself unable to accept his position. Return the money he has advanced, thank him for his kindness but make it quite clear that you have thought twice about taking up secretarial duties with an undertaker. Then return to your room and prepare yourself for your final proficiency. Brush up on grammalogues and advanced phraseology — I remember Mr Sissley telling me that you were weak on the Halving Principle — and then arrangements will be made for you to sit the examination on Saturday morning next at nine a.m. sharp at the academy. I will be there in person, and if he is free of commitments so I feel sure will Mr Sissley.'

That wasn't what she wanted. In fact it was quite the reverse. Now that she had made the break she just wanted to leave the whole of the past year behind, and that included both Gathercoles and the family in Sefton Park. She was even glad that Arnold Openshaw had disappeared from her life. All she wanted now was to be left alone to start again. On her own. To make her own decisions, handle her own affairs, pursue the goal of success in her own way. Very slowly she picked up her old suitcase and walked towards the door.

'Thank you, Miss Gathercole,' she said. 'I'll be there next Saturday at nine.'

CHAPTER NINE

'Barbara, Barbie, Baby, Babs . . .' Uncle Harry ran his fingers yearningly up his wife's arm, then slipped them inside the loose lacy neck of her tea gown. Music made by a small string orchestra down on the terrace mingled with the lazy sigh of the sea and drifted up through the open balcony window of the Marlows' hotel suite.

'Don't do that, Harry, it makes me want to scratch.'

'You shouldn't look so delicious.'

'Why don't you go for a walk? Find the boys or something.'

'The boys are on the Cossingtons' yacht.'

'Will they be back for dinner?'

'I expect so. Babs, darling . . .'

'Yes, Harry, I *know.* But it's too hot.'

'Not if I unfasten your gown. Oh, my sweet, sweet girl, how lovely you are . . .'

'Oh really. Harry, I don't *want* to.'

'Yes, you do. You know you do, really and truly . . .'

For a moment she resisted, fighting his climbing body with hands, elbows and knees. She turned her face away from his urgent lips, then abruptly capitulated and lay inert as a bolster. He might have been entering a mousehole in a tree trunk, seeking admittance to some jealously guarded crevice in a stone wall, and when the poor ridiculous business was over Babs said: 'If you've squirted all over my lace, Harry, I'll be absolutely livid.' The string orchestra began to play Offenbach.

Beloved Babs. Despite being the mother of two — no, three — children, she was the abiding virgin, the thrillingly, eternally unattainable. She was naturally pure and chaste, fresh and lovely as a Madonna lily, and, rebuttoning his fly, Uncle Harry could only marvel at the disparity between his wife and his niece. Above all else he revered and understood immaculacy in women.

Lying with closed eyes his thoughts turned to Cassica. The furious indignation had faded now and he felt no more than a weary aversion. Her bouts of sullenness alternating with a propensity for argument had been sufficiently trying without the additional embarrassment of unashamed carnality, and he was relieved that she had left the shelter of his doors; the fact of her absence more than compensated for the not ungenerous allowance he proposed to make her until she reached the age of twenty-one, which would be in . . . in . . .

'My darling,' he said. 'When is Cassica's birthday?'

From the other side of the bed Babs made a weary, bruised sound. 'May, I think. Why?'

September, October, November, thought Uncle Harry, counting inaudibly. No more than eight months. How tempus fugits.

He wondered what Cassica was doing now, at this very moment, then fell asleep lulled by the music and the sea and the teasingly elusive scent of Chanel. Soon it would be time to dress for dinner.

* * *

Mona Marlow was also lying on her bed, but in her case it was because there was nothing better to do. In the home run by nuns this was the hour allotted for silent contemplation, and those who had nothing in particular to contemplate lay on their beds and either dozed or stared blankly at the ceiling.

She hasn't been for two weeks now, thought Mona. Two whole Sundays when everyone had a visitor but me. I suppose she doesn't like me anymore. Well, I can't really blame her. I mean, no one likes me very much, so I don't see why she should. But oh it was nice, her coming here. I used to like laughing and talking with her and letting everyone see that she was my friend.

Becoming aware that her eyes were wandering in the direction of a certain crack in the ceiling, she shut them quickly. The crack was like the shape of a horse's head, and there was even a small smudgy mark that looked like an anguished eye. On nights when the horse horror was very bad she could still see the crack even though there was no light in the room. It would seem to superimpose itself on the darkness and press its dreadful wordless accusation down against her forehead; she would feel it banging against her skull like frightened hooves, like big demented heartbeats, and then the screams and cries of all the horses torn by shell splinters, pierced by rifle bullets and left bleedingly impaled on barbed wire would start ringing louder and louder until the sounds bounced from wall to wall, collided with one another and then finally amalgamated in one vast and violent sound that would bring one of the nuns running.

'Turn over on your other side, you were dreaming again—'

'I wasn't — it was real—' Dry mouth, sweating body, pleading, trembling hands.

'You had two helpings of prunes and custard at supper. I saw you. Now straighten your nightdress, lie on your other side and ask the Blessed Virgin to protect you from the sin of gluttony . . .'

'But my head's banging and banging—'

'It's a bilious headache, that's all. Go to sleep, and by morning it will be gone.'

Since Cassie had been coming to see Mona, the torment seemed to have abated; she had thought about the horses less, and when she did so the tearing agony of mind was greatly diminished. The pity and the horror were still there, yet in manageable form. But now the physical pain part of it was coming back again, the thought of it filling the lonely hours with silent dread and she knew that before long the thing would once more be out of control.

Please, Holy Mother, I beseech you send my friend to visit me next Sunday. She needn't come for the whole hour, just ten minutes would do, but oh let her be here and smile at me and hold my hand and make me brave, world without end, amen.

But the prayers didn't work. Probably because she was C. of E. instead of R.C.

* * *

Down on the Pier Head the lights from an arriving ferryboat were glinting on the twilit water, jostling, blending, drowning and then reforming like chips of coloured glass. The sound of someone playing 'Sweet Adeline' on a melodeon drifted towards the landing-stage before being brutally cut off by the rattle of chains and the crash of gangways. Day trippers to New Brighton began to file ashore, sun-reddened families with picnic baskets and buckets and spades and, watching from the shadow of the overhead railway, Arnold Openshaw thought she might be on this boat, for all I know. After all, she's got to be somewhere.

Twice he had called back to his old room, braving the tight-lipped censoriousness of his ex-landlady in order to find out if there was a letter from her. She had promised to write, but even so he had been a fool not to insist upon knowing where she intended to go. The suspicion that she had no definite destination in view was an unhappy one and he tried hard to reassure himself that Cassie was far too level-headed to suddenly rush off into the unknown after what had obviously been an upset with her family. Most painful of all, however, was the suspicion that she hadn't written because she hadn't wanted to; she didn't want to keep in touch with him because he was too dull and uninspiring. It was almost a relief to wonder whether Mrs Handsworth could prove spiteful enough to destroy any letter that had arrived, and although his gentle soul shrank from such a thought it was difficult to forget her wrath on the morning following Cassie's clandestine visit.

'Three hairpins,' she had said, holding them aloft between the tips of her fingers. 'Three women's hairpins, Mr Openshaw, and all of them found in your bed.'

'Oh, I say—'

'Not one, Mr Openshaw, but *three.*'

She made it sound as if each hairpin had belonged to a separate woman and a wild neigh of laughter burst from Arnold even as the sickening shock of her words dizzied him. It seemed to compress him, to force him down into the flowered linoleum like a weed among the roses.

'I think I can explain, Mrs Handsworth—'

'Unless you've taken to wearing a bun in bed, Mr Openshaw, I don't think you can. I am a clean-living woman in a clean-living house, Mr Openshaw, and I will be obliged if you will pack your case. I would like the room free for cleaning and disinfecting by dinnertime.'

He was now living in a room in the next street. The house was run by an Irish family who ran an illicit still up in the attic which they referred to lovingly as the *crayt'r,* and their cheerful comings and goings brought him to the rueful conclusion that three or more women churning about in his bed at the same time would worry them not at all.

The last of the trippers disembarked from the ferry and plodded towards the tramcars waiting to take them home to Toxteth and Fazakerley, Kirkdale and West Derby. The twilight deepened, the pubs opened, and an oily smell rose off the Mersey and mingled with the scent of sewage and summer-warmed soot.

He wished that he could have kept the hairpins. That in her righteous wrath Mrs Handsworth might have dropped them on the floor or even flung them in his face; he would have retrieved them, stroked them tenderly back to self-respect and been able to feel that he possessed at least some tangible, personal and everyday part of Cassie Marlow. But the hairpins had gone and so had she, and Arnold crossed over into Water Street and began to make his way home.

* * *

'We must not be late to bed,' Emilia told Wilfred. 'To all intents and purposes tomorrow is going to start like an ordinary working day.'

'Think she'll turn up?'

'She promised. And the girl is no fool.'

All the same, she seems to get herself into foolish situations, Wilfred thought.

He and Emilia were watching the last of the sunset flush from Red Rocks, a haphazard outcrop of sandstone draped with seaweed that lay a little beyond Hilbre Point. The tide was out, the firm sands ridged like the interior of a dog's mouth. To the right of them the three islands, Hilbre, Middle Hilbre and the Eye, lay in silent mulberry-coloured shadow.

'You've never done this before, have you, Emilia?'

'Done what, loved one?'

'Made a special dispensation for an erring pupil.'

'You make me sound like the pope.'

'D'you honestly think she's worth it?'

A long silence broken only by the twick-twick cry of a low-flying sanderling.

'One can never be sure. On the whole I'm inclined to think yes.'

'And you're right, more often than not.'

'She has a difficult background. I know little of her parents, but from what her uncle said they were rather ineffectual. They both died within a few weeks of one another and she was then sent — pitchforked, if one may put in crudely — into a milieu that must have seemed very strange to a girl still in mourning.'

'She was lucky to be sent to Gathercoles.'

'I understand that she had already won a place at Cambridge.'

The sunset faded to indigo; the sky turned a soft emerald green before surrendering to the dusk.

'Beggars can't be choosers,' Wilfred said.

'Oh, what a melancholy observation . . .'

They sat in silence, watching the coming of evening and listening to the strange, lonely little cries of sea birds settling for the night. The sound of the sea was so faint that it might have retreated beyond the rim of the horizon.

'I still think she may do well in the long run.'

'There's nothing wrong with her intelligence, certainly.'

'It's a question of whether she has the drive. Plus the perspicacity to see that a position with an undertaker is a ludicrous waste of effort.'

'We personally have never sent anyone to an undertaker, have we?'

'Perish the thought. No, I fear we put them in the same class as publicans and fishmongers.'

'Alfreda Morris took temporary employment in a public house.'

'Alfreda Morris has now been placed with the Royal Maritime Insurance Company as junior shorthand-typist. I believe she commences her duties next Monday.'

The first star. One hesitant needle tip stabbing through the greeny-violet. A sudden tiny splashing in the rock pool close by; a sign that some unimportant creature had seized another, and was about to dine.

'My behind's getting stiff.'

'Yes. We had better go before the light fades completely.'

'Give me your hand, darling.'

'I can manage.'

'Don't get your skirt wet.'

'Where are you, Wilfred? I can't see you anymore . . .'

'I'm here, close by you, my darling . . .'

Perhaps I was an idiot, Emilia thought next morning. After all, I have had any amount of promising pupils passing through my hands before Cassica Marlow. Why was I so insistent that she should return to take her final certificate? Was it belief in her, affection even, or merely a subconscious business urge to ingratiate myself with her uncle who is rich and powerful and an undoubted source of prestigious employment for young Gathercolians? After all, I am but a humble cog in Liverpool's vast commercial machine.

Sitting at her desk she stared down at her ringless hands. The office was dusty, the air heavy and listless with holiday boredom. Even the pillbox girls were away on their annual week's holiday. Through the open door she heard the clock down in the hall strike ten, then the sound of footsteps.

'She won't be coming now,' Wilfred said gently.

They waited in silence for another hour, then relocked the academy and took the next train back to Hoylake.

* * *

Mr Hoskins was about Uncle Harry's age, a smallish, neatly shaped man with beady eyes and a high forehead surmounted by a luxuriant crop of russet-coloured curls. His funeral parlour was a double-fronted building halfway down Mount Pleasant, its two windows furnished with black velvet curtains drawn back to reveal a pair of large stone urns tastefully filled with white wax flowers. Appropriate gloom predominated, only the small office where Cassie worked being lightened by sunshine coming through from the dusty-white masons' yard where angels and crosses, and headstones in the shape of open books, and yards and yards of curbing were cut and hammered, gouged and chiselled six days a week from sunup to sundown. The masons were very conscious of social distinctions and always touched their powdery caps to the young lady in the office, although the two men who worked down in the basement at the more grisly side of the business acknowledged her presence with no more than a distant nod.

The work was not particularly difficult and after a certain amount of initial confusion Cassie soon got the hang of it. Orders, invoices and advice notes for new consignments of granite and marble had to be dealt with, and oak, elm and deal constantly restocked for the coffin shop at the end of the yard. The carpenters were as deferential as the masons, and only the two stablemen in charge of the six black horses had the impertinence to wink at her.

No one, she swiftly discovered, ever actually died. They fell asleep, or passed away or passed over, or were gathered up, caught up or, even more fancifully, rocked to sleep in the bosom of the Lord; yet beneath the whispered euphemisms beat the healthy pulse of shrewd commerce.

'Dear Sir,' dictated Mr Hoskins at manageable speed, 'we beg to acknowledge receipt of your kind enquiry of the 10th instant re our range of funeral services and have pleasure in enclosing herewith our brochure, from perusal of which it will be seen that we have a wide and comprehensive range of interments suitable to all pockets. All arrangements placed in our hands are carried out with sympathy, dignity and reverence, and efficiency is our watchword. Hoping to receive the honour of your further instructions in this sad matter, we remain, dear Sir, yours faithfully . . . and on the brochure, Miss Marlow, will you be so good as to make a note to the effect that black plumes are five shillings extra.'

Mr Hoskins was always very nice to her, but he used to stare at her a lot and one afternoon when she gave him his letters for signature he reached out his hand and inadvertently touched her bust. He immediately said that he was sorry, and Cassie gruffly accepted his apology. It didn't happen again.

Remembering the awful despotism of Arnold Openshaw's landlady she had searched for a room let by a landlord and had finally met with success. The man who owned the house in Upper Parliament Street, just round the corner from Catherine Street, asked her to provide two references, which she did (writing them herself in the ladies' room of the Bon Marche), plus a week's rent in advance, and left it at that. He didn't even live on the premises. The house was very quiet, and only the occasional soft footfall going past her door told of any other presence save her own. Her room was on the ground floor, with a small kitchen built into a cupboard under the stairs and the use of bathroom and lavatory on the first floor.

And every morning she awoke in the narrow bed and thought exultantly I'm free — I'm free! I'm an independent woman well on the way to success! She loved making her own bed before she left for the office and leaving everything neat and tidy (cup and saucer washed, art. silk stockings hanging to dry over the geyser), and in the evenings she made a great thing of preparing toasted cheese and setting the table with the beaded cork mats she had found in the drawer.

The euphoria lasted for three weeks or more, and the first real sign of its fading came with the dying of the long days and the subtle lengthening of the evenings, and with the increasing frequency with which she found herself thinking about people from the past. She wondered what they were doing up at The Mount, how the other girls from Gathercoles were getting on and whether poor old Arnold Openshaw had realised his ambition of becoming the secretary of a Labour MP. The one person she preferred not to think about was Miss Gathercole herself, because she should have let her know that she had changed her mind about taking the exam.

On her way to and from the office she never met anyone she knew, but if anyone did happen to smile at her in the street it was impossible to smile back without the fear of being considered common. So she remained straight-backed and poker-faced, every inch the new, purposeful young businesswoman who made her own decisions and kept her own council.

The weekends were the worst. A bit of shopping on Saturday afternoon, a walk in Princes Park on Sunday morning, and that seemed to be that; she rearranged her room several times, began to knit a silk jumper but kept dropping stitches, then went through a spell of haunting the shabby little bookshops in Brownlow. Hill. She bought a copy of Milton's *Areopagitica* because it was cheap, the collected works of Rider Haggard in a sixpenny edition and a copy of Browning's poems, and when for the first time since leaving school she read the lines *Grow old along with me! The best is yet to be* the thought that she was growing old all on her own almost brought tears to her eyes.

The house was close to a junction at which five roads met, and sitting in the window, chin in hand, she became a spare-time tram watcher. Small, brown and either-ended like earthworms, they bored their way through the melancholy twilight with a single yellow eye gazing steadfastly ahead, their antennae snapping and crackling and emitting occasional showers of blue sparks along the overhead cable. She began listening to their clear, high-pitched feminine voices accompanied by the rhythmic clang of the bell that was like the beating of a metallic heart. They became like friends to her, and she began jotting their serial numbers down on a piece of paper which she kept under the clock, and the highest one she ever saw was tramcar number 992, which had a dent in one side.

Tramcars humming contentedly along Upper Parliament Street from Smithdown Lane; singing and sighing down the hill to the Pier Head and to the mournful chorus of tugs on the river; tramcars glittering and triumphant like mobile gaslit conservatories; tramcars surging like brown swans in a backwash, like schooners with the wind in their rigging, and during that autumn she learned that the distant late night cry of a tramcar is the loneliest and most desolate sound in the world.

Every morning at first light she was awakened by the rattle of iron buckets and the slosh and rasp of scrubbing brushes on front doorsteps; Liverpool's step-girls, engaged at sixpence per week per flight of steps, were a raucous, red-armed race in sacking aprons who scrubbed and hearthstoned and bawled cheerful obscenities to one another across the street. She learned that the old, black-shawled women who sold lemons in the vicinity of Lime Street station were known as Mary Ellens and she even began to recognise some of the ex-servicemen who sang in the streets, but none of the other inmates of the house betrayed the slightest desire to become acquainted with her. They didn't appear to be acquainted with each other, for she never heard the sound of voices outside her door; merely the occasional swift, soft footfall of someone going out or coming in. She watched them from her window, and it was obvious that they too were straight-backed and poker-faced businesspeople who didn't smile or speak because of the fear of being thought common. And they were all older than she was.

Then suddenly she remembered Mona. And that tomorrow, Sunday, would be visiting day.

It was many weeks since she had been to see her, and the mere thought of having a social project in view made Cassie's spirits soar. She hurried to the shops to buy chocolate, some more tooth powder in case Mona needed it, and a bunch of chrysanthemums, and when she arrived at the home and was shown into the visitors' room Mona looked so blank and apathetic that it made her feel a bit irritated.

'I'm awfully sorry I haven't been for so long, but I have been a bit busy, you know. I don't live with your parents anymore but I've got a little flat all of my own — well, I suppose it's more of a room with cupboard attached really, but it's jolly nice. And I've also got quite an important job — I'm in sole charge of the office of quite a big establishment, and I—'

'I'm not allowed to have second helpings anymore,' Mona said. 'It makes me dream.'

'Oh? Well yes, you do look a bit thin, Mona.'

Cassie sat looking at her, and pity took the place of irritation. The shadows beneath her eyes made them look larger than ever and there were hollows in either side of her neck.

'Never mind, I've brought you some chocs.' Cassie dived into her handbag, and Mona's hare lip quivered painfully before being obscured by her hand.

'Now you must eat them all yourself and not give any away — and I've brought you some more tooth powder and these flowers to put in your room. I always think chrysanthemums smell of cats, but they're a nice colour and just think, it won't be all that long before we start getting daffodils again, will it?'

She rattled on, trying to stem Mona's tears with a barrage of words.

'One of these days you'll have to come and see my little flat, Mona. We'll have to ask permission for you to come and have tea — there's a nice table and some comfy chairs — and then we could go for a walk in Princes Park where they've got a lot of swans and things . . . and oh, we could have a really ripping time, couldn't we?'

Mona's tears were now beyond control, yet she cried very quietly, as if she were an expert. No sobs or even sniffs, just large iridescent tears sliding down her cheeks and dropping on to the front of her woollen jumper.

'Oh, Mona, you poor girl, I can't stand you being in here . . .' Blinking furiously, Cassie passed her handkerchief to Mona who wiped her eyes with it and then passed it back. 'It's absolutely wicked to shut you up when you're so nice and so gentle . . . oh, don't cry, duck, you're starting me off . . .'

They sat close together, knees touching and heads bent, and the murmur of constrained visitors' conversation was pierced by the sudden squawking of a fat old woman in a bathchair. A nun rustled over to her and wheeled her swiftly away.

'Mona,' Cassie whispered, taking her hand and squeezing it hard, 'come back with me now. When it's time for me to go, just get up and come with me and no one'll notice. Have you got a coat handy?'

Mona shook her head.

'Can you arrange to get one? Don't bother about anything else, I've got spare nighties and things — just take *a chance* and *come* . . .'

'Sister Magdalen would be angry—'

'Blow Sister Magdalen. Mona, you're coming — you can't stay in this awful place anymore, and I'll take all the blame. I don't mind — in fact I'd quite enjoy it. But you'd look funny going out without a coat so try and think how you—'

'We keep our garden coats in the back lobby—'

'Where's that?'

'Through the refectory and along the passage.'

'Right. Now listen, Mona, in a few minutes we'll start saying goodbye. Then you come to the door with me, and while I go out through the hall you just go quietly and get your coat and — is there a way out of the lobby into the garden?'

Mona nodded.

'Could you get to the front gates without being seen? I'll walk down the drive and all you've got to do is just sort of meet me very quietly. Do you think you can do that?'

Bleakly Mona nodded again, but a little warmth seemed to be creeping into the hand that Cassie was still squeezing fiercely.

'Good. It's worth trying, and now we've decided, you won't suddenly change your mind, will you?'

Another shake of the bent head.

'So wipe your eyes then, and blow your nose . . .'

No one seemed to take any notice when Cassie stood up and began saying goodbye in a rather hearty voice. She patted Mona's shoulder and told her that she would come again next Sunday, and Mona raised her huge, blurred eyes and said, 'That would be very nice. Thank you.'

She accompanied Cassie to the door, and without turning to see which way she went, Cassie crossed the cold echoing hall, nodded graciously to a lurking nun and rejoiced inwardly when she saw from the front door that an autumn mist was already beginning to obscure the outline of trees and bushes. Casually she sauntered down the overgrown drive, and when she reached the gates a figure stepped hesitantly out of the damp and hazy gloom. Without speaking they walked out into the road that led to the railway station, and in less than half an hour were drinking tea and eating vanilla slices in front of Cassie's gas fire.

* * *

It was an insane thing to have done, yet it was high time someone attempted to improve poor old Mona's ghastly way of life, and reconsidering her somewhat high-handed action, Cassie remained impenitent.

Once coaxed over the threshold it seemed as if Mona could neither eat nor drink enough, and she edged her chair nearer and nearer to the fire until her cheeks flared red and her brown lisle stockings smelt of singeing. They made a fresh pot of tea, and after the vanilla slices Cassie set to and made a plateful of fishpaste sandwiches.

'It's like a little nest in here,' Mona said, looking round. 'Like a warm, private little bird's nest.'

'And you're free to share it,' Cassie said very earnestly. 'It's lovely having you here.'

'But they won't let me stop, will they?'

'I don't know. We'll have to see.'

'Would you let me stop, if they would?'

'Yes.'

Outside the mist thickened, shrouding the home-going tramcars and dripping from the iron railings, and comfortably ensconced between two chairs Cassie looked across at the dim shape of Mona in her bed and thought well, I daresay we could manage somehow. There's going to be an awful row anyway, but if Mona wants to live here and I agree, surely they can't just cart her away by force. For one thing, she's over twenty-one . . .

'Cassie?'

'Yes, dear?'

'I do hope God will forgive me for what I've done.'

'If He starts getting shirty, refer Him to me.'

'Oh, Cassie, what an awful thing to say . . .'

They wouldn't be able to go on living in this room; they would have to find somewhere bigger. And Mona would have to find something to do during the day . . . She more than liked Mona, she loved her, but there would be difficulties.

'Cassie, you do believe in God, don't you?'

'Yes, of course. But I'm not frightened of Him, any more than I'm frightened of your father.'

'And it *will be* all right, won't it?'

'Yes. Hush now, dear, I'm thinking.'

By the following morning Cassie had made three decisions. The first was not to go to the office that day, the second was to send a telegram to Mr Hoskins advising him that she was suffering from a sick headache, and another telegram to Sefton Park telling them of Mona's whereabouts. The third decision was to sit back and see what happened next.

They ate breakfast by the fire. The mist had cleared, the step-girls had clattered away and the world seemed full of a bright new promise.

'There goes dear old 307,' Cassie said, glancing through the window. 'She's on the Wavertree run.' But she didn't bother to jot it down.

Swiftly she washed the breakfast things, tidied the room and then prepared to slip across the road to the post office. It occurred to her that it would be prudent to take Mona with her, and Mona insisted with deferential tenacity upon polishing their shoes before they went.

They sent the telegram, then went for a stroll up Princes Road, where the leaves were falling thickly and a man with a hurdy-gurdy was churning out Gilbert and Sullivan, and it was all so wonderful to Mona that she gave a happy little skip, and when an old gentleman smiled at her she smiled back and didn't remember to put her hand over her top lip until it was too late.

Returning home down Granby Street they bought a bag of fruit drops and then a meat pie and some apples for lunch, and they were walking arm in arm along Upper Parliament Street when Cassie noticed the big Daimler drawn up outside the house. And the sudden chill in the pit of her stomach told her that if she wasn't actually frightened of Uncle Harry, she was a little apprehensive of meeting him again.

'Now, don't worry,' she urged Mona as they drew nearer. 'And whatever happens, remember that you've always got me.'

Nibbs was sitting at the wheel, gazing impassively ahead, and they found Uncle Harry standing at the foot of Cassie's bed dressed in a dark overcoat with a velvet collar.

'How did you get in here?' Attack seemed the best form of defence.

'Nibbs rang all the bells until someone answered, and you had carelessly omitted to lock your own door. Now then, Mona—'

'So my telegram didn't take long to arrive,' Cassie said chattily, and, taking off her coat, nodded to Mona to do the same.

'You needn't bother to remove it, my dear,' said Uncle Harry. 'You will not be staying.'

Mona made a crushed little sound, and began slowly to refasten the buttons, her head bent low.

'It so happens,' Cassie said, 'that I want her to stay. And as she wants to stay, I don't think you can stop her.'

'Abduction is a criminal offence, my dear Cassica.'

'I didn't abduct her, she came of her own free will—'

'You were instrumental in removing her from the care into which I, as her legal parent and guardian, had placed her—'

'But she's grown up! She's old enough to please herself!'

Oh Lord, she was losing her temper again. Why is it, she thought despairingly, that I can never talk to him without shouting? It must be because he's so pompou . . .

She and Uncle Harry were facing one another and, drawn up to her full height, Cassie was able to look down on to the top of his head. There were a few freckles beneath the thinning hair.

'Mona must return to Huyton,' he said slowly and quietly but very emphatically. 'The Mother Superior and her staff have been extremely anxious since they discovered Mona's absence and it was fortunate that I knew instinctively where to look for her—'

'I'd no intention of keeping it a secret. That's why I sent a telegram—'

'Which presumably arrived after I left for my office. No, Cassica, I'm afraid that your propensity for domineering will only succeed in antagonising people, and I'm afraid my poor daughter is likely to suffer for it in the long run.'

He went over to the window and tapped on the glass. Nibbs came up the steps and Uncle Harry went to the front door to let him in.

Mona didn't cry. Neither did she look at Cassie. She just stood silently with her head bent and Cassie watched impotently as she left the room with Nibbs, who held her arm with gentle deference and called her Miss Mona.

She was surprised when Uncle Harry saw them out to the car and then returned, closing the door behind him.

'Now, Cassica,' he said. 'I believe you were on the point of offering me a cup of tea.'

She felt like weeping when he said that. Perhaps because Mona had gone despite all her brave promises to protect her, and even perhaps because Uncle Harry looked suddenly very old and rather ill.

So she went out to the cupboard under the stairs where the smell of Cherry Blossom boot polish still lingered, and she made a pot of tea and took it back to where Uncle Harry was standing by the window with his hands clasped behind his back.

'I've forgotten whether you take sugar.'

'One.'

They sipped in silence, then he said: 'Are you quite determined to go on living in this fashion?'

'What's wrong with it?'

'Nothing is wrong that I can see. It's merely rather limited.' He looked round him, and Cassie became aware that the penny-in-the-slot gas meter had a squalid air.

'I don't plan to live here for ever. Any more than I plan to remain in my present situation.'

'I was rather startled to hear that you were conferring the benefit of your secretarial training on an undertaker.'

'A funeral furnisher and monumental mason.'

'Still planning the great success, my dear?'

'Oh, yes.'

'In what direction?'

He was looking at her with kindliness, as if he had forgotten the scene down by the lake that day, and it was suddenly tempting to say I don't know; that's the trouble. It would have been very nice just at that moment to ask for an old person's advice instead of resenting his interference. But the moment passed with the memory of Mona, and then the shocking unfairness of being blamed for Babs's misdemeanours. Despite Uncle Harry's rich and influential urbanity he was just a pathetic old man in love with an expensive but disreputable woman. If anyone needed advice, he did.

'I've got it all planned,' she said proudly. 'I know exactly what I'm doing.'

'And after next May you will be quite capable of managing without my allowance, I take it?'

She wanted to say I can manage without it now, thanks; but she didn't. For one thing, it wouldn't have been true.

'Yes,' she told him. 'That'll be fine with me.'

They stared at one another rather emptily, conscious that any desire to establish closer contact was dwindling to a pinpoint. She asked if he would like another cup of tea. He said no thank you.

'By the way, why are you not at your office today?'

'I told them I was ill because I wanted to spend the day with Mona.'

'Mona . . .' Her name hung on the air like a sigh.

'Why can't she come to see me sometimes? I'd look after her, and it'd give her something to do.'

Uncle Harry placed his cup and saucer on the tin tray. Preparing for departure he drew from his overcoat pocket a pair of pale chamois gloves and began to put them on.

'How would you like her to spend Christmas with you?'

'What — here?' Surprise held her rigid.

'Yes, of course. I daresay we have a folding bed or something of that nature up at The Mount. But you must be quite sure, Cassica, that you are prepared to take on the responsibility. Mona is a dear girl, and despite whatever you may think we are deeply devoted to her, but a great deal of patience is required in looking after her. In dealing with her foibles, for instance. Perhaps on second thoughts—'

'Oh no, let her come — please! I'd enjoy having her, and I think she likes being here—'

'The strain would not be too great for you, Cassica?'

'No, of course not. We get on very well together — it doesn't take much to make her happy . . . she said this place was like a little nest.'

'Perhaps it could be arranged for Nibbs to bring her on Christmas Eve, and she could return to Huyton on the evening of Boxing Day. I will consult the Mother Superior—'

'She *must* let her come! We could have tremendous fun because Mona asks for so little—' Enthusiasm sparkled. 'I could cook a little Christmas dinner — does she like crackers or would they frighten her? — and then perhaps she, or even both of us, could come to tea with you all on Boxing Day! What about that?'

Uncle Harry smoothed the chamois gloves over his knuckles. 'I'm afraid that would not be possible. Aunt Babs and I are spending Christmas in St Moritz this year with the boys.'

The sparkle died, but not enough for it to show. 'Fine,' she said. 'Top-hole.'

When Nibbs returned from depositing Mona back in Huyton he rang Cassie's doorbell. Uncle Harry picked up his bowler hat.

'Goodbye, Cassica my dear. I will keep in touch.'

'Goodbye, Uncle Harry. And thank you.'

'On the contrary, thank *you*.' A brisk peck on the cheek, a brief whiff of gentleman's eau de cologne. Had he forgiven her? (Had she forgiven him?)

One of her nameless fellow-occupants coming along the street as the Daimler slid away from the kerb stared after it in deferential astonishment.

CHAPTER TEN

Bare trees now, soot-blackened twigs etched sharply against a weeping grey-brown sky. Fog on the river and the hoarse cry of tugs; the moan of foghorns, the cold wet framework of the overhead railway and the cold wet feet of the down-and-outs who huddled beneath it.

By the end of 1920 the unemployed of Liverpool totalled more than thirty-seven thousand but the post-war boom was still confidently expected, and in Bold Street a man with a racking cough was dressed up as Father Christmas and employed at sixpence an hour to open the motorcar doors of lady and gentlemen shoppers.

And the shops were twinkling with tinsel and red ribbons and cottonwool spread out to look like a fall of virgin snow, and Cassie, searching avidly for a present for Mona, was torn between a book about animals and a nightdress case in the guise of a Pierrot doll. In the end she decided on the book.

The spirit of Christmas shopping quickened and intensified, and standing outside a poulterer's shop hung with a dense feather curtain of dead chickens and geese, turkeys and ducks, all strung up by the ankles and still dripping a little blood on to the pavement, she finally decided on a chicken that weighed in at four pounds and cost three and six with head and feet thrown in.

Shining electric light in the main thoroughfares, gaslight in the side streets and naphtha flares illuminating the market stalls. She bought potatoes and onions and a cabbage, some tangerines and a box of dates; some sausages to go with the chicken and a box of crackers reputed to contain fancy hats and tasteful novelties: then a fruit cake with white icing, and as a final, almost defiant gesture a sprig of mistletoe from which the berries were already parting company. She had very little money left but it didn't matter and, hurrying to catch the tramcar in Church Street, she dropped a threepenny bit into the cap of a poor legless man propped in a wheeled soapbox with a little dog that sat up and begged.

And it was strange how it all brought back the memory of Jessica; how it took her back to the old Walham Green days of wresting the maximum from the minimum and treating each purchase as if it were a transaction of life-or-death importance. The knowledge that she had been entrusted with the responsibility of her cousin Mona, if only for two days, made her glow with pleasure.

Mr Hoskins had formally closed the administrative side of his business at midday on Christmas Eve ('Things are reasonably tranquil now, Miss Marlow, but we must gird up our loins in readiness for the influenza fatalities which undoubtedly lie ahead of us . . .') and just before she left he gave her a pair of silk stockings in a holly-green box, and then unlocking the cupboard in his desk poured two small measures from the bottle of Hall's wine only normally administered to those suffering acute pangs of bereavement.

'I wish you a very jolly Christmas, Miss Marlow!'

'Thank you, Mr Hoskins, and the same to you.'

He was a strange old thing with his darting eyes and mop of springy russet curls; sometimes his country hedgerow appearance and careful old-world courtesy made him seem like a creation of Beatrix Potter. Yet no one from Miss Potter's world would mention the word *loins* in front of a young unmarried woman any more than they would fleetingly caress her bottom. Which Mr Hoskins had done — once.

But it was very thoughtful of him to give her a pair of real silk stockings and she planned to wear them on Christmas Day.

During the previous weekend Uncle Harry had confirmed that Mona would be arriving after tea on Christmas Eve, and Cassie sped home with the shopping; the first thing she did was to inscribe a loving message inside the animal book, then wrap it in tissue paper and hide it away in readiness for tomorrow. She unpacked the chicken, shuddered at the sight of the head and feet and put them in a basin; then took them out again and threw them thankfully away. The tiny kitchen was not over-equipped and she had never cooked an entire meal before, but she saw no reason for apprehension.

And when Mona stepped inside the front door her eyes were shining under the old sheltering hat brim and she seized Cassie in a tremulous child's embrace and gasped 'I'm so happy . . . so *awfully* happy!'

Nibbs came in too, carrying Mona's suitcase with one hand and a wicker hamper in the other, then went back to the Daimler to fetch the canvas folding bed. He helped them to erect it, then stood looking at it doubtfully.

'No one gave me any orders about blankets or pillows, miss.'

'Don't worry, Nibbs, we'll manage easily.'

He shook Cassie's hand and wished her best respects for the coming season and there was marked tenderness in his eyes when he said, 'Goodbye, Miss Mona. Have a nice time and I'll call for you at five o'clock on Boxing Day.'

'Oh, can't it be later?' Her hand went up towards her lip.

'I'm very sorry,' Nibbs said. 'It's what the lady at the convent said.'

'Oh well, never mind.' Cassie smiled brightly at Mona while Nibbs picked up his chauffeur's cap and departed.

'Well — here you are at last!'

'And it's Christmas Eve!'

'So take your hat and coat off, Mona, and let's get busy . . .'

They began by hanging up the paper chains Cassie had bought one lunchtime and then tied the bunch of mistletoe to the light fitting that hung in the middle of the ceiling.

'So now if anyone wants to kiss us, they jolly well can!'

'I don't think anyone would kiss me.'

'Rubbish. Why not?'

'This frightens people.' She touched her lip.

'Anyone who's frightened of you isn't worth kissing, so there.'

'Oh, I don't mind,' Mona said cheerfully. 'I got used to being like this years ago.' It was the first time she had mentioned her disfigurement, and Cassie felt as if a small victory had been won.

There was not enough cupboard and drawer space for Mona to unpack her suitcase properly, so she removed her nightgown and spongebag and pushed the rest back under the bed. Then Cassie's attention was caught by the wicker hamper.

'Is that yours too?'

'No. I think it must have come from home.'

They opened it, and among the wood shavings found a Christmas pudding, a large mince pie, a box of liqueur chocolates and another box containing Carlsbad plums. There was also a bottle of claret, a bottle of Luncheon sherry, a corkscrew, and a little note saying, 'A Merry Christmas from The Mount'.

'Well, well.' Cassie was uncertain whether she felt pleased or patronised. More the former than the latter, she finally concluded.

'Listen!' Mona held up her finger. 'I can hear people singing.'

They pulled back the curtains, and carol singers from St Saviour's church over in Huskisson Street stood hunched and shrouded in their own breath under the lamp post, tilting their music towards the light as they sang about peace on earth and goodwill to all men. And just then the first big curly flakes of snow began to fall.

'It's all too beautiful to be real . . .'

'Mona,' Cassie said, 'I'm going to make this a Christmas to last you for the rest of your life.'

* * *

'I don't think its legs should stick up like that, do you? They don't look natural.'

'Don't people tie them together with string?'

'Oh no, I shouldn't think so, dear. It'd taste.'

There was barely room for two people in the kitchen at the same time, and because it was under the staircase Cassie always had to stand with her head bent. The chicken was lying in the roasting pan on top of the gas stove.

'Perhaps they'll go flat as it cooks.'

'In the meantime,' said Cassie, 'they stick up too much for it to go in the oven.'

They looked at one another very seriously, then began to giggle.

'I have to admit that I've never actually cooked a chicken before,' Cassie said finally. 'But there can't be much to it, can there?'

They peeled the potatoes and washed and chopped the cabbage, then Cassie mixed a little flour and water in a basin for gravy while Mona pounded a knob of butter and some sugar in another basin for brandy butter.

'Only we'll put some of your father's sherry in, instead of brandy.'

'Cassie,' Mona said, 'what are we going to boil the pudding in?'

'Ah.'

'We've only got two saucepans and I don't think either of them is big enough.'

'Go and get the pudding and let's see.'

Mona did so. The first saucepan was obviously far too small, and the Christmas pudding slid into the second one as if it were a second skin, and then refused to come out.

'Hold it upside down while I catch it—'

'It still won't! Wait while I bang it on the floor—'

Panting, they managed to extract it.

'Couldn't we warm it in the oven with the chicken?' Mona suggested.

'I suppose it's possible. But I always remember the ones at home boiling in a saucepan, don't you?'

'Well, no . . .'

Footsteps above their heads made them pause. 'Hang on a minute,' Cassie said, and went out into the hall.

She knew the man coming down the stairs by sight; a pale, secretive individual who lived on the first floor, not far from the bathroom.

'Excuse me,' Cassie said brightly, 'you couldn't lend us a large saucepan, could you?'

'Good morning, Miss er.' He stood looking at her apprehensively. 'I'm not sure . . . perhaps. I was just coming down to collect my milk.'

'Please don't hurry.'

'No. No . . .' He scuttered to the front door. 'I will have to see . . .'

Cassie retreated to the kitchen again and was busily pricking the sausages with a fork when the man reappeared cautiously round the doorway and proffered a small bucket.

'I'm afraid this is all I have. It's quite clean.'

'Oh.' Cassie and Mona looked at it doubtfully. 'It's for our Christmas pudding.'

'In that case,' the man said with a little more authority, 'it will need a lid.'

'We've only got two saucepans and two lids and we need them for other things.'

The man blinked his pale eyes at them without speaking, then retreated upstairs again. He returned with a large plate with *Souvenir from Glastonbury* inscribed on it.

'Oh, it seems a pity . . .'

'Don't worry,' he said. 'It was never a favourite.'

Under his instructions they put water in the bottom of the bucket and placed the pudding in it, and then he dropped the plate carefully into position over the top. It fitted perfectly.

They thanked him again, hoisted the bucket on to the top of the gas stove and lit the flame. The man remained hovering on the threshold.

'I've seen you lots of times,' he said to Cassie, 'but I've never enquired your name. Mine is Frampton.'

'Cassica Marlow. And this is my cousin Mona.'

A shade self-consciously they all shook hands, then to Cassie's surprise the man asked whether they would care to take a glass of sherry in his room at twelve o'clock. 'Miss Dawlish and Miss Hammond will also be calling in.'

Cassie accepted on behalf of them both, and Mr Frampton vanished like a pale shadow with his half-pint bottle of milk.

In the end they secured the chicken's legs with a piece of tape, and the bird was sizzling in the oven when they combed their hair and tidied themselves in readiness for the coming conviviality.

Mona asked anxiously whether she should polish their shoes but Cassie said not to bother, then asked Mona if she would like to powder her nose. A little hesitantly Mona said she wouldn't mind trying, and the result made her sneeze so violently that they both became convulsed with mirth.

Up in Mr Frampton's room Miss Dawlish and Miss Hammond were already *in situ,* standing close together with small glasses of sherry held formally at breast height.

Mr Frampton introduced Cassie and Mona, and everyone wished everyone else a merry Christmas. It was strange suddenly to be on social terms with the other occupants of the house — 'those of us who are here; Mr Talbot-Jones is away for three days and poor Miss Zimmerman is in hospital with her legs . . .'

Miss Dawlish wore rimless spectacles and cotton wool in her ears while Miss Hammond, a little younger, had her hair parted in the middle and a slight tendency towards goitre. But they were quite friendly, and Cassie learned that they were both schoolteachers, Miss Dawlish teaching divinity in Dingle while Miss Hammond taught maths in Wavertree. Mr Frampton was in insurance. Encouraged by this information Cassie said that she was a personal private secretary, and when they asked to whom, gaily took the plunge and said to an undertaker. Their faces froze a little, but they said how interesting, then turned their attention to Mona.

'Mona is at home,' Cassie said quickly, and thought my golly, what a world of difference between home and A Home . . . She saw the way they avoided looking at Mona's top lip, but Mona sipped her sherry and began talking to Mr Frampton about squirrels. She seemed amazingly at ease.

Mr Frampton's room was larger than Cassie's but darker, with a lot of old-maidish knick-knacks standing on little tables decorated with burnt pokerwork. From behind a beaded curtain came the discreet smell of roasting chicken, the soft glub-glub of a simmering Christmas pudding. He poured a little more sherry into each glass, and with great animation Cassie told Miss Dawlish that the undertaking business was very interesting apart from being very necessary.

'It grows on you,' she said loudly, because of Miss Dawlish's cotton wool. 'I don't mind admitting that I was ever so squeamish at first, but after a while you stop thinking in terms of dead bodies and corpses and ghosts and all that rot and just think of them as clients, same as anyone else.'

'Have you ever seen one?' Miss Hammond edged a little closer.

'Not to actually *contemplate* as you might say, but I've passed them in the passage on their way up to the chapel of rest many a time and I just think to myself oh yes, there goes dear old M 142 — they all have serial numbers, like trams—'

'Trams?'

'Yes, haven't you noticed? As a matter of fact I started collecting them when I first came here because I didn't know anybody — tramcar numbers I mean.'

'M 142,' repeated Miss Dawlish. 'What does the M stand for?'

'Male,' replied Cassie. 'Like F for female.'

Although he was still talking about squirrels, Mr Frampton's ears turned red. Miss Hammond began to laugh on a shrill note and Cassie put down her empty glass on one of the pokerwork tables and said: 'Well, it's been lovely, but I think we ought to go and see how our chicken's getting on. We had to tie its legs together with tape and the knot might have come undone—'

'Yes, I must go too,' Miss Dawlish said hastily. 'This afternoon I am going to sit with poor Miss Zimmerman for a while.'

Outside Mr Frampton's room they all wished one another a merry Christmas once again; smells of roasting chicken crept from behind Miss Hammond's door opposite and drifted down from the second floor where Miss Dawlish lived. Steam clouded the landing window.

'Oh, weren't they all nice!' Mona exclaimed when they were back on their own territory. 'That man Mr Frampton had a red squirrel for a pet once, and in the winter it hibernated in an old hatbox on top of his wardrobe!'

Her eyes were very bright, and with the sensitive quivering of her deeply segmented top lip she looked more than ever like some shy, gentle creature enticed indoors from the woods. How easy it is to make her happy, Cassie thought fondly. And how easy it is to love her.

In the oven the chicken was turning a gratifying shade of brown although the roasting potatoes were still rather hard. The Christmas pudding had boiled dry and was emitting an acrid smell, but they added more water from the kettle which seemed to console it.

'While we're waiting I think we'll open your father's bottle of wine,' Cassie said, pouncing on it. She drove the corkscrew in and then pulled, and the cork broke off half way.

'Oh gosh, look what's happened. Now what do we do?'

'Screw it into the bit that's left,' Mona suggested.

Cassie did so, and staggered backwards when the corkscrew flew out minus the cork. In the end she poked it down into the wine, which made it difficult to pour but didn't seem to impair the taste.

They carved the chicken, made the gravy and divided the sausages and the vegetables between them. Sitting at the table close to the gas fire they pulled crackers, put on their fancy hats and laughed themselves silly over the tasteful novelties. Everything they said seemed enormously, significantly funny, and the short cold day was already dying by the time they had eaten two helpings of Christmas pudding with the burnt part at the bottom cut off.

When they had washed the dishes and restored the kitchen they went for a walk. Last night's snow had melted, leaving the streets black and shining, and it seemed as if they had the whole of Liverpool to themselves.

Grove Street, Falkner Square, Abercromby Square; their footsteps echoing, their voices hushed. There were no tramcars, no motors, not even any singing ex-servicemen.

'What's London like?' Mona asked.

'Much the same as this, only bigger. And of course, much nicer.'

Although Cassie's somewhat abortive trip to London had cured the worst of her homesickness, she was still occasionally conscious of a yearning to go back. To make a more determined, less precipitate attempt to re-establish herself in the city of her birth, where people said *parth* and *barth* and were not touchy about what other people thought of them.

'One day I'll take you there. When I've made a real success of things we'll go to London for a holiday and I'll show you Buckingham Palace and Big Ben and the Tower of London. There's a nice little hotel where I stay called the

Bluebell where they know me and always give me the very best attention. And then one night we'll go to the theatre . . .'

They turned into Bedford Street, walking arm in arm.

'I've never been to a theatre.'

'Oh, you've got such a lovely lot to see and do, Mona dear.'

'Yes, I have, haven't I?'

When they arrived home Cassie shovelled some more pennies in the meter and they relit the gas fire. They drew the curtains and made a pot of tea, but they didn't want to eat much.

'What would you like to do tomorrow? We could go across on the ferry, if you fancy it. We'd have to wrap up warm.'

'Yes, Cassie. I'd like that.'

'We'll have cold chicken for lunch and then we'll set off early because you've got to be . . . or maybe we'd better go on the ferry in the morning.'

'Yes.'

Something seemed to dwindle and die. There were four crackers left and they pulled them unsmilingly, as if taking part in a solemn ritual. They admired the fancy hats but didn't put them on.

'Isn't it a scream to think of us all cooking our separate chickens and boiling our separate Christmas puddings this morning?' Cassie said with an effort. 'You'd think the two old girls would have got together with Mr Frampton and made one big do of it, wouldn't you?'

'Perhaps they don't really like each other.'

'But they all look so beastly lonely.'

'I thought they were all so nice though, Cassie.'

'Yes, of course they were. Terribly nice . . .' But the word *lonely* seemed to take on a life of its own; to buzz about the room like an irritating and insistent little fly. It made one wonder how many lonely people were sitting behind the dignified Georgian facades of Liverpool's more refined areas.

Yet the day ended very pleasantly. At bedtime they made some cocoa and sat in front of the fire in their nightgowns and Mona had the animal book on her lap while Cassie made a half-hearted attempt to get on with her knitting. They didn't talk much, but the silences were tranquil.

They retired to bed shortly after eleven, Mona kneeling by the side of her bed with her hands clasped together and her eyes closed while she thanked God (and, because of the Convent Home, the Virgin Mary) for giving her such a lovely day, and looking at the ivory-coloured soles of her upturned feet Cassie thought honestly we get on so well together we might as well be sisters.

As they had done on the previous night, they divided Cassie's blankets and pillows between them and then covered their beds with their coats, while upstairs on the second floor Miss Dawlish inserted fresh cottonwool in her ears, adjusted her pink hairnet and thought what nice girls; I wonder if I should invite them to the school handicraft exhibition?

* * *

But no one could dispute the fact that the day had gone, had finally gone, and that tomorrow would be only little more than half a day. Even now the minutes were ticking past, slipping through the fingers like sand. Clench them tight, screw them shut, press harder and harder, but still they trickle away.

The house is so quiet I can hear my heart beating. Am I the only one awake? Mr Frampton, Miss Dawlish and Miss Hammond, all in their separate rooms, their separate cosy beds. How nice they all were. And tomorrow they will be having cold chicken for lunch like us. We forgot to give Mr Frampton his bucket back. And his plate that we used as a lid. Perhaps he'll come down to collect them and we can give him a glass of sherry. Having a glass of sherry is very nice. Supposing Cassie kissed him under the mistletoe? What would he do, what would he say? I wouldn't want to kiss anyone under the mistletoe; I don't like kissing people because I can't do it properly. But I like hugging people; people I love. And I love it when Cassie hugs me . . .

Cassie's asleep. I can hear her breathing. How many breaths does she take in a minute? . . . about fourteen or fifteen, I should think. If I breathe at the same rate that she does . . . in . . . out . . . in . . . out . . . perhaps I'll go to sleep too. Perhaps I've already been to sleep and I've woken up again. How funny it would be if I was really asleep now, and only dreaming that I'm awake . . . Oh, Cassie, *Cassie* dear . . .

Silence deep as a well; thick as velvet, black as a nun's habit. The soft rapid pulse of nuns' feet in the corridor. Foggy breath hanging in the air, sharp noses reddened with the cold. It's always cold there. *Turn over on your other side, you were dreaming again. You had two helpings of tapioca, didn't you? How many times have I told you about the sin of gluttony? Our Lady won't love you. God won't love you. Cassie won't love you, or have you to stay with her any more . . .*

My heart's thumping enough to make the bedclothes move. It's echoing all through me, it's beating against my forehead like hammers. Like *hooves!*

'Cassie, I don't feel well . . .' Tongue parched as an autumn leaf. Sitting up, rocking to and fro, head clasped in hands.

The horses are back. The agony and the terror. The screams and the pounding of guns. The flailing of huge, tormented limbs through gusts of angry white smoke. Tangles of harness, tossing manes, blood-flecked lather and big yellow teeth bared in scream after scream after scream. Save them, save them — oh somebody stop the noise and the madness and the killing and the pain and let the poor horses go free !

Out of bed now. Shivering, panting, forehead clenched in sweating hands. Cassie, oh please Cassie, help me . . . Am I really saying this or am I only thinking it? Cassie, Cassie . . . no, I mustn't wake her, she'll think I'm mentally deficient and in any case there's nothing she can do. Nobody can do anything when the horses come back. But oh, Cassie, if only . . .

Go and get a drink of water. Put the light on in the kitchen and the horses will go away. But do it now, quickly — while there's still time. There's not much time before your head bursts open and all the red blood comes pouring out with the noise and the pain and the terror . . .

The click of the door. Did it wake Cassie? I hope it didn't, but oh, if only it did . . . still breathing so calmly . . . in . . . out . . . in . . . out . . . the hall, where's the stairs? Follow the line of the banisters and yes, here's the door — oh please Holy Mother Heavenly Father stop the noise the screams the hooves — the *hooves!*

Snick. A flood of light. Everything tidy and nice if only I can reach it through all the pain. Clean cups and saucers, the cocoa tin, Mr Frampton's bucket. Look, these are the real things, not the war. The war isn't real because it's all over. All over amen.

She meant to get a drink of water, but she didn't feel thirsty now. She didn't feel anything. Just cold and empty and isolated as she always did in the convent and in all the other places except here. Yet even the happiness of this place wasn't enough to keep the horses away. They had followed her here as they followed her everywhere with their screams and shrieks and beating hooves. And although they had gone now, they would be back. She knew now that wherever she was they would always come back because what had happened had been real — more real even than standing here in Cassie's kitchen — and what had happened to them could never be undone. It was no use saying the war was over, because it had *happened,* and the earth's atmosphere would always be full of the agonised ghosts of all the millions of horses who had died. Wherever she went she would never escape. The torment would go on and on; she knew that now.

She made her preparations very quietly and calmly: removing the rack from inside the oven and propping it against the wall; closing the kitchen door and sealing the crack beneath it with crumpled tea towels. Cassie's gingham apron was lying by the draining board and she held it lovingly against her cheek for a moment before folding it into a neat square and placing it on the floor of the oven. She switched off the light, turned on the gas and lay down with her nightgown tucked tidily round her ankles.

The oven smelt pleasantly of roast chicken, of Merry Christmas, and the horses would never come back anymore.

* * *

There were no flowers, no mourners apart from the family, and certainly no black plumes. Not even any black horses. Just a plain coffin without an inscription sliding silently from a motor-hearse with oval windows and the blinds drawn down. Because suicide was a criminal offence it was doubtful whether a clergyman could have been found to officiate at her burial in consecrated ground without the aid of Uncle Harry's wealth and influence. In the end the vicar from St Clement's obliged, rather briefly and worriedly, and she was laid to rest in Toxteth Park Cemetery, but in a little space close to the workhouse wall and well away from everyone else.

As if she'd contaminate them, Cassie thought, and dug her chin deeper in her coat collar.

Standing by the graveside she seemed to be beyond feeling, certainly beyond the palliative of tears. Her eyes had been as dry as stones since Boxing morning. The discovery, the sickly stench, then the curtains billowing wildly and the panic-stricken rushing to and fro; Mr Frampton in his dressing-gown and Miss Dawlish without her teeth. The hopeless wait in the hospital, the dogged refusal to leave without Mona and then finally the telegram to St Moritz.

Babs was wearing sables and a black hat with an impenetrable veil. Uncle Harry in spats and his coat with the velvet collar had his arm round her because she had caught a bad cold on the boat coming back, and Desmond and Lionel standing on either side of their parents, suddenly very tall and silent, their pudgy baby boy faces set like cold suet.

Their attitude towards Cassie seemed curiously ambivalent; they spoke to her — Babs even managed a quick squeeze of her gloved hand — and Uncle Harry's sole reference to Mona's death was *this sorry business*. They made no accusations of negligence or irresponsibility on her part; they heaped no recrimination on her head, but neither did they try to comfort her or draw her back into the family circle.

And although her own feelings towards them were equally unclear, she knew that if anyone should speak disparagingly of Mona and of what had happened her fragile self-control would snap. She too was able to present a reasonably calm surface, but beneath it lay a deeply searing bitterness. My only fault was to sleep too heavily; your fault goes back over a period of twenty-eight years.

They parted at the cemetery gates with vague smiles and evasive glances. They said do let us know if you want anything and when the weather improves you must come out and see us. She said yes thank you, I will, and all the real things remained unsaid.

She went back to the room in Upper Parliament Street and somewhere upstairs a door banged hastily. No one had spoken to her since Mona's death; the little budding friendships begun in the spirit of Christmas and the sipping of sherry had failed to take root. Genteel good taste had been outraged and there was no pity, not even any curiosity, in the scurrying figures with discreetly averted faces. But it didn't matter because she too wanted to wipe them from her mind; in particular she wanted to wipe away the memory of her own vivacious chatter about undertakers and their clients.

Mona's one-eyed doll was still in the drawer and she put it in a carrier bag together with the animal book, then left the house again.

She walked down towards the towers and domes of the Pier Head, and the ferryboat *Daffodil* was in. She bought a return ticket and went up on deck where the gulls were screaming and sweeping low overhead. She took her hat off and stuffed it into her pocket and as they moved out from the landing-stage the wind tugged at her hair and loosened it from its pins. It was stingingly cold.

There were not many other passengers about, and when they reached mid-river she held the carrier bag over the side and then slowly let it drop. It disappeared for a moment before floating clear, and the doll emerged from the open mouth of it with its grubby white frock spread around it. The book sank, taking the carrier bag with it, and a flock of gulls wheeled and squawked as they hungrily probed the doll's edibility. Then they left it, and it too began to sink, its bobbing face lapped by the muddy water until it disappeared from sight. Cassie stayed hunched against the rail with her hair streaming loose until they returned to Liverpool.

She didn't want to go home. Neither did she want to go to work because she had already decided to give in her notice. After what had happened, the death trade was not for her.

Cramming her hair back under her hat she left the *Daffodil* and boarded a tramcar for Mount Pleasant. It was now four o'clock and almost dark.

Having recently returned from supervising a funeral Mr Hoskins was sitting dressed in his black tailcoat. His top hat lay upturned on the filing cabinet.

'Good gracious, Miss Marlow, have you been indisposed? I haven't seen you since Christmas Eve!' He looked at her peevishly.

Cassie stood by the door. 'I'm very sorry, Mr Hoskins, but I've just called to hand in my notice. I'm afraid that due to a change in my personal circumstances it will no longer be possible for me to remain in your employ.' Voice very steady, eyes still dry.

'Leave? You want to leave?' He looked at her in amazement. 'Why?'

'I've just told you, Mr Hoskins. There's been a sudden change in my personal — well, not just in my circumstances but in my whole outlook. Something I experienced during Christmas has made it quite impossible for me to even contemplate working with a — working here. I'm very sorry.'

She should have stopped then. Just shaken his hand and said goodbye and walked out, but now that she had started talking she couldn't stop.

'Something unbelievably terrible happened over Christmas and as long as I live I'll always feel that I'm to blame. I persuaded them to let her come and yes all right we did have a lovely time on Christmas Day — at least, I *thought* we did — but during the night when I was asleep — sound asleep and I didn't hear a thing — she went out to the kitchen and she — and she . . . oh, I can't even bear to say it . . . she . . .'

As if released from some unendurable pressure the tears sprang out and poured down her cheeks. Hot and furious she dragged her hat off again and her long hair fell down and her nose started running but she still couldn't stop talking. 'For as long as I live I'll always see the terrible picture of her lying there curled up like a poor little homeless cat . . . she must have felt so alone and unloved to do a thing like that even though I'd tried — I'd tried so *hard* to make everything nice and homely and lovely and happy for her — and not because I was *sorry* for her but because I loved her . . . I really *loved* her . . . and I thought she *understood* . . .'

'Now, now, my dear. Try not to—'

'I've just come from her funeral and it was absolutely horrible . . . no one there but us and it was all so hole-in-corner and a cheap and terrible coffin — worse than our Poor Law ones — I was so *ashamed* — and it just seemed as if they couldn't get her buried and out of sight fast enough — not a single floral tribute and nobody cried — we just stood there and when it was over simply walked away and left her . . .' Gushing tears, racking sobs and a weight of grief that was beyond her strength to bear.

Still sitting at his desk Mr Hoskins held out his arms to her, and like a fool she rushed across the room straight into them.

CHAPTER ELEVEN

'Strictly between you and me, Mrs Hoskins has trouble with her colon. More often than not it's got her laid up.'

'Oh dear. Is it very painful?'

'She says it is. But I've always taken the view that pain is all a matter of how you approach it. Some of us are more philosophical than others.'

'Yes, I suppose so.'

'And the same thing applies to death.'

'Yes.'

Cassie and Mr Hoskins were sitting in a secluded corner of the lounge of the North Western Hotel. They had just eaten a large dinner. A string orchestra composed mainly of elderly ladies was playing a Grieg potpourri, while across in the ballroom a jazz band was playing ragtime. It was warm, sweet-scented and agreeable, and in the softly opulent lamplight Mr Hoskins looked very nice in his stiff shirt and dinner jacket. Cassie was wearing a skirt of non-committal length and a low-necked lace blouse with tassels round the bottom.

'Take our poor Tommies, I tell her. Four solid years of being blown up, shell-shocked, gassed, eaten by rats in the trenches — they didn't complain.'

'More coffee, sir?' A cruising waiter filled their tiny cups with a flourish.

'I used to live next door to a chap who was gassed.' (And I also knew someone who gassed herself voluntarily. Who lay down and put her head in the oven because she didn't want to go on living anymore.)

She still couldn't reconcile herself to Mona's death, or to the bitter knowledge that Christmas Day, far from cheering her, must secretly have had an adverse effect. (Why didn't I notice — why didn't I *see?)*

'There's going to be a coroner's inquest,' she said aloud. 'I'll have to go.'

'A mere formality, that's all.' Mr Hoskins squeezed her hand comfortingly.

'I still can't get over her doing that. I mean, without even talking things over with me first.'

'Mrs Hoskins sometimes speaks of doing away with herself but it's only play-acting, I'm afraid.'

'Oh gosh, you don't want her to—'

'No, no, of course not. I just want the poor woman to be happy.'

'And can't she be?'

'Not with her colon trouble, apparently.'

Having squeezed Cassie's hand Mr Hoskins remained holding it under the table. Holding it, kneading it, and pressing her cuticles back with the ball of his thumb.

'The trouble is,' he said, 'that we are both givers, you and I. We are the type to give ourselves unstintingly in the service of others. Day after day, year after year we pour out our love and devotion until there comes a time when the well runs dry. We are parched and exhausted.'

'Yes, that's just how I feel—'

'A new well must be dug, or a new spring discovered. In other words, what we both need is a little sympathy.'

'Yes.'

'Which is why I saw no harm in our having an evening off together. A nice leisurely dinner in nice surroundings and the balm of a little mutual sympathy. Dear little girl, how fetching you look in that blouse.'

'Thank you, Mr Hoskins.'

'Percy.'

'Percy.'

'I knew we would find a great deal in common, quite apart from business, which is why I booked us in for the night.'

'You did say separate rooms though, didn't you?' Her index finger was becoming sore from his attentions.

'Yes, yes, as I told you. But it would have been a pity to end the evening by going home in the cold, alone.'

'This must be costing ever such a lot,' Cassie murmured.

'I have two gravel pits in Nantwich, as well as my establishment in Mount Pleasant.'

'Oh. I didn't know.'

'I am quite a man of substance in my way. Which is why I feel confident that I can offer you a little consolation in your sorrow — as indeed you can do the same for me.'

'How, exactly?' Cassie looked uneasy, and Mr Hoskins gave a merry little chuckle.

'All I ask is the pleasure of your company.'

The dinner had been very nice and Mr Hoskins had been very kind, but she was beginning to feel sleepy. She wished they could say goodnight and go to bed now.

As if divining her thoughts Mr Hoskins removed his pocket watch, snapped it open and said, 'Good gracious me, how the evening has flown! Time to think of retiring.'

Threading their way through the palm trees they left the lounge, crossed the marble foyer and entered a lift, and the first thing she noticed when he unlocked the door of room 310 was that it contained a double bed of formidable proportions. The second thing she noticed was that her little attaché case was lying next to Mr Hoskins's Gladstone bag.

'Oh look, they've made a mistake—'

'Yes, how stupid of them.' Mr Hoskins surveyed her cautiously. 'How very stupid.'

'This must be your room. Where's mine?' No longer sleepy, Cassie stood poised for flight.

'I will speak to the reception clerk.' Mr Hoskins tripped blithely over to the telephone and unhooked the receiver.

'Give me reception. Is that the clerk? This is Mr Percival Hoskins and there has been a mistake in my booking. I asked for two single rooms for a young lady and myself and you have given me one double. I insist that you change it immediately . . . I beg pardon? I'm afraid that what you suggest is quite out of the question. No, no. The young lady and myself are . . . *full?* Surely you must have another room to offer? You haven't? In that case it is up to you to find me alternative accommodation of a suitable nature in another hotel . . .'

It was a good performance; a quite impressive display of virtuous indignation, except that he was holding down the receiver hook.

'It doesn't matter,' Cassie said tonelessly. 'We'll have to make do.'

She could have walked out. Just said a frosty goodbye and trudged back to Upper Parliament Street, but suddenly the thought was more than she could stand. The place was so full of Mona.

'Nothing will occur,' said Mr Hoskins, smoothing the turned down sheet. 'I promise you on my honour that nothing need occur.'

'All right.'

'But you do love me just a little, don't you, dear? As a friend, I mean.'

'Umm.'

'I love *you* as a friend. And we mustn't forget what we said about the balm of a little mutual sympathy . . .'

I am about to be deflowered, thought Cassie. No use beating about the bush, he had it planned all along. The only thing that really annoys me is that he thinks I'm too feeble-minded to suspect anything. Honestly, it's hardly flattering.

'I tell you what we'll do,' Mr Hoskins cried happily, 'we'll put a bolster down the middle of the bed—'

'There will be no need for that, Mr Hoskins—'

'Percy—'

'Percy—'

'Oh, my dear little girl in your dear little blouse . . .' He darted across to her and, reaching up his arms, clasped them round her neck. He began to kiss her, then suddenly released her and said, 'The bathroom is just behind you. Whilst you are making your preparations I will be waiting.'

Cassie marched into the bathroom carrying her attaché case and locked the door. She didn't quite know what Mr Hoskins meant by his reference to preparations so cleaned her teeth, then in order to give herself a little more time decided to have a bath. She lay in the warm scented water for a long while thinking if Mona hadn't killed herself I wouldn't be doing this. Because of what Mona did, nothing seems to be real anymore. And certainly nothing matters any more . . .

She wondered how much it would hurt. Then while she was drying herself remembered the pleasant tingle of eroticism she had felt that night in poor old Arnold Openshaw's bed. If she was going to be horrid she would have preferred being horrid with someone a little younger than Mr Hoskins — Percy — but it was her own fault for casting herself into his arms in the first place. As ye sow, so shall ye reap, thought Cassie, and crisply nightgowned and smelling of dentifrice marched resolutely back into the bedroom. And halted abruptly.

A total stranger was sitting in the bed. A little shrunken beady-eyed creature with a cranium bald as a bird's egg and the blankets held close to its chin. It was smiling at her expectantly even as her horrified gaze transferred itself to the familiar bunch of auburn curls capping the bulbous mahogany bedpost.

'Oh *no*—' She retreated, and Mr Hoskins leaped from the bed with dreadful agility and sped towards her, stark naked.

She flew to the door, wrenched it open and tore along the thickly carpeted corridor. There was no one about, but the distant rattle of lift gates filled her with fresh panic and she bolted through a door marked Private and slammed it shut behind her.

The place was in total darkness and she leaned back against the door for several minutes, panting and listening for the sound of pursuit. There was none, and it occurred to her that even in the grip of ungovernable lust it was unlikely that any man would rush mother-naked through an hotel in pursuit of his prey. She began to breathe more easily, and when her searching hand encountered the light switch she discovered that she was in a small windowless room containing cleaning equipment: brooms and brushes, a vast and complicated vacuum-cleaner and yellow dusters spread along the hot pipes. To her left was a pair of wooden clothes pegs hung with white aprons and mob caps.

She began to laugh silently and hysterically, and in spite of the hot airlessness of the room found herself shivering uncontrollably. There was no lock on the door so she sat on the floor with her back against it and her knees drawn up under her chin, and although her situation was ludicrous in the extreme she would sooner have died than return to room 310.

A chambermaid found her at six the next morning with her head pillowed on a pile of dusters and one of the aprons spread over her like a sheet. Blurred and confused, Cassie embarked on a complicated explanation concerning a difference of opinion with her father in 310 and being too upset in consequence to find her way back to her own room but the chambermaid gave her a weary, patient smile and said wait here, madam, until the gentleman's gone and I'll fetch your clothes for you.

It looked as if she had seen it all before.

* * *

And the months which followed proved to be some of the grimmest of Cassie's life. Not only had she forfeited her job, she was also asked to vacate her room in Upper Parliament Street because the other tenants had complained about living in close proximity to someone involved in the scandal of a suicide case. It wasn't nice, they said.

Apart from the hurt of seeing faces so recently friendly returning to the old careful impassivity, she was quite relieved to go. The ghost of Mona would always cling to the place and more than once she had almost been driven to seek solace from the family in Sefton Park. Look us up when the weather improves, they said, and let us know if there's anything you want. But she knew they would have no comfort to offer, and the weather was still wintry. In any case, she had her pride.

So when they met at the inquest she smiled bravely, and as soon as the verdict of unsound mind was delivered slipped quietly away without saying goodbye.

She found a cheap room in a back street not far from Gambier Terrace. The furniture was sparse, the kitchen no more than a gas ring standing on a tin tray, and the window looked out on to the Bricklayer's Arms, a small dingy pub where fierce fights and wild singing kept her awake on Saturday nights.

Her landlord was an unemployed docker, his wife a small, harassed woman with the regulation black shawl pinned tightly across a hollow chest, and their poverty was awesome. Yet the plight of the family in the basement was worse; a man, wife and child existing on food vouchers from the Poor Law Guardians, paying half a crown a week for rent and living by the light of one candle. The basements of Liverpool were becoming filled with people like the Kellys; once the domain of fat firelit cooks and drowsing off-duty parlourmaids, they were now more often the foetid rat-runs of those most perilously near destitution. Basements were cheaper than attics, and those who took up residence in them seemed quickly to assume the slinking furtiveness of vermin, of pale and hungry rats shivering at bay in dark corners.

Although her own finances were at a very low ebb, Cassie allowed herself the sombre satisfaction of not giving

Uncle Harry her new address. The allowance he made her was only due to continue for a few more weeks, and the sooner she acquired complete independence the better. Every day was spent in job-hunting, but, like the dockers, the shipyard workers and the cotton-spinners, unemployed shorthand-typists met with no more than bored indifference.

'I take it you have your certificate of proficiency?'

'Er . . .'

'References?'

'Well, no. Due to a slight difference of opinion with my previous employer . . .'

'In that case we cannot see our way even to putting you on our list. Good day.'

Employees had no business having differences with those who employed them and, suddenly revolted by the smugness, the prim gentility of those who worked in offices, she made a second attempt to become a shop assistant and this time succeeded. It was in the haberdashery department of one of the big stores.

Having been down to one meal a day for almost six weeks her old black mourning dress fitted her again and she wore it every day because black was the uniform colour for shop assistants everywhere. She worked behind the ribbon and lace counter with a sad, sallow woman called Norah, and when they were neither serving customers nor tidying the drawers of merchandise she and Norah stood to attention with their arms folded behind their backs. They were opposite the button counter which was run by Norah's friend, an angular woman with iron-grey hair and a disparaging sniff. Her name was Miss Chaucer, but Norah always called her Ciss.

The work was trivial but not unduly arduous, although at first the long hours of standing made her legs ache. During the night the muscles seemed to stiffen, and when she first got out of bed she could scarcely stand. Norah advised her to massage them with witch hazel, which she did, and in time the pain wore off.

But none of the others seemed to like her very much. Once again they thought her London accent stuck up, and if she had cherished any theories about shopgirls being less preoccupied with social status she was speedily disillusioned. Office girls were disliked because they too were all stuck up, but their most withering contempt was reserved for the servant class, which was immediately below their own. A rusty black dress had nothing whatever in common with a cap and apron, and although female shop assistants earned a pitiful wage they clung to gentility as fiercely as any shorthand-typist. Life became narrow, petty and almost unbelievably boring.

'I want some bébé ribbon for my camisole.'

'Certainly, madam. What colour have you in mind?'

'Blue. It must be blue. Oh no, no, not *that* blue!'

'A little paler, madam? We have a very nice bébé in powder—'

'Too wishy-washy. Show me something else.'

'Certainly, madam. Our line in sky is quite popular.'

'Too wide. Have you the same thing only narrower?'

'Only in a different shade, madam. We have a nice soft green in the width you prefer—'

'Green? On my camisole—'

Have puce then, madam dear, to match your complexion . . .

As a relief from the tedium of selling ribbon Cassie turned her attention to the friendship of Norah and Ciss; it was a deeply tormented one, evidently of long standing, and seemed to bring little joy to either of them. Norah appeared vague, timid and prevaricating, while Ciss suffered from extreme jealousy. Conversation ranged from veiled innuendos to bitter accusations on the part of Ciss, and patient, lukewarm denials on that of Norah. Because any form of chitchat between employees was heavily frowned upon, they pursued their sad rambling arguments in whispers, which might, when Mr Venables the floorwalker was out of earshot, rise occasionally to a dispirited mumble.

'I was watching you, Norah. And I know what you were thinking.'

'I wasn't thinking anything.'

'Yes, you were, Norah. And I think you knew that I knew what you were thinking.'

'How did you?'

'There you are, I've caught you out. You *were* thinking, weren't you?'

'But what makes you think I was thinking *that?*'

'You coloured up, Norah.'

'No, I didn't.'

'Oh yes you did, Norah. You definitely coloured up.'

'Well, it wasn't because I was thinking what you thought.'

'No, but I know you, Norah.'

'No, you don't. Not really.'

'Oh yes I do, Norah. I know you inside out . . .'

Someone in the staff canteen told Cassie that Norah and Ciss had been planning to go on holiday together since the summer of 1916, but had never done so because they could never agree upon their destination.

Then one Saturday afternoon a young woman with bright red hair stopped at the ribbon counter.

'Ooh hullo, Cassie! Fancy seeing you!'

It was Effie, late of the Gathercole Academy, and pleasure at seeing her overrode any twinge of social embarrassment on Cassie's part.

'Effie — how nice!'

'Don't tell me you're *wairkin'* here?'

'Yes.'

'What's happened to your shorthand and typin', then?'

'It's a long story—'

'Well, what time d'you finish wairk?'

'Six.'

'Meet you in the Kardomah at five past.'

'Make it half past. We have to do our dust covers and everything.'

'Right-oh. Ta-ra, then.'

Effie Morris with her vigorous red hair, quick eyes and harsh northern sense of fun. She was wearing a tweed costume with a rabbit fur collar and her stockings had fancy-work clocks up the sides. She looked cheerful, prosperous and self-confident and, sitting opposite Cassie over toasted cheese and a pot of tea for two, came straight to the point.

'For Chrissake, love, why don't you cut your hair off?'

As a Liverpudlian who pronounced work *wairk* it might have been assumed that she would pronounce hair *hair*; but no, it was called *hur*.

'Nobody's got long hur these days. At least, nobody under the age of thairty. I know a nice fella who wairks in a posh salon and he'll cut your hur for nowt if you give him a bit of encouragement. An' your skairt's too long, petal. Only maiden aunts are wurring them that length.'

She appraised Cassie's appearance with all the sorrowful diligence of a tax inspector faced with an undeclared bankrupt, and instead of annoying Cassie it made her laugh.

'I'd have cut me hur if only I'd had *fur* hur. Y'know, long golden cairls hangin' down me back, like—'

'Gerraway — you're really lairnin' to talk proper at last!'

They giggled helplessly, ordered more tea and a plate of fancy cakes and Cassie wiped her eyes and said you don't know just how much I'm enjoying this.

'Been having a hard time of it?'

'Yes, in a way.'

'What's happened to your stuck-up relations?'

'A lot of it was my fault, I suppose.'

'Want to tell?'

Cassie did so, with a certain amount of impromptu editing. The time for compulsive and repetitive monologues about Mona had passed, and while speaking frankly about having worked for an undertaker she remained silent about the debacle in the North Western Hotel. But under the influence of hot tea and iced cakes and Effie's critical attention, her spirits began to rise for the first time for weeks. And with them, imagination blossomed.

'Yes, all right, undertaking has its ups and downs as a business same as any other, but I wanted to make a success of it. I mean, what's wrong with being the first woman undertaker? Instead of a lot of boring men in baggy black, why not women in black riding habits? Top hats and veils and little nipped-in jackets and long skirts and thin boots with pointed toes? Women are much more sensitive and sympathetic than men, and I still think that a lot of discriminating people would sooner have their loved one laid to rest by nice compassionate women.'

'So why did you leave?'

'My employer and I didn't get on. He probably recognised me as a threat.'

'It would take a lot of money,' Effie said thoughtfully. 'God knows how much a hearse would cost.'

'Exactly. That's why I'm selling ribbons.'

'Well, you won't aim enough for the first down-payment, doing that.'

'I know.'

Effie poured the last of the tea, then broke into the small, depressed silence by saying: 'Money's the most important thing in the whole wairld, and the sort of money I want can't be aimed with a typewriter, not unless I hit some rich old man on the head with it and pinch his wallet.'

'What are you going to use instead?'

'Me pairsonal charm.'

'Oh, Effie.'

'Listen, petal.' Effie leaned across the table, her eyebrows arched like ginger caterpillars. 'Women have got something that men haven't got, and, being men, it's what they want, see? Most men sort of hate women because of this and they'll always do the dairty on them if they get the chance — *after* they've had what they want — so to my mind that leaves women in the clear to do the dairty on *them*.'

'You mean, after they've—?'

'Well, it's up to the women, isn't it?'

'Well . . .'

'So listen, stop selling effing ribbon and get your hur shingled and your skairts shortened and go back to secretarial wairk with some nice old gentleman.'

Cassie sat thinking deeply, then said: 'I'd rather get rich some other way.'

'There isn't any other way,' Effie said remorselessly. 'Effing men have seen to that.'

'Do you remember that chap Arnold Openshaw?'

'Who? Oh — him.'

'He said that capitalism is an atrocity.'

'What's that got to do with it?' Effie looked blank.

'It's got to do with the immorality of trying to extract more than your fair share out of what's available. Instead of trying to grab all we can for ourselves we should try to spread it around a bit more fairly.'

'That's daft—'

'I used to think so, but the woman in the basement where I live goes to the bread shop with the baby's bassinet because they're on food vouchers and she doesn't like people seeing her walk home with the big special loaf that everyone recognises as Poor Relief bread, so she wraps it up in an old shawl and pretends it's the baby. I think that's awful.'

'Why doesn't she do something, then?'

'What can she do? She's already got TB.'

'I dunno. Chuck a brick through the Lord Mayor's window — or get herself set up as a lady undertaker—'

'Oh, Effie, you are *hard!*'

'No I'm not, just practical. Listen, petal, people wairn't put on this airth just to be nice to each other, any more than animals were. And the last thing they want is to have all the same amounts of everything dished out to them every week. There'd be no ambition then, they wouldn't even bother to gerrup in the morning. The whole wairld's built on the idea that if you don't grab it someone else will . . . while you're busy bein' nice to some poor old down-and-out someone else'll be busy pinching your effing handbag—'

'Yes, but if only—'

'Ah shurrup, love,' Effie said. 'You've got a helluva lot to lairn.'

Nevertheless, she insisted on paying Cassie's share of the bill as well as her own and as they parted harmoniously, exchanging addresses and arranging to meet again in the near future, Cassie suddenly asked her what effing stood for.

'It's short for fornicating,' Effie said. 'What d'you think?'

A bitter east wind was blowing and the man standing outside selling matches had a long string of mucus waving from the end of his nose.

He could at least wipe it, Cassie thought, and ignoring his pathetically extended cap went home to consider the problem of her appearance.

* * *

I don't want to look like Babs; not even if I could afford to. And in spite of what Effie says, I don't want to be like her mentally, either. She's what Effie wants to be. So it stands to reason that I don't want to look like Effie, either. Effie as she is now, I mean. I think rabbit's awful. I don't think you ought to have fur at all until you can afford at least squirrel; just have tweed or velvet, or something. Effie's nice, but she's inclined to be common. I don't want to be common, whatever happens.

Which leaves me with the alternative of looking like Ciss and Norah. Which I suppose I already do, a bit. Black drags you down. It's much more than the colour of mourning, it's also the colour of servility; of meek but proud poverty — black doesn't show the dirt; black is unassuming; black goes with everything. Arnold was right when he talked about the deliberate ploy of putting all the serfs in uniform; khaki or cloth caps for the men and white aprons or dingy black for the women. By their raiment shall ye know them, without the bother of having to ask.

But Effiie's right too, it's daft selling ribbon. An act of wilful masochism on the part of someone who passed university entrance. Nobody ever became successful through selling yards of ribbon and broderie anglais. Ciss has been selling buttons for fifteen years and look at her. She can tell real mother-of-pearl from imitation, but that's about all.

ST PETER: Well now, Ciss — or rather Miss Chaucer, I should say — what reason have you to offer for expecting a place up here rather than one down there?

CISS: I would be able to tell Our Father whether the buttons on His heavenly raiment are real oyster pearl or only got up to look like it, sir.

ST PETER: I commend your humble approach, Miss Chaucer, so you may come in, but I doubt whether you will ever have an opportunity to see Our Father, let alone examine His buttons; only a very small place can be allotted to you at the very back of the hall . . .

And sooner or later I start thinking about Mona again; Mona in her old-fashioned hat with the big brim to hide her face; her woolly jumpers and cardigans and her lace-up shoes. She could have been beautiful, even with her lip. She *was* beautiful in a way — even more beautiful than Babs because she had no artifice. But why oh *why* did she do it? Did I get Christmas Day all wrong? Every time I see horses in the streets I think of her. Big shining quivering carthorses with their feet ringing on the cobblestones and it's funny how she never mentioned them; only seemed sorry for the ones that got killed in the war. But I don't believe she was mad, she just had a social conscience like Arnold. And she was just lost and unhappy as I am, because I can't decide what I want to be, how I want to be, and which way I want to go.

Can it really make any difference how you do your hair? Whether your hem's higher or lower by a couple of inches? Shouldn't people accept me for what I am? But what am I? And how much does it matter, anyway? How long before I'm dead and forgotten like Mother and Father? Like Mona . . .

After weeks of cold winds and spiteful rain that tormented the daffodils in Princes Park and penetrated the inadequate clothing of the poor, early summer came in hot and strong. Chilblains on the earlobes of the step-girls healed and faded, and even the Mersey raised a hint of blue sparkle to match that of the sky.

In skimpy skirt and smoothly bobbed hair beneath a hat shaped like a teacup, Cassie tripped up the steps of the Gathercole Academy in Hockenhall Street and asked if she might see Miss Gathercole.

'Ooh, I'm afraid Miss Gathercole's busy, miss. Can I take a message, like?' Same maid called Mavis, same starched cap and apron and adenoidal singsong. She didn't recognise Cassie.

'Yes, you may take a message,' Cassie said graciously. 'Perhaps you will tell her that Miss Marlow has called to say that she is now available to sit for her final certificate of proficiency at any time convenient to her good self. Perhaps I may come in and await the favour of her reply?'

Deeply impressed, Mavis showed her into the hall. Same shadowy garden-seat green; same big stained-glass window with Grecian women carrying jugs on their heads, same distant murmur of voices, clicking of typewriters. Cassie stood motionless, facing the impressively carved staircase. She heard a door open and, although she tried not to, she began to smile.

Because today was her twenty-first birthday, the day upon which she was legally considered capable of making her own decisions and ordering her own affairs in a sensible, rational manner.

CHAPTER TWELVE

'Hit, hero, hope, hammer, are all examples of the upward *h,* and the upward *h* is used in preference to the downward because it joins so neatly to most of our other outlines. The downward *h,* as I said earlier on, is used firstly when *h* follows upward *l* or a horizontal stroke, as for instance in the word *unhook* . . .'

The scrape of chalk across blackboard, and thirty pairs of eyes diligently following its progress; cotton frocks, strap-and-button shoes and little-girl bobs held in place by tortoiseshell hairslides.

'So you should now be able to write *In order to unhook the hero we must first hit him on the head with a hammer* . . .'

Someone at the back of the class stifled a giggle, and Miss Marlow, chalk in hand, raised a deprecatory eyebrow.

'Is there anything wrong, Marjorie?'

'No, Miss Marlow.'

'In that case, why titter?'

Marjorie mumbled an apology, and, waiting for them to finish transcribing the words she had dictated, Cassie thought there are times when I still can't believe that this is really me.

Miss Gathercole's reception of her had been somewhat frigid on that afternoon more than a year ago.

'Your final certificate? Have you not left it a little late?'

'Well, I just wanted to be absolutely certain that—'

'Certain that what, pray?'

'Certain that I'd get it.'

'What have you been doing in the meantime?'

'Studying, Miss Gathercole.'

'Hmm.' Scepticism gleamed. 'What became of the golden opportunity offered by the undertaker?'

'The time came for me to better myself,' Cassie said primly. 'To reach for higher things, as it were.'

'You will not reach higher things in the secretarial world until you have learned not to prevaricate,' Emilia said. 'Not only do you prevaricate, you also on occasion behave with quite incredible obstinacy, and it is difficult to say which of the two is the more irritating. And I see that you have also become a flapper.'

Hands clasped behind her back, head bowed and lower lip caught behind front teeth, Cassie realised that she had automatically reassumed the humble posture of scolded schoolgirl, which was ludicrous at her age. Hastily she straightened up, looked Miss Gathercole in the eye and said: 'In that case, I see no point in either of us wasting any further time.'

'Are you really sure about taking your final?' Emilia relented a little. 'Are you brushed up on advanced contractions, confident at a hundred and sixty words a minute?'

'Yes.'

'And you are equally confident of your typing?'

'Yes.'

'In that case I will see whether something can be arranged.'

Having spent all her available time assiduously revising and practising, Cassie passed the shorthand tests with ease but only scraped through the typing. Mr Sissley was in the office when Miss Gathercole handed her the engraved certificate. He looked at her with an amused smile and asked what she proposed to do now.

'Find a new situation, Mr Sissley.'

'Easier said than done, these days.'

'Yes. I know.'

They both sat contemplating her in silence, then Mr Sissley asked what type of situation she would prefer. 'Banking, legal, shipping?'

'Beggars can't be choosers, can they?'

'I seem to remember you as an ambitious young lady,' he said mildly.

'I didn't know any better.'

Curiously depressed, she put the certificate in her handbag and prepared to depart. 'But thank you all the same for allowing me to—'

'It is just within the realms of possibility,' Miss Gathercole said, 'that we might be able to offer you a temporary post at the academy.'

'*Here*?'

'Miss Whittaker — doubtless you remember her — is taking up an appointment on our behalf in the Scilly Isles. She is to become personal private secretary to an ornithologist, one of several persons of substance who have applied to us for staff of a particularly high calibre.'

'Oh. Will she like that?' Cassie had no very strong memories of Miss Whittaker, who had taught touch-typing and assisted Mr Sissley with shorthand tuition.

'The appointment carries great prestige. Both the academy and Miss Whittaker herself are proud that she should be given the honour of filling it. Lord Gunter Blake, of whom you may have heard, is famous for his study of the great shearwater, but I understand that he has now turned his attention to the razorbill — Miss Whittaker is *very* keen.'

'How jolly. So you mean, I'd be—'

'Under the personal eye of Mr Sissley and myself, where you would be allowed to try your hand at a little rudimentary teaching, but a great deal of your time would be spent in marking exercises and helping with the general running of the establishment. As I have already mentioned, the appointment would be of a temporary nature, the hours would be from nine until six and the remuneration modest but sufficient. Perhaps you would care to think the matter over and telephone me tomorrow morning between the hours of nine and ten.'

Flushed and incredulous Cassie mumbled that she would do so, then on reaching the door turned round to face them both and said: 'I've already thought. Thank you very much, I accept.'

She didn't quite know what made her do it. Any more than she knew what had prompted them to make the offer, and not for the first time she thought ashamedly of that Saturday morning when she had deliberately ignored her appointment with them.

But now, having accepted, she could only hope to compensate for past misdemeanours by offering extreme efficiency coupled with almost devout conscientiousness, and so in the weeks that followed she worked cheerfully and tirelessly at every allotted task. In regulation dark blue smock with a bow at the neck she treated the students with sympathy, the rest of the staff with tact, and was not at all averse to such mundane little jobs as sticking on stamps and going to the post. Once when the boilerman was away with kidney trouble she even took on the additional role of stoker, and the startled Mr Sissley had almost to remove the shovel from her hands by force.

'My dear Miss Marlow, this is no work for a young lady!'

'Oh honestly, it's nothing! I quite like a bit of hard physical exercise—'

'But you are taking on menial work—'

'When the ship's in trouble,' Cassie replied gallantly, 'it's all hands to the pump, Mr Sissley.'

He agreed and, trying not to laugh, ordered her from the scene.

But she was pleased with herself and with everyone around her, for in one magical bound she had left the drab world of haberdashery and in her own estimation at least was something superior even to a full-blown secretary. If she ignored the subject-matter she could even persuade herself that she was some sort of junior university professor — there was not a vast difference between a smock and an academic gown — and as soon as her finances permitted, she left the room in the back street near Gambier Terrace and took one in Huskisson Street where there was no muffled sound of TB coughing nor wailing of sick and underfed children.

She set herself assiduously to woo Miss Gathercole, not only because her alliance was now very important, but also because she had begun to like her. No longer a pupil, with a pupil's automatic resentment of authority, she was able to assess her more clearly, and although the distinction between employer and employee was at all times rigorously adhered to, she was beginning to find evidence of a profoundly warm and humane personality behind the Alexandra fringe and stately phraseology.

Yet on the day when Emilia graciously offered her a permanent place on the staff of the Gathercole Academy ('Your progress has been monitored with scrupulous care and it is felt that most shortcomings can be eradicated with experience'), she was conscious of a strange heart-sinking. Perhaps it was the word permanent.

'The waird pairmanent's lovely if it means six hundred a year and not havin' to wairk,' Effie said. 'But that only happens in the pictures.'

Cassie agreed and tried to stifle the curious twinges of dissatisfaction. It occurred to her that she ought to be in love, and she spent a week or so contemplating Mr Sissley as a possible object of desire. Although he was old he was very jolly and she liked his natty style of dressing, but the alchemy failed to get going. It didn't seem to work for him either, for in spite of coquettish glances and dropped handkerchiefs he appeared to remain sunnily indifferent to her as a woman.

And outside Gathercoles, the worldwide depression was still deepening. British newspapers sought to cheer the two million unemployed with descriptions of famine and cholera in post-revolution Russia, and to amuse them by quoting the story of girls in a Swiss soap factory who were wrapping tablets of their product in Austrian treasury notes. They gave little space to the man in Runcorn who was jailed for stealing two herrings, or to the bands of barefoot children swarming round the gates when Liverpool's remaining dockers came off shift to beg for any uneaten sandwiches. Still, a brilliant fancy-dress ball was given at the Philharmonic Hall by Lady Russell and Mrs Fredk Stubbs in aid of the Seamen's Friendly Society, and Mrs Harold Marlow's name was prominent among the list of guests. She went as Columbine, and her Pierrot was Mr Douggie Marshall, the well-known young golfer.

Then on the Monday before the academy reopened for autumn term, something dramatic occurred.

Strolling down from Huskisson Street towards the Central Library, Cassie became aware of people standing on street corners as if they were waiting for something to happen. A slight hush seemed to have fallen. She turned into Lime Street where the traffic was barely moving and a dense crowd of pigeons flew up with a clatter of wings as if death were in the vicinity.

Then she saw the multitude massed on the plateau in front of St George's Hall, silent and motionless and listening to the voice of a man who stood poised on an improvised dais. She saw his toylike fist beating the air, heard the shuffling of feet and the low drone of agreement, saw the thoughtful listening faces. They were all men, cloth-capped and drab-suited, and they were everywhere; even perched astride the huge ornamental lions.

There was something deeply impressive about such a large mass of people; a sense of power seemed to come from their very orderliness. There was no sign of police, and the driver of a stationary tramcar rolled a cigarette as he watched the proceedings.

Checking the inclination to go over and listen with the crowd Cassie walked on, and at the far end of the plateau turned left towards the library. And then it happened, swiftly and horribly, so that no one was ever able to say with certainty how it began. She heard the sudden thunder of feet, the bawling of a frightened crowd, and realised that they were coming her way. Clutching her library books she ran across the road but the human torrent overtook her and swept her along, elbows in her ribs, boots stamping on her feet. She screamed, and struggled to remain upright, and in the mad confusion saw the police, truncheons upraised, smashing their way through the bobbing sea of faces. The man next to her went down, silent as a crumpled sack, and those behind him swore as they sprawled over his body. The library books were torn from her grasp and she screamed again as a police horse reared with dancing, dangling hooves, and foam from its excited mouth splashed on to her coat like a patch of white lace.

'Come on, lads!' roared a voice and Cassie found herself lifted by the crowd and tossed like flotsam in a stormy sea in the direction of the Walker Art Gallery, which was next to the library. For a few minutes she fought against the tide with elbows and fists and kicking feet, but it was useless. The most she could do was try not to fall.

They poured across William Brown Street in a clatter of boots and a rattle of prancing hooves while the blows smashed down from the truncheons and the blood spurted. She heard a woman's voice screaming imprecations and they swept up to the doorway and remained there, massed and struggling like a swarm of furious bees, then burst inside the great hallway, Cassie with them, and there was a second's relief in the idea of having reached sanctuary. Then unbelievably the blows began again, and the majesty of marble splendour and civic pride was desecrated by the stench of rage and terror and mad-eyed scrambling and the smack of fists and the thump of truncheons, and all the sounds mingled and merged, echoed and re-echoed up the staircase and along the galleries, and uniformed attendants made confused attempts to assist first one side and then the other. A panting man on his knees close to Cassie lugged desperately at the blue-clad leg of a policeman and finally succeeded in toppling him. Like a busy housewife the man sat on the policeman's chest and began squeezing his windpipe as if he were wringing water from the weekly wash. A young man in a clergyman's collar lay with blood running from his head.

With one shoe lost and her hat gone Cassie backed away and a whirling fist caught her on the side of the face. She staggered, and dizzy with pain and horror almost fell over a man with thick black hair who was sitting on the floor weeping bitterly. She had never seen a man weep before — hadn't even realised they could — but the sight of his helpless child's tears made her sink down on the floor beside him. And in all the violent pandemonium raging about them she put her arms round him and held him and he laid his head against her breasts as if she were his mother.

'Don't cry — it'll be all right—'

'I was only listening — thass all I was doing—'

'I know, I know. Don't cry . . .'

She managed to extract her handkerchief from her pocket and bending over his shock of hair began to wipe his eyes. He smelt of poverty, of mutton fat and sweat, then she saw blood on her handkerchief. A policeman stumped over to them.

'Gerrup—'

'He can't. He's hurt—'

'You can gerrup too, miss. We don't want women in this.' He began to tug at the man's legs. 'Come on, gerron your feet . . .'

Another policeman appeared, they took a leg each, and lying on his back the man slithered across the floor like a sledge over the ice. Fresh contingents of police were arriving and the place was now cleared of all except those incapable of movement. Blood gleamed stickily on smashed white faces and, catching sight of the jammy mess where a man's front teeth should have been, Cassie felt a singing in her ears, a sickness in her stomach, but before she keeled over someone seized her round the waist and jerked her upright.

'Cassie! Cassie, for God's sake what are you doing in here?'

In the seconds before the singing, stinging blackness wiped everything out she found herself looking into the incredulous eyes of Arnold Openshaw.

* * *

'What were you doing in there?'

'On my way to the library. What were you?'

'I'd helped the LUWCM to organize the meeting. I came up from London a few days ago.'

'Is that where you live now?'

'Yes, mostly.'

'Oh. No wonder we never seem to meet.'

'But I thought you were somewhere in London, too. That's where you went that time, wasn't it?'

'Yes, but I came back. And when I went to look for you, you'd gone.'

'Oh, Cassie . . .'

They were sitting in a steamy little café in London Road. After the mêlée they had found Cassie's shoe lying in the gutter, not far from one of the library books, but there was no sign of her hat. The ambulances and the Black Marias had departed, the Walker Art Gallery was being swabbed and cleansed by indignant janitors and the pigeons had settled back on the deserted plateau outside St George's Hall.

'Cassie, it's so nice to see you.'

'It's nice to see you, too.' She spoke soberly, and without smiling because her face was beginning to stiffen on the side where it had received the blow. 'And what does LUWCM stand for?'

'Liverpool Unemployed Workers' Committee Movement. Our slogan is Work or Maintenance and our first aim is to improve the Poor Law Relief scale.'

'Good idea.' She remembered the Kellys.

'We plan to abolish the shame of food coupons and we're campaigning for a cash rate of thirty shillings a week for every family of man, woman and one child.'

'Thirty bob's a lot of money.'

'We can afford it. This country's one of the four richest in the world but those in power don't propose to part with an extra penny until it's taken from them by force. And we're prepared to do that if necessary.'

She looked at him without speaking.

'We're pledged to get rid of the injustices of the present system, and if it entails a certain amount of civil upheaval we're still prepared to go ahead and to continue the struggle for the things we believe in.'

'Tell me something. Who's we?'

He leaned a little further across the table and said: 'I've joined the Communist Party, Cassie.'

'What happened to the Fabians?'

'So far as I'm concerned they've smothered themselves under a blanket of intellectual waffle. They're all words and no action — I just got sick of waiting for something decisive to happen. Besides which, for all their earnest good intentions they're socially out of touch with the workers.'

'I saw a man crying this afternoon. He looked just like a little boy.'

'Why don't you join us? Help in the struggle—'

'I don't know,' she said. Then added inconsequentially: 'My face hurts.'

'I think you're going to have a black eye. Was it a policeman who hit you?'

'I don't know, I didn't see. Anyway, what difference would it make?'

'The police are oppressors of the under-privileged. They're part of the system that's based on one rule for the rich and another for the poor. In a country that boasts of its freedom we should be free to hold meetings in public places, we should be allowed to air our grievances. We should be listened to, and not pursued and assaulted as if we were criminals.'

Arnold had remained much the same in appearance except to have become a little thinner and a little more threadbare, but he had become a lot more intense. The eyes behind the small wire-rimmed spectacles had developed an hypnotic quality.

'Yes, it was awful,' Cassie murmured. 'Something ought to be done.'

'You could help—' He seized her hand between the teacups. 'Commit yourself, Cassie. We've already got some marvellous women working for us — Mary Bamber, and her daughter Bessie . . . Put yourself outside the social confines of Sefton Park—'

'I did that a long time ago, but it was nothing to do with politics—'

'Everything's political, you can't escape it! Every time we eat a meal or sleep in a comfortable bed we're making a political statement, we're accepting a system that has food and beds for some but not for others—'

'What d'you want me to do then, sleep on the floor?'

'No, of course not, silly girl. I'm suggesting that you help us to ensure that everyone has a bed, a decent meal and a pair of watertight boots—'

'Oh, you make it all sound so easy!' Already she was beginning to feel the old, irritated impatience with him. 'I think it's far better if we all try and help ourselves, and that includes being helping and loving — you don't say anything about being loving, only about being *fair* — to all the people close to us personally. Take care of the pence and the pounds will take care of themselves, sort of thing.'

'We had an estimated crowd of four thousand people at the meeting this afternoon, and they all came because they were looking for someone, for *something* that will help them overcome the hopeless, demeaning poverty that grinds them all down—'

'But I can't *think* in terms of four thousand all at once!' Cassie snatched her hand away and cradled her throbbing cheek with it. 'They all become faceless and nameless — I'm just not big enough, noble enough. Of course, I'm sorry for them, and I know more about poverty than you think, but

I'd far rather concentrate on one or two people at a time, like my cousin Mona—'

'How is Mona, by the way?'

'Dead. She killed herself. And in spite of what you say it was nothing to do with poverty or politics it was just because no one had ever loved her, they'd just stuck her away in homes and places because they didn't like looking at her hare lip—'

Her voice began to shake. She saw the waitress looking at her with idle curiosity. 'I'm going now. Thanks for the tea—'

Arnold stood up too, hastily scraping back his chair and fumbling for money in his trouser pocket. He looked pale and very distressed.

'I'm awfully sorry — I didn't know. Poor Mona . . .'

Without replying Cassie threaded her way rapidly between the other tables while he paid the bill. He caught up with her on the pavement outside.

'Listen Cassie, you haven't told me anything about yourself. Where you live and work—'

'I live in Huskisson Street and I work at—' She turned to face him, glaring at him ferociously with her one good eye; the other was now closing to a purple-coloured slit. 'I work in that pillar of bourgeois respectability known as the Gathercole Academy—'

She hurried away.

'You forgot your library book!' He pounded after her.

'Thank you—' She snatched it and broke into a run.

'Cassie — listen to me!'

He caught her arm and drew her urgently into the doorway of a tobacconist's shop. They were almost at the corner of Lime Street.

'Cassie, I've no money and no immediate prospects but I'm in love with you — will you become engaged to me?'

Her mouth fell open. She closed it, then swallowed hard. 'No, Arnold, of course not.'

'Don't you love me? Not even a bit?' The anxiety in his expression was hard to face.

'No. Well yes, I do as a friend—'

'Mightn't it develop into something else?'

Like 'flu developing into pneumonia, she thought distractedly. 'No, I don't think so. But please don't think I'm not—'

'I know I haven't really any right to ask you because of my lack of all the things that make good reliable husbands in the capitalistic sense. But I do love you so, Cassie, I always have done . . .'

Unable to look at him anymore she fixed her aching gaze on the shop window display. Gold Flake, Craven A.

'It's awfully nice of you . . .' What else could she say? She tried to smile.

'It's not nice of me at all, it's just the truth. I can't help loving you any more than I can help breathing. And Cassie, I'm sorry if I bore you with politics, I'll honestly try not to, but somehow you seem to epitomise everything that's beautiful and worthwhile and idealistic — you're all the lovely things I want to fight for—'

'And you'd like to share me with four thousand down-and-outs?'

'What's that got to do with it?' He looked blank, almost stupid. 'Oh, I see — a joke.'

'Wasn't a very good one.'

'Oh, Cassie . . . look at me, Cassie . . . I'm not much good at proposing or anything like that, but if you could just sort of — well, help a bit—'

'But I don't want to be proposed *to*!' She was worried, exasperated and a shade tearful. 'I've said no, and I mean no. I don't want to get engaged to you or to anyone else. Thank you for the honour, Arnold, but I only want us to be good friends.'

He stood looking at her for a long sad moment, then gently took her arm. 'I'll see you to the tramcar.'

Mercifully it arrived almost immediately and he handed her up the step with heart-breaking solicitude. The tramcar was number 385 and used to be on the Lodge Lane run, and it was terrible that she could remember such trivialities when a man had just offered her his hand and heart.

* * *

Although the incident on St George's plateau was given little coverage in the press it marked a significant point in the history of post-war struggle for realignment.

A previous gathering on the Exchange Flags, that private, hallowed square at the rear of the Town Hall, had passed without incident; no police presence, no charges of trespass, so it was therefore assumed that a meeting on the public site of the plateau would not be regarded as an offence.

Afterwards, there were varied accounts of what really happened; some claimed to have seen hundreds of police with drawn truncheons rushing from the nearby Sessions Court while dozens of mounted policemen charged into the crowd deliberately to cause pandemonium. To pursue the defenceless unemployed into the Walker Art Gallery — some even insisted that police horses had been ridden into the entrance — was seen as an act of calculated provocation on behalf of the authorities and the resultant mood was one of understandable bitterness.

Yet, others claimed to have heard one of the meeting's organizers suggest an invasion of the art gallery ('Come on, lads, it belongs to us, anyway'), and suddenly fearful of incipient anarchy the police had been forced to take action.

So the result was one of mutual recrimination and muddled rancour mingled with a certain gloomy satisfaction on both sides, and a large and bellicose out-of-work docker named George Garrett, eager to keep the torch of revolt alight, organized a series of daily marches which disrupted Liverpool's traffic as the eight thousand strong procession wound its way through the main streets. But there was no trouble, no temper-flaring, and the police who accompanied them were patient, even sympathetic. Lady shoppers grew accustomed to the Work or Maintenance placards bobbing along Ranelagh Street and Church Street, and the stout, sweating police sergeant who headed the procession became known to the men who marched behind him as Adequate Maintenance, which they later shortened to Comrade Addy.

In fact it was all in danger of becoming too friendly and too cosily prosaic, which was why in the middle of October, Arnold Openshaw was sent back to Liverpool by the National Unemployment Movement to help organize the first Unemployment March to London.

* * *

'As we here at Gathercoles pride ourselves on furnishing young secretaries-to-be with a complete training for their chosen career, it stands to reason that this must also include the subject of general deportment.

'Now the word deportment comes originally from the Latin *deportare*, meaning to carry, and in English has come to mean far more than merely walking with a graceful carriage. Deportment is another word for conduct. And no young secretary worth her salt would ever demean herself by slipping into any form of questionable conduct in an office, where it is more than likely that she will be working in the company of men.'

Emilia paused and studied the young faces in front of her. Wide-eyed, alert, and very serious, they stared back at her.

'We will take first of all the matter of attire. This must be simple, modest and practical. No bows, no frills, no jewellery. A secretary prides herself upon being indispensable but invisible, and therefore dark clothes are preferred. Navy blue is the colour most universally approved, and this may be relieved by the addition of white collar and cuffs which may be bought in detachable form from any good haberdasher. These must naturally be kept sparkling white, and many of my old girls make a practice of removing and then washing and starching their collars and cuffs the moment they reach home in order to have them ready for the following morning.

As for the rest, skirts of modest length (and *do* not sit with your legs crossed in front of your employer), sensible shoes that do not squeak, clean hair in a simple style, and I cannot stress too strongly the importance of personal cleanliness; many a first-class shorthand-typist has failed to make the grade simply because she *offends*.'

Another pause. The small wise eyes under the Alexandra fringe; the sudden unaccountable blush of a girl in the back row who had been experimenting with mascara.

'And now, our behaviour. On this subject my advice to you is simplicity itself: When in doubt, don't. Do not prevaricate, do not complain, do not gossip, do not giggle. You may have the misfortune to work in proximity to the type of man who has an unfortunate penchant for questionable jokes and innuendos. Do not listen. Get on with your work. That is what you are there for. And if any man should attempt any form of familiarity, tell him firmly that you are not interested in his attentions. Just tell him quietly and politely that he is wasting valuable time which could be put to better use.'

'Yes, Miss Gathercole . . .'

Emilia ended with a short homily on the subject of chastity ('Immorality shows in your face, and in due course may well show itself elsewhere'), then dismissed them with a regal wave of the hand.

Crossing the big dark green hall, she came upon Arnold sitting on a chair twiddling his hat on his knee.

'Good gracious.' She stopped abruptly. 'Are you not Arnold Openshaw?'

'Good afternoon, Miss Gathercole.' He rose to his feet. 'Yes, and I'm very sorry to intrude—'

'Not at all. I am always delighted to welcome back an old pupil. I have fifteen minutes to spare so you must come upstairs and tell me all about yourself. Have you in fact become a male secretary?'

She led the way and he followed unwillingly. Seating herself behind her big desk she motioned him to a chair. The office was as he remembered it from his initial interview;

perhaps a little more cluttered with books and papers, perhaps a little dustier.

'In a way,' he said, 'although male secretary is perhaps rather a loose term.'

'For whom do you work?'

'I hope eventually to carve a political career, Miss Gathercole.'

'In Parliament?'

'That, or its equivalent.'

'It is high time we had another Lord Salisbury.'

Arnold smiled non-committally, then said: 'As a matter of fact, Miss Gathercole, I called to ask whether—'

'I believe it was Lord Salisbury's third ministry that introduced the Workmen's Compensation Act — most necessary, I always thought.'

'I quite agree. But I was wondering—'

'You look a little furtive.' Emilia eyed him beadily. 'Are you trying to tell me that you are some sort of radical?'

'I am of a socialist persuasion, Miss Gathercole,' Arnold said resignedly. 'And therefore work for a cause in which I believe.'

'Am I right to understand that your creed discourages you from eating meat?' She was looking at him now with more curiosity than disfavour. 'Personally I am not against minority beliefs provided they remain within the bounds of propriety.'

'Thank you, Miss Gathercole.' Feeling like a gauche student he began to twiddle his hat again. 'But I really called to ask whether I could—'

'My own personal creed has always been that of self-help, and I have striven to teach those in my care that the most satisfying rewards are those which have been worked for honestly and conscientiously. But when there is no work available then the government must make plans to provide it. Why else do we employ them?'

'Exactly—'

'After all, it is perfectly simple to envisage schemes whereby people with no work shall be moved to places where they can be re-employed, perhaps in another capacity. Everyone who can possibly afford to do so must be prepared to employ at least one other person; two parlourmaids instead of one, four gardeners instead of two. Local councils must play their part, and with the aid of twopence on the rates must double the number of people employed in schools, in hospitals, in museums and public parks. Huge armies of men could usefully be employed scrubbing the soot off our municipal buildings — and what an aesthetic bonus that would bring! No, no, take it from me, there is no such thing as the unemployment problem; there is merely the lack of initiative problem.'

Emilia smiled at him briskly, then rose from her desk. 'And now, I must go. Thank you, Arnold, for the courtesy of your visit. It was most interesting to listen to all your news and views, but take my advice and disregard the vegetarian ethos of your creed. What a man chooses to eat is a private matter between himself and his stomach, and from your increased thinness it is obvious that a large rump steak would do you nothing but good.'

They shook hands and Emilia herself opened the front door and waved him off down the steps. He spent the rest of the afternoon walking with stony eyes and clenched jaw round the dockside slums where five or six families shared one privy and one outside water tap, then returned to the corner of Hockenhall Street shortly before six o'clock and waylaid Cassie as she was leaving.

'Oh, Arnold, no—'

'Oh yes, Arnold, yes—' Masterfully he folded her arm in his and set off with her across Dale Street.

'We're not going to another political meeting, are we?'

'No, we're going to the Bear's Paw for a meal. I've just sold an article to the *Statesman* for a guinea.'

* * *

'I have a feeling that he is still trying to press his suit with Cassica,' Emilia said over supper. 'That was the real reason for his call.'

'Were you sympathetic?' Wilfred helped himself to a little more potato.

'So-so. He is a nice boy, but totally unskilled in the art of manipulation.'

'Isn't that to his credit?'

'In a *political* career? Dearest heart, his enemies will eat him alive. To mix metaphors, even I can run rings round him. And he will need more than a little manipulative skill if he is to get anywhere with Cassica—'

'Manipulative skill or devilish wiles?'

'A spring in one's gait and a flower in one's buttonhole can scarcely be described as devilish wiles, but I fear that a courtship heavy with political dogma and social conscience will cut no ice with our Miss Marlow. She is ambitious, but not in that sense.'

They finished their meal in silence, for the subject of courtship was close to that of marriage, and marriage was one of the few topics carefully avoided in the grey Gothic house hidden from the world by tamarisk and evergreen.

CHAPTER THIRTEEN

Yet the incident in the Walker Art Gallery had made a strong and lasting impression upon Cassie. It was the first time she had seen the face of mass violence, and sometimes the thud of truncheons on skulls still seemed to sound in her ears. But it was the man who had clung to her and wept who haunted her; she wished she knew his name and address so that she could take him some cigarettes and ask what else she could do to help. She found herself searching the faces of the men in the streets, although it was doubtful if she would recognise him again. All she could remember was the shock of black hair and the thin trembling body beneath the sour-smelling jacket.

She was still seeing Arnold occasionally, and if she was refusing to attend political meetings her sympathy for the cause was now rapidly increasing. Arnold wanted to lend her books to read — Marx, Engels, Lenin — but she dismissed them impatiently.

'I know all that — I can see it all in the streets. I want to *do* something!'

'We desperately need more women on some of our committees—'

'Oh damn committees! I want to go on the big march—'

'The one to London? Oh, Cassie, I'm afraid that's quite impossible.'

'Why? I'm a jolly good walker, and besides I could help cheer people up.'

He shook his head, his smile loving. 'It's only for men.'

'Oh, trust *them*! What about all the unemployed women, have they just got to stick at home?'

'Dearest girl,' he said, 'we're talking about a march of almost two hundred miles. We'll be sleeping rough and eating in soup kitchens for three weeks. The discipline will be harsh and only men who are sufficiently fit will be allowed to volunteer.'

'Are you sure you're fit enough to go? You're dreadfully thin, Arnold, and your cough's come back . . .'

She stood looking at him, and for the first time perceived that there was a funny and rather sad sort of nobility about him. If his ears hadn't stuck out she could almost have loved him. Perhaps even married him, in time.

'I'm perfectly fit,' he told her. 'And a good deal tougher than I look.'

The march to London was planned to begin on Sunday 29 October and Cassie helped to sell copies of a broadsheet containing new words set by George Garrett to an old hymn tune.

Outcasts are we from factory
From workshops, mine and sea.
Despised by those who use our blood
To save their property . . .

She felt strong and fierce, standing outside the Children's Infirmary in Myrtle Street, and when a group of ex-servicemen on crutches moved slowly along the gutter she gave each of them a copy for nothing provided they stopped singing 'Sweet Adeline' and substituted what was rapidly becoming the official battle hymn of the Liverpool unemployed.

They thanked her, and obediently agreed to do so.

And the desire to participate in the London march increased, not merely because she wanted to help but because her feelings for Arnold were now also deepening. At last the scales were dropping from her eyes and she was seeing him as he really was: a luminous visionary, and an intellectual prophet. A Gentle Jesus in wire-rimmed spectacles who loved all the world but most of all loved her, and she hugged to herself in happy secrecy the first delicious stirrings of reciprocal emotion. She was in love at last.

She confided some, but not all, of this to Effie one evening over cups of tea and Eccles cakes in front of the fire.

'Go, then,' Effie said. 'Gerron with it.'

'Women aren't allowed.'

'Go as a man, then.'

'You're spoofing. How can I?'

'You'll get a man's suit for half a crown in any pawnshop.'

Cassie giggled. 'And what would I do about work?'

'Send them a wire saying you're down with 'flu.'

'Oh, Effie, you *are* dreadful !'

They laughed and joked about Cassie dressing up as a man, but that night she dreamed that she was herding an enormous flock of white geese along a wide straight road lined with strawberry beds. The air was filled with the harsh nasal sound of their voices and the soft plap-plap of their feet, and she had to keep running from one side of the road to the other to prevent them from grazing among the strawberries. She felt tired, deathly tired, and when she tried to restore her strength by eating a handful of fruit she found it bitter and unpalatable. She longed to lie down and sleep, and tears of exhaustion were rolling down her cheeks when finally she saw the tin church that was their destination. She redoubled her efforts to marshal the geese, and when at last they were all safely herded inside they turned into a great crowd of laughing happy people, men, women and children, and they all cheered her and the tin church became miraculously transformed into a marble palace with a big golden banner saying Success, Success! suspended from between two pillars.

It was all so beautiful and so joyous that she hated waking up.

* * *

Liverpool was not the only city to take part in the 1922 March of the Unemployed. The first contingent set out from Glasgow for London on 17 October, and the complete force was due to arrive in London on 17 November.

'I must warn you,' said a letter from the General Secretary of the British Empire Union to the Under Secretary of State, *'that the March of Unemployed and the mass demonstration at the Marble Arch and in Trafalgar Square will prove, from certain sources of information at our disposal, to be a much more dangerous and sinister movement than on the surface it appears to be. We understand that this March is being generally organized by Labour-Socialists and Communists throughout the country, and they hope if possible to incite the marchers to destruction of property and looting during their progress . . .'*

The masters and matrons of the Poor Law Institutions echoed this profound disquiet when they wrote to the president of the Poor Law Association saying that they were quite unable to deal with a sudden and massive influx of tired and hungry men, all of them demanding shelter and a meal on any one specific night: *'How shall we accommodate them all? We are only able to give shelter in our casualty wards for two or three single cases per night . . .'*

The letter was sent on to the Home Office, who curtly replied that this was a Health Office matter. And so the buck was passed, but when the Liverpool contingent moved off to the accompaniment of cheers and speeches and the rattling of collection boxes by, among others, the young square-jawed Bessie Braddock, there was a rare feeling of optimism and the Work or Maintenance banners were raised with pride.

Joe Haggie was one of the men who had received a free pair of boots and socks from the Poor Law Guardians, and although his feet were gratifyingly warm and dry he could feel a sore place on his heel after the first ten miles. He ignored it and continued to step out bravely, and his mind went back to the old days of marching at ease with the Lancashire Fusiliers. Long straight French roads lined with poplars, and ahead of them the deep growl of war. A bad time, a wicked time, but the comradeship and the jokes had made up for a lot of it. He was lucky to have come through.

But through for what? To march all the way from Liverpool to London to present a petition to Parliament asking for work. His war medals clinked on his breast — Peggy had sponged and pressed his suit — and although he loved her it was nice to be away for a bit. Life in one room got them both down at times, particularly with Peggy being in the family way, and although she had tears in her eyes when he kissed her goodbye, he knew that she would be glad to see the back of him for a bit. He had made a good little cradle with rockers out of an orange box and she wanted to get on with lining it and hemming little squares of blanket without him getting under her feet all the time. Dear little Peg, she was his queen.

The lad marching next to him hadn't got much to say. Neither had he got any medals. Too young to have been in the war seemingly; he just trudged along with his head bent and his chin buried in a white muffler.

'How's your feet?'

'All right.'

'Takes the first fifty miles to gerrum hardened up.'

The lad nodded, hands stuffed deep in pockets. From somewhere at the back of the marching column came the jaunty sound of a mouth organ, and when it began to play 'Tipperary', Joe seemed to feel the old familiar weight of a Lee Enfield against his shoulder. It made him smile.

They stopped that night in a village hall outside Northwich, and sympathetic locals had set up a soup kitchen with thick barley broth and hunks of bread and cheese, and the vicar made a speech of welcome and blessed them and the work they were doing.

'If we wos wairkin' we wouldn't be doin' this,' someone pointed out, but the atmosphere was good-humoured, and only the lad buried himself deep in his blanket and refused to respond when Arnold, one of the sub-marshals, came round wishing them all a good night.

Onward comrades, organize—
Burst the ruthless chain,
Solidarity shall prove
Our quest is not in vain . . .

Sometimes it would be a solitary voice singing, other times the roar of voices would drown the rhythmic crunch of boots. They marched through villages where people ran to their doors to stare, and at Wolverhampton they were joined by a fresh contingent who swung into step with them, and who picked up the chorus of George Garrett's battle hymn:

Marching on with hearts undaunted
Workers, sound the drum!
Let the tyrants hear our voices
Victory will come!

But the songs and jokes faded with the change of weather which set in when they were within fifteen miles of Coventry. Last leaves torn from the creaking trees reminded them that this was savage November, and the rain fell steadily, pitilessly, and Joe Haggie forgot about marching in step and shuffled like an old man because wet socks had now rubbed both heels raw.

'Let's see 'em,' the lad said gruffly that night. 'Come on, get your boots off.'

Joe did so, sitting down on the chill straw that furnished the barn in which they were to sleep.

'They're going septic.'

He was a lad of few words, and always spoke with his head bent beneath the baggy cloth cap. He pushed his way out to the tap that stood in the greasy farmyard and soaked his handkerchief in cold water.

'There's some cocoa on the brew.' It was Arnold, and although the lad coloured slightly, he nodded without saying anything.

He bathed Joe's heels as well as he could, and Joe looked down on the long careful fingers stroking away the dirt and bits of grit.

'How's that feel now?'

'Champion. What's y'r name, lad?'

'Bill.'

'Have a fag, Bill.'

'Ta.'

Joe rolled a couple while the lad eased the socks over the inflamed feet. They lay back side by side, smoking the poor little fags thin as darning needles and listening to the incessant rain drumming on the roof. Joe started thinking about Peggy and the baby.

'No smoking in the barn.' Arnold's tired, harassed face appeared over a mound of hay. 'We're only allowed to use it provided no one strikes any matches.'

Obediently they pinched them out, and the lad rolled over on his face as if he were sulking.

'Cocoa and bully beef,' Arnold added, looking at him curiously. 'Look sharp, or you'll be too late.'

On the following day there was a marked increase in coughing and sneezing, and marching through Rugby the lad suddenly broke away from the column and darted into a chemist's shop and onlookers raised a thin cheer as he rushed out again with a large paper bag hugged close to his chest.

'Six packets of aspirin, six tins of Fuller's Earth and four big bottles of cough linctus!' It was the most he had ever said all at one time, and Joe Haggie shoved an affectionate elbow in his ribs and said if he was so rich, what was he doing on a hunger march?

'They gave 'em me for nowt!' The lad's voice rose on a shrill note of triumph.

And although he was so young, shy, sheepish, taciturn, he seemed to be developing a strange influence among them.

During the late afternoon of the following day an elderly man marching at the rear of the column fainted, and it was the lad who gave instructions about propping him up with his head between his knees while he unbuttoned his collar, rubbed his hands and patted his stubbly white cheeks.

'Come on, ole lad . . . brace up. Not far to go now . . .'

Some of the others tried to get him on his feet, hauling him up as if he were some obdurate old tree fallen in a gale, but the lad said leave him, *leave* him until he's ready . . .

And all the time the rain wept endlessly on the dark sodden figures tramping through the puddles, the mud and the miserable slime of late autumn on their way to the House of Commons. The target of twenty miles a day became reduced to fifteen or even less, and on the morning they walked through Helmdon one of the Liverpool men, whose cough had been no more than a monotonous smothered crunking, suddenly haemorrhaged. Like the flowering of a giant red poppy the stain spread and soaked the muffler knotted under his chin and the lad supervised laying him on a groundsheet and then sped for help to the nearest house. He was taken to the local infirmary on the back of a farm cart and when Arnold saw the lad perched on the tailboard holding the man's hand he asked sharply where he thought he was going.

'With him.'

'There's no need for that. The infirmary will look after him.'

'He's not going on his own.'

One or two men remained gathered round while the rest began to move off.

'Please obey my orders. It's essential that we have a full turn-out when we get to London, and if I let one off the others will want to follow.'

The horse between the shafts began to move forward and, cold, wet and worried, Arnold seized the lad's arm and jerked him off the tailboard. He stumbled and his cap fell off into a puddle.

'*Cassica*!'

'Yes, I know.'

There was nothing more she could say. One of the men gave a delighted guffaw, then began to run towards the retreating column with the news.

'I thought I expressly forbade you even to think of coming—'

'Yes, you did, Arnold, but I had to because — well, because . . .'

The rain, which had dwindled to a seeping mist, began again. Suddenly lost for words, Cassie picked the cap out of the puddle, shook it and then put it back on her head. They stood facing one another in the middle of the road while the cart rumbled off towards the infirmary.

'Arnold, I came because I wanted to help the cause, and because I know now that I love you.'

'Where did you get those ridiculous clothes from? And what sort of a girl are you to think you can sleep and eat and everything among a crowd of men?' He seemed extraordinarily angry.

'I love you, Arnold.' Perhaps he hadn't heard the first time. 'And as I just said, I came because I wanted to help, and to share the hardship with you all—'

'You did nothing of the sort.' With a wave of his fist he indicated to the fascinated bystanders that they should rejoin the rest of the marchers. Unwillingly, they slouched off.

'You came because you thought it would be *fun*. Because you're the daft, fickle, irresponsible sort that thinks all this is just a game, just a bit of light-hearted frivolity. It's just fun to you, dressing yourself up in worker's clothes, trying to speak Scouse in a deep voice, pulling the wool over these poor chaps' eyes, making a mockery of them so that you can go back to Sefton Park and have a jolly good laugh—'

His fury seemed to be increasing. She had never seen him like this before; never even known that he had it in him to *be* like this. Loving admiration fought with resentment, and the rain dripped off the peak of her cap on to the toes of her boots.

'Arnold, you can't really believe—'

'I can believe anything of your sort. No decency, no pity—'

'When it comes to pity,' she retorted, stung, 'I didn't notice you showing much for that poor chap gushing blood. Or for the old boy who fainted just because he was too blooming weak to stand up because you insisted on making him walk too far in one day—'

'The object is not to straggle along as if it were a choir outing—'

'No, but it's you that's hard and cruel, not me—'

'I never said you were hard and cruel — I called you daft, fickle and irresponsible—'

'Oh shut up, Arnold Openshaw, you make me sick! You're a typical man — you know it all yet you achieve nothing. You're full of beastly stupid facts and figures and dogmas and creeds but you don't really care about people as people. As individuals. You don't know or care that Joe Haggie's wife's expecting a baby or that the man who plays the mouth organ's poor old mother's been carted off to the asylum because she thinks she's turning into a dog and she's afraid she'll bite people — you don't talk to people and make friends with them because all you really want them to be is just a lot of numbers — a lot of stupid arid figures that you can shout at the government in the hope that one day they'll make you president or whatever it is after you've had your tinpot revolution and done away with our King and Queen—'

He hit her. But even in his blazing anger it was not across the mouth, which was where he thought he wanted it to be; it was an awkward, incompetent jab somewhere in the region of her shoulder. Even so she lost her balance and fell down. Her cap slid off again. He picked it up and squashed it back on her dripping, rat-tail hair, then hauled her out of the puddle and back on her feet.

'You're wearing trousers with *flies*!'

'What other sort *are* there?'

They faced one another through the lashing rain, lips drawn back, pulses hammering. They were alone now, the column of marching men no more than a dingy smudge in one direction, the horse and cart a slow creeping shadow in the other.

'Go away,' he snarled at her, rain peppering his glasses. 'Go back where you belong and here's your train fare out of Party funds, which'll make your Sefton Park bigwigs laugh harder than ever—'

The coins splashed at her feet. Shaking with rage, she bent to retrieve them. She flung them back, and one of them struck him on the chin.

'Save them for hiring another church hall for another soppy Communist speaker. I managed to walk all the way here, I'll bloody well walk back!'

They plodded off, separately, and the coins lay where they had fallen. As a sum of money it was no more than a paltry amount, but it would have bought a week's bread for a child.

* * *

Wilfred Sissley withdrew the thermometer from beneath Emilia's tongue and, squinting, tilted it towards the light.

'Almost normal now, but not quite.'

'I want to get up.'

'Not until it's ninety-eight.'

'I feel so tired of lying here.'

'Poor girl, I'm sure you are. But if it's down to normal by this evening I'll let you come downstairs for a little while. We'll have a nice log fire and the curtains drawn and we'll listen to some music. How about Galli Curci?'

'I would rather have a string quartet.'

'Then you shall have a string quartet, my angel. May I suggest the Beethoven third for delicate cheerfulness? And then how about a bowl of bread and milk with lots of sugar and a pinch of cinnamon?'

'Oh, loved one, am I being a terrible bore?'

'The day you bore me will be the day the heavens fall.' He placed the thermometer on the discarded breakfast tray, then plumped up her pillows and smoothed the blankets. He gave her the morning paper, kissed her forehead, then said: 'I must shave and dress.'

She reached up to put her arms round his neck. 'Shall we hear the quartet first?'

He shook his finger in mock admonition, kissed her again, then went down to the sitting-room to find the record. The gramophone was on the table in the bedroom window; he set it playing, then sank down on to the chair by her bedside. They listened, absorbed and at peace, and the last movement was almost at an end when the front doorbell rang.

They looked at one another, startled and strangely apprehensive. Tradespeople rarely called, and never on a Saturday morning. The bell rang again, vigorously, and without speaking Wilfred went down to answer it.

In the porch he found Cassica Marlow holding a large bunch of shaggy chrysanthemums and smiling expectantly. Her smile faltered when she saw him, and her features seemed to fly apart as the significance of his silk dressing-gown and slippers and tousled hair became inescapably clear. He could do nothing to help her, or to help himself and Emilia, so he smiled as breezily as possible and held out his hand.

'Well, well, what a nice surprise!'

'I heard when I got back from — from being ill that she'd got 'flu as well, so I thought I'd bring a few — Miss Gathercole does live here, doesn't she?'

Sympathetically he watched her struggle to assimilate the terrible facts. Mr Sissley in Miss Gathercole's house. At ten thirty in the morning. In pyjamas and dressing-gown.

'We both live here,' he said, because there was no point in saying anything else. 'Would you like to come in?'

She stepped inside and he closed the door, shutting out the boom of the sea.

'I'm — I'm sorry I've — perhaps I'd better go . . .' She stood clutching the flowers, large-eyed and distraught.

'Nonsense, I'll make some coffee. I say, what beautiful flowers. Look, do sit down and I'll—'

'No, I won't stay—'

'Cassica dear,' he said, gently taking the flowers from her, 'it's too late to retreat now, isn't it? So sit down for a moment and I'll take these up to Emilia and see if she's awake.'

He went up the stairs in a soft rustle of silk, and Cassie sat on the edge of the hall chair with her mouth slightly open and her mind completely blank. She stared at the clothes pegs with their assortment of male and female hats and coats, at the pictures on the wall, at the silver salver on the oak table but none of it made sense. Miss Gathercole and Mr Sissley living together in sin. But no, they couldn't possibly be. They must be brother and sister. Or cousins, or at the very least just very good friends. For one thing they were far too old. But even so, Mr Sissley in his pyjamas in Miss Gathercole's house . . . Her thoughts scrabbled like frenzied mice in a box.

'Would you like to come up?'

She raised her head and saw him standing halfway down the stairs, his hand resting on the banister rail and his figure outlined by the watery sunlight seeping through the landing window. It made her think of the big stained-glass window at the academy and Mr Sissley — old Dapper Dan with a carnation in his buttonhole — skipping up and down the stairs so cheerful yet so carefully formal and courteous while *she* majestic as the *Mauretania* and immaculate as a Mother Superior . . .

'Come along, Cassie, she wants to thank you for the flowers.'

She left the chair and went towards him, slowly and rather gropingly because her eyes were suddenly full of tears. He had never called her Cassie before and she remembered once almost being in love with him.

He opened the door of the bedroom and the first thing she noticed was that the bed was a double one. Emilia was lying in the middle of it, propped up on a bank of pillows with her Alexandra fringe curling on her forehead as usual but her back hair tied in a plait that was tucked down the neck of her nightdress. She was holding the bunch of flowers with a hand adorned by a narrow gold wedding ring.

'Good morning, Cassica.'

'Good morning, Miss Gathercole.'

Stifling an hysterical desire to laugh, Cassie managed to stammer a few words of conventional sympathy for Miss Gathercole's indisposition.

'Thank you very much for the flowers. Most kind.'

'Not at all, Miss Gathercole.'

'I am extremely fond of chrysanthemums, particularly the bronze variety.'

'Yes, I like them too, but I always think they smell a bit of cats, don't they?'

'I confess I have never noticed.'

Although Emilia spoke with her usual stateliness Cassie was certain that she detected a slight tremor of uncertainty, and indeed it would surely take a woman of brass to remain impervious to being found *en flagrant delit* — well, practically — by an ex-pupil and junior employee. Smiling at the woman in the bed with sudden kindness she remembered all the routine homilies, all the dire warnings about ogling in the office, of sensuality in the shorthand-typist . . . Her kindness increased.

'I hope Mr Sissley likes chrysanthemums, too.'

'Mr Sissley,' replied Emilia from her pillows, 'prefers roses. Particularly *Gloire de Dijon*, of which you may have heard.'

'And I think that this is a cue for Mr Sissley to put this magnificent bouquet in water,' Wilfred said, removing it from Emilia's grasp. 'I also think that a pot of fresh coffee is indicated.'

Quietly he left the room.

'Do sit down.' Emilia indicated the chair by her bedside.

'Look, Miss Gathercole,' Cassie said. 'I'm truly sorry about blundering in and — and upsetting things. First of all I thought I'd just drop you a note saying get well soon — after all, I know just how beastly 'flu makes you feel — and then when I woke up early this morning and the sun was shining I thought oh drat it all I'm going to get up and do my shopping first *thing*, and when I was walking past Central Station I saw the flower stall and it suddenly seemed a good idea to buy some and just hop on a train with them. I knew your address because of Christmas cards and all that, but I honestly didn't mean to — well, drop any sort of brick as it were . . .'

Emilia smiled. And very slowly put out her hand. I've got her, thought Cassie, taking it and pressing it reassuringly. We'll have no more of the old hoity-toity from now on. I feel rather sorry for her in a way . . . well, I mean, let's be magnanimous . . .

'And your own influenza is now completely better?' Emilia's hand lay relaxed as a sleeping cat's paw.

'Oh, yes thanks. Awful at the time, but you soon get over it.'

'I am very glad you got over it in time to take part in the Hunger March.'

The cat had awoken. The paw slipped gently from Cassie's grasp and took up the folded newspaper lying on the counterpane. Without haste Emilia removed her pince-nez from the bedside table and clipped them to the bridge of her nose. She began to read aloud.

> *A cheery diversion was caused on the march to the capital by the discovery of a young lady masquerading in men's attire. Believed to be a friend of Mr Arnold Openshaw, one of the organizers, it is not clear whether she wished to experience at first hand some of the discomforts of walking twenty miles a day in wind and rain, or whether she regarded her participation as a light-hearted spree. But whatever her motives, this tall and comely young lady was regarded with admiration by her fellow marchers, who described her as a plucky lass.*

Cassie stared down at her lap, then unobtrusively pulled her skirt further over her knees. Through the closed bedroom door came the faint smell of coffee, through the closed window the faint boom and wrack of the sea. Time itself hung suspended.

'It is impossible not to feel pity for the unemployed,' Emilia remarked at length. Again, without haste she laid aside the newspaper and replaced her pince-nez on the bedside cabinet. Then rather surprisingly she reached for Cassie's hand. She held it on the counterpane and began pressing it. Reassuringly.

'And the plight of unemployed women must be even more pitiful. All those millions of women who must now fend for themselves — the poor, lost generation whose men died in Flanders, how sad it is to think of them queuing patiently for situations however humble and demeaning, pleading for even a microscopic wage which will do no more than keep the breath within them. I pity unemployed women from the bottom of my heart, Cassica.'

'Yes.'

'In the same way that I rejoice with the fortunate minority employed in situations carrying a more than adequate remuneration. As for the three per cent of women — it cannot be more — who not only receive an adequate remuneration but have the additional good fortune to be honoured and trusted in a situation that offers interest, variety, and the genuine concern of an altruistic employer — all I can say is that they should count their blessings daily and strain every nerve to be worthy of their hire.'

'Yes.'

'Ah, but I was quite forgetting that you yourself have had first-hand experience of unemployment, Cassica, and that you are therefore better qualified to speak of the humiliation than I. But in your case, I am perfectly certain that it was no more than a fleeting experience which we can put down to youthful inability to see the wood for the trees. You are naturally endowed with far too much common sense, let alone ambition, to let such a thing happen again.'

'No. Yes.'

'And now I think I hear Mr Sissley coming with the coffee, so we will say no more.'

With a final squeeze Emilia released Cassie's hand, patted it gently and then laid it aside like some poor little creature from which the last drop of blood had been teased.

* * *

She had won again. She always did. Even with the scandal of her private life laid suddenly bare she had contrived to turn the situation to her own advantage. Resentment mingling with reluctant admiration and a slight desire to laugh preoccupied Cassie as she strode along the deserted promenade.

The tide was retreating now, drawing back from the drenched ribbed sand with a sighing, sucking noise. She leaned over the iron handrail holding her hat in her hands while the wind seized her hair in damp playful fingers and ruffled it into a tangle of salty curls.

They had both been surprisingly nice to her as they drank coffee and ate biscuits up in Emilia's room — or rather, Emilia and Wilfred's room — asking her if she liked music, had she ever been to Hoylake before, did she like swimming and so on; no mention was made of Hunger Marches, never once did the conversation veer even marginally close to socio-political matters, and covertly studying his bland sunny smile Cassie wondered whether Wilfred even knew of the newspaper report. She wondered whether Emilia would point it out to him or whether she did in fact consider the episode finished and done with. With such a strange and complex woman, one couldn't be sure.

She walked further, reluctant to turn back in the direction of the railway station, and once more she began thinking about Arnold Openshaw. His wild unreasonableness and thin-lipped rage still had the power to astonish her, but now the whole mad excursion had already taken on an air of unreality. The newspaper had questioned her motive for joining the march, and she could only say that what had felt at the time like a genuine commitment to a cause had somehow leaked away. She still cared about Joe Haggie, about the old man who had fainted and the one who had been taken to the infirmary, but she still couldn't see any connection between them and the books and pamphlets and ghastly speechifying so dear to a good socialist's heart.

'People, not statistics,' she said to a mean-eyed seagull perched nearby. 'Even you are a person worthy of individual consideration and respect.'

In the meanwhile, she was once again back at the starting point. Success was still eluding her, and so was love. She realised now that she could never be in love with Arnold Openshaw however hard she tried. Perhaps the only tremor of love she had ever felt was for the poor broken man who had wept in her arms in the Walker Art Gallery, and perhaps that was the only tremor a cruel and unjust fate intended to allow her.

The outlook at that point was very bleak.

CHAPTER FOURTEEN

Liverpool, 1928. The new Anglican cathedral was continuing to rise on its hillside above the river and there was talk of doing away with the big Brownlow Hill workhouse, although no government had yet succeeded in halting industrial decline and the hardship inseparable from it. The General Strike had come and gone, solving nothing, and in spite of growing acerbity between Left and Right, Protestant and Irish Catholic, the ordinary Liverpudlian pursued his own affairs unmolested, like the man who patrolled the vicinity of Church Street with a placard saying Vaccination is Performed with the Devil's Tool.

It was still a city rich in diversity, with the floating fairyland of the Cunard luxury liners providing the sables and pearls of the shipping magnates' wives; oysters at the Adelphi, champagne before a charity concert at the Philharmonic Hall; glowing velvet, gleaming satin, old men with rigidly starched fronts and old ladies with sagging backsides and a manservant to wait on the Pekinese.

And somewhere between the pomp and the penury came the shorthand-typists and the junior secretaries, tripping briskly down Water Street, Dale Street, Castle Street, in their strap shoes with Cuban heels, their art. Silk stockings at one and eleven a pair, their navy blue or chocolate brown dresses with prim white collars and cuffs and washable mackintosh circles tacked under the arms in case they offended.

They were brave and giggly and skittish; learning the tango and the Charleston and dreaming about sheiks and Ramon Novarro and setting their hair in water waves and polishing their nails on pink Cutex cubes that washed off quicker than soapsuds. And in spite of being the girls of the lost generation they all hoped to marry; if not a prince, at least someone kind and reliable and nice-looking who would rescue them from the fate of becoming personal private secretaries, that race of thin-lipped, thin-hipped super-competent and miserably soured old maids who lived in neat little service flats with Mother and a cat, and who had nothing to look forward to except a pension of thirty shillings a week and a neat little gravestone that said Miss Vera Bloggs, Spinster of this Parish who Died Wondering. They didn't want to end up like that.

But some of Liverpool's shorthand-typists of 1928 were not content with hoping to marry someone kind and reliable, and putting up with Dear Sir-ing in the meantime. One of them was the red-haired Effie.

'Effie, there's a lovely boy in the accounts department who wants to take me out.'

'Gerraway!'

'I think he's serious, Effie.'

'How much does he aim?'

'How should I know, we never talk about things like that. But ooh, he's got a lovely smile . . .'

'I'd settle for anything on two legs if it aimed five pounds a week.'

'*Effie* — all you think about is money.'

'Wharelse is there?'

'There's love, Effie. True love . . .'

She had seen a lot of girls get engaged to boys with lovely smiles who worked in accounts departments or drawing offices or technical divisions. She had seen the stars in their eyes (so much bigger and brighter than the poor little diamond in their engagement rings) and had listened to their endless plans for the future. And their futures were all so long in coming — saving for this, saving for that, learning to cook and waiting for the day when they could exchange the drudgery of the typewriter for a sink full of washing and a baby screaming in the back bedroom.

'Men are all right,' Effie said, 'but they'll do you down, if you let them.'

'So what's the answer, Effie?'

'Be one jump ahead.'

The only person who never appeared shocked by her views was Cassie Marlow. They still saw one another quite frequently, Cassie now living in a three-roomed flat in Falkner Square while Effie occupied a cavernous bedsitter over an ironmonger's shop in Granby Street.

'You've gorra get hold of the chaps with the brass,' Effie said.

'And what are you offering in exchange?'

'Me body.'

Cassie started laughing, tried not to, then laughed harder than ever.

'What's wrong with me body?'

Standing in a tin bath, scrawny as an ill-fed pullet, Effie stopped ladling water over herself and glared at Cassie challengingly. Two fierce tongues of red hair protruded from either armpit and her Lady Fayre bath cap gripped her eyebrows like sticking plaster.

'Nothing's wrong with it, Effie dear. From what I can see it's got all the essentials, and in all the right places.'

'Well then, stop laffing . . .'

Up until recent times it had been very difficult for decent girls to meet decent men without being introduced by an intermediary. Teashops were too primly censorious, pubs were forbidden ground to unaccompanied females, and none worth her salt could allow herself to be accosted in the street or on a tramcar. The rules were beginning to relax but they still had a long way to go — until, that is, the glorious advent of the Rialto.

Lavish, exotic, white-domed like a mosque, it arose on the corner where Upper Parliament Street meets Catherine Street, and there had never been anything like it before. It contained a large cinema with a screen worthy of Cecil B. de Mille's most colossal epic, and at the top of the wide marble staircase was a restaurant and a ballroom where the semi-élite of Liverpool could glide in sophisticated decorum to the music of the Collegians' Dance Band. Dinner jackets, beaded evening dresses that hung from the shoulder, husbands and wives celebrating birthdays, anniversaries; formally engaged couples, he with brilliantine, she with diamante hairslide, holding hands beneath the wickerwork table, smiling and whispering *soon . . . soon . . .*

But it was the Saturday afternoon tea-dance that was God's gift to nice girls who wanted to meet nice men.

They hunted, very discreetly, in pairs, and at first Cassie was unenthusiastic about accompanying Effie.

'I can't dance.'

'Gerroff — you used to go to dances at the Adelphi in your palmy days.'

'I only went once, and then I did it all wrong.'

'Well, now's your chance to do it right. Come on, I'll be the man—'

She stuck a record on the portable gramophone, enfolded Cassie in a grip of iron and trundled her round the room. They quick-stepped, slow-stepped, waltzed and tangoed and it made Cassie remember the blue chiffon evening frock and the feathery aigrette she had worn at the New Year's Ball. Her so-called palmy days seemed a lifetime ago.

The Rialto ballroom was vast and dim, a Sahara of gleaming sand-coloured floor beneath a huge prism of cut glass which at climactic moments slowly revolved and showered the dancers with little chippings of multi-coloured light. The walls were painted with vague, feathery trees relieved here and there by clumps of hollyhocks and ladies in poke bonnets, and the waitresses with dinky bows in their hair carried their tea-trays through trelliswork archways entwined with paper roses. There were no windows, so nothing to spoil the illusion that everyone was foxtrotting in some dim garden-paradise where it never rained and there was no unemployment problem.

The band sat on a dais framed with more trelliswork and paper roses, and on Saturday afternoons they all wore white flannels and blue blazers. They were very doggish and sporty with plastered-down hair, and the one who sometimes stood up to sing the refrain in a soft wobbling voice with an Oxford accent used to wink at Effie but she never responded. He was not the sort of prize she had in mind.

But the Rialto tea-dance had an insidious allure, and after a few weeks Cassie found herself pleasantly at home among the wickerwork tables and chairs, the pots of pale China tea and dainty sandwiches. She discovered that she enjoyed dancing after all, and initial unease at being asked to dance by strangers gave way to amused and tolerant acquiescence. There was no harm in it, and it was much better than sitting at home reading.

Effie, however, seemed to become totally consumed by this new dream world, and although Granby Street was only a stone's throw away she would disappear into the Ladies' upon arrival and devote a good fifteen minutes to rearranging her appearance, tweaking at her hair, powdering her nose and flattening her caterpillar eyebrows with index fingers dipped in Vaseline. Every movement was performed with the sly concentration of a poacher setting a snare; then, finally satisfied, she would join Cassie at their table and engage her in animated conversation while her hungry red-brown eyes raked over the other tea-dancers, sorting the wheat from the chaff.

'He looks nice, over there.'

'Where?'

'That chap sitting on his own.'

'He's going bald.'

'Bald men are often rich. He's smiling at you — smile back.'

'If you want him, you can do the smiling—'

'Ooh, come on, chicken, let's dance past him . . .'

Bald men, hairy men; tubby men with little hot hands and thin men with soft damp ones. They all asked if they might have the honour and passing one another to the heady pulse of 'Yes, Sir, That's my Baby' — Cassie in the arms of a man with a monocle, Effie in the arms of one with a military moustache — they would smile triumphantly at one another and feel glad that they were women.

Then Cassie noticed that Effie was becoming increasingly engrossed in the four people who sat at the table nearest the band. They too were there every Saturday afternoon, and to begin with Cassie wondered why they never danced with one another; two men and two women, they were all young and good-looking and vivacious and well dressed, with gold cigarette lighters and jade green cigarette holders lying among the tea things.

'They're in the pen,' Effie whispered.

'In the what?'

'Pen. They're professionals, and you have to buy a ticket if you want to dance with them.'

'What a waste of money when people can have us for nothing.'

'Rumour has it they're willing to do more than dance.'

'Oh, Effie, how ghastly!'

'Is it?'

Effie continued to stare, absorbing every detail of dress and mannerism. She watched them on the dance-floor, weaving skilfully and gracefully in and out of the throng, smilingly at ease like royalty among the lesser orders. And her eyes went back again and again to the rich and careless little baubles that littered their table. She went without lunches for a week and bought herself a mother-of-pearl cigarette case and every Saturday morning stocked it with ten Turkish cigarettes.

* * *

One early evening when Cassie was walking home from Gathercole's a voice behind her said: 'My God, if it isn't dear old Minnehaha!'

She turned and recognised her cousin Desmond.

He raised his trilby, then took her arm and tucked it companionably in his. 'Where are we off to?'

'Please yourself where you go. I'm going home.'

'In which case, it pleases me very much to come with you.'

On the way he insisted upon stopping at an off-licence for a bottle of sherry, and when they reached Falkner Square he sent his hat skimming merrily across her living-room and said what a ripping little place.

'A poor thing, but mine own.'

'Oh, Minnie, how dour you sound!'

She looked at him in surprise. 'Do I? Put it down to weariness at the end of a working day.'

'Are you glad to see me?'

She stood considering him while she slowly removed her hat and coat. 'Well, I suppose more nonplussed than anything. I mean, as cousins we're not exactly close, are we?'

'Then tell me where the glasses are and I'll give you a sherry. And then you'll feel as glad and close as anything.'

They sat down opposite one another at the gate-legged table in the window, and from the tall trees in the square came the sound of evening birdsong.

It was almost eight years since they had met, and the clumsy lumpish undergraduate had become smoothed into a personable and pleasant young man. She remembered that she had always preferred him to his elder brother Lionel.

'So how do you occupy yourself, Minnie dear?'

'I'm a teacher. And you?'

'I'm about to become a farmer.'

'What were you before that?'

'What you might call an explorer. I explored stockbroking at the pater's request, had a look at accountancy, tried the world of the prep school master, but we live in strange and unsettling times and it isn't always easy for a young chap to find his niche. Have you found yours, by the way?'

'Yes, thank you,' she said rather primly. 'I teach shorthand at the place where I learned it. It suits me very well.'

'Does it, really?' He sat looking at her with unabashed interest. 'I visualised you doing something rather more startling.'

'Oh? Such as?'

'I don't know . . . the stage perhaps. Or getting involved in some great movement or other.'

Funny he should say that. But she stared down into her sherry, refusing to be drawn.

'How's the family?' she asked.

'Don't you ever go and see them?'

'No. Not now.'

'Can't say you miss much. I don't go home all that often.'

'They were very kind to me,' she said formally.

He refilled their glasses without replying and, listening to the last sweet notes of a thrush, they both became conscious of the years that had passed. And how little they knew of one another.

'How's Lionel, by the way?'

'Oh, splendid chip off the old block. He's about to be made a junior partner in the old firm.'

'I expect Uncle Harry's pleased.'

'Highly gratified, no doubt.'

The conversation languished. There's too much ground to cover, Cassie thought. It's all too much of an effort. When he's finished his sherry he'll get up and go. Then to her own surprise, heard herself asking if he'd like to stay for some supper.

He accepted with alacrity, and they made poached eggs on toast and he laid the table with cheese and biscuits and celery and refilled their glasses again. On impulse she lit the candle in the little brass candlestick she had bought in a junk shop for sixpence.

'What made you think I'd want to go on the stage?'

'Your masterly handling of the big scene. I still cherish the memory of you standing down by the lake in your drawers, telling everyone where they got off—'

'Oh, I didn't! I just got a bit cross, but it was Uncle Harry who had all the best lines—'

'I'm not so sure. *I hate, loathe and abominate the idea of being a damned secretary in my Uncle Harry's damned office . . .*'

'I didn't really say that, did I?'

'My memory's word perfect. And then you chucked your shoes in the lake and hit me on the head with one of them—'

'Serves you right for being in the way—'

Suddenly they began to laugh, easily and delightedly like two old friends.

'Oh, Minnie, what an absolute topper you were! You've no idea how I wanted to hug you — to clasp you to my damp and dauntless bosom—'

'Never mind that, you could at least have stuck up for me. All those awful accusations your father made about me being immoral and everything weren't true, you know.'

'Of course they weren't. And he knew that as well as everyone else . . .'

She stared at him over the rim of her sherry glass. 'So why did he—?'

'To ease the pain of Mother, I suppose. He must have had an intuition about her almost from the beginning but he's always suppressed it and refused to let it develop into even so much as a suspicion. Babs is perfect, and to acknowledge that she eats young men alive would kill him.'

'So you know about . . .'

'Everyone knows, and they have done for years. It's just that it's never actually spoken of.'

'It must be strange to be loved so much.' The sherry was beginning to make her feel wistful and introspective. It was also diluting her hatred of Uncle Harry.

'I'm perfectly certain that someone must love you terrifically.'

'No, they don't.'

'Not anyone? Ever?' He looked genuinely amazed.

'No. Well, there was somebody, but he's gone. We had an awful row with a lot of people looking on in the middle of the road. It was dreadful.'

'He'll come back.'

'Actually, he did. He came back about a year later and said he was sorry—'

'He doesn't believe in rushing things.'

'He lives in London,' Cassie said. 'And is rushed off his feet with political things.'

'Anyhow, what happened?'

'He said he was sorry, and although I was too, I was a bit beastly to him. I don't like Liverpool much and I don't think I'll ever really belong, but I don't belong in London anymore now. I've left it too late. And in any case I don't think that I could be sort of half-married to a man who doesn't really think in terms of one single person at a time. I mean, he only really loves the masses. To him, there's something almost holy about people when they're in droves.'

'So he's gone again?'

'Yes. Have some more cheese.'

'I've eaten over half of it already.'

'I can get some more tomorrow.'

It was quite dark now and the window reflected them sitting with their elbows on the table on either side of the little gold candleflame.

'Life's awfully strange, isn't it? You and I sitting here, after all this time.'

'You've no idea how scared of you Lionel and I were. We used to dodge you because we didn't know what to say.'

'You seemed so distant and supercilious . . .' Then she could no longer keep her mind from the last time they had met. The wind blowing cold across Toxteth Park Cemetery, the hasty, embarrassed little huddle of black-clad family round the grave at the foot of the workhouse wall. Mona. She wanted to speak her name, to speak words that would warm her memory and help to keep it alive. Yet the words refused to form.

'I suppose I'd better be going,' Desmond said without moving.

'I'll make some coffee first. By the way, you haven't told me where you live.'

'At the moment I'm putting up at the Grove Hotel in Mount Pleasant.'

'Oh, not far from where I—' But she didn't want to talk about undertaking, either. 'It's better than home, is it?' she asked, instead.

'Infinitely.'

'Have you got a girl?' Not that she was really interested.

'Not at the moment. There have been one or two encounters of what you might call a light and trivial nature, nothing more. Come on, let's finish the sherry.'

'I can't, I feel rather stinko as it is. And I've got to get up in the morning.'

'You haven't been to bed yet.'

'Give me time.'

'When you do go, Minnie dear, can I come with you?'

'No, of course you can't.'

They were leaning very close to one another across the table. The candleflame had become no more than a sleepy flicker that stretched up every now and then as if it were yawning.

'Oh, go on, Minnie . . .'

'Certainly not. The very idea . . .'

The last honeyed whisper of a saxophone in the Rialto ballroom: 'God Save the King' coming grandly from the cinema downstairs. Pub doors locking, footsteps receding, wavering voices upraised in song: *Oh, I love the dear silver that shines in your hur, And the brow that's all furrowed and wrinkled with cur* . . . then empty streets and only the scutter of a small night wind. Liverpool darkness, warm, sooty and companionable; Liverpool sleep undisturbed by the faraway keening of an all-night tram, the lonely bellow of a ship waiting for the 3 a.m. tide.

* * *

'You're joking!'

'No I'm not, it just seems funny the first time, that's all—'

'Funny isn't the word for it—'

'Lie still then—'

'Well don't lie on top of me, I can't breathe—'

'Oh, Minnie, don't be daft. Surely you know—'

'Of course I know. What d'you take me for?'

'Wait a minute, put your other leg *there.* Now, is *that* better?'

'Yes. A bit . . .'

'Oh, what an adorable girl you are, Minnie. Adorable . . . adorable . . .'

'Ow, you've got your elbow on my hair—'

'I'm just looking at your face. It's so beautiful and strong and fierce—'

'Like an Alsatian—'

'Shut up. Look, shift your other leg a bit, can't you—'

'You just told me to put it there—'

'No, the other one. Jesus, it's like trying to seduce a centipede . . .'

The bed shaking with laughter. Then shaking with the other thing, and Cassie thinking so this is it. This is really it. This is the thing nice girls don't do until their wedding night. Or shall we say, the nice thing girls don't do until . . . How strange and primeval and tumultuous . . . Oh glory, I'm floating . . . *floating* . . .

* * *

'He's my cousin,' she said to Effie a couple of days later. 'But it's not serious.'

'And you mean you're . . .'

'I'm what?'

'You know.'

'Yes, I'm fornicating, Effie dear. I hope I don't get in the family way.'

Effie stared. 'Don't tell me you're not taking precautions?'

'Well, no. I haven't really had time to sort of find out—'

'A piece of sponge,' Effie said, 'soaked in vinegar.'

'Going to be a bit crowded in there, isn't it?'

Desmond had been coming to Falkner Square each evening, sometimes staying all night and gliding swiftly away at first light in order not to compromise Cassie with the neighbours. They made love hectically, tempestuously, in between jokes and laughter and bottles of grocer's wine, and the post-coital peacefulness enabled them to talk openly and frankly about the darker things.

'I'll never know how much I was to blame for Mona's death.'

'Tell me about it, if it doesn't hurt too much.'

She told him, lying on the bed in her petticoat and without her knickers on, slowly passing one long shapely leg up and down his creased grey flannels.

'I wish I'd known her better,' he said, 'but she was hardly ever at home and then of course we both went away to school. So I just grew up with the idea of a funny shadowy sort of sister whom no one talked about.'

'Weren't you curious about her when you grew older?'

'I can remember making a conscious effort to be nice to her once when she came home for a few days in the hols. I must have been about fourteen. We went for a walk through the park and she kept trying to hold my hand and talk to me about all the horses being slaughtered in the war, and I didn't know what to say. I mean, it wasn't *my* fault. And I can remember feeling hot and uncomfortable and wishing she'd let go of me — in the end I think I simply did a bunk. Not very noble, I'm afraid. I disliked myself for it afterwards, but it also made me dislike her for putting me in that sort of position.'

'Somewhere along the way I must have let her down, too. Perhaps she thought I was going to do a bunk as well.'

'So she got in first, by doing a permanent one.'

'It's all about responsibility, isn't it?' Cassie's thoughts went back to the Unemployment March; to those who took part and to those who organized it.

'Yes. Pity we don't get a second chance.'

'So long as we keep on living there's always a second chance.'

He pulled up her petticoat and began kissing her abdomen, encircling her navel and then moving slowly down towards the crisp black hair.

'I say, what a funny smell—'

'Oh? What sort?'

He raised his head, nostrils dilating. 'I don't know. A bit like fish and chips.'

'The woman upstairs cooking supper,' Cassie said dreamily. 'Go on with what you were doing.'

Their affair had been in progress for a little over two weeks when he broke the news that he was leaving Liverpool on the following day. Her first reaction was one of dismay, then she remembered about the farm he was going to run and asked where it was.

'South Africa. I thought I told you.'

The furthest she had imagined was Devonshire or Scotland. 'Yes, of course you did. I'd forgotten.'

'I'll miss you, Minnie dear.'

'Shall I come and see you off at the quayside, waving a tear-sodden handkerchief?'

'We sail out of Tilbury,' he said. 'And I don't think a wet handkerchief would wave properly.'

He asked her to see him off from the train, and up until the very last minute she thought she wouldn't go in case she cried, and even hurrying under the steam-filled roof of Lime Street station was suddenly afraid that Babs and Uncle Harry might be there too. They weren't, and she helped him to stow his haversack under the seat of the London train while the porter dealt with the two big suitcases.

'But why South Africa?'

'It's nice and warm,' he said.

They kissed goodbye, but it was nothing like the kisses they had exchanged in the Falkner Street flat. In place of ardour there was tenderness, and in their eyes the reassurance that friendship lives longer than passion.

She cried when she reached home. Not only because she would miss him, but because once again she had not succeeded in falling in love. At least, not in the way the poets described.

* * *

Dear Sir, we beg to acknowledge receipt of your letter of the 29th ultimo with regard to your esteemed order for one 'Jupiter' lightning conductor. This is now to hand, and we are pleased to state that our installation engineer is now in a position to call upon you at any time to suit your convenience . . .

Effie's fingers danced over the keys as her hot brown eyes flicked over the shorthand notebook open on the desk beside her. Sod lightning conductors. Sod the job, and the typewriter and the stupid sod who invented them. Sod them all.

From all over the office came the sound of typewriters, brisk as the rattle of grapeshot. Little bells pinged, and every now and then the boss's buzzer sounded; one jab for Edith, two jabs for Effie and three jabs for Mary. Do not hesitate to call upon us should there be any further service we can render in this matter. We have the honour to remain, dear Sir, yours faithfully.

The junior coming in with the tea. Three cups without saucers on a tin tray; one communal teaspoon and the sugar in an old Bovril jar.

'Stan's picked up a lovely wireless second-hand. It can get Hilversum.'

'Ooh, where's that?'

'I don't know, but it's gorra lovely jazz band.'

'I'm thinking of doing away with me fringe.'

'What for?'

'Me mother says it hides me eyes.'

'Ooh, my friend's got lovely eyes. He wants to get engaged but I said no.'

'They've got stockings in Blacklers for eleven pence-three-farthings.'

'Each?'

'No, you daft thing, a *pur*!'

I know the ones she means, I've seen them; they're plated lisle and they're the colour of Mersey mud. I wouldn't be seen in them to save me life. One of these days I'm having nothing but pure silk. Pure silk next me skin and a bath every day and me hur set in big loose waves and not little frizzy cairls as if I've been stood out in the rain all night. I'm getting out of here, it's no better than the Royal Maritime. But I'm not just finishing here, I'm finishing with this whole lark. Shorthand typin' gets you nowhere, that's why I'm finishing . . .

She went to the Rialto tea-dance that Saturday with Cassie and they both sat at the table next to where the pros sat laughing and talking and scattering their bright little bijoux among the cucumber sandwiches. They didn't talk much, Cassie sitting with her chin on her bunched fist picturing Desmond playing deck quoits and dressing up as Father Neptune or whatever it was they did, while Effie gazed thunderously at the girl pro who was wearing seductive georgette with floating panels and her hair tucked behind her ears which gave her a dangerously exotic look.

They danced with the one or two gentlemen who invited them, but mostly with one another, and with the voluptuous rhythm of the tango throbbing in her blood Cassie thought I suppose I can see now why chastity is considered a good thing; once you've gone beyond the bounds and then stopped, it's awful. I ache with wanting. I can't think about anything else.

Life had now become pale and curiously static, like the world inside a goldfish bowl, and on some nights when she couldn't sleep she would think I'm like Babs; I remember how shocked I was, and now here I am thinking and remembering and dreaming and longing to be horrid again with her own son.

CHAPTER FIFTEEN

'But we have always served Madeira and Bath Oliver biscuits,' Emilia said with her eyebrows raised. 'And I confess that I see no good reason for change.'

'What about a few canapés?' suggested Wilfred. 'Smoked salmon, and things.'

'Smoked salmon in the middle of an industrial slump strikes me as insensitive,' Emilia said. 'Not to say downright common. But then, my moral sensibilities are said by some to be too highly developed for my own comfort.'

'I would never dream of questioning your sensibilities, my darling,' Wilfred said gallantly. 'Madeira and Bath Oliver biscuits are more than adequate, considering the times in which we live.'

'I fear for our dear country under the leadership of this Mr Ramsay MacDonald.'

'It is time the socialists had a turn, Emilia. We must wait patiently to see what they will do.'

'One thing is certain. They can scarcely do less than that incompetent idiot Baldwin.'

'Mr Baldwin was at least honest when he said that there is no easy solution to unemployment. If there were, surely he would have implemented it, if only for selfish reasons.'

'This government is bound to collapse,' Emilia grunted. Then added: 'Two bottles of Madeira? Or had we better have three?'

'Let us say two bottles, and two in reserve. And perhaps we could spread the Bath Olivers with a little *Patum Peperium*?'

'We will see. These final decisions must not be hurried.'

For some years past it had been the custom for Emilia and Wilfred to invite their staff up to the office for a small social gathering in celebration of the academic year's end and the commencement of the summer holiday, and with the passing of time this had come to include one or two old pupils of merit who kept loyally in touch with their alma mater, and a handful of rather staid personnel managers who had been applying to Gathercoles over the years for reliable and competent young shorthand-typists. It was an occasion of gravity and rather careful decorum and always took place at lunchtime on the day the academy was finally closed down until September. Cassie had been attending these functions since her inception as a member of staff, her initial enthusiasm cooling a little with the years until by 1929 she approached them in second-best frock and with a smile of no more than pleasant vagueness.

But this year's little gathering was destined to have a character all of its own; a flavour, a particular bouquet that would remain unmatched by any other vintage before or after, and those participants who lived on to experience more complex and more petulant times would recall Gathercoles' end of 1929 summer term as epitomising all the innocent gaiety of a golden age.

The mood of it began with Emilia herself, who woke early. Watching the play of light on the bedroom ceiling she remembered that this was the last day of term and that dear little Miss Whittaker, who had been lent by the academy to Lord Gunter Blake for ornithological purposes, was now back from the Scilly Isles and had promised to be present among the guests. She had been away far longer than originally envisaged, and although she had said nothing so far about taking up her old position, which in the meanwhile had been filled by Cassica, Emilia was not worried, for she had a delightful surprise up her sleeve. Miss Williamson, Miss Whittaker's erstwhile colleague and fellow instructor, had only last week confided the fact of her impending engagement to the gentleman who was personal private assistant to the Clerk of the Lancashire County Council, so her position on the staff would fall vacant in due course. This could therefore be offered to Miss Whittaker, thus leaving Cassica in the same position as hitherto, and this in turn would leave dear Miss Sturgeon, who taught book-keeping, in *her* same position.

My staff, thought Emilia fondly, and all of them in their rightful positions which they have earned by their own industry and application. As I am loyal to them, so have they remained loyal to me. She looked forward with maternal pride to making the announcement of Miss Williamson's engagement.

Wilfred awoke, stretching and gasping and rumpling his cheerful yellow hair which still had no more than the odd thread of silver.

'Last day of term, loved one.'

'So it is.' He disappeared briefly in a paroxysm of noisy yawns.

'Furthermore, I have an announcement to make.'

'Yes, I know. Miss Williamson.'

'No. This is a private one.'

Wilfred emerged from beneath the sheet with smiling eyes. He smoothed his hair in an effort to appear, even in bed, the acceptable model of a legal, fully-recognised partner in Liverpool's most august commercial academy. *Gathercole & Sissley*. How the name tripped off the tongue. How often during the past twenty-odd years he had thought of it, not so much in terms of avarice but as a means of binding Emilia and himself into some sort of official relationship. It seemed an alternative to the tender ties of marriage, which were still being denied them, and it would not be his fault if being made a partner brought certain financial advantages. He loved Emilia with a single-minded simplicity that had never faded, never once faltered; at the same time, he would have loved to own a Daimler open tourer.

'Tell me, my darling.' Dispensing with dignity he cuddled up to her and his fingers found the rigorously buttoned front of her nightgown.

'Don't do that, dearest. You will make me cold.'

'I was only counting them. Do tell me the news.'

'I first opened my academy in 1891,' Emilia began, clearing her throat, 'and for two years before that I was teaching clerking, as it was then called, in two rooms. It is therefore a matter of fact as well as a matter of quiet personal pride that I have now been pursuing my chosen profession for forty years.'

'Forty years,' repeated Wilfred reverently. 'And so, you are thinking of marking the occasion by some special act of an official nature?'

'Yes, I am. In fact, I have already done so. I have ordered a cake from Reece's.'

'Oh, how splendid.' Fingers at rest on the buttons of her nightgown, eyes closed in resignation; Gathercole still just Gathercole without the Sissley. From somewhere in the distance his ears seemed to catch the expensive chug-chug of a receding Daimler.

'Is that all?'

'I think it is quite sufficient,' Emilia said. 'That, and a little savoury something on the biscuits.'

He raised his head and kissed her cheek. 'Bless you, my darling,' he said, 'and my most loving congratulations on your fortieth anniversary.'

The big brass geyser in the bathroom was a recalcitrant creature, apt to explode in a dramatic blue flash when lighted taper was applied; bottles would be blown off the shelf, and on more than one occasion Emilia, clad in hairnet and kimono, had been forced by its flames and fumes to retreat across the landing. On this particular morning, however, it behaved with commendable docility and, bathed, dried and dressed in corsets, bust bodice and petticoat, she stood before the mirror curling her fringe with the irons heated by the row of blue flame teeth while it heated Wilfred's bath water.

Forty years a teacher of commercial subjects . . . ! Here I am at sixty-two, she thought, well past my prime yet still a reasonably commanding figure. My eyes seem to have become a little smaller, but that is only due to the collapse of certain unimportant muscles in the vicinity; my skin is still smooth, my lips still full if I remember to pout them a little, and my hair is still lustrous and plentiful. All in all, I must be grateful for such mercies as time and a benevolent Creator have allowed me. I seem to be ending with far more than I began, and although modesty would naturally forbid my boasting that I am in any way personally responsible . . .

A little puff of smoke arose from the curling irons. Dexterously she detached them and applied them to another portion of fringe. No, all things considered she looked very well indeed, and to mark this special day she resolved to wear the agate brooch Wilfred had given her. Dear Wilfred. Her small eyes shone with tenderness as she thought of him. No man could ever have proved more of a boon and a life's treasure, and gaily tossing a handful of gravel-like bath salts into his bath she sailed back to the bedroom vowing that on her fiftieth anniversary she would make him a partner in the Gathercole Academy.

Gathercole & Sissley, she thought. How elegant it would sound. Her mood of calm happiness lasted throughout the morning. As classes had ended the day before there were no pupils on the premises, but there was a certain amount of ritual paperwork, of checking, filing, tidying, locking and latching to be got through before the academy could officially be termed closed.

By twelve o'clock the white damask tablecloth had been spread over Emilia's desk, and the two portraits on the wall opposite looked down upon the large fruit cake, the Bath Olivers coated with chicken-and-ham paste, the polished glasses and the two bottles of Madeira.

'On second thoughts, it might be advisable to open a third,' conceded Emilia, twitching at a small bowl of flowers. 'Not only is it my personal celebration, but we have also Miss Williamson's engagement to think of.'

'Plus the return of Miss Whittaker from the Scilly Isles.'

'And the commencement of the summer holidays! Mr Sissley, I think that you and I will drink a quiet little toast before our guests arrive . . .'

Wilfred poured, and they touched glasses.

'Darling Emilia, I love you so.'

'Hush, my loved one. Remember where we are.'

They drew apart, guilty as two adolescents, as they heard a tap on the door. It was Cassie.

'Is there anything more I can do, Miss Gathercole?'

'Where is Mavis? And is she wearing a clean cap and apron?'

'She looks impeccable in clean everything, and she's hovering in the hall ready to open the door to people.'

'Dear Cassica,' Emilia said impulsively. 'How well that frock becomes you.'

'Thank you, Miss Gathercole. I think you look rather splendid, too.'

They stood contemplating one another gravely while Wilfred poured a third glass of Madeira.

Although the hideous threat naturally posed by Cassie's impromptu visit to the Hoylake house had been answered by a swift counter-threat by Emilia, neither had taken advantage of her situation. Instead, both waited with apprehension during the weeks which followed for evidence of the other's duplicity — Emilia listening for covert sniggers and watching for scandalised parents to remove their daughters from her establishment, and Cassie expecting the private interview that would end in her dismissal. But in fact both of them strove hard to maintain the illusion that all was the same as before, and instead of opening a painful chasm between them it became apparent that Cassie's social blunder had created an unacknowledged bond.

For the first day or so after discovering that Miss Gathercole and Mr Sissley were living in sin together, Cassie had been too amazed and bemused even to think of telling anyone else. Only once during the course of the following weeks had there been a moment of temptation to confide the earth-shattering scandal to Effie; the desire to share the secret with her, and to be able to laugh at the two naughty old things was, for an instant, almost overwhelming, yet something made her keep silent. Whether it was loyalty or mere selfish prudence she didn't know, but the desire for gossip passed and now whenever she thought of the relationship at all it was with a certain protectiveness.

Miss Gathercole still had the power to antagonise with her shrewd perceptions and unassailable self-assurance and on more than one occasion Cassie had made a serious study of the job column in the *Liverpool Echo* — had even applied for one or two — yet something continued to hold her; sometimes it seemed like inertia, and sometimes like the dreary caution that debilitates girls who are no longer in their first careless flush, but whatever it was she could read the knowledge of its existence in the astute currant eyes of her employer. As for Wilfred, his manner towards her was precisely the same as it had always been, yet she could never forget his touching concern for her on the day she inadvertently put her foot through his and Emilia's private world.

She could only suppose that in a funny sort of way she was rather fond of them both, and that they must be fond of her, which was why they were offering her a glass of Madeira in advance of their other guests.

'Your very good health,' she said.

'And yours, Cassica,' they replied graciously.

The first guests seemed to arrive in one black-suited, stiff-collared clump; Mr Gladstone (a distant relation of *the* Mr Gladstone), who was in shipping; Mr Furnival who was in sugar, Mr Sandhill, marine insurance, and little Mr Torrey who wielded considerable power in the chamber of commerce.

Led by a starched and polished Mavis they proceeded across the hall and up the staircase with impressive dignity, and when they reached the office Mr Furnival, who was something of a fop, raised Emilia's hand to his lips and kissed it.

Miss Williamson sidled in wearing a mauve dress with a bunch of cotton daisies pinned on the shoulder and her neat hair clipped in place by a tortoiseshell hairslide. Love had made her very pink and excitable and she tended to spray saliva when she giggled.

'An *irreplaceable* member of my staff,' Emilia said. 'She will be sadly missed by us all.'

'Sounds as if you're dead,' Cassie muttered, and Miss Williamson tried to trap her giggles in a little lace hanky.

Three ex-pupils arrived; Doris and Peggy and Fiona. They were all private secretaries to men in important positions, and daintily nibbling Bath Olivers they looked round at the rich tobacco-coloured walls, the cluttered accumulation of books and box files and said really, the dear old place hasn't changed at all, has it? They looked like (and, indeed, *were)* the sort of girls who could do 160 words a minute shorthand.

Miss Sturgeon appeared, having locked away the book-keeping equipment and dusted the blackboard for the last time until September. Still stout, still cheerful, when offered a glass of Madeira by Wilfred she said thanks muchly, Mr S., I don't mind if I do.

The only guest who had not so far arrived was Miss Whittaker, and when Emilia saw the door open again she prepared a warm smile of welcome. But it was not Miss Whittaker, it was a cadaverous girl with a lot of blazing red hair and a bottle wrapped in tissue paper tucked under her arm. It took Emilia no more than three seconds to recognise Alfreda Morris, a pupil contemporary with Cassica. She also recognised that Alfreda had gate-crashed her little gathering, but the joyousness of the day coupled with a glass and a half of Madeira forbade her to speak of it.

'Alfreda, my dear child, what a pleasure!'

'Ooh, I'm ever so sorry, Miss Gathercole, I didn't know you'd got something on, like. I only meant to call for Cassie, and got sort of swept up—' She indicated the bottle. 'I just bought this on the way for us to celebrate the end of tairm . . .'

'Put it on the table, dear,' Emilia said. 'I am quite sure it will come in useful.'

Effie did so.

'It is always so rewarding to have old pupils flying back to the nest. Are you in your same position, dear? You must tell me.'

'Yes, roughly,' Effie said.

'And what are your prospects?'

'Fur to middling at the moment. But I've got me eye on vurious altairnatives.'

'How wise. But you must do nothing precipitate, Alfreda. We are living in difficult times . . .'

Effie found Cassie over by the fireplace, topping up Fiona's glass.

'Here, I'm going to get tiddly if you keep doing that!'

'Do you good.'

'I say, you teach here, don't you?'

'That's right.'

'What's it like?'

'It's absolutely ultra-spiffing—' Cassie added a little more to her own glass with a bright smile and her eyes crossed. Fiona moved away to tell Doris that Cassie was up the pole.

'Well, look what's blown in — good old Effing Effie—'

'Don't call me that here! Jesus, Cass, why didn't you warn me about coming? I feel a right twerp—'

'How could I, when I wasn't expecting you?'

'I'd bought a bottle of gin and I thought we'd go back to my place—'

'Have you come into money?'

'Yes, in a way.' Effie leaned closer, her hot breath fanning Cassie's cheek as she tried to make herself heard against the rising crescendo of conversation. 'Listen, petal, they've taken me on in the pen!'

'The what?'

'The pen. You *know,* the Rialto—'

'Effie!' Cassie gazed at her aghast. 'Have you given up your job?'

'No, of course not. It's lightning conductors in the daytime and dancing at night.'

'You'll kill yourself—'

Wilfred came over. Heartily he shook Effie's hand and said how nice it was to see her.

'Nice of you to have me, Mr Sissley. I'm sorry if I—'

'Rather special this year. Miss Gathercole is celebrating forty years of teaching—'

'I mean, I didn't know you'd got something special on—'

'Added to which, there's Miss Williamson . . . a double celebration for us . . .'

Conversations were becoming increasingly fragmented as the noise level grew, and Cassie was the first to see Miss Whittaker easing her way through the animated groups of guests. She appeared somehow larger than before, and her hair looked different. I do believe she's had it touched up, Cassie thought. That's what ornithology does for you.

Over the heads of the others, she watched Emilia greet her, pressing Miss Whittaker's hands between her own, then uncovering them and staring at the left one which lay limp and glittering on her palm. Her eyebrows rose higher and higher until they disappeared beneath the Alexandra fringe. Minutes later someone clapped for silence, and Emilia's voice cried, *'Friends!'*

Silence fell, and with glasses in hand and crumbs of Bath Olivers littering bodice and waistcoat alike they contemplated the regal figure of the academy's principal.

'Dear friends,' said Emilia, 'we are here today not merely to mark yet another ending of my academic year, but to celebrate other and more personal triumphs. We will take the least noteworthy first; this concerns myself, and the chance discovery through the perusal of old files that I have now been teaching commercial subjects for a period of forty years.'

Smilingly she raised her hand against the cries of *'Bravo!'* and *'Impossible!'* 'I have to admit to my own sense of astonishment that time should pass so swiftly, but all I wish to say on this particular matter is that if I have succeeded in planting the feet of merely a *few* young women on the rungs of the commercial ladder that will lead them to success, then my work has not been in vain . . .'

Applause. Cries of *'Hear, hear!'* And over in the corner Wilfred swiftly opening another bottle of Madeira. This was the fourth, and unknown to Emilia there were a further three lined up behind the wastepaper basket.

'And now to more exciting news. Many of you will be familiar with my extremely charming and able colleague Miss Williamson, who has been teaching the art of Pitman shorthand-writing to my pupils for some years now. Miss Williamson, you will be delighted to learn, is to be married this coming September to Mr — to Mr ah Herbert Glover of the Lancashire County Council, and in presenting this small gift on behalf of the Gathercole Academy, my dear Miss Williamson, all I can do is to wish you every joy, and to console myself with the knowledge that my loss is Mr Glover's gain.'

More applause. Emilia handing an envelope to Miss Williamson, who blushed and giggled and fired a small volley of saliva over Mr Gladstone. At Wilfred's suggestion they all raised their glasses and drank to the health of the future bride and groom.

'And if that were not sufficient excitement for one day,' continued Emilia, 'I have some especially wonderful news with which I myself was only made conversant some ten minutes ago. My other dear and valued colleague Miss Whittaker, who for some time now has been on loan in an official capacity to Lord Gunter Blake, the eminent ornithologist, has returned from the Scilly Isles with the glad tidings that she too is about to be married!'

Gasps. Little murmurs. Surreptitious sippings. Enjoying herself enormously, Emilia raised her own glass and moistened her lips before dropping the bombshell.

'And who, you might well ask, is to be the lucky man? I will tell you. It is no less than Lord Gunter himself. Our dear Miss Whittaker is in fact about to become Lady Blake of Tarleton Tracy!'

There was an especially searing gasp from Doris, Peggy and Fiona. Effie looked thunderstruck for a moment, then gave a raucous cheer. Everyone cheered. They raised their glasses again — and again — and it was Cassie who finally made herself heard above the rapturous uproar.

'Listen, everybody, listen! I've got my camera downstairs — let's go out in the garden and take some snaps!'

Glasses in hand they hurried down the stairs, some a little unsteadily, with Mr Furnival endeavouring to kiss Miss Sturgeon as they went — 'Don't feel left out of things, my dear, there is still plenty of time . . .' and out in the little paved garden the late July sun sparkled on the old flagstones and sooty leaves, and its genial holiday warmth raised their spirits even higher.

With her box Brownie in one hand, Cassie tried to marshal them all into some sort of order, then became aware of the girls from the pillbox factory sitting on the fire escape, watching and munching their miserable bread and cheese. Overcome with sudden affection, she called to them to come down.

They looked awkward and abashed and shook their heads.

'Come on — come down! Come and have your picture taken—'

'Yes, come on — do come!'

Although in the past they had always appeared so brash and so common, now it was like trying to coax a litter of timid little kittens down from a tree. They hesitated, bit their lower lips, mumbled excuses about being in their overalls, and it was not until Emilia herself stepped forward and told them sharply not to shilly-shally that they did as they were told.

They crept down one behind the other while Wilfred and Effie sprinted back to the office for the rest of the bottles and some more glasses, and it became one of those times when the world stands still and leaves everyone free to love everyone else.

They mixed and mingled happily and without constraint, calico overalls and pin-striped trousers; girls with engagement rings, girls with none. They laughed and joked, sipped and cheered and ate the cake from Reece's, and they used the whole reel of film to record for posterity the day when the class barriers fell in Hockenhall Street. And when the bell rang for the pillbox girls to return to work they insisted on first linking hands with everyone round the old fig tree and singing 'Auld Lang Syne'.

They went back up the fire escape, waving their hands and crying Liverpool's immortal term of farewell: 'Ta-rah . . . ! Ta-rah, love . . . !'

There were tears in everyone's eyes.

'Splendid, splendid girls,' Emilia murmured, many hours later.

'Salt of the earth . . .'

'And I think we managed very nicely on two bottles of Madeira — or did we breach a third?'

'Not altogether certain . . .'

'And by the way, what was in the one that dear Alfreda brought for us?'

'Lemonade,' Wilfred said, eyes closed, head swimming. 'Just fizzy lemonade, my darling.'

* * *

Within two months Effie had an amber cigarette holder, a gold cigarette case and lighter, and a gold powder compact. At least, they looked like gold, which would do for now; the next ones would be solid 18 carat with engraved monogram.

'God, I'm fed up with Gathercoles and all those stupid girls.'

'Come in the pen with me, then.'

'I can't. It's not what I want.'

'What *do* you want?'

'That's the trouble, I don't really know.'

'Strikes me you want another fella.'

'No, I don't.'

'Well, shurrup grumbling.'

'What I want,' Cassie said finally, 'is success on my own terms. I want to achieve it myself, through my own perspicacity.'

'What's perspicacity?'

'It's — oh, it's vision, it's the ability to recognise the golden chance when you see it — and then the ability to grab it and make a great success of yourself.'

'In that case we both want the same thing.'

'We have the same *goal*,' Cassie said, 'but I think we part company over the way we're prepared to achieve it.'

'Ooh, God, you're so bloody pompous—'

'I'm thinking of going back to London.'

'You're always saying that, but you never go.'

'When I think that I won a place at Cambridge—'

'Where they all say parth and barth—'

'Oh, shut up, Effie. Let me be fed up in peace, can't you?'

'I know why you're fed up. It's because you're thairty.'

'Well, you're going to be thirty next year.'

'Maybe,' Effie said. 'But a lot can happen before then, can't it?'

In fact, Effie's outlook had never seemed brighter. Still working as a gruff but competent secretary by day, she lived for the evenings when the lights went up outside the Rialto, illuminating the twin white domes and the giant hoardings that advertised Gloria Swanson, Al Jolson and the wonders of talking pictures.

It was so warm inside, and it smelt so nice. It was so big and rich and beautiful with its white marble and black wrought iron, and at last she belonged there. The commissionaire always touched his cap and said good evening, miss.

Mounting the staircase in one of her two cut-price evening frocks — Bold Street models would come later — was like mounting towards heaven, that soft-padded place with sweet music and kind lighting where rich men fell in love with poor girls and lifted them out of the Depression and the dole queues and having the week's tramcar fares stacked on the mantelpiece and always dipping into it for something else like stockings or a hair-trim or an extra bun for lunch.

Her ballroom dancing was now as competent as her shorthand-typing, and like the others in the pen she adopted a pseudonym; as Jim was Maxim, Ron was Rudie and Gladys was Tanya, so Effie after due consideration became Mitzi. The others were quite nice to her in a casual sort of way, and all observed a strict code of conduct about not pinching each other's clients. For they all had their regulars; Tanya had a silent flint-faced man on Tuesdays and Thursdays and was always booked for the evening of Fridays (which was Residents' Night) by a funny old fella whose jowls bounced in rhythm with his nimble little feet.

Ron who was Rudie (and boyish) had a collection of elderly ladies who liked to pat his cheek, and Jim's (that is, Maxim's) regular every Monday was a thin and exquisitely dressed woman in her fifties who danced with him hungrily, as if she had been shut away in a box all week. Her name, she said, was Babsie.

It cost a shilling for three dances, and if the pros were kindly disposed towards one another it was partly because of the need to present a united front against the common enemy, that bumptious little runt up there on the bandstand wagging his silly baton and thinking he was Jesus Christ Almighty. For it was he who literally called the tune, and who thought nothing of cheating footsore pros by playing four tunes straight off, instead of only three. It's just that the mood was right, he would say. I only did it because the mood was right and I didn't want to break the spell.

Then Effie, who was now Mitzi, acquired her own regular, and that was when it all started happening.

He was a black-haired man, not all that old (she put him at about forty-five), with sallow good looks and a gold eyetooth that flashed when they danced together beneath the big cut-glass prism. He had a fascinating accent with a sort of lisp to it and he told her that he was Spanish and that his name was Lopez.

'You are a beautiful girl, Mit-thi.'

'Thanks. You're not so dusty yourself.'

'Where I come from all the girls are dark. Your hair is a wonderful colour, Mit-thi.'

'Ginger.'

'Ginger, no no. It is bold and brilliant and very, very rare. It denotes a girl of great passion.'

'Uh-huh.'

'Are you a passionate girl, Mit-thi?'

'Try me,' she said laconically.

He took her out to dinner, and she learned that he held an important diplomatic post at the Argentinian consulate in Liverpool.

'I thought you said you were Spanish.'

'My family is dethended from Pedro de Mendoza who founded Buenos Aires. We are one of the first original families in Argentina.'

'Gerraway . . .'

He was very attractive, he tangoed marvellously, and she became indignant when Tanya dismissed him as an oily little dago. She found herself sticking up for him, and when he gave her a gold bangle almost fell in love with him. Almost, but not quite, because she knew what rotters men were.

He asked her how much she earned, and she said not much. And because she had put a down-payment on a fox fur cape in Swears & Wells, went on to tell him how she had to spend her days slaving in an office in order to pay the rent and keep her poor old gran in a posh home at the seaside. He asked which she preferred, dancing or typing, and she said well, dancing, for God's sake.

'That is because you are a passionate girl, Mit-thi.'

'I can be. When I feel like it.'

'I know a plathe where you could earn a lot of money and be adored and admired for your wonderful danthing.'

'Oh?' Hands carelessly busy with pseudo-gold cigarette case and lighter.

'You would be the only girl with red hair, Mit-thi, and you could become very rich and famouth.'

'Oh? Where?'

'In the capital of my country. In Buenos Aires.'

'You're daft.'

But gradually it appeared that he was not. He told her that in Buenos Aires there was a wonderful hotel with a theatre and a ballroom where they would pay almost incalculable salaries to beautiful English girls with red hair in order to dance with them. Just dance; no more. As a matter of fact the hotel in question was owned by his sister Carla, who is very sweet and simpatico like yourself, and she would insist that you live with us in our family and be loved and looked after and carefully chaperoned just like the daughter of any big and splendid family. And you would forget all about offices and hard work and grey skies and poverty and be able to send much, much money home to England for your grandmother to live in luxury until the end of her life . . .

'Go on, pull the other one.'

But he showed her photographs of himself taken with his mother and father, his uncle the duke, and his sister Carla; and of his house, which was enormous and white and ornamented with curling wrought iron just like the Rialto.

'What else would they want me to do? Don't tell me just dance the tango?'

He reached for her hand, covered it with his own soft white one and gazed deep into her eyes. And he told her very quietly and emphatically that Argentina was a Roman

Catholic country where all women were sacred. They were honoured and respected, cherished and highly esteemed not only for their beauty but for their brains as well. In Argentina the virtue of women was venerated, was regarded with wonder and reverence and extolled in poetry and song, but — his hand slipped a little way up her arm — he was not able to swear before the Virgin that she might not receive a very good offer of marriage. Because she was, after all, so very beautiful and radiant and clever and simpatico.

She didn't believe any of it. She thought the whole thing was a scream, and told him so. But somehow the idea of it kept her awake at night.

CHAPTER SIXTEEN

'There aren't many Spaniards in Liverpool, you know.'

'No. I daresay.'

'Which makes him right exotic.'

'Effie,' Cassie said, 'a Neanderthal would be right exotic riding a bike down Dale Street, but that'd be no good reason for throwing in your lot with him.'

'What's an effing Neanderthal?'

'Oh, never mind. Just a figure of speech.'

They discussed it endlessly; the pros and cons, the possibility that it might be the chance of a lifetime against the old story of girls always getting caught by men and done the dirty on.

'I've never met a man yet, chicken, who isn't ready to do you down.'

'Maybe he's different.'

'Aah, they're all the same. They're all bastards.'

'But just suppose this one isn't?'

There were times when they seemed to change sides; Cassie arguing for, and Effie against. Once, worn down by the to-and-fro, Cassie asked if she could meet him in order to judge for herself, but Effie proved curiously evasive. He's busy, she said. He's very busy wairkin' in his consulate-thing . . . It was as if she were already part of some sort of conspiracy.

Cassie got fed up with it and left her alone. It was during a period of maximum dissatisfaction with the Gathercole Academy — Emilia was proving exceptionally high-handed, and the lady teacher engaged in place of Miss Williamson was obsequious and mousily prim and wanted Cassie to join the Church of England Temperance Society. In a fit of rebellion she applied for an audition with the Liverpool Repertory Company. They asked her how she was on Shaw and Shakespeare. Fine, she said. They gave her a dog-eared script of *Romeo and Juliet* and she turned over two pages at once and cried: 'It was the nightingale and not the lark that pierced the fearful shadow of thy bottom . . . of a tomb.'

'Thank you, dear,' they said. 'If we've an opening we'll let you know.' So she took a taxi back to Gathercoles and had a short sharp row in the hall with Emilia because she was late.

'We are here not only to teach but to set an example.'

'I am paid to teach, but my private life is my own.'

'Not if it extends into the hours for which you are engaged to instruct my pupils.'

'If my work is considered unsatisfactory, perhaps you will kindly inform me.'

'I am informing you now.'

'Then I must ask for my cards.'

'They are in the office. Pray see me when the academy closes.'

Snip-snap, snip-snap, like two pairs of scissors. Two women, one still young and the other growing old, glaring at one another in the thundery light coming from the stained-glass window; Emilia harassed and crotchety because Wilfred had just been notified that he must find alternative accommodation for his wife, as the nursing home in which she had lain for so many years was to be closed. *Why can't she die? Why doesn't she die?*

How awful if I get to look like her when I'm old, Cassie thought. It's something I've got to avoid at all costs . . .

Yet they patched it up, and a few days later Emilia graciously admitted that Cassie had a certain flair for coaxing the best out of the more dim-witted pupils.

Winter set in early that year, soft weeping rain turning to icy needles that stung the face and crunched underfoot. Wounded ex-servicemen, their medals a little tarnished now, still hobbled and limped and crept along the gutters with caps extended, and one of the daily papers printed a reader's letter saying that they earned far too much with their mournful dirges and had no right to batten on the good nature of ordinary decent people who had to work for their living the hard way.

Standing at the tram stop opposite John Lewis's one raw Saturday morning Cassie became aware of a familiar figure standing with back turned a little ahead of her. Thin shoulders bowed beneath a thin overcoat, a trilby hat with the brim turned down all round and the rain dripping off, and when he turned his head a little, a pair of small round metal-framed spectacles hooked over large ears. The tramcar arrived, and in the flapping of folding umbrellas Cassie all but lost sight of him. She climbed the stairs, and sitting hunched against the steamy window on the brown slat seat was Arnold Openshaw.

She sank down beside him panting, in a flurry of raindrops.

'Arnold!'

'Cassie Marlow! Well, I never.'

'How are you? Oh, Arnold dear, how *are* you?'

'I'm fine — and you?'

'Topping, thanks.' She groped in her wet handbag for her fare.

'Here, let me—'

'No, I wouldn't dream of it—'

'How far are you going?'

'Home. I get off at the corner of Grove Street . . .'

The ding-ding of the tramcar bell. The sharp ping of the ticket machine slung across the conductor's chest.

'Thank you, Arnold. That was awfully nice of you.'

He smiled and rubbed his woolly glove across the window. 'Do you mind if I smoke?'

'No, of course not. Listen, Arnold, I'm sorry I was so nasty the last time—'

'When was that?' He sounded tired, dispirited, almost uninterested.

'When you came back after the march. You were so nice and forgiving and everything and I do realise now that it was mostly my fault. I shouldn't have gone—'

'Oh, that. That's all right, Cassie.' For the first time he turned to look at her as he stuffed tobacco into a briar pipe. The odd raindrop still dripped from his hat brim into his lap and his eyes were kindling with affection. 'It's all so long ago now.'

'Yes, I know, we're getting quite old. And I worry—'

'You mustn't do that.' Laying the unlit pipe on his knee he took her hand and pressed it briefly. 'It's all over now.'

'And you're not fed up with me anymore?' It was strange how much it mattered.

'No, of course not, you silly girl.' He released her hand and fumbled in his coat pocket for matches.

'Are you back in Liverpool for long?'

'No, only for a couple of weeks.'

'How's the cause these days? And your work and everything?'

'Oh, the struggle goes on.'

'Are you winning?'

'We will in the end. Capitalism is doomed and only socialism can take its place. Worldwide socialism is the only answer. It's inevitable.'

'I just can't visualise everyone everywhere placidly agreeing to the same system. I mean everybody's so different, and they seem to hate the idea of being in agreement about quite little things, never mind—'

'Cassie dear.' He lit his pipe, put away the matches and took her hand again. 'Don't let's talk politics. It only spoils things.'

'Yes, I agree.' She smiled at him fondly through the haze of smoke. 'The hell with politics — come back and see my flat and I'll cook us some lunch. I've got a nice little place in Falkner Square.'

'I'm afraid I can't. You see—' He let go of her hand again. 'I'm married now.'

'Married?' The tramcar gave a pained scream as it swung round into Catherine Street. 'You — married?'

'Yes. For over a year.'

'But, who to?' The shock almost winded her. She felt sick. 'Oh, Arnold . . .'

'To a very nice girl called Betty. We shared the same digs in Clapham. She was an elementary schoolteacher, and we found we had a lot in common.'

'Like politics?'

'She's politically active, yes.'

'Where is she now?' (I don't want to meet her, I don't want to meet her.)

'She's sitting downstairs.'

'What, on this tram?'

'Yes. She doesn't like smoke.'

'Oh. Oh, well.' There was nothing more to say. Shattered and suddenly painfully bereft, Cassie got up from the seat. 'This is where I get off, as you might say.'

'Goodbye, Cassie dear.'

'Are you happy?' She shouldn't have asked, but she couldn't help it.

'Yes. We're both very happy indeed.'

'That's good. Well, goodbye then, Arnold.'

'Goodbye, Cassie.'

She lurched away, clinging to the backs of the seats as the tram jolted to a halt. She paused for a moment before alighting and looked through to the inside of the tram where the passengers sat facing each other in two long rows. They were mostly women; fat and thin, old and young; women with babies, a woman with a bundle of washing.

And one of them was Arnold's wife, the woman who had had the cheek to appropriate what for so long Cassie had regarded as her own.

* * *

She had to tell someone, and the obvious person was Effie. Without bothering to go home she went straight to the bed-sitter over the Gransby Street ironmongers but there was no reply to her knock, just a bony-kneed little girl sitting on the stairs reading a comic who said the lady's out, missus.

She walked back down the street, looking in open shop doorways for the thatch of insolent ginger hair, the angular figure clad in garments partly chic and partly back-street market ('Won't be long now, petal, before I'm all of a piece, like . . .') but there was no sign of her. Thrumming with the desire for a heart-to-heart Cassie turned reluctantly in the direction of Falkner Square.

Oh, Effie, you could have knocked me down with a feather. I felt my heart give this terrible leap when I only *thought* I saw him at the tram stop, then when I saw that it was really him I nearly died. Because he's the boy I've loved all along, Effie. I knew it, in that split second. And now after all my years of secret loving and caring, hoping and yearning, Effie, here I am cast off like a glove. Flung aside like an old *shoe*. Oh, Effie dear, the pain, the *pain* . . .

The pain made her ravenous. Without bothering to remove her hat she slung a knob of lard into the frying pan, swirled it round and then broke three eggs into its sizzling centre. Brutally she mashed them around until they solidified, then tipped them on to a plate. The rest of the fat she absorbed into a hunk of bread.

No, I'm kidding, Effie. I don't feel any pain. Why should I? I'm not the sort to. Arnold Openshaw — a lower-class name with delusions of grandeur — has never meant anything to me. He may have been a proud Communist and all that but his private emotions were servile. Oh, you'd never believe how he grovelled. I could have wiped the floor with him. Trodden on his ears — and God knows they were big enough . . .

Having consumed the eggs and fried bread at the kitchen table she then ate two bananas washed down with a cup of strong tea and felt much better. Calmer. Less tragic, and at the same time less coldly vindictive. She lit a cigarette, lay back on the sofa and tried to read *Vogue*. But it was no good. She couldn't settle, couldn't concentrate for thinking about Arnold Openshaw being actually married. To a woman. To a woman called Betty Openshaw. What was she like? Blonde or brunette? Pretty, or just passable? All he had said was that she was an ex-schoolteacher, politically active. And that she didn't like the smell of smoke. She wished now that she had stayed on the tram until the next stop and given herself more time in which to scrutinise the faces of the inside passengers.

Restlessly she wandered round the flat, then on impulse hurried back to the bedroom and changed into a dark crêpe de Chine frock. She powdered her nose, applied some lipstick, pressed two sleek kiss-curls against either cheek, then hurried off with mackintosh and umbrella towards the Rialto.

The tea-dance was already in progress, the floor fairly crowded. A waitress with a tray balanced high on the palm of her upturned hand showed her to a small and inconspicuous table against the wall.

'Meeting a friend, are you, madam?'

Aware that unaccompanied females were looked upon with disfavour, Cassie gave her a level stare and said what awful weather we're having.

Sitting back in her green wickerwork chair she scoured the floor for Effie. She caught sight of her, magnificent beneath a carefully arranged coiffure of blazing red, sailing briskly before the saxophone-wind with an elderly pinstriped man clinging to her harsh bosom like an undersized sailor lashed to the rigging of a schooner.

Cassie tried to catch her eye as she swept past. Effie didn't notice. The waitress reappeared with a pot of tea for one and a salver of little sandwiches decorated with mustard and cress. 'When your friend arrives, I will repeat the order,' she said.

'I'm most grateful.'

'Not at all, madam.' She marched away, stiff as a protestant at a papal jubilee.

Repeatedly Cassie tried to catch Effie's attention. At the end of the three dances she saw her relinquish hold of her pin-striped client and then flash him a brief smile of professional saccharine sweetness before strolling back to the pros' table. She leaned back in her chair and lit a cigarette, inhaling deeply, and although Cassie waved to her she didn't see. Another client presented himself at the table and she was off again.

Rio Rita—
Life is sweeta, Rita,
When you are near . . .

A bald man approached Cassie and asked if she would care to dance. Watched beadily by the waitress, Cassie politely declined. She poured out another cup of tea, and the need to tell Effie about Arnold Openshaw became increasingly urgent. She couldn't wait. Effie, listen, what do you *think?*

The throbbing sobbing of saxophones. The wailing of a violin. The chap who sang the refrain plunking at the strings of a banjo, and the leader, smart, winking, dinky, doggish, with patent leather hair and a wide white smile waving his baton up there on the stand framed in gold trellis, paper roses and painted hollyhocks in the marvellous make-believe summer garden where everyone was rich and happy and mysteriously beautiful in the cunning, caressing light.

The third time Effie returned to the table by the band the waitress had just brought a fresh pot of tea. She poured one, lit another cigarette, and squinting vampishly through the smoke suddenly beheld Cassie standing in front of her.

'It's something when it costs me a bob to damn well talk to you.' She slapped the dance ticket down among the little gold trinkets. Involuntarily the pro called Rudi rose to his feet.

'No, not you, thank you. Her.'

'You can't sit here, chicken, the manager doesn't like it—'

'Well all right, let's *dance* then—'

Effie stubbed out her cigarette with a sigh and rose to her feet.

'You'd be much better off with me, dear,' Rudi said, sinking back again.

'What makes you so sure?'

Watched with a certain amount of bland curiosity Cassie and Effie took to the floor. It was a quick step.

'Listen, Effie, I had to talk to you. What d'you think?'

'Gathercoles has burnt down.'

'No — Arnold Openshaw's gone and got married!'

'Gerraway—' Their feet collided. 'Look, who's leading who?'

'Oh, you do it. I met him on a tram, Effie, and you could have knocked me down with a feather—'

'I thought he was in London.'

'So did I. To be quite honest I hadn't actually been losing sleep over him, but when I saw him so unexpectedly—'

'Left foot — your *left*—'

'Sorry. Yes, when I saw him so unexpectedly, it had quite a catastrophic effect. I couldn't seem to breathe for a minute or two, and then I realised that I do really love him, Effie. *That* way, I mean.'

'And now he's married someone else.'

Strutting, stepping, gliding and sliding, Cassie wished that Effie could be a little less matter-of-fact. Love wasn't something you could lightly dismiss, particularly when you were thirty. And she had loved Arnold, and still did; she had been a long time recognising it, but now the pain of it throbbed like an illness and she wished they weren't doing a quick step. It was too brutally bright.

Then she remembered Effie's Lopez.

'How's yours?'

'My what?'

'Your Spanish chap.'

'I told him to sling his hook.'

'And did he?'

'Haven't seen him since.'

Effie had always been of a laconic disposition, but now the sophisticated world of the Rialto had added a coating of blasé world-weariness that Cassie half-admired and half-disparaged.

'Well, that's all right then. But I thought you'd like to know about Arnold—'

'Why didn't you come round to Granby Street and save yourself a shilling?'

'I did, but you weren't there. You're never in, these days.'

'Too busy—'

'Making money?'

'Christ, chicken, shift your feet . . .'

By the end of the third dance they were laughing and joking in the old way.

'See that fella over thur?'

'Aye.'

'Well, he's bin married three times and his last wife was Tairkish.'

'Gerraway!'

'Aye. An' in Tairkey they like big fat women, so they just sit round on the floor all day eating Tairkish delight and ooh, they don't ever do any wairk . . .'

They parted fondly, Cassie having invited Effie to lunch at Falkner Street on the following day.

She made a shepherd's pie and put a blancmange to set overnight on the cold kitchen window ledge. She bought a bottle of wine at the off-licence and woke up next morning to the bells of St Saviour's and thinking no one could go on, if it wasn't for Sundays. Arnold forgotten, she was glad she had invited Effie to lunch.

But Effie didn't arrive. The shepherd's pie had a golden crust, the blancmange had set and everything else was ready, but still no Effie. Cassie sat in the window sipping a little preliminary gin and orange and watching for the red bonfire of hair coming round the corner from Grove Street. She waited, cursing, until two o'clock, then with a sudden rush of anxiety put on her coat and hat and dashed round to the bedsitter above the ironmonger's shop.

The door was on the latch. *'Cooee — Effie!'* Silence, and a curious brooding stillness hanging over the clothes and the dance shoes and the Harlequin doll on the bed and the teapot still half full of cold tea.

But no Effie. The child with the thin knees was lingering shadowlike at the bend in the stairs and Cassie asked if she had seen Miss Morris this morning. The child shook her head, then bolted back into the gloom. So Cassie went home again, now more intrigued than perturbed.

In the meantime, Effie had not arrived at the flat. The shepherd's pie was beginning to get dry, so Cassie sat down to eat on her own, and thought if she does come now all she'll get is a cup of tea and a biscuit.

For the first time she could remember, Sunday was stretching itself into an infinity of boredom, and after lunch she flung herself bad-temperedly into the chair with the *Sunday Despatch*. A small column on the front page caught her eye:

> *The evil of White Slave Traffic is once more rearing its ugly head and young British womanhood is again under threat, particularly in our seaports and big cities. Young girls have been reported missing under mysterious circumstances in London, Birmingham, Manchester and Liverpool, and others have recently reported having been importuned by strange men, and occasionally women, with the promise of interesting and lucrative work in foreign countries, notably those of South America. Our police force is investigating each case with scrupulous care but the secret, sordid world of the White Slaver is difficult to penetrate, and baffles even the most astute . . .*

She read it again. Then dropped the paper in her lap, and slowly and dreadfully the facts began to fit together.

'And have you informed the police of your suspicions?'

'No, not yet. I wanted to talk it over with you, first.'

'I am flattered.'

'That wasn't my intention — I just thought you might have some advice about what to do next.'

'During the course of my career I have become acquainted with many varieties of human activity, but I am thankful to say that the practice of white slavery has not been one of them.'

'I'm sorry I bothered you.'

'Come now, there is no call for peevishness.'

It so often went like that between Cassie and Emilia; one of them in a mood of trustful affection which the other would destroy with an involuntary rebuff. They rarely seemed to manage an encounter in the same frame of mind; above all, they never seemed capable of sustained detachment, or neutrality. Sooner or later one always upset the other, and while Emilia shook her head over Cassie's inability to progress beyond irritating and precocious schoolgirl, Cassie was not slow to mutter criticism of Emilia as the eternally bossy headmistress.

'I was not being peevish.'

'No, dear, of course you were not.'

Suddenly capitulating, Emilia folded her arms on her desk and looked at Cassie from under her fringe. The academy was silent except for the muffled stamp-stamp of machinery up in the pillbox factory. The classes had ended, the students had gone home and Cassie would have gone home too if it hadn't been for a powerful urge to seek advice from Emilia. They both made a conscious effort to start again.

'I'm very worried about her. I know she's quite old enough to take care of herself, but from the tales you hear about White Slave Traffic it sounds as if no one would stand a chance if they'd really got you marked down, what with nice old ladies digging hypodermics into girls' legs in cinemas—'

'It is a mistake to believe all one hears, particularly of a lurid nature. Just repeat to me the facts concerning Alfreda herself.'

Cassie did so, trying to make Effie's involvement with the Rialto ballroom sound as if it were based on a fondness for physical exercise. She repeated all she knew about Lopez, about his blandishments and exotic promises, and ended with the disappearance of Effie without any of her personal belongings.

'I called round there again last evening and she still wasn't back, and first thing this morning I telephoned her office and asked if I could speak to her and they said she hadn't come to work.'

'Yet you say she appeared to have severed her relationship with this South American person?'

'That's what she told me, and she always speaks the truth. So it makes me think that perhaps he *is* a white slaver, and meeting with rejection made him turn nasty.'

'Has she no family?'

'Yes. I've never met them, but I believe they live in Birkenhead.'

Emilia sat thinking. 'We must get into touch with them first. They are Alfreda's lawful next of kin, and it is up to them to decide what steps to take.'

'I don't know their address—'

'Presumably the constabulary will be willing to help us there—'

'Wouldn't it be quicker just to tell the police ourselves — about our suspicions, I mean?'

'We must not be too precipitate. For one thing, I am perfectly sure that there will prove to be a logical reason for Alfreda's so-called disappearance, and for another, it would be distinctly unwise for us to raise a hue and cry without first warning her parents. After all, it is quite within the realms of possibility that that is precisely where she is. At home with her family in Birkenhead.'

'Without telling anyone? Without turning up for lunch with me yesterday?'

'A sudden summons. An illness, a family drama; these things generally happen without warning.'

'Yes. I suppose you could be right.'

'So go home now, Cassica, and try to free your mind from worry. And if you should find that Alfreda has returned in the meantime, perhaps you would be good enough to telephone me at Hoylake. Here is my private number.'

They parted. On the way home Cassie called round to Granby Street again, but the door was still on the latch and there was still no Effie. There was not even any sign of the shadowy child. The shops of Granby Street were mostly small, humble and gaslit, but they all bore some token sign of the coming season of goodwill; mince pies in the baker's and mistletoe and tangerines in the greengrocers, but Cassie walked on with eyes averted.

Although she wasn't exactly the mourning type, Christmas for her had become synonymous with tragedy, and as a result it would only add to her profound sense of unease about Effie.

* * *

But Emilia took the news of Effie's suspected abduction with far more concern than Cassie would probably have given her credit for.

She discussed the matter with Wilfred, and when she had succeeded in tracing Effie's family it was he who volunteered to go and see them. She awaited his return with anxiety, fearing some form of mass hysteria on the part of the elder Morrises, but in reality their reception of him had been cool and their reaction to the news of Effie's disappearance no more than one of mild surprise. They said that she had always gone her own way and seemed prepared to leave it at that. Very politely Wilfred pointed out that going all the way so South America, possibly against her own will, could perhaps be a matter of some concern, but once again they shrugged their shoulders and said that our Eff could always look after herself.

It was a small terraced house bursting with people of all ages; a black-clad grandmother rocking a perambulator, wiry red-haired children climbing on the furniture, eating buns and screaming friendly abuse at one another, and a short fat man with ginger freckles and braces hanging at knee-level who offered Wilfred a Guinness and said if you do get to hear anything about our kid, we'd always like to know.

He left them to their noise and their unshakable imperturbability with relief.

Emilia then interviewed the police, saying that an ex-pupil of outstanding ability who had overcome the handicap of a family background that was both uncouth and uncaring had disappeared from her accustomed milieu in mysterious circumstances. They made a careful note of all she told them and promised to look into the matter, but without waiting for proof of their conscientiousness she then paid a call on the Argentinian consulate and discovered, after a certain amount of stilted courtesy on both sides, that they had never recently employed anyone on their premises with the Christian name of Lopez.

'What now?' Wilfred asked, as he and Emilia sipped Ovaltine in front of the fire.

'Alfreda has been missing for seven days,' she said. 'It is therefore time to acquaint the Home Secretary with our suspicions.'

She wrote to him herself, typing the letter on one of the academy's six new Remingtons with a touch impeccably even and phraseology appropriately convoluted.

Sir, I have the honour to address you with regard to the probable whereabouts of an ex-pupil of the above academy, which, as you will note from perusal of our letter-heading, is an institution long noted for the excellence of its standards in connection with the teaching of Pitman shorthand-writing, typewriting, book-keeping and general office procedure. I must stress, however, that our care for Gathercole pupils, both past and present, extends far beyond the realms of fitting them for a business career; we make a point of continuing to take a benevolent interest in their welfare for so long as they care to remain in touch with us, and it will thus be readily understood that the sudden disappearance in what can only be termed circumstances both sinister and ominous of one of our Old Girls has filled both my establishment and myself with considerable alarm . . .

It was a long letter, giving a personal description of Effie (tall, Titian-haired, of good deportment, etc.) and listing her past employers, including the manager of the Rialto ballroom on a spare-time basis.

She then sat back and waited.

'Why didn't she stay with the Royal Maritime Insurance, where we first placed her?'

'Because she was an ambitious, volatile girl, rather in the same mould as Cassica. Which is probably why they were friends.'

'I don't think much of this being a public dancer, or whatever they're called.'

'We must remember that resourcefulness is not always compatible with dignity, loved one.'

'How wise you are, my darling . . .'

Five days later Emilia received a letter regretting that the Home Secretary had no knowledge of the whereabouts of Miss Alfreda Morris, but that if such knowledge should become available he would he pleased to acquaint Miss Emilia Gathercole of the Gathercole Secretarial Academy with it.

She wrote back rather tartly, asking whether in the cloistered confines of Westminster they were aware of the problem of White Slave Traffic. There was a pause of ten days before the same gentleman wrote back, cautiously admitting that the subject of Slave Traffic, White, had indeed been brought to the notice of HM Government, but that so far, no policy save that of watchfulness had been adopted. But at the first sign of any fresh development in a situation both complex and delicate, she, Emilia, could rest assured etc. etc.

The dignified phraseology almost outdid her own and she crumpled the letter into a ball and threw it across the breakfast table. Then she retrieved it, smoothed it flat and added it to the carbon copies of her own letters that she had filed in a buff folder with Effie's initials pencilled on the front.

On 22 December it began to snow and, becoming aware that Cassica was looking rather pale and listless, she did something that she had never even contemplated doing before. On the spur of the moment she invited her to spend Christmas Day in the carefully guarded retreat she shared with Mr Sissley.

CHAPTER SEVENTEEN

'I called in at Swears & Wells the fur shop yesterday,' Cassie said, 'and so far as I'm concerned the final proof that something's happened to her came when they said they'd got this fox fur cape which was all paid up except the final instalment, and that she'd never been back to collect it.'

A blazing coal fire. Shadows twinkling on the tree hung with little silver bells. Cups of China tea and slices of Christmas cake balanced on replete and tranquil laps.

'So I paid the final instalment and the manageress gave me a receipt and said they'd keep it safely until she went back to collect it.'

'Which will be any day now, mark my words,' Wilfred said from the depths of an armchair.

'I once had a sable stole,' Emilia said dreamily, 'which I inherited from my maternal grandmother. But my father's sister, with whom I lived for a time, considered such things effete and threw it to her foxhounds.'

'I do hope she's all right. Effie, I mean.'

'Human nature is remarkably resilient.'

'Yes, I know. And it's all very well for me to believe that when I've just had a nice Christmas Day in the company of—'

'Friends, shall we say?'

'Employers and friends,' Cassie said. 'And I'm very grateful, because mostly I prefer to ignore Christmas.'

'My dear child.' Emilia poured a little more tea. 'Why should that be?'

The room with its white painted walls and windows heavily curtained against the inquisitive world outside seemed to encourage confidences. Accepting another cup of tea Cassie fought against the temptation, then heard herself telling them about Mona. And about that other Christmas with its bravado of paper chains and mistletoe, the man who lent them a bucket in which to boil the pudding inviting them to his stilted little sherry party, and all the primitive, primary-coloured happiness of Christmas Day ending in — ending in . . .

She told them, her head sunk low, two-thirds of her longing for their understanding and, even more contemptibly, their love, while the remaining one-third said where's your pride? For God's sake, where's your pride?

Wilfred and Emilia sat immobilised. They might almost have died.

'I'm sorry,' Cassie said finally, out of the long firelit silence. 'I didn't mean to depress you.'

They said very little; certainly nothing platitudinous like it wasn't your fault, you did what you could, she's better off now and at peace. Yet their understanding seemed to fill the room, and to help heal the old aching grief.

When the day was considered officially over they consulted the train timetable and insisted on walking with her to Hoylake station. The snow had cleared, leaving a starlit sky and the invisible sea growling like an old dog in its sleep. They walked on either side of her, Emilia wearing a toque surmounted by a chiffon scarf tied under her chin, and it was impossible to remain unaffected by the sense of loving strength that came from them. It would be quite wrong ever to think of them as two naughty old things furtively living in sin when they had a dignity, and above all the kind of radiant serenity that could only come from a devotion deepened and finally brought to perfection by the passing of the years.

Perhaps that's what I'm looking for, Cassie thought, and will never find; it's called success in love.

* * *

She thought about it again the following day when the weather had turned milder and brought with it dank yellow-grey garlands of fog. Even at midday the light was no more than a pale smear touching the soot-encrusted houses. The streetlamps were still lit and she walked from one to the next, listening to the echo of her footsteps and drawing the florist's paper closer over the heads of the white carnations she was carrying.

She reached Toxteth Park Cemetery with its dripping trees and dim, marble angels, and was very close to the unmarked grave over by the workhouse wall when she saw that someone was already standing at the foot of it; silent, motionless, a shrouded hump looming darkly in the fog. Her heart began to beat uneasily.

'Hullo — Uncle Harry?' She drew level.

'Cassica . . .'

He was wearing a black bowler hat and a silk scarf folded in the neck of his overcoat. They stood silently assimilating their mutual surprise, then Cassie removed the paper from her flowers and moved forward to lay them at the head of the grave.

'A thoughtful act. I am very grateful.'

'There's no need to be. I come every year.'

'You still think of her?'

'I'll never forget her.'

'No.'

They spoke very quietly, almost in whispers, yet the fog seemed to lift their words and hold them eerily suspended. They continued to stand there, wanting to move away and yet unable to do so. The constraint between them made it impossible to speak of Mona except in a politely trivial way, yet standing by her graveside it was equally out of the question to broach an alternative subject.

Finally, it was Cassie's giving an involuntary teeth-chattering shiver that released them.

'My dear, you're cold. I have my car outside, let me drive you home.'

They turned away and looking back after only a few paces could catch no more than a faint glimmer of Cassie's white carnations through the melancholy fog.

'No Nibbs?' The car was a rather sporty Lagonda and Uncle Harry eased himself behind the wheel.

'Nibbs is still with us, but I decided that the time had come when I should show a little more self-reliance. He taught me the rudiments of driving and I now consider myself to be of capable but not yet virtuoso standard.'

They moved cautiously into Arundel Avenue, Uncle Harry wiping a gloved fist against the murk-laden windscreen.

'Which way?'

'I wish you wouldn't bother. I can easily walk.'

'Not in this weather, don't be foolish.'

So she told him Falkner Square, and he replied that when he was a boy he used to visit an aunt who lived there with a parrot called Livingstone.

'It's all flats now, of course.'

'Yes,' he said, 'the age of littleness is already upon us.'

Although the fog was clearing in places he drove very slowly and carefully. 'Strange to think it's Boxing Day.'

'I hate Christmas now.'

'Because of Mona?' Away from the cemetery they were able to speak of her.

'Yes, I suppose so. Although I spent yesterday with some very nice friends in Hoylake. She's also my employer, incidentally.'

'Oh — Madame Gathercole. Splendid old gorgon, isn't she?' He negotiated the turn from Bentley Road into Granby Street, bumping the kerb very slightly. 'I didn't know she was married.'

'She isn't,' Cassie said. 'She lives with a cousin.'

'She's become one of the characters of Liverpool's commercial world, over the years. And she seemed very fond of you when I called on her.' She noticed how courtesy forbade him to add *when I was seeking your whereabouts in order that I might pay you an allowance.* 'What a long time ago it seems.'

'I'm in my thirties now.'

'Any sign of a young man?'

'Not really. At least, none that I would want to spend the rest of my life with. This is my place — can I offer you a drink?'

He seemed to need little persuasion and accepted a small glass of sherry. (Which was a good thing, because sherry was all she had.) It occurred to her that things were not as they should be when a family man had time on his hands on Boxing Day.

'How's Aunt Babs these days?' The words came easily, for she had forgiven Babs her sins of omission a long while ago.

'Oh, in excellent health. She often speaks of you.'

'Does she? That's nice.'

'Now that the boys are gone, she busies herself with charitable work. I sometimes suspect that she works too hard, but you know your aunt. She is still filled with restless energy, but of course she has more to give of herself than most people.'

'Yes. I remember.'

They sipped, eyeing one another cautiously, speculatively. Cassie remembered that she had always quite liked Uncle Harry, and in spite of his pomposity had rather sympathised with him for being married to Babs.

'But I want to hear about you, Cassica. There must be more to your life than teaching Miss Gathercole's pupils and showing hospitality to an old and rather irascible uncle.'

She smiled. 'I don't find you irascible. In fact, I've often wanted to apologise for the way I behaved when I was living with you. I must have seemed dreadfully precocious and ungrateful.'

'You were lost. A sad little fish in an alien pool, and I'm not at all sure that it isn't I who should apologise to you.'

I shall cry in a minute, she thought. She poured them both a little more sherry and asked brightly how the boys were.

'Lionel is now my junior partner and has become engaged to Moira Eggleton, who is the daughter of Sir Maurice Eggleton the cotton man. They seem very well suited, and Babs and I are delighted.'

'And Desmond?'

'Ah yes, Desmond. If one is to be honest it must be admitted that he caused a certain amount of perturbation to begin with. Didn't seem to know his own mind. In the end he opted for farming in South Africa, and I have to own that I became rather impatient when at the last minute he started some nonsense about changing his mind. I rather gather he had met a girl somewhere, and of course there was not the slightest chance of his marrying and taking her out there. I had set him up in a small citrus farm in the northern Transvaal and although it had cost me a great deal of money there were no facilities for a young wife. The whole idea was totally impractical, and I had to tell him so.'

'How is he now?' Her watch lay in her lap. She picked it up, squinting hard at the dial. 'Do you hear from him?'

'Oh yes, but only irregularly. He seems to have settled down.'

'And he's still not married?'

'No, no. He has promised not to think of marriage until he has made his way and the farm is showing a profit. We still expect him to do well, in due course.'

'To be a success . . .' Aware that he was looking at her curiously, she said: 'I think my watch has stopped. Can you tell me the right time?'

He snapped open the gold hunter that she remembered. 'Ten minutes past twelve, exactly.'

'Listen, Uncle Harry, will you stay for lunch? I've got some nice ham, and a mince pie that I can't eat all by myself—'

She suddenly wanted him to stay more than she had wanted anything in her life. The desire to get to know him, to make friends and to reach beneath the carefully groomed self-esteem to the rather nice, troubled man, was almost painful in its intensity. But he rose from the chair, set down his glass and said that he must be going.

Feeling grey with disappointment she said: 'The last time you came to see me you brought Mona. Nibbs carried the folding bed in, and Mona was like a happy little girl.'

'I was very fond of my daughter, you know.'

A few years ago, moral indignation would have prompted her to demand why in that case he allowed her to be locked up and treated as mentally deficient? The temper inherited from her mother would have flared and there would have been red cheeks and harsh words and an end to any possibility of the quiet give and take of ordered conversation. Now that she understood more, she found that she had fewer words with which to express it.

'Yes, I'm sure you were.'

'Life is never simple.'

'Divided loyalties, and all that.'

He stood in the tiny space that constituted the hall, holding his gloves and his bowler hat. She caught the elusive whiff of gentlemen's cologne.

'I wish you would come and see us, Cassica my dear.'

'Well, I've often meant to, but—'

'Please,' he said. 'It would mean a lot to both of us. Now that the boys are gone, we see little of young folk, except of course those whom Babs is involved with in the course of her social work.'

'I can't really picture Babs doing social work.' She parried. 'What sort is it?'

'She helps with the running of a charity concerning the training of boys from poor homes for the ministry. Some sort of off-shoot from the Church of England, I understand.'

'She's become religious?' The idea was startling.

'That may have something to do with it, although she is not demonstrative about her beliefs. But she has a great gift for organization and I am glad that she has something to occupy her.'

'Yes. It sounds wonderful.'

'So when may we expect you?' He placed his gloves inside the upturned bowler and began tossing them up and catching them, as if he were making pancakes. 'What about seeing the New Year in with us?'

Something made her evasive; pride, possibly. 'I'm going to a dinner-dance with some friends.'

'Ah yes, I daresay. Young people have their own celebrations arranged.'

It was strange how sad a pompous man could look. Pity made her say, 'But I could manage this Sunday afternoon. Would that do?'

He said that he would send Nibbs with the car at three o'clock but she insisted that she would rather walk. He kissed her cheek, and the urge to renew acquaintance with him override her reluctance to return to the scene of former disasters.

The fog had cleared, and she watched him drive cautiously to the end of the square. Going back into the flat she began to wash the two sherry glasses, then on second thoughts washed Uncle Harry's and refilled her own. She carried it over to the armchair and sat down with her feet tucked under her. Sipping, she began thinking over what he had told her about Desmond. Was I the girl? I suppose I'll never know . . .

The thought made her fumble for her handkerchief.

* * *

Emilia unhooked the last of the little silver bells from the Christmas tree and laid it carefully alongside its brothers in the cottonwool-lined box. She detached the Bethlehem star from the summit and the tree stood stark and brownish-green, its fallen needles littering the carpet beneath it.

A melancholy time, she thought. The death of one season and not yet the birth of another. I wonder if I should make some marmalade?

A north-west wind had dissipated the last shreds of fog and the heaving sea was making a sullen moaning sound outside the windows. Gulls like bits of white rag soared and screamed over the creaming waves and, lost in her own thoughts, Emilia failed to hear the telephone ringing out in the hall.

She was wondering whether a personal interview with the Home Secretary might not perhaps bear more fruit than a mere letter. She was quite prepared to travel overnight to London . . . Sir, I beg to request the honour of a private interview regarding Miss Alfreda Morris, who has already been the subject of correspondence between us. While hastening to reaffirm my gratitude for your past interest in the matter of her inexplicable disappearance I have to confess that I am not entirely satisfied that every diplomatic stone has yet been turned . . .

Oh, these girls, she thought. Why do I continue to worry about them when they have long since passed through my hands? There is Rhoda who has jumped out of an excellent position with the Prudential into some ridiculous place where they bore holes in strips of metal for little boys to play with — Meccano, is it called? — and poor Vera Potter in a sanatorium, they say both lungs are affected — and I still cannot help thinking about Cassica's cousin . . . Oh, how it all niggles and naggles . . .

Sitting on the arm of a chair and absently stirring the fallen pine needles with the toe of her shoe she was unaware of the door opening behind her. It was only gradually that she became conscious of another presence in the room, of someone standing motionless and staring at her in silence.

She turned swiftly, with a little gasp.

'They have just telephoned,' Wilfred said, 'to say that my wife has died.'

He walked towards her stiffly, like a man in a trance, and the tears running down his cheeks were turned to diamonds by the shining radiance of his smile.

* * *

Getting off the tramcar at the end of Smithdown Lane, Cassie walked through Sefton Park in the direction of The Mount. No traffic; silence, except for the low throbbing of the wind. Expensive trees bowing over expensive garden walls, her footsteps falling lonely as pennies on a church offertory plate.

There was something disturbing and upsetting about coming back and she wished that she hadn't agreed to do so. To divert her thoughts she tried to catch glimpses of the old, schoolgirlish Cassie; the noisy, bouncy, mutinous Cassie who seemed to have developed into a remarkably dull and prosaic form of school teacher. I used to laugh such a lot, she thought, with Desmond and Effie — Oh, God, Effie where *are* you? They've re-let your bedsitter, did you know? — and I've got your things packed up in two suitcases and a tea chest back at my place . . . Her mind shied away from the laughing and the careless happiness with Desmond; she hoped she wasn't the girl he had wanted to marry, yet at the same time it was rather wounding to contemplate the thought of someone else . . .

She began walking up the long drive that led to The Mount with shoulders back and head erect.

Hannah opened the door. A few grey hairs threaded the neat bob beneath the starched cap, otherwise she looked exactly the same.

'Good afternoon, miss.'

'Hullo, Hannah. How are you?'

'Nicely, thank you, miss. Madam's in the library.'

The scent of hyacinths and woodsmoke. The softness of thick carpet, the discreet silver chime of a distant clock.

'Cassica, my dear.' Uncle Harry came from the direction of his study wearing a velvet jacket. He helped her out of her coat and she couldn't help thinking of the last time she was here, dashing across the hall choked with tearful indignation, suitcase in hand, goodbye — goodbye — I hate you all! — She saw him watching her quizzically.

'Is it nice to be back?'

'Yes,' she said, beginning to smile. 'Yes, I think it is.'

'Your aunt has got one of her charity boys here,' he said, leading her across the hall by the elbow. 'She has developed such a range of practical knowledge that they tend to burden her with their problems at all hours. Her patience is remarkable.'

'Coco, *darling!* — what an *age* it's been, you dreadful standoffish old thing!'

Thin silken arms twining round her neck, the fragrant whiff of Chanel and a soft lock of hair brushing her cheek.

'Hullo, Babs,' Cassie hugged her back, then they drew apart, scrutinising one another.

'Coco, what a *dazzler* you've become! Tall and slim and madly chic — you've more than fulfilled my wildest expectations!'

'You're not looking so dusty either—' (But oh, Babs, age is catching up with you. Your neck's gone stringy and your mouth's sunk in at the corners . . .) They embraced again, laughing breathlessly while Uncle Harry watched approvingly.

'Come along in by the fire, the weather's so utterly beastly—'

Babs tugged at her hand and they went through to the library where the silver tea tray was already in place.

'Now, Coco, you must promise me never to go away for so long again or I shall be very cross, but in the meantime tell me all your news — you must have *oodles* — and oh, by the way, this is one of my poor little LBs — I do charitable work, you know, oh yes, I'm almost a missionary, darling — Jack, come and meet my niece—'

A young man rose obediently from the sofa with outstretched hand and a wide smile that vanished with lightning speed when he recognised Cassie. She recognised him too: it was the professional dancer from the Rialto who went by the name of Maxim.

They shook hands and managed to say good afternoon, and, for Cassie, risk of incredulous laughter was increased to danger point by the rapid Morse-like batting of Maxim's eyelids and the urgent pressure of his fingers as he silently pleaded discretion. She decided to torment him a little first.

'This is your LB?' She turned to Babs enquiringly. 'What does LB stand for?'

'Lay brother, darling,' drawled Babs with her guileless little-girl smile. 'Now go and sit down by Harry while I pour the teazle.'

Shallow Royal Doulton teacups filled with Earl Grey and a thin sliver of lemon. Little scones filled with Devonshire cream and home-made jam; a plate of puff pastries and a large coffee and walnut cake with icing. Maxim — or rather, Jack — nibbled quickly, nervously, while darting glances at Cassie, and Babs remarked on the sheer awfulness of some people not always having enough to eat.

'I quite agree,' said Uncle Harry. 'Although conversely, we must not blind ourselves to the virtues of abstinence. I believe that practically all known religious regard a period of fasting as beneficial to the soul. A form of cleansing, as it were.'

'I think Babs was referring to lack of money rather than any form of asceticism,' Cassie said. 'Which is it in your case, Jack?' She gazed at him with eyes almost as innocent as those of her aunt.

'A little of both,' he replied weakly.

'And when do you take your vows?'

'In the thing I'm interested in we don't have to.'

'No,' she said very thoughtfully. 'No, I suppose not. I believe only doctors and solicitors and bona fide vicars have to take vows—'

'Speaking of soliciting,' said Babs animatedly, 'they say it's positively unsafe to walk along Lime Street late at night.

The most obnoxious insults are constantly hurled at one by women with little dogs and dreadfully sinister men who carry knives — I believe they're called ponces—'

'Really, Babs,' Uncle Harry said, 'this is a highly distasteful subject, particularly coming from the lips of a gentlewoman—'

'I *do* apologise, although now Harry's a JP I feel that I ought to take a certain wifely interest in sin, don't you? Have another scone, Harry dear.'

'It's certainly not a good thing to talk about sin in front of Jim — sorry, Jack,' put in Cassie, equally animated. 'It could be very harmful for his moral sensibilities.'

'I'm quite capable of looking after my own moral sensibilities, thank you.' Jack shot her a vindictive look.

Away from the soft lights and sweet music of the Rialto ballroom his allure was considerably diminished. He had pale eyes and acne scars.

The worm's beginning to turn, Cassie thought. We'd better be careful. Her eyes met those of Babs, and she tried to establish from them whether she realised that she and Jack were not total strangers. If I don't give the game away, she told herself, it won't be for the sake of either Babs or Jack; it'll be for that poor dignified old cuckold Uncle Harry.

By the time they reached the coffee and walnut cake it seemed that every remark, however harmless, had now become loaded with dreadful significance. Babs asked Cassie in a silvery little voice whether she had ever felt the urge to take up charitable work on her own account, and with a suppressed smirk Cassie replied that, for her, charity began at home. An immediate vision of lying in bed with Desmond filled her mind, and catching sight of Uncle Harry's suddenly suffused face wondered with a stab of horror whether he could have guessed her thoughts.

But he was choking on a crumb, and in her relief she put down her own cup and saucer and walloped him on the back with unnecessary force. His plate flew from his hand into the fireplace.

'*Really,* Harry,' said Babs, aggrieved, 'how can you expect the young to look up to you?'

'What a daft thing to say to someone in imminent danger of spifflication,' cried Cassie through a haze of semi-hysterical tears.

'I think you mean suffocation,' Jack said, munching stolidly. 'The two words are often confused.'

Uncle Harry gave a last high barking cough then steadied himself and took a cautious sip of tea. He wiped his eyes and blew his nose.

'Thank you, Cassica. Most kind.'

'A case of kill or cure,' Babs said.

'*Cassica,*' repeated Jack, now bent on a little retaliation. 'What a funny name.'

'It is from the Greek, therefore lost on those deprived of a classical education,' said Cassie. Then added: 'Something tells me that you yourself have more than one name.'

'Oh? Really?' He stopped munching and stared at her challengingly.

'But I may be confusing you with someone else. Like a friend of a friend whose name was — Maxim, was it?'

'Coco darling, how curiously spinsterish you sound,' said Babs. 'Anyone for more tea?'

They all declined, so she rang the bell for Hannah, who glided in to remove the tray and then, after a slight tightening of the lips, the shattered fragments of plate from the hearth.

Uncle Harry snapped open his watch. 'Well, I daresay that as a young man you have arrangements of a pressing nature for this evening?' he said to Jack, and Cassie, who had calmed down, thought dear God, don't let's start again.

'I must be going too,' she said.

'I'll walk down with you, then,' Jack said, flicking her a meaningful look.

'Yes, do, Jim. That would be nice.'

It was obvious that he wanted to talk to her, presumably about his part-time role of under-privileged divinity student, and, for her part, Cassie was rather keen to talk back to him. About Effie.

'Oh no, Coco, you can't go yet — you've only just come!' It was also obvious that Babs had no intention of leaving them alone together if it could be avoided. 'Say bye-bye to Jack and come back by the fire—'

'Yes, I believe that Hannah is under the impression that you are staying to dinner,' Uncle Harry said.

They were all standing up now, Jack edging towards the door, and it was impossible to gauge from Uncle Harry's tone and facial expression whether he was in on the conspiracy as well. Or if he was weaving a little conspiracy all of his own.

In the end she had to stay. Babs saw Jack to the door, and when she returned to the library Uncle Harry welcomed her back as if she had just returned from an arduous and rather dangerous journey. He prodded the fire into a blaze, dusted his hands on his handkerchief and then moved briskly over to the drinks table.

The evening passed pleasantly. Babs, a little tight, was gay and amusing and Uncle Harry was genially acquiescent, and Cassie found herself enjoying their company even while being aware of a tautness between them. By the end of dinner she was certain that the reason for their insistence on her presence was not altogether altruistic; they needed someone to act as a buffer between them.

Saying goodbye to Babs she promised to go and see them regularly, then Uncle Harry drove her home.

A small cold moon lay high over the trees of Sefton Park, its silver light glittering on the frosted puddles. They drove in silence until they turned from Mulgrave Street into Upper Parliament Street, then Uncle Harry said: 'I still love her, you know.'

So of course he knew about Jack. As doubtless he knew about all the others, and it was love, not stupidity or even pride, that compelled him to join in the pathetic charade. *Babs is perfect,* she remembered Desmond saying, *and to acknowledge that she eats young men alive would kill him . . .*

It was hard to know what to say. Perhaps he didn't want her to say anything. But when they stopped outside the Falkner Square flat, she touched his hand and said: 'I can't help loving her, either.'

* * *

Upon hearing of the death of Wilfred's wife, Emilia's first reaction had been to fly with him to the nearest registry office. During the week that passed between demise and burial, however, she realised that it would be selfish to subject him to further strain, even of a joyous nature, so soon after the melancholy stress unavoidably involved. After all, he had to watch his health.

She began thinking in terms of a spring wedding, but when spring came found herself procrastinating.

'I can't help worrying about this man Herr Hitler.'

'He won't be coming, sweetheart!'

'Perhaps not to our wedding, but I believe that he has designs on our country.'

'Oh nonsense, Emilia! But even if he had, wouldn't it feel safer if we were actually married?'

She had to concede that in a wholly illogical way, it would. 'Very well, loved one, August.'

'Not before then?'

'It will take me until August,' she said rather sharply, 'to get *ready.*'

'Oh, my darling Emilia, I love you so—'

'And it is because I love you too, dearest, that everything must be perfect.'

Perhaps Herr Hitler will die, she thought. Or perhaps there will be a bloodless coup and he will be replaced by a more magnanimous regime.

For things seemed to worry her more, these days. A case of petty pilfering among the academy pupils had upset her in a way that would have been unimaginable five years ago, and the whereabouts of Alfreda Morris continued to nag like a splinter at the back of her mind.

She was also becoming rather stout, and although she corseted firmly there seemed to be less and less definition between bust and hips. I am sixty-seven, she thought crossly; a ludicrous age at which to contemplate becoming a bride.

Apart from Wilfred, the person who seemed closest to her these days was Cassica. The rebellious pupil the know-it-all miss had matured into a poised, practical woman upon whom she could rely at the academy, and whose company she and Wilfred enjoyed for the occasional Sunday lunch out at Hoylake. Cassica, of all her girls, now seemed most representative of the Gathercole spirit; willingness combined with steadiness; efficiency coupled with modesty — and sometimes she would look back on the old harum-scarum days with an indulgent smile. In retrospect, even Cassica's lamentable spell in the undertaker's office appeared touching and somehow rather praiseworthy.

And for Cassie herself, life had undoubtedly entered a more placid stage. Teaching shorthand had become a routine she seldom thought to rail against; although her salary was still modest it was sufficient to finance two weeks' holiday each summer; she went to Dartmoor with a girl who worked in the City Library, explored a portion of the Welsh coast on her own, and one year went back to London and found it painfully disappointing. Once again, no one spoke to her or smiled at her in the street. The only person she was able to establish the smallest contact with was the waitress who served breakfast in the small Bloomsbury hotel, and she only wanted to complain about her varicose vein. She began to understand why Londoners had earned a reputation for being stuck up, and although she still didn't care much for Liverpool it seemed to offer a cheerful raucous welcome in comparison with London's stately indifference.

She had several good friends, and even a boyfriend of sorts. His name was Godfrey Gibson-Rose and he lived on a private income in a carefully furnished flat in Rodney Street. Pale grey carpet, mushroom-coloured walls, stone jugs full of bare twigs in the winter and an original pencil sketch by

Degas over the fireplace. He was older than Cassie and rather good-looking in an etiolated way, with long pale fingers and long feet clad in pale suede shoes, which in those days were considered a little depraved. He always called Cassie my *dear,* and although he seemed to enjoy her company, he never made love to her. A light and graceful kiss on the cheek was the most he aspired to, and although in the early days she had tried to persuade herself that she was in love with him she wasn't really — and so it didn't matter. They went to concerts at the Philharmonic Hall and he taught her to appreciate Brahms, which was of more lasting value than rolling about on a bed together.

She had heard nothing from either Desmond or Effie and had seen no more of Arnold. She thought of them all at times, and of Arnold perhaps a little more frequently because of the events in the world outside. So much seemed to be wrong, and so little of it put right by the ever-increasing army of zealots who noisily peddled doctrinal cures for the ills of mankind in every newspaper and at every street corner.

Only Westminster seemed mute, and when Palmer's Shipyard up in Jarrow was put into liquidation and the town left to contemplate its own extinction, the President of the Board of Trade merely roused himself sufficiently to say that Jarrow must work out its own salvation.

Hitler had become Reich Chancellor the previous year, and on Cassie's thirty-fifth birthday the young son of the caretakers who lived in the basement swaggered forth in a black shirt which he had bought by post for five shillings. He tried to sell her a copy of *Der Stürmer* and she told him to run away and play. He did and helped to terrorise elderly Jewish shopkeepers in the Myrtle Street area by painting swastikas on their windows.

But at the Rialto Jeanette MacDonald was fluting like a nightingale in the dark of the cinema and, while Eden was having a series of glum talks with Mussolini on the subject of Abyssinia, people up in the ballroom were learning the Impetus Turn ('a very useful figure in the slow foxtrot'). The pros in the pen were still flashing their artificial smiles, but Cassie never went back there again. Because she could do nothing more about it, she didn't want to be reminded of Effie and her probable fate, any more than she wished to contemplate the spectacle of Babs dancing with Jack or Maxim or whatever his name was.

In the autumn of 1936 when the abdication crisis was at its height, she decided to write a novel in her spare time. It was to take place at the time of Waterloo and the heroine's name was Constance Arbuthnott. Several of Godfrey's rather bloodless friends were on Liverpool's artistic fringe; one had chipped a lump of stone into a strange shape and called it *Configurations,* while another wrote small bleak poems which occasionally found their way into the *Poetry Review.* Someone else knew Ivor Novello, so all in all the prevailing disposition was one of sympathy with creative struggle. They told her that it was high time someone revived The Novel, kissed her cheek and left her alone to get on with it.

It was harder than she had imagined, with strings of inaccurately chosen words bunching themselves into awkward unrhythmical sentences, yet even as she scribbled amendments or hurled crumpled sheets of paper in the direction of the wastepaper basket she was conscious of a powerful urge to continue. Sometimes, on a good patch, it almost seemed as if her mind was being invaded by the restless ghost of some other powerful but unknown story-teller.

She worked hard at it during the long winter evenings, only marginally aware that a new wave of zealots had joined the International Brigade and gone off to fight for the Republican cause in Spain. At teatime on 26 April 1937 the Luftwaffe's Condor Legion bombed the small cultural centre of Guernica and almost obliterated it. The rest of the world woke up, if only briefly, and began to speak of plans for adopting Basque refugees. Cassie reached chapter sixteen, and the bitter realisation that Constance Arbuthnott was no more than a cardboard figure, a paste-and-scissors job by courtesy of Hardy, Dickens, and all three Brontes. She tried to tear it up but it was too thick, so with a dull sense of *déjà vu* put it in a fishmonger's carrier bag and took it down to the Pier Head and let it fall over the side of the landing-stage.

'Ay, chook, you've dropped yer supper.' A man in a cap eyed the sinking object hungrily.

'Yes, I know.'

'Well, warra waste.'

'Not really,' she said. 'It was very indigestible.'

But the south-west wind brought with it a hint of summer; the old sweet scent of lush Welsh pastures and little wildflowers that managed to float intact among the soot and grime and the heavy stench of the Scottie Road slums. Between the clouds the sky was a marvellous blue, and it stirred the office girls of Dale Street and Castle Street into the purchase of sixpenny face-packs which they hoped would remove the dinginess of winter and leave in its place complexions radiant as apple blossom.

It also stirred Emilia into renewed contemplation of matrimony, and with a sudden lift of the heart she decided that she and Wilfred should be made legally one on 18 May, which, unbelievably, would be the thirtieth anniversary of their first meeting.

CHAPTER EIGHTEEN

'I was watching you, Norah. And I saw how you coloured up.'

'When did I?'

'When that man asked you the way to Wines and Spirits.'

'He made me jump.'

'No, he didn't, Norah. You coloured up for another reason.'

'You'd better tell me what it was, then.'

'You don't need me to tell you.'

'Well, don't then.'

'No, I won't. I won't say any more. But you and I both know what it was that made you colour up like that . . .'

'I wish to see some ecru lace,' said an authoritative voice. 'No more than two inches wide.'

'Certainly, madam.' The appropriate box laid on the glass-topped counter. The stiff cards of lace unwound and displayed over Norah's listless fingers.

'That's dainty, madam . . .'

'Umm. What else have you?' Small eyes sharp behind clip-on spectacles. Grey Alexandra fringe curling beneath green velvet toque.

'This one's novel, madam. But quite dainty in its way . . .'

Emilia bought six yards. Then turned her attention to insertion lace, broderie anglais and the narrow satin ribbon that went with it.

'Will that be all, madam?'

'Thank you, yes.' A sudden smile of surprising sweetness. 'And thank you, miss, for your trouble.'

'Not at all, madam.' And poor Norah colouring up again while Ciss watched tormentedly from between the cards of novelty buttons.

The store was gaily decorated with spring hats and sunshades and caught at last by the joyous fever of impending nuptials Emilia spent a considerable sum of money in a very short time. Four new nightgowns, the high collars and long sleeves of which she proposed to lace-trim herself; two new bust bodices, a new pair of white satin corsets and four new pairs of knickers with elasticated legs. She bought petticoats and stockings and shoes, and the wedding frock she finally chose was of navy blue silk with a tiny white floral pattern and a little coatee to match. The hat, that final and most important adornment of all, she proposed to buy from Madame Louise in Bold Street.

Her busy mind planned and replanned ceaselessly. A small luncheon party at the house — no, on second thoughts at an hotel. It was no use saying *family only* as neither she nor Wilfred had any, and, because the long years lived in voluntary seclusion had prevented the formation of friendships among Hoylake people, there only remained the loyal and affectionate staff from Gathercoles who, so far, had no inkling of the bombshell about to be dropped.

Because of a sad childhood followed by long years of reticence, Emilia had come to enjoy secrets. She felt that she was almost at the very peak of happiness now, with her trousseau purchased, the wedding date fixed and the outside world still in total ignorance. But the greatest secret of all was the one she hugged to her bosom with almost unbearable delight, for she had been to see her solicitor about Wilfred's partnership in the academy, and the legal papers were now ready for his signature. As they were the most precious thing she had to give, they were to constitute her wedding present to him and she proposed to keep them in total secrecy until their wedding morning.

With a fresh little surge of joy, she ordered the wedding cake from Reece's and decided that each of the poor girls from the pillbox factory should be given a tiny portion to place beneath their pillow, in order, so the superstition went, that she might dream of her future bridegroom.

'Upon opening my fly I have found a small matter outstanding which I am sure you will deal with promptly and expeditiously,' Wilfred read aloud. He looked over the top of his spectacles at the attentive class. 'Doris dear, I think you must have misheard my dictation, but, in case you didn't, it is impossible to interpose a vowel sign between the *l* hook and the curved stroke to which it is applied. In other words, what I dictated was the word file, not fly.'

Doris went pink, and scuttled up to retrieve her test paper.

'Otherwise excellent,' Mr Sissley added kindly.

It was the final class of the day, and when the last of the test papers had been discussed and distributed and a new exercise set for that evening, Mr Sissley dismissed them with a courteous smile and a wave of the hand.

For a man of sixty-five he was still remarkably spry, loose-limbed and erect. Although his hair had faded from cheerful buttercup yellow to a silvery primrose it was still thick and plentiful, and his eyes had lost none of their optimistic sparkle. He continued to dress with elegance and to wear a carnation in his buttonhole, and students frequently remarked that he must have been quite a lad in his time.

'He still is,' said a girl called Winnie Sage, watching him from the tram stop. 'Look, he's going off with Miss Marlow.'

'They're only walking the same way.'

'That's what you think. He's had his eye on her all winter.'

As it happened, Cassie was going back to Hoylake with Wilfred because he and Emilia had invited her to supper. On average she now lunched or supped with them about once a month, but this particular invitation, issued only ten days since the last, had something faintly mysterious about it. Both Wilfred and Emilia were exhibiting signs of a strange and covert excitement which was manifesting itself in the form of clandestine glances, sudden conspiratorial little smiles and, particularly on the part of Emilia, a new and buoyant animation that pleased the pupils as much as it puzzled the staff.

Miss Sturgeon said that Miss Gathercole was planning her retirement, and, although Cassie made a pretence of agreeing, privately she wasn't so sure. For it was obviously something which equally involved Wilfred, and she could only suppose that whatever impediment there had been to their marriage had now been removed, and that they were about to get spliced.

So she set off for Hoylake with Wilfred on that late afternoon of late spring, Emilia having intimated that she would be spending the day engaged in the preparation of a special meal. Yet as Wilfred gave no sign of there being any reason for celebration, so Cassie was equally determined not to betray any undue curiosity. To be on the safe side, however, she was wearing the new straw hat she had bought from the Bon Marche to cheer up last summer's coat and skirt.

'It's charming,' Wilfred said, sitting opposite her in the train. 'And it takes me back to your wide-eyed ingenuous days.'

'I don't believe I ever had days like that.'

'Oh yes you did, in between being as haughty as blazes and as contemptuous of poor old Sir Isaac Pitman as only a young woman cheated out of university could possibly be.'

'I must have been a pain in the neck,' Cassie said. 'I don't know how you put up with me.'

'We couldn't have done,' he gave her a loving smile, 'if it hadn't been for the charm of your wide-eyed ingenuousness.'

'Something's making you seem extra happy, Mr Sissley.'

'It's the spring combined with the prospect of a good supper. And after all these years, I suggest that you start calling me Wilfred.'

She thanked him and said she would, and when the train halted at the stop before Hoylake he impetuously seized her hand and said, 'Come on, Cassie, let's walk along the sea front — we'll be home almost as quickly as the train!'

The tide was just on the turn and, although the sky had large patches of blue, the sea was a muddy brown as if news of the coming summer hadn't yet reached it. It smacked against the sea wall and then withdrew, a thick lather of bubbles clinging to the sand for a moment, and everywhere was the old familiar sense of cleanliness; houses and trees and even the roadway washed and bleached by wind and salt water. There was no one about.

'Hilbre looks ominous at this time of day. Have you ever been to it?'

'Yes, once. Emilia and I set off in a hired pony and trap and we stayed there eating our sandwiches and watching the birds until the next low tide. We enjoyed it no end, and we've always meant to go back, but—'

'But somehow there's never time,' she said.

The breeze caught at her hat and threatened to dislodge it. Hastily she grabbed at it.

'Steady the Buffs!' Wilfred laughed, then added, 'No, it's a bore how quickly time passes. They say the happier you are the faster it goes, and I must admit that life plus Emilia have been very good to me. And by the way,' he stopped abruptly, and stood etched against the heaving sea, 'thank you for never prying.'

She stopped too and stood looking at him very seriously; pale grey chalk-stripe suit, red carnation, thick hair ruffled by the wind and his Burberry raincoat carried folded over his shoulder.

'You both mean a lot to me,' she said. 'And it's taken me a long time to realise it.'

They began to walk on and had reached the Hoylake promenade when again the breeze snatched at her hat and this time it went skimming over the iron handrail and into the sea. With a cry of vexation she watched it bobbing like a merry little boat in the shallow trough of two waves.

'Oh, *damn!*' He said it for her. 'Never mind, I can rescue it—'

'No you can't — it's hopeless—'

'Here, hold this—' He dumped his raincoat in her arms, then ducked with agility under the handrail. On the other side the wet stone wall dropped straight down to the sea.

'Mr Sissley — Wilfred — please don't bother! It's not worth getting your feet wet—'

'Look, it's coming to the top of a wave, and when it breaks it'll leave it stranded and I can grab it before—'

'Don't, please . . . it doesn't *matter* . . . !'

Crouching on the edge of the wall with one hand still holding the rail he looked up at her like a merry schoolboy. 'Of course it matters, you ninny! We can take it home and get Emilia to dry it in the oven — whoops, here we go!'

Her hat rode to the peak of the wave and hung there poised for a moment. It was a big wave that had been slowly gathering itself, and even as she implored him to get up she remembered something about every seventh wave being bigger than all the others. This was going to be a seventh wave.

'Mind you don't fall!' she shouted, and the words seemed to be blown back into her mouth by another gust of wind.

A trickle of creaming foam escaped from the wave's crest before it broke and ran towards the wall. Still holding the handrail Wilfred stretched outwards and downwards. His fingers touched the brim, lost it, grabbed again, and then the wave began to recede, taking the hat with it. A narrow strip of streaming sand showed for a moment at the foot of the wall. The hat had retreated, and was now becoming a part of the next wave. There was an awful fascination in the slow heavy rhythm of swelling, cresting and falling, and Cassie, mute now, stood gripping the folds of Wilfred's raincoat.

The wave built and built. It seemed now that the last one had only been of average size. This, without doubt, would be a seventh. It held the straw hat poised on its sharp peak, balancing it like a circus performer, then allowed it to slide down towards the shore for a second before smothering it in a torrent of foam. Readjusting his position Wilfred crouched with one foot braced against the wet sea wall, and when the hat suddenly danced back into view he lunged at it and fell.

Cassie screamed. Flinging the raincoat aside she thrust herself under the handrail and half jumped and half slid down towards him. The wall was not a very high one, and as the wave hit the foot of it she saw Wilfred lying on his back in the swirling wash of foam. It covered him completely for a moment and then withdrew, and he went on lying there as if it were too much trouble to rise.

'Wilfred!' She gasped as the cold water lashed her calves. 'Wilfred — get *up*!'

His eyes were closed. Floundering through the receding foam she grabbed at the front of his jacket. She snatched at his hand and began urging him to get up, quickly, before the next wave. Already it was massing itself, little silver-brown crinkles gathering into a smooth and glassy shoulder of water ready to project itself over him.

But he remained motionless, cold spray on his closed eyelids. She began tugging at him, letting go his hand and hauling at him by the lapels and then reaching down and trying to lug him along with her arms round his waist. The next wave toppled and seethed down over them both, splashing the crown of Cassie's bent head as she heaved and strained at Wilfred's inert body. The water covered him again for a moment and then withdrew with a hiss, and he lay in a tangle of lace — 'Wilfred — Mr Sissley — for God's sake get up or you'll *drown*!'

But he was knocked out. Unconscious. Panting and gasping she let go of him and began splashing back towards the wall with the idea of climbing back to the promenade and screaming for help. But the next wave was already forming so she stumbled hastily back to him and, unable to shift him, knelt down and tried to shield his face from its impact. It broke over them both and she crouched gasping and sobbing with her desperate eyes pressed against the poor sodden carnation in his buttonhole.

The wave receded, washing his hair sideways across his forehead and she raised his head in her hands and shouted at him in a voice cracking with terror. He gave no sign of having heard. A little pink shell was washed into his limply curled hand and she suddenly saw how dark everything about him had become. The pale grey suit was now almost black, and his primrose-coloured hair the colour of waterlogged seaweed.

The next wave broke gently, and curled round him with little fingers that seemed filled with a strange and loving tenderness; little fingers that wanted nevertheless to carry him away from the shore and out to where a gleam of sunlight had turned the chopping waves to glittering pewter. She stood up, cupping her hands against her mouth and shrieking, 'Help — help meee . . . !'

There was no reply, she didn't expect any, so she peeled off her sodden coat, crumpled it into a rough pad and thrust it under his head to keep it clear of the next wave. Then she waded stumbling back to the wall and, scrabbling for the handrail, hauled herself to the top.

Unbelievably there was still no one in sight. Sobbing and shivering she ran across the road to the houses on the other side. Her cold fingers fumbled with the catch on the nearest gate and the sedate garden path seemed a mile long. She hammered on the door and it was a long, long while before anyone answered.

'Yes?' A middle-aged man in a cardigan and slippers looking at her as if she were selling something he didn't want.

'Please can you help — telephone — someone's in danger of drowning—'

'I was just listening to the news—'

'For Christ's sake, man, help me!'

Grumbling and without haste he followed her down the path leaving the door on the latch. Without waiting for him she flew across the road leaving wet footprints and a scattering of salt water drops to where Wilfred's raincoat lay abandoned. Grasping the handrail she looked down and he was still lying there, washed by a new wave of creamy lace that reminded her with mad irrelevance of the froth on a glass of beer.

'Look — there he is!' Suddenly she was too frightened to go any closer. It wasn't the cold or the fear of the sea, it was the fear that Wilfred would suddenly sit up and reproach her for deserting him. She clung to the handrail as if it were the last glimmer of hope in a world gone mad.

The man in the cardigan and slippers plodded away from her and she opened her mouth to shriek abuse at him, then saw that he was heading for the steps that led down to the sands. She and Wilfred hadn't seen them, hadn't bothered to look for them. Of such trifling omissions are tragedies born. With gritted teeth and wet hair slapping her cheeks she willed the man to hurry . . . for Jesus Christ's sake hurry . . .

She saw him hesitate before descending from the final step on to the thin border of drenched sand left by the last wave. She saw his slippers darken and slowly fill with water, and then she saw his blurred white face when he turned to look up at her.

'He's dead. It's no use, he's dead . . .'

* * *

Because he was dead there was no point in taking him to hospital, or to anywhere but home.

A policeman, the man in cardigan and slippers, and two other men who had somehow appeared, plus Cassie sobbing and shuddering and vomiting sea water on the hall floor; they laid him on the drawing-room carpet, eyes still closed and drowned carnation still in his buttonhole. The smell of dank salt sea water overpowering the seductive scent of roast duck, and Emilia small and white-faced with shock kneeling by the body and chaffing its hands in stunned silence.

They tried to coax her away, rough, kindly hands on her shoulders, but she suddenly shook them off violently. And the violence increased to madness so that she beat her fists on the sodden jacket and cried, 'Come back — *come back*!'

Cassie, now recovered a little, tried on her knees to hold and support Emilia, but Emilia fought like a cornered animal with a face wild and almost bestial in its agony. *'Come back to me — come back — I've made you a partner*!'

Shocked and aghast they all waited and listened to the repetition of that magic word 'partner' as if it might perhaps contain some secret element capable of breathing life back into the sodden pitiful object when all forms of artificial respiration had failed.

'Try to calm yourself, madam,' the policeman said finally. 'Go with the young lady and try to keep calm.'

So they both went into the dining room where the table was laid for three and the candles ready for lighting. Cassie stood by the sideboard, her salty clothes drying stiffly on her body while she held Emilia in her arms, bracing herself against the mountainous sobs and strangled cries.

'Sshh-sshhh . . . quiet now . . .' She had never tried to pacify a babe in arms but this was what it must be like. Cold, shivering and deeply shocked, she tried to distract Emilia with words, with stroking and rocking and holding and loving, with little baby-words and whisperings, and sometimes it seemed as if Emilia had succumbed; beneath the disordered Alexandra fringe she seemed to be listening, to be taking in sense, then her head would come up and her old face, blotched and distorted, would spit hatred and wild accusations at Cassie, at Wilfred, at God, and at anyone she could call upon to listen. The duck burned in the oven and the fire in the drawing-room died.

They took Wilfred away. Cassie stayed on alone with her, eyes smarting with tears and fatigue as she alternately held and fought the old woman rendered insane by loss. Dully she thought how amazing it was that the old could feel such pain.

At about three in the morning Cassie succeeded in persuading her up to bed. There was no chance of getting her to undress but she agreed to rest for a while under the quilt. Sitting on the foot of the bed she waited for Emilia to sob herself to sleep. Hiccoughing now, and clutching a drenched handkerchief as a child would clutch it's mother's hand, she grew quieter, the storm-blotches fading on her face, but when Cassie gently tucked the quilt closer before tiptoeing downstairs she woke again and began pawing like a wounded, blinded animal at the empty pillow beside her. 'Come back . . . Come back to me . . .'

In the end Cassie spent the rest of the night lying on Wilfred's side of the bed, trying to ignore last night's proximity of him and trying to accustom Emilia to the agony of knowing that he would never be there any more.

'Loved one — oh, my dearest loved one, I had a terrible dream . . .'

'Sshhh-sshhh — go back to sleep now, darling . . .'

How extraordinary to call her darling, Cassie thought, removing the poor old fingers groping at her face in the dark. Sick with tiredness and with pity she held Emilia in her arms and thought I'll never know anyone in the whole world as intimately as I know you. What's between us now is far more intimate than the thing with Desmond; this has forged some terrible kind of bond between us that neither of us will be able to break . . .

They slept uneasily for an hour or two, and when the first pale streaks of dawn silvered the room Cassie woke up and inched herself cautiously off the bed. Aching with stiffness and with misery she went down to the kitchen to make a pot of tea.

Outside, the next tide was already on the ebb.

* * *

Wilfred had died not from drowning but from a heart attack, and the reason why they had invited her to supper was because they intended asking her to be chief witness at their wedding.

And while Cassie was assimilating these facts, Emilia, very pale but once more in control, was striving to absorb the knowledge that Wilfred's heart attack had almost certainly been caused by the exertion entailed in trying to rescue Cassie's hat.

The Gathercole Academy was closed for the day of the funeral ('We mourn the passing of a loyal colleague and trusted friend . . .') and after that it was business as usual. There was no alternative. But the strange old building in Hockenhall Street remained full of his presence; the sound of his laughter and his light footsteps on the stairs, the gleam of his cheerful yellow hair illuminated by the big stained-glass window on the landing. Emilia refused to have the small desk that he had used removed from her office, so that it remained opposite her own with its contents undisturbed. It took many weeks before she could steel herself to contemplate the portrait of him that hung next to her own, but in the meantime there was no question of having it taken down. Staff and pupils treated her with more than usual deference and tended to speak to her in hushed voices, but no one except Cassie knew of the depth of her bereavement. Wilfred's post was not advertised and no attempt was made to find a successor, and if anyone found it strange they made no comment for Miss Gathercole's tendency towards parsimony was well known.

During the weeks that followed, the relationship between Emilia and Cassie was troubled and unstable. The memory of the hours immediately following Wilfred's death was seared ineradicably on both their minds, and alone at night both would relive them again and again, sometimes with gratitude and pity, but more often with hatred and unendurable pain. Both were aware now that they had come too violently close on that night ever to hope of regaining a calm compatibility.

During times of especial bitterness it was impossible for Emilia not to blame Cassie for the tragedy; although she had not been a witness, she could see in her mind's eye the stupid irresponsible girl urging Wilfred to rescue her new straw hat and Wilfred, against his better judgement, courteously doing as she asked. Sometimes she hated Wilfred too, and in her anguish would castigate him as well for being vain and easily flattered, and at the blackest times of all could even allow herself to suspect that they had been having a flirtation. Alone in the Hoylake house she would sit for hour after hour in the darkness, listening to the sound of the sea while she explored all the suspicions and possibilities that grief had dredged up from the depths of her mind. Sometimes she couldn't stand the hiss and smack of the waves and would feverishly thrust plugs of cottonwool into her ears, or else try to shut it out by playing the gramophone.

Then at other less angry times it seemed as if the sea were her only friend; that all her happiness had been lived to the sound of its voice at the end of the garden, and during late evening when the holidaymakers had gone home she would stand by the handrail on the seafront and watch its bland summer face and think that to leave it would be to relinquish her most precious memories of Wilfred.

Soberly she thought about suicide. She was old now and had no one to live for. Then lassitude set in and she couldn't be bothered. It was simpler to go on living, to float dreamlike through the days, submitting to the routine and the discipline that she herself had instigated so many years ago.

In the end it was her first love that saved her; the Gathercole Academy still needed her and there seemed little point in throwing away her life's work in useless mourning. Although privately she had always been sceptical of God's existence and had thus no great conviction that she and Wilfred would be reunited in an after-life, she felt increasingly that he wanted her to go on presiding over the commercial education of Liverpool's young ladies, and to continue the task of placing them, when qualified, in suitable positions with Liverpool's most exalted businessmen.

So she picked up the reins again, and a girl called Lucy Nixon reached a speed of 175 words a minute in a five-minute shorthand test given personally by Emilia; another girl lost both her parents in a train crash outside Runcorn and had to be helped re-establish herself in the home of her married brother and his wife; a new boiler was installed in the basement at Hockenhall Street in readiness for the coming winter and when Cassie went down with shingles Emilia took her a bunch of grapes and a copy of the new Priestley novel.

'How do you feel?'

'Sore round the waist and not very well generally.'

'They tell me that shingles are caused by the nerves.'

'I'm not surprised.'

They sat guardedly observing one another in the Falkner Street flat, Cassie in her dressing-gown with her feet propped up on a leather pouffe.

'I must say you look rather pale. What has your general practitioner prescribed?'

'Aspirin and plenty of rest. Can I make you some tea?'

'I will make it myself,' Emilia announced, 'if you will direct me to the kitchen.'

Pompous old faggot, thought Cassie, listening to the subdued tinkle of cups and saucers on the other side of the wall. Still, I suppose it's kind of her to bother.

The sense of monumental weariness that Emilia had suffered and finally managed to conquer was now afflicting Cassie. The horror of Wilfred's death had had a slower but possibly equally destructive effect because she could now only see it as the final and most supreme example of her own ineptitude. She had implored him not to rescue her hat — a fact she still found impossible to communicate to Emilia — but because she was essentially ineffectual he had taken no notice of her. All her relationships, however happy and well meaning, ended in catastrophe because of her basic ineffectuality. Mona and Effie, and to a lesser degree Desmond and Arnold. And now poor Wilfred. Everyone she touched she smeared with disaster; it was quite possible that the death of both her parents could be laid at her door (was I the immune carrier of Spanish 'flu?)

Oh, God, she had prayed recently, just make me a good friend to people and we'll forget the success thing . . .

It was a pity that she and Emilia were powerless to comfort one another, but a door had slammed shut on that terrible night they had spent holding one another and weeping, and to make any reference to it now was quite impossible. I must leave here, Cassie thought; leave Gathercoles and Liverpool and start again somewhere else, but the same dreary sense of lassitude that had afflicted Emilia prevented her from making the effort. And so here they were, locked fast in a deep and painful relationship where only work or trivialities could be spoken of.

'I hope I have done everything correctly,' Emilia said, coming back into the room with the tea tray. 'I found what appeared to be tea in a little tin box and Bourbon biscuits in a glass jar.'

'Thank you. I'm very grateful.'

'There is no need to be. The sick are always worthy of our patience and forbearance.'

Emilia at her most sonorous, her most high-flown impossible. I'm on the verge of hating her, Cassie thought, and this time I'll never swing back to liking her again. I'm no longer young, and my emotions are getting set in their ways.

'A little milk, or do you prefer it *au naturel?*'

'As it comes, thanks.'

'This is the first time I have seen your little flat.'

'I hope you like it.'

'The view over the gardens is most restful.'

'That's why I took it.' Cassie gave Emilia a sombre look. 'I value restfulness.'

'Are you content to resume your position at the academy in September?' Emilia took a cautious sip of tea.

'Why, are you thinking of replacing me?' The words came sharply.

'Of course not. I have always found your work highly satisfactory, but I must admit that during the course of last term I noticed a certain falling off in standard—'

'Hardly surprising, is it?'

They were so close now to the forbidden subject. All they had to do was to mention his name, to speak of the misery and the sleepless nights, but Emilia took another small sip of tea and said: 'Miss Sturgeon has purchased a small motorcar and has learned to drive it during her holiday. She sent me a picture postcard of Brixham harbour.'

Cassie murmured conventional surprise, and thought why don't I do that? Buy a horse and cart or a caravan or something and just clear off, permanently . . . She sat thinking about it and making little plucking movements at her waist.

'It is advisable not to scratch because the blisters are liable to become inflamed. Have you tried boracic powder?'

'No.' You insufferable old busybody.

'I will call at the chemist's shop and ensure that they send some round.' Emilia rose, patted her queenly bosom and prepared for departure.

'Thank you for coming.'

'Not at all. I hope you will soon be well again, dear.'

'Thank you, Miss Gathercole.'

They stood looking at one another a trifle wistfully. Cassie was on the verge of asking Emilia to stay for a second cup of tea and then saw that she hadn't finished the first one, while Emilia drew on her gloves and thought I must leave her to the restfulness she spoke of so pointedly.

So they said goodbye until autumn term, smiled, and left it at that.

CHAPTER NINETEEN

And the slow dragging half-life continued, for Cassie at any rate, until the following spring when Emilia sent for her and asked whether she would care to accept a temporary teaching post in Luxembourg.

'Luxembourg? You mean, where the *Count* comes from?'

Emilia permitted herself a token smile. 'Strangely enough, the gentleman in question does compose music, I believe, but his name is Dr Kremer, not Lehar.'

'But I've never been abroad—'

'So here is your chance.'

'You honestly mean there's a Luxembourg composer who wants to learn shorthand and typing? But in what language and—' She sat blinking. 'It doesn't make sense.'

Emilia removed a thin sheet of writing paper from its envelope, unfolded it and began to read through it again.

'Dr Kremer, who was apparently given the name of my academy by a member of the Gladstone family' (how the august name rolled off her tongue) 'has an invalid daughter who wishes to learn typewriting in order that she may assist her father in the preparation of his memoirs. They are being written in English, although Dr Kremer informs me that he and his daughter normally converse together in French. I foresee the engagement lasting in the region of six months, and if you decide not to accept the post I shall quite understand. I will try my best to find a substitute, although I fear that neither Miss Sturgeon nor Miss Killigrew, who has been with us for a mere six months, is quite up to the general standard required.'

'But I can't possibly decide straight away—'

'There is no need to. I can give you until Monday morning.'

'But today's already Friday—'

'Yes. I am aware.'

'But what about everything here? My job, my flat, my friends? I've got some geranium cuttings I can't leave—'

'Think about it,' Emilia said. 'Weigh up the pros and cons and decide over the weekend whether or not you wish to avail yourself of Dr Kremer's offer.'

'What do you advise me to do?'

Cassie's eyes met the small wise ones opposite. If I advise you to take it, they said, you will no doubt suspect me of trying to get rid of you. If I advise you not to, you will probably feel that I wish to thwart you. Either way you will no doubt silently accuse me of busy bodying.

'It is entirely up to you, Cassica.'

'In which case I can only promise to consider it.'

'Do that.'

So she considered it deeply and earnestly while she did her ironing, her weekend shopping, cooked her Sunday lunch, went for a walk round the square and then sat down in the armchair with her feet tucked under her, smoking innumerable cigarettes and drinking endless cups of tea. Sometimes it seemed a marvellous idea, the chance she had been waiting for, and she decided to seize it with both hands. She started planning the clothes she would take, wondering about a passport, and then on impulse hurried out to the public phone box and rang up Uncle Harry to ask for his advice. But Uncle Harry and Babs had gone away for the weekend and when the new maid asked if she could take a message Cassie said no thanks, it's not important.

She decided that she wouldn't go. Couldn't go. She was becoming middle-aged and set in her ways. She knew nothing about Luxembourg and didn't want to teach a composer's invalid daughter how to use a typewriter. And she couldn't leave her geraniums.

In the end it was waking up to the paralysing boredom of another drizzling Monday morning that forced the decision. She lay staring at the clean blue Gathercole smock hanging on the wardrobe door and listening to the woman in the flat upstairs arguing with her husband. The smell of frying kippers assaulted her nostrils. The clank of the step-girls' buckets receded, and left room for the adenoidal singsong of the caretaker talking to her cat ('Bairty') out in the hall. And away over in Grove Street the metallic whine of tramcars stuffed with shop-cleaners, office-cleaners and all those humble domestics who did their best to mop and polish a clean pathway through the damp, dust and smuts in readiness for their social superiors whose own drudgery began at nine o'clock. She told herself that nothing could be worse than Liverpool on a wet Monday morning, and when she reached the academy went straight up to Emilia's office and told her that she had decided to accept.

Emilia, still in hat and coat, looked suddenly relieved and pleased. I've caught her off-guard, Cassie thought, and it's easy to see that she wants me to go. Strangely enough, the realisation hurt.

'I will cable Dr Kremer immediately,' Emilia said, 'and between us we will settle the details.'

'I think I've now reached the age when I might be trusted to settle my own details,' Cassie pointed out.

'You, my dear Cassica, will have your time fully occupied in making personal arrangements. You must remember to interview your landlord, cancel the milkman and the newsagent, sit for your passport photograph and buy a new costume. Personally I think navy blue linen — cool, but not too summery, for we are not yet fully conversant with the Luxembourg climate and mistakes can entail needless expense . . .'

Her unstinted advice goaded Cassie almost beyond endurance, but shortly before explosion point Emilia suddenly made her a present from the academy petty cash of ten pounds for contingencies and offered to take care of the geranium cuttings until her return.

'They like a sunny window ledge and watering twice a week.'

'Both of which they shall have.'

'Quite a *lot* of water, but they mustn't actually *sit* in it.'

'I will ensure that they are all in bloom when the time comes to reclaim them.'

Cassie wondered a shade apprehensively whether Emilia would ask her out to Hoylake for a final supper before her departure; she had not been back since the night of Wilfred's death and was uncertain about how unnerving she would find the experience. But no such invitation was issued, and they said goodbye down in the front hall on Cassie's last day. Everyone else had left except Queenie, Mavis's successor, and she scuttled away like a mouse glimpsed in the larder.

'Well, Cassica my dear, *bon voyage.*' Emilia extended her hand. 'Come safely back to us.'

'Do you really mean that?'

It was a daft thing to ask, but it was suddenly very important to know where they stood in relation to one another. Emilia, however, parried it with another question.

'You do want to come back to us, don't you?'

They stood looking at one another even as they continued slowly to shake hands. A beam of greenish late-afternoon light filtered through the stained-glass window and caught the brooch that Wilfred had given Emilia.

'Yes,' Cassie said finally. 'But do *you* want me to?'

'Why shouldn't I?'

'Because of — what happened.'

'We must try to think of it as a bond between us.'

At least they had managed to refer to it, however indirectly. Perhaps next time would be easier, and then one day they would be able to speak of Wilfred's death with something, approaching equanimity.

'Goodbye, Miss Gathercole,' Cassie said finally. 'See you in six months' time.'

'Remember to inform me of your safe arrival. I shall be anxious.'

Emilia opened the front door and stood there unsmilingly with her hand raised in what looked like a benediction, as Cassie walked away.

* * *

She arrived in the city of Luxembourg at six in the evening, having dozed on the Channel steamer and assiduously watched the train-side scenery all the way from Ostend. She was met by a chauffeur who had mastered her name but apparently little else in English except the word 'please'.

'Please?' He held open the rear door of the yellow Panhard, and when he had loaded her luggage on board, and she had said thank you very much, he returned the compliment with a stiff little bow. 'Please?'

Cassie smiled again, then after a moment's consideration said: *'Merci.'*

Which seemed to satisfy him, for they drove off through the narrow streets and she sat back watching the buildings and the trams and the people and thinking that it was like arriving in Liverpool all over again.

But the house was very different from The Mount. Set just within the boundary of a lush city park of lawns, flowerbeds and fine trees, it fronted a boulevard kept at bay by a double gate and high railings overspilling with a luxuriant tangle of wisteria. Yet the small front garden had a white table and chairs set out under a chestnut tree whose pink blossoms brushed the upper windows, many of which had ornate white shutters drawn down over them. The house itself was a large stone edifice with a turret and steep slate roofs, and it wore a sleepy yet somehow watchful look as she climbed the flight of steps up to the front porch.

'Please?' The maid who opened the door was a fresh-faced girl in a cap and apron. She smiled, and Cassie decided that she might as well start as she meant to go on.

'Good evening,' she said with polite deliberation. 'My name is Miss Marlow and I have come from England by arrangement with Dr Kremer.'

The maid's smile increased and she indicated that Cassie should step inside. Cassie did so and became instantly aware of two things. The first was the sound of piano music and the second was the subtle and discreet aroma of good cooking.

The hall was very large, with a tiled floor and a huge iron lantern hanging down the well of the curved staircase. Then a door opened, and a girl leaning heavily on two sticks came towards her.

'Miss Marlow, I am enchanted to meet with you.'

It was difficult at first sight to tell her age; she could have been anywhere between sixteen and the mid-twenties. Her fair hair was bound in a thick smooth plait round her head and her face had the pale, finely chiselled and rather dreamy look of invalidism. She moved with difficulty and yet with a strange grace, and Cassie saw that beneath the ankle-length skirt she was wearing surgical boots.

'Miss Kremer . . . how do you do?'

The girl balanced on one stick while they shook hands. 'You must be tired after your journey. Let us go into the salon and drink some tea.'

The piano music stopped, then after a short pause began again in a series of runs and trills.

'Is that Dr Kremer?'

'Yes. He has a pupil with him.'

The room they entered was warm and cluttered with pictures and china, books and embroidered cushions. It led into a large and ornate conservatory where the plashing of water could be heard but not seen through the luxuriant vegetation.

'Please to sit down, Miss Marlow.'

The girl indicated a chair and, feeling like Jane Eyre at her first encounter with Adele Varens, Cassie sank rather dazedly into it. A table set with an ornate tea tray was drawn up by the chair opposite and, laying aside her sticks, the girl seated herself.

She poured a little tea into two small cups and there was a touching grace about her slow careful movements. She spoke English with an accent, and the placing of each word with such gentle exactitude produced an effect of old-fashioned charm. She told Cassie that she had visited England several times with her father, accompanying him on concert tours when she was a little girl.

'That was after my mother died, and before I became ill. My father commenced his musical career as a concert artist and only turned to composition later.'

'I see.' Cassie wanted to say something more warming, more intelligent, but constraint prevented it. Being abroad felt very strange.

'Tell me something of yourself, Miss Marlow,' the girl said politely. 'I should like to hear.'

What, precisely? Cassie wondered. That which isn't reprehensible will be very boring.

'I'm afraid I'm a fairly humdrum person,' she finally admitted. 'My parents died when I was young, I went to Liverpool to stay with an uncle and aunt, and although I had won a place at university it seemed more sensible to take up secretarial work. I am now a teacher at the academy where I was originally a pupil.'

'That is very interesting,' the girl said. Gravely they both sipped a little more tea and the plashing of water in the conservatory made Cassie wonder whether it would be considered uncouth to ask where the lavatory was.

'I expect you will wish to see your room,' the girl said finally.

'Thank you. That would be very nice.' (Oh, Lord, I'm getting as quaintly stilted as she is.)

The girl tinkled a silver bell that stood on the tray and the maid reappeared. The girl spoke to her in another language, the maid bobbed a curtsey and Cassie followed her upstairs.

Her bedroom was on the first floor and overlooked the park. Although it was furnished with massive mahogany furniture, oil paintings and a large crucifix, the general effect was one of solid comfort rather than heaviness. Her bags had been unpacked and her clothes laid neatly in drawers containing lavender bags. There was an adjoining bathroom with flowery *art nouveau* tiles, and a bidet which Cassie eyed warily from the safety of the lavatory seat. I am a stranger in a foreign land where they have a bias towards suppositories and washing their behinds. I hope I'm going to like it here, that's all . . .

To cheer herself up, and because there seemed nothing else to do in this large, strange house, she had a bath. Then she put on her green crêpe frock with the squared shoulders and vee neckline and went back down the wide shallow staircase in time to see a smallish, white-haired man crossing the hall. He was rubbing his hands together and humming a tune, and instinct told her that this must be her new employer. He looked old and fairly harmless and suddenly reassured she marched up to him, held out her hand and said: 'How do you do, Dr Kremer? My name is Cassica Marlow.'

* * *

'My wife was a remarkably attractive woman,' Dr Kremer said, much later that night. 'By which I propose to infer that she was a woman of remarkable attraction.'

'Yes. I'm sure.'

Supper had been a superb and rather dizzying amalgam of asparagus and Ardennais ham, of chicken in wine sauce with tiny new potatoes, followed by cheese in infinite variety and then a rich *tarte* with baby strawberries nestling in a rich bed of confectioner's custard served with thick yellow cream, the like of which probably hadn't been seen in Liverpool since Victoria's heyday. There had also been a lot of light and fragrant white wine.

'She came from Vienna.'

'Really?'

'Her father's signature was appendaged to Austria's ultimatum to Serbia.'

'Gosh.'

'On 23 July 1914.'

'Yes . . . I suppose it must have been about then.'

'Aha, Miss Marlow, you are interested in the march of history?'

'Yes,' said Cassie. 'Very interested indeed.'

It seemed like ten years since she had left Lime Street station for Dover and the cross-Channel steamer. Her eyes pricked with tiredness and a kind of regurgitating pulse beat in her midriff. Dr Kremer's daughter had excused herself before the coffee and hauled herself off, presumably to bed. How wise.

Cassie and Dr Kremer were now sitting in rattan chairs in the conservatory, where mercifully the trickle of water no longer provoked reminders of bodily functions. Soothed by it, Cassie surveyed her host and between long sleepy blinks noted again the cloud of soft white hair, neatly trimmed but worn a little longer than was usual. The face beneath the hair was pale pink and rather cherubic, with a quick twinkling smile that could vanish at the touch of a serious thought. He was not very tall, but of a neat continental build, she decided.

'I met your Mr Gladstone in my aunt's salon in 1894. It was in an area called Kensington and Mr Gladstone was a remarkable man of eighty-five years. He drank tea and ate hot toast with butter and shortly afterwards he resigned the premiership. Not I understand on account of my aunt's tea and toast, ha ha, but because age had laid a natural weariness on him. I was a young student at the time and had come to London to hear Joachim.'

'Oh yes, I've heard of him . . .' It was a pity that there seemed to be so many small — well, smallish — men about, but of course she had long ago become accustomed to being taller than most of the opposite sex and now it no longer troubled her.

'Are you interested in music, Miss Marlow?'

'I like listening to it, but I don't play anything.'

'Capital, capital! Composers and performers owe their lives to people who are content to sit and listen.' The cherubic twinkle was back. He reminded her of a mixture of Einstein and Father Christmas.

'And talking of music, Dr Kremer.' She jerked herself awake. 'What exactly is it that you want me to do now that I'm here?'

He sat back in his chair and laced his fingers together.

'During the progress of a long musical career I have witnessed many things of a surprising and wonderful nature. They have now become history. I have seen the decline of the Romantic movement, have been present at the birth of Impressionism and have lived to hear the twelve-tone system at work. It was I who gave the first recital in Luxembourg of Debussy's *Six Epigraphes Antiques* in 1917 and I am proud to have helped guide the footsteps of the young Honneger in Zurich. I have known as intimate friends such masters as Richard Strauss, Igor Stravinsky — whom I once advised on the choice of an oculist. I remember — dear, foolish Fritz Kreisler, and many, many others.'

'Did you ever meet Brahms?' she asked, and thought dear God, he's nearly as pompous as Emilia.

'Brahms? In Vienna, but only fleetingly, during the year he died.'

'How amazing — all those famous names . . .'

'I have been blessed with great good fortune, which is why I propose to express my gratitude by setting down my memories before it is too late. It is to be a book of memories and impressions, and my darling Josianne, who as you see is unable to lead the life of a normal young woman, is most desirous of helping in its construction and wishes to prepare the manuscript for the English publishers who have expressed their interest in it. And you believe, do you, that six months will be sufficient time for her to perfect her understanding of the typewriter under your guidance, Miss Marlow?'

'Oh, plenty. In fact I can't help thinking it's a bit extravagant, hiring me just to teach one pupil—'

'That is for me to say,' there was a touch of arrogance about him, 'but in the meantime we will commence tomorrow. I have purchased an English typewriter to match our English tutor, ha ha, and you will find that my Josianne is always at her best in the mornings. So in the meantime, Miss Marlow, it is my pleasant duty to escort you to bed.' Briskly he removed the empty coffee cup from her hand.

'Thank you very much, Dr Kremer, but I think I can find my own way.'

Nevertheless she took his proffered arm and allowed him to escort her up the staircase. But she really was quite a lot taller than he was and the whole thing felt ridiculous, so she comforted herself by rehearsing the stinging rebuff she would administer when he tried to enter her bedroom. No thank you, Dr Kremer, I am here as an employee and I prefer that our relationship should be kept on that level . . . you may have met Brahms and had an aunt who entertained Gladstone but by God, sir, that cuts no ice with me. I once knew an undertaker who had the same ideas as you and, believe me, he got nowhere. Absolutely nowhere at all . . .

They halted outside her bedroom door and sliding her arm from his Dr Kremer shook hands with her, gave a little bow, bade her goodnight and went serenely on his way.

3 June 1938
Dear Miss Gathercole,

I arrived at Dr Kremer's house last evening after an interesting but uneventful journey. Luxembourg looks rather a picturesque old place with lots of big houses and trees and everything seems rather old-fashioned and slow, which is restful in some ways but I imagine could get on one's nerves. Still, I suppose I haven't been here long enough to form a proper opinion.

Dr Kremer seems quite a nice old gentleman and his daughter is a very pleasant girl. The latter is some sort of cripple, but I don't know any details. She goes out in a wheelchair but uses two sticks indoors, poor thing. You would roar with laughter if you saw the typewriter — a vast old Royal *with a lot of gold twirls and twiddles painted on it, but it works all right and Dr K. is very proud of it because it's an English one. We had our first lesson this morning and I think Mdlle K. will soon get the hang of it. Quite honestly I think it's going to be a waste of time and money my spending six months on one pupil but, as I say, it's early days yet.*

The food is very nice but a bit rich and they drink a glass of wine with every meal except breakfast. I often hear Dr K. playing the piano in the music-room; he has one or two advanced pupils apparently, but although he started out as a pianist he's now more interested in composing. The weather is quite hot but all the women still seem to wear hats and gloves when they go out. Will write more fully in a day or two. I hope all's well at the academy — it all seems so far away and I miss it very much — please write, it would be lovely to have a letter and all the news.

Yours very sincerely, Cassica Marlow.

* * *

7 June 1938
Dear Miss Gathercole,

You'll be pleased to know that I'm beginning to find my way around here now, and slowly getting used to the idea of being on the Continong. Father and daughter tend to speak French to one another (but Luxembourgisch to the servants) and although they speak good English as well, I'm now plucking up courage to try a bit of my schoolgirl French on them. They're very courteous and don't laugh, although they correct me sometimes, which is a good thing of course. By the time I come back I hope to be bi-lingual!

Mdlle. is getting on quite well with her typing — I'm sometimes tempted to make a real job of it and teach her Pitman as well, but she tires easily. I'm still not sure what's wrong with her but gather it's some sort of wasting disease of the muscles. She has good days and bad days, but never complains. She and her father go to Mass every Sunday and sometimes during the week as well, so perhaps that helps her in some way.

Yesterday we went out to the forest in the car where there are lots of big rocks and pine trees and it's all very beautiful but not as good as Scotland. Dr K. and I took turns in pushing Mdlle. in her wheelchair and once when I was pushing it he hid behind a tree and then sprang out on us shouting Cuckoo! I felt a bit embarrassed — after all, he must be nearing sixty — but it made his daughter laugh, which was the main thing. I'm slowly coming to the conclusion that continental people are rather more childish than we are.

Must close now as we're going to a recital of chamber music in a friend's house and Dr K. is going to play the piano part in the 'Trout' quintet, which will be nice. Must change my frock and do something about my hair, it won't lie down flat since I've been here.

Lots of love to everyone, and all the best to you,

Yours, Cassica.

* * *

24 June

Dear Miss Gathercole,

Thank you very much for your letter and it's marvellous news about Brenda Chadwick becoming secretary to the Lord Mayor. There's a pat on the back for Gathercoles if ever there was one! Congrats to all concerned.

As for me, I'm still plodding along with my one and only pupil, although plodding's hardly the word for it; life here is very full of interest and Dr Kremer and his daughter seem to treat me like one of the family and I've met some quite interesting people, mainly musicians and people who enjoy music very much, and also an Austrian ex-countess who was very sympathique but not much to look at; she had bandy legs and a set of very large china teeth. Although the Continent is so huge compared to Britain, this particular bit of it is very cosy and parochial. Everyone who is anyone in Luxembourg knows everyone else who is ditto, but they don't seem so much snobbish as just rather dignified and slow-moving. All the same, it will be very nice to be back home again.

Love to everyone,

Always, Cassica.

* * *

29 July

Dear Miss Gathercole,

Sorry I haven't written for so long. Josianne (as I'm now permitted to call her) has begun typing bits of her father's manuscript; very slowly of course, and I can't always resist correcting the spelling etc. In some ways she reminds me of my poor cousin Mona but without her physical deformity. In fact she's rather beautiful in a vague, pre-Raphaelite sort of way. As for His Nibs he's busy transcribing somebody else's music for the piano; Liszt was always doing that, and personally I think it's wrong; they ought to write something of their own and not hide behind other people.

In ten days' time we are off to stay in the family's country house, which will be rather nice after the heat of the city. I haven't seen it yet but gather it's an old mill surrounded by woods. The servants are already busy packing up and Romain the chauffeur is transporting trunkfuls of linen etc. People on the Continent never do anything by halves.

I'm addressing this to you at Hoylake because I imagine the academy's broken up for the hols by now. I still get bouts of homesickness, although I have to confess that I rather like it here.

Have a good rest, and think of me sometimes,
Ever, Cassica.

* * *

Although the gaps between letters were steadily increasing, Cassie was still enjoying writing to Emilia. Not only had distance promoted a new affection, it was also very pleasant to be able to impart — in a breezy, throw-away style — something of the life in Luxembourg. And not just the social occasions, the small dinner parties, the recitals given for friends in the grand salon, but the particular flavour of the place itself.

She described the window boxes spilling over with geraniums and dwarf marguerites, the stately dowagers in hats and gloves promenading with their dachshunds, the melodious tolling of church bells and the sensation that each day was a long and rather graceful progression that began when the city streets were swept and watered at sunrise and ended past midnight, when the last shutter had been lowered and the parks given over to the nightingales.

She also took some snaps (this is our house, taken from the opposite side of the boulevard, this is the Grand Duke's palace, which isn't a patch on Buckingham Palace and neither could their guardsmen hold a *candle* to ours). Yet for some reason she failed to enclose any of either Dr Kremer or of his daughter. Noting the discrepancy, Emilia wondered whether she liked them too much to part with them, or not enough to merit wasting film on them in the first place.

She wrote back, sitting at a table beneath the feathery profusion of tamarisk, her face shielded by a flat straw hat that gave her the look of a wise and venerable tortoise. It was very hot and still in the garden, and the presence of the sea could be sensed rather than heard.

7 August 1938
My dear Cassica,

How pleasant to receive your letter and the enclosed snapshots. They are very interesting, and it is most kind of you to think of me. The colourful window boxes remind me that your geranium cuttings are now in flower; I planted them out in my garden as I feared the roots were becoming restricted in their rather small pots, but you shall have them back when you return in the autumn.

Life is very quiet and peaceful here in Hoylake — the trippers seldom venture in this direction as they prefer the open-air swimming pool and the bandstand; speaking of which, I hear that a girl from the greengrocer's shop recently won some sort of singing contest there and has been offered a situation with a dance band. If it is the girl I am thinking of she is very plain, poor child, with spectacles and greasy hair. But I daresay modern beauty aids could come to her assistance.

I spend my holiday in reading and pottering in the house and the garden. I find that I have rather less energy these days, but my health continues to be excellent.

She laid aside the pen and allowed the letter to run on in her head: Sometimes I miss Wilfred so much that I can scarcely bear it. The garden and the house are so full of him, so alive with memories that I can hardly endure to live here anymore. I make up my mind to sell the place, to get away from the noise of the sea, but memories are all I have. To lose them would be to lose everything. So I go on alone, hoping that tomorrow the healing will start, that I will reach some kind of spiritual convalescence, but in the meantime I am getting older and even ordinary things bother me more. I do not understand about electric fuses, I am afraid if I hear a strange noise at night, there are mouse droppings in the pantry yet I am too squeamish to set a trap . . .

If only she could write the truth, could pour out her feelings in a torrent of tear-streaked words and post them off to Luxembourg knowing that they would be understood and pitied and that a return letter would arrive bulky with loving consolation . . . Brushing a small insect from her sleeve she took up the pen again:

> *All in all, life is very kind to me. Yesterday I received a postcard from Miss Sturgeon who is touring in Scotland with her little motorcar, and I read in the Post that a charitable organization has arranged to send two hundred under-nourished children from the dockside areas to Morecambe for a week. The only sad news I have is that the pillbox factory above my own establishment is threatened with closure due to lack of orders. It would be much quieter without it, and some of the girls, one has to admit, are not all that one might desire; nevertheless, it would not be the same without them.*
> *Have you received any intimation from Dr Kremer regarding the termination of your duties with his daughter? I think we envisaged the end of October, but should he be willing to dispense with your services before then, I should be very pleased. However, we must bear in mind the old saying that he who pays the piper calls the tune.*
> *With all good wishes,*
> *Yours affectionately, E. Gathercole.*

* * *

So far, Cassie had regarded her ultimate return to Liverpool with a kind of placid satisfaction. The weeks spent in Luxembourg had diminished the sense of boredom and petty frustration just as surely as they had obliterated the smell of kippers; then one day something catastrophic and totally unexpected happened, and it changed everything.

With all the terrified disbelief of someone falling over a precipice, she fell in love with Dr Kremer.

CHAPTER TWENTY

It happened at a place called Montdorf-les-Bains on the day before they were due to leave for the country.

They had driven out there with Josianne's canvas chair folded against the front passenger seat and Cassie was given to understand that the place was some kind of spa, less famous now for its waters than for its social appeal. One went to Montdorf to admire the gardens, to sip tea and listen to the orchestra, but most of all to see and be seen.

Grandly ornate and now opulent in high summer, the place rippled and flowed with silk-clad women arm in arm with formally attired escorts; hats and gloves, uniformed nurses in charge of starched children, and invalids like Josianne nodding and smiling to one another as they were wheeled along the sandy paths between the rose beds.

'Good *afternoon*, Dr Kremer . . . such a *pleasure* . . . !'

Smiles and handshakes; stiff little bows, and Dr Kremer touching with his lips the hand of a blancmange-like widow.

Some spoke in French, others in German, and switching adroitly from one to the other Dr Kremer answered courteous questions about his health, his music, his daughter — and, accompanied by politely curious glances in Cassie's direction — the young lady from England.

The orchestra was playing Massenet in the grand pavilion where afternoon tea was being served.

'I love this tune,' Cassie said dreamily. 'What is it?'

'It is from the second act of *Thaïs*. Very, very charming.' Dr Kremer hummed an accompaniment while reaching for another éclair.

'For myself, I prefer *Manon*,' Josianne said.

'I love it all,' sighed Cassie. 'All the music and the visual beauty, it's like stepping back to the turn of the century.'

'In the evenings it is full of ghosts, like Versailles or your Hampton Court.'

'But they are not kings and queens, they are wheezing old notaries and their waddling old wives.' Josianne's merriment caused people at the next table to stare. She turned pink, and her father shook his finger at her.

'You are causing perturbation, my child, and upsetting the smooth workings of the gastrics all around you.'

After tea they wandered further through the grounds, Cassie pushing the canvas chair as they followed the winding path up through the woods. The declining sun was making long shadows on the lawns below, but the air was very still and warm. Music floated up to them, and when the front wheel of Josianne's chair became momentarily obstructed by a tree root Dr Kremer placed his hand on top of Cassie's and helped her to push it clear.

It was a soft, gentle, small hand, with a few little golden whiskers just below the knuckles. She turned her head to look at him, and fell hopelessly in love for the first time in her life.

The power of it seemed to knock the breath out of her. Somehow she managed to keep on walking, but with face averted because instinct told her that what had happened must have made her look different. Everyone would know, so she stared into the glowing trees, trying to breathe normally, and beneath all the tumult and confusion prayed with all her strength that he would let his hand remain on hers. He did so, only releasing it with an affectionate little pat when they left the woodland path and turned towards the waiting Panhard. Romain sprang to attention with a click of the heels, and dazedly Cassie thought here we are, back to normal. Now the feeling'll go away . . .

But it didn't. Pressed against him on the back seat of the car she was blazingly conscious of the warmth of flesh beneath the pin-striped trousers. Why *him*? What am I going to do? Why didn't I feel like this with Desmond or poor old Arnold, or anybody . . . ? She sat with her eyes closed and listened to the murmured conversation between father and daughter.

'*Qu y a-t-il, mademoiselle?*' She could feel his breath on her cheek as he turned to look at her.

'*Je suis un peu fatiguee. C'est rien.*'

The house on the boulevard already wore a closed, abandoned look. Most of the rooms had the shutters down, and groups of dust-sheeted chairs appeared locked in a private world of their own. Up in her room Cassie stood with her forehead pressed against the window and thought with increasing amazement why him — why *him*?

He was old and foreign. And small. (Well, smallish.) The first two were bad enough, but to fall in love with a man who, let's be honest, only came up to your shoulder was ludicrous in the extreme. She felt exasperated, like someone who had caught measles at an inappropriate time and place, and told herself that if she had been such a fool as to fall in love, the best thing she could do was to fall out again, and smartly.

No. Not possible. Any attempt to stifle this new and wonderful richness of feeling would make her ill. She would become a neurasthenic, either pinched and embittered or perhaps uncontrollably aggressive, and this, common sense could not allow. She was here because she had a job to do, and the most sensible way to deal with the problem was to admit her feelings to herself but to no one else. So she did, and immediately she wanted to laugh, to pirouette, to do her hair a different way; being in love filled her with the promise of endless secret enchantment and, changing her frock for dinner, she assured herself again and again that being in love was her own private business and nothing whatever to do with anyone else. It was all perfectly simple.

So she sailed downstairs with her hair parted on the opposite side, and her sparkling vivacity made Josianne catch at her hand and say: 'Happily, you are not tired any more, mademoiselle?'

'No, I'm feeling absolutely fine now.'

Dr Kremer was pouring three glasses of port for an aperitif. She sensed him looking at her in mischievous appraisal and her heart started thudding.

'It is the prospect of a holiday from the ordinary life,' he said. 'Tomorrow you will find yourself in a new world, mademoiselle.'

He handed her a glass, and their fingers touched.

'I already have,' she said hoarsely. 'And to celebrate it, do you think you could both call me Cassie?'

They did so ('Casseee'), but although she had already been calling Josianne by her Christian name as befitted their pupil-teacher relationship, Dr Kremer made no move to suggest that she might call him Eugene. But it didn't worry her, because the new inner freedom she had granted herself allowed her to call him Eugene in her thoughts. Eugene darling Eugene, my very own darling *darling* . . .

Dinner was a less elaborate meal than usual and there was an informal picnicking air, with most of the silver put away and the curtains taken down in readiness for the annual cleaning. They took coffee in the music-room and before lowering the lid and locking the Steinway Dr Kremer played a wistful little piece that stole through the big room like a sigh.

'I've never heard that before. What was it?'

'*Berceuse pour. Josianne*,' the girl said, sitting motionless in the wheelchair. 'Papa wrote it two days after I was born.'

'It was beautiful,' whispered Cassie, and pressing her hands together under the folds of her frock thought oh, God, oh, God, if only he'd write something with all that love in it for *me* . . .

19 September 1938
My dear Cassica,

I have not heard from you for some time and cannot help being prey to a certain anxiety. Are you well, and is your situation with the Kremers still satisfactory? I am also feeling considerable disquiet in regard to the present political circumstances in which we find ourselves. For a long while now I have been suspicious of Herr Hitler, and I find his claim to the Czech Sudetenlands deeply disturbing. The stupid man has no earthly right to them at all, and as France is pledged to assist Czechoslovakia and we are pledged to assist her, I very much fear that sooner or later a second world war will ensue. What is the general climate of opinion with you? What are Dr Kremer's thoughts on the matter? As an educated and no doubt intelligent Continental, presumably he must have some.

Here at my establishment autumn term has begun well, although not without what one might call an undercurrent of unease. Several girls' fathers are helping to dig trenches in the parks and many of them are taking part in civilian field exercises designed to equip them with the necessary experience should war come and Hitler send over his bombing planes. However, we must not concentrate on gloomy prognostication to the exclusion of everything else. I am in good health; the lassitude and slight tendency towards dyspepsia that had previously troubled me seem to have disappeared.

The girls in the pillbox factory are now on what is termed short time, but it appears that no definite decision regarding their fate has yet been made.

Please write to me when you can spare the time,
Your affectionate friend, Emilia Gathercole.

The letter arrived at the house on the boulevard and remained there for ten days before being forwarded by the somewhat torpid servant left in charge. On the evening that Cassie read it, Neville Chamberlain had already arrived at Berchtesgarten in his Super Lockheed 14 and was in conference with the Reich Chancellor, but news of it had not yet penetrated the dream world of Entesmillen.

Standing close to the bank of the Mullertal, the old stone house known as Ducks' Mill was far removed from the strident discord of political machinations; Napoleon, the Kaiser, Hitler . . . all of them mere temporary ripples on the face of the deep pool that lay beneath the remains of the old mill wheel.

The house itself was large, and the best rooms with their heavily timbered ceilings and white-washed stone walls were furnished with agreeable simplicity, while the remainder, damp, shadowy and faintly mysterious, remained as storerooms or servants' quarters. A grand piano (carefully wrapped in blankets during the winter) stood open by the window that looked out on to the splashing boulder-strewn Mullertal.

Half-shrouded by trees, the place had a wistful, dreamy quality that was totally in accord with Cassie's mood. Mesmerised, she wandered from room to room, standing in the open doorways and watching the play of sunlight as it filtered through the leaves on to the tiled, rug-strewn floors. She explored the woods, silent except for the distant murmur of the river or the sudden echoing shriek of a bird, and the beauty of everything was intensified, deepened and made marvellously significant by the fact of being in love.

If Dr Kremer — Eugene — had guessed the state of her feelings towards him he gave no sign; on the whole she imagined that he remained safely in ignorance and loved him the more for it. Despite his fame and breadth of experience he was still too modest to suspect his own powers of attraction, and although he now kissed her hand sometimes when they said goodnight it was the charming, light-hearted kiss of friendship. And at this stage, his friendship was still sufficient; if he had flung himself at her feet with violent protestations of love it would have shattered everything.

Although the three of them were ostensibly on holiday they had taken their work with them, and the long tranquil days were punctuated by the sound of piano-playing and typewriter-clicking. Dr Kremer's memoirs had been completed some months before, and sometimes when Josianne felt too tired Cassie would type a dozen or so pages for her and follow with loving concern his descriptions of childhood and dawning interest in music. Rest periods were spent either in walking, with Cassie and Dr Kremer pushing Josianne in her wheelchair along the more accessible lanes and tracks, or else in dreamy solitude. Cassie read Emilia's letter of 19 September sitting on a large smooth boulder in the Mullertal's midstream, with her cotton skirt pulled down over her knees but her head tilted at an attractive angle in case Eugene should be looking at her from one of the windows.

Digging trenches in the parks? Well, so what? They wouldn't start another war, not after the last one. The plight of the girls in the pillbox factory made more impact, although a couple of nights later she dreamed that chanting blackshirts with flaming torches were marching through the woods and setting the trees on fire. At breakfast she ventured to ask Eugene his opinion of Hitler and his National Socialism.

'A plague of flies that will pass with the ending of summer,' he said. He was wearing an open-necked shirt with a flowered cravat, and his rosy-cheeked good-humoured charm moved her so much that she had to look away. A week later when they drove into Haller she bought a picture postcard and sent it to Emilia, writing it at the table of the outdoor restaurant where they had lunched on grilled trout.

Wish you were here (trite, but true). Dr K. has started to compose a major new work to be given its world premiere at a big charity concert next year. The bit I've heard sounds awfully good. J. & I are still typing merrily. Sorry to hear about the girls in the p.b. factory & wish I knew the answer, but if economists can't come up with anything I don't see how people like you & I can. Will write more fully later. Yours ever, C.M. PS. Try not to worry about Hitler; he & his ilk are nothing but a plague of flies.

'Tell me about the lady to whom you write, Casseee.' Josianne was absently outlining wine stains in spilt salt.

'Miss Gathercole? Oh, she's quite a nice old girl. Dreadfully English and a bit prim really, but I can't help being fond of her. I suppose I ought to be getting back to her and her secretarial academy. After all, you're a fairly competent typist now.'

'We will miss you.'

'Really?' Cassie gazed at her hungrily. 'You and your father — you really would?'

'Whereas we were once two people, we are now three,' Josianne said almost inaudibly.

'I've grown very fond of you, Josianne.'

In the early days it was reasonable to suppose that some of Cassie's affection for her must have been a result of her feelings for Eugene — a case of whatever belonged to the beloved was automatically rendered beloved also — but the girl's philosophical acceptance of her malady, her sudden gaiety and fits of happy giggles made her easy to love on her own account. During the weeks spent at Entesmillen the three of them seemed to have become more and more like a self-contained little family and lying in her carved peasant's bed at night Cassie would listen to the babbling voice of the river and think father, mother and daughter. I know Josianne feels like that, but I wonder if Eugene does too?

* * *

Mr Chamberlain had returned from his meeting with Adolf Hitler and Peace in Our Time was the catchphrase echoed with relief by those who remembered the 1914–1918 war, and with scepticism by those who also remembered but no longer believed in the efficacy of a signed piece of paper.

Emilia was one of these. Even if it had been typed on Gathercole-crested paper by her own hands she would have remained doubtful of its value. She was doubtful of a great many things these days, and of herself most of all. The cracks that had appeared in her self-confidence were gradually widening, and on nights when sleep failed to come she sometimes looked back with hollow amusement on all the years she had spent in nursing the academy and building it to its present state of apparent eminence. Why? What for? What was the use, ultimately, of doing anything? The most important factor of her life she had consistently neglected, overlooked, thrust aside until she was less preoccupied with more mundane things; despite all her supposed acumen she had made a point during the past thirty-one years of putting the cart before the horse.

He had died without being made a partner. Without being married to the woman whom he had loved and honoured and served with such devotion. Sometimes the knowledge of her selfish stupidity was like a grinding pain deep in her insides and she would sit on the edge of the bed with her arms clasped round her knees, rocking to and fro and groaning aloud. She began to associate mental suffering with the quantity of food she ate, and found that after a week of living on milk and arrowroot biscuits she could think of Wilfred with less anguish. As the summer faded she heated the milk and added a pinch of sugar. She lost weight, but bundled in cardigans and a grey alpaca shawl it was not immediately noticeable.

'When I went into her office this morning,' the new shorthand teacher said, 'she was sitting huddled in her chair and she looked the living image of old Queen Victoria.'

Autumn brought falling leaves and drizzling rain and they tried to cheer her up with little anecdotes about the students, but Emilia continued to sit with her hands folded and her chin sunk on her breast. She was waiting for Cassie to return.

* * *

Eugene Kremer dotted a couple of crotchets, considered them gravely, then laid aside his pen although the music continued to ripple through his mind like the Mullertal below his window.

The holiday was at an end, and they were also due to leave Entesmillen for the house on the boulevard. He was not altogether sorry; the time spent in peaceful seclusion had resulted in the first rough sketches of the composition he intended for next year's concert, but now the chill damp of autumn was creeping through the stone walls and although the woods were ablaze with colour the nights were cold. In spite of the agreeable company of Josianne and Cassie he was also looking forward to a wider social circle.

He left his desk and went over to the window. It was a grey, rather misty day and Cassie was standing on the river-bank throwing pebbles into the water. Although her back was turned towards him there was a hint of dejection in the droop of her shoulders. What an amazingly tall girl she was; so tall, so big-footed, so English . . . He was very fond of her.

Still watching her, he remembered that she was due to return to England. What a pity. Not only had she performed the task of teaching Josianne the mysteries of the typewriter, she had also proved a charming companion. Josianne would be desolate. Above the music flowing in his mind his thoughts continued to dwell on the matter. He would miss her too. Therefore, something must be done. Some plan must be put into action to keep her in Luxembourg for a while longer; for the winter, say. With pursed lips and agile fingers drumming a tattoo he continued to gaze at her, then suddenly smiled. Under the cloud of soft white hair it was like the smile of a mischievous cherub.

'Casseee!' He opened the window, and hearing his voice above the sound of the river she spun round as if she had been shot. 'Casseee, I wish to speak with you, please.'

Dropping the last of the pebbles she hurried indoors. Seeing her close to, he noticed that her hair was glittering with droplets of water.

'How foolish are the English,' he said, 'with their liking for cold and wet.'

'It's just the mist. I'm certainly not cold.'

'But it is bad to be wet.' He went over to her and placed his hands on her shoulders, reaching up to do so. Cassie winced, and instinctively bent her knees a little more. 'Your shoulders are wet. Unless you wish to have a cold you must wear a mackintosh in the rain.'

'Yes, you're right. I'll remember to do so in future.' She looked down on him, suddenly laughing and happy.

'But it is not that of which I wish to speak.' He removed his hands from her and sat down on the piano stool. 'When are you planning to leave us and return to England?'

Her laughter died. 'It's really up to you, Dr Kremer. I don't think Josianne needs me any more now in a teaching capacity, so . . .'

'You are wrong, we both need you.' He ran his hand lightly over the piano keys.

'Oh. Thank you. I mean . . .'

'So, my dear Casseee, I have a proposal to make to you. I wish in fact to propose.' He examined the word 'propose' as if it were an interesting new gadget. 'And I propose to you that you remain with us in order to help Josianne with the preparation of my memoirs. You have made her a virtuoso of the typewriter, that I know, but there are days when it is difficult for her to work because of her malady. Also I begin to realise that the English I use is not always sufficiently correct and it would be of great service if you would make the necessary corrections as the work proceeds. Now then, tell me what you say?'

He looked up suddenly, and caught the expression in her eyes. I love you, it said, and I want nothing more than to stay with you for the rest of my life.

'I'd have to think about it, Dr Kremer,' she said, turning her head away. 'And of course I'd have to consult my employer — Miss Gathercole, I mean.'

'Consult with her, then. Go away and write to her now. Tell her that Dr Kremer needs you urgently to help with his memoirs and that you will return to her in the spring like a swallow, ha ha!'

Meek as a schoolgirl she left the room, and Dr Kremer thought yes, I am very fond of her. She is funny and English and nice and I am very, very fond of her. So is my Josianne. We do not wish her to go away.

He went back to his desk, briskly struck out the dotted crotchets and began again.

* * *

Christmas in Hoylake. Grey-green waves heaving their bulk against the wall of the promenade. The scream of a hungry gull and a small rapt child pushing a brand-new doll's pram. Tall, decorated Christmas trees standing outside the porches of big houses and the wind moaning through the tamarisks that partly concealed Emilia's home.

Still wearing her dressing-gown and slippers she was sitting by the fire unwrapping the small gifts given to her by the academy staff on the day term ended. Lavender water from Miss Killigrew, who was Miss Williamson's successor, and a tartan-covered box of shortbread which Miss Sturgeon had obviously put by from her motoring tour of Scotland. Dear Miss Williamson (who was now Mrs Herbert Glover) had sent a small book of comforting rhymes by Wilhelmina Stitch, and she had also received a tasteful watercolour of a long-billed dowitcher from Sir Gunter and Lady Blake.

Christmas cards from pupils past and present crowded the mantelpiece and the window ledge and romped along the top of the bookcase, but there was nothing from Cassica. Perhaps bad weather had delayed the posts from Luxembourg.

It was time to begin roasting the small chicken she had bought, but instead she switched on the wireless and then poured herself a modest glass of Madeira. Silvery choirboy voices filled the room, singing of peace on earth and goodwill to all men. She wondered whether Adolf Hitler over in Germany had the audacity to share the same sentiments.

Lulled by the music and the warmth of the fire she dozed, the glass of Madeira untouched and the chicken, naked, cold and unloved, still lying on the kitchen table.

No one sends Christmas cards on the Continent (Cassie wrote to her eventually), *they only have New Year ones. I hope you received the one I sent. I really meant to write earlier on but the days just fly and there's so much to do. I went to Midnight Mass with Eugene and Josianne but didn't actually partake as I'm not* R.C. *But it was all very colourful and the music was lovely; over here they seem to have much higher standards for all sorts of things than we do.*

I hope you're keeping well and not working too hard. How's everyone at the academy? I can't imagine any startling changes taking place. Eugene is working on the orchestration of his Idyll ardennais ready for the big concert; apparently it'll be one of the big social events of the year. He'll be conducting it himself and we're naturally all very excited. I'm nearly halfway through typing and editing his memoirs and finding them absolutely fascinating; I'll have to buy you a copy of the book when it comes out. In the meantime forgive haste, and do drop me a line some time. I haven't heard from you for ages and I'd really love to hear all the news.

Yours ever, Cassica.

It was a breezy letter, cheerful to the point of rank insensitivity, and it successfully hid the real state of things so far as they concerned Cassie.

Not only was she still in love with Dr Kremer — and she no more addressed him as Eugene than he called her chérie — but her feelings had now deepened into a raw painfulness that she was finding increasingly difficult to conceal. The adolescent joy of being in love had largely faded, and in its place had come a deep-seated misery, a nagging sense of insecurity as the weeks passed, and it was no longer sufficient for all the love to be on her side. Now, she needed desperately that he should love her back, and spent a large proportion of her sleepless nights in analysing and brooding upon each word, glance or gesture she had received from him during the day. There were times when a certain smile could send her hopes skimming above the treetops, then a sudden terseness would send them plummeting like a shot bird. She developed a suspicion that he thought her necklace of red glass beads common, so gave them to one of the maids. She realised for the first time that men probably dislike being seen with women who are taller than they are, so developed the art of walking upright but with bent knees whenever he was in the vicinity. Love was giving her a meek, hangdog look and, although he was as charmingly cheerful as ever, she laughed and chatted less in case he should think her *farouche*. She wished she knew more about music, instead of merely liking it.

And, as if to make a deliberate nonsense of this painful, yet carefully courteous, relationship, she was working for six hours a day on his memoirs; poring over his tiny rapid handwriting, passionate to learn everything that he was prepared to tell, and then going back over it sentence by sentence in order to cleanse his grammar of all imperfections, his prose of any hint of the outlandish.

At this pre-publication stage she knew more about him than anyone else, save possibly Josianne; hungrily she consumed anecdotes concerning his student days and lingered over light-hearted confessions of a love of cafés and girls, and when he introduced his future wife, Marthe Schaus from Wiesbaden, she sat alert, pen at the ready, so that she might strike out anything unseemly or ill advised. Although she hated Marthe Schaus, her first duty was to protect her because she had once belonged to him, yet there was little need for interference because she remained throughout no more than a shadowy background figure. Perhaps (pale ray of hope) he hadn't been all that fond of her.

The Luxembourg winter was raw, cold and grey, and the rain fell unremittingly. Cassie bought herself a new winter coat and an umbrella, but didn't go out much. Josianne caught a chill during the early days of March and three weeks later Mr Chamberlain abandoned his plan of appeasement and announced that Britain would support Poland should she be attacked. Cassie read an account of it in a week-old copy of *The Times* and, strangely heartened, told Dr Kremer over supper that she thought it prudent to return to Liverpool and her old job at the academy.

'Prudent? Please, what is prudent exactly?'

'Wise.'

'And why is it wise to leave my daughter and myself and my memoirs half-finished?'

'You and Josianne are as finished as you're ever likely to be,' she said, attempting a joke for the first time for weeks, 'and as for the memoirs, I'm still waiting for you to redraft chapter nine as you promised.'

'Did I promise?'

'Yes. Three weeks ago.'

He looked cross and petulant, with pink cheeks puffed and lower lip out-thrust. 'I am too busy. It is not possible. You must redraft it yourself, Casseee.'

'But it's not my place—'

'Of course it's your place. And your place is here, with me and with Josianne.'

'You can't make me stay.'

'Of *course* I can't make you stay, you foolish creature. How could I lock you up without everyone knowing? And if I did, what good would it bear?' He looked crosser than ever. 'No, no, I can only hope that you will stay because you are needed, and because of ordinary affection.'

My affection is not ordinary, she thought despairingly. It's tearing at me like some damned terminal disease. But oh, would I really have the strength of mind to leave him? To condemn myself to not seeing him every day?

'You just want me to stay until the book is finished, then?'

He stopped looking cross and took her hand. 'Finish the book,' he said, twinkling at her, 'and then there may be other plans to discuss.'

What sort of plans? For the life of her she daren't ask, yet it required a huge effort of will to remain silent. Instead, she searched his face under cover of a smile, and when he bent to kiss her hand a lock of his white hair brushed the front of her dress.

'Wait and see,' he said, as if she had spoken. And as if he understood her anguish.

CHAPTER TWENTY-ONE

'I've lost my faith, that's all,' Arnold Openshaw said.

'Meaning that you never had much to start with?'

'Enough for the loss to hurt.'

He and his wife were sitting at the kitchen table of their London flat. It was a top-floor room with a black gas stove in the corner opposite the sink. The table was covered in leaflets, papers and pamphlets and his wife was addressing envelopes in rapid, impatient handwriting. Arnold looked at her short-clipped hair and bumpy skin and thought how nice-looking she used to be.

'So I'm resigning my Party membership, Betty.'

'Just like that?'

'I'm afraid so.'

'May I ask why?'

'I've already told you,' he said wearily. 'I can't go along with the doctrine of force, and neither can I accept orders from another country. My idea was a British communist party, not a Russian one.'

'Geographical as well as social barriers will be swept aside because world domination is what we're pledged to.' With a swiftness born of long practice she folded a leaflet and thrust it into the envelope. 'In the meantime, you could help with these.'

'Sorry.'

She looked up at him sharply. 'You mean you're not going to?'

'I mean just that.'

She tucked the envelope flap in and flicked it across to the others. 'I despise you, Arnold.'

'Yes, I know,' he said, and it didn't matter anymore. Betty, the Party, and all the old ferocity of purpose seemed aimless, pointless and a vast waste of time. I took a wrong turning, he thought. Somehow, I've got to retrace my footsteps and start again.

He reached for his pipe and tobacco tin.

'Please don't smoke in my presence, Arnold.'

'I'm going out,' he said. 'Don't wait up for me.'

* * *

Cassie and the two Kremers spent Easter at Entesmillen, but this time the three of them were not alone. A group of orchestral players was also staying in the house, and spent a major part of each day with Dr Kremer in the music-room. Torrents of music blended with the torrential spring rush of the river while Cassie sat upstairs working over the second half of the memoirs manuscript a section at a time before typing them.

Several musicians had brought their wives and children but none of them spoke English and, having exchanged courtesies with Cassie and listened politely to her still somewhat idiosyncratic French, they left her in order to chatter among themselves. But they were very gentle and charming with Josianne, who seemed temporarily to have lost interest in her role of Papa's typist and now preferred to sit reading fairy stories to a group of small girls and boys who listened spellbound and invariably begged for more.

But it was Cassie who helped her to bed each night, unfastening the more inaccessible buttons, removing the surgical boots and then helping her to swing the white matchstick legs up on to the bed. With her long plait of hair brushed out and clouding round her shoulders she looked very fragile and ethereal, and the night she put her arms round Cassie's neck and whispered 'Oh, Casseee, we do love you so . . .' Cassie hugged her back and said 'I love you, too.' And in spite of all the other people in the house, the strange impression of being mother, father and daughter was still very strong.

The highlight of June was the concert arranged for the evening of the 23rd and was to take place in the ballroom of the mansion belonging to the Austrian ex-countess. A champagne supper was to follow, and proceeds from the sale of tickets were earmarked for the relief of leprosy in the Belgian Congo. All the *haut monde* was to be present and Radio Luxembourg was to broadcast the second half of the concert which contained the first performance of the *Idyll ardennais* conducted by the composer himself.

Luxembourg dressmakers, pins between lips, fussed with darts and plackets, folds and pleats in the gowns of well-proportioned ladies while elderly valets sponged and pressed the evening dress of elderly bankers and lawyers and medical men. Chandeliers were feather-dusted and fresh orchids arrived from the Côte d'Azur. Nerves tightened and tempers snapped, and everyone was far too occupied to hear the rumble of political thunder echoing from the direction of Danzig.

Given the task of supervising Josianne's toilette, Cassie persuaded her to wear a long voile dress with little pink flowers on a violet background, and for herself she chose black velvet in order to provide a dramatic effect among all the pastels and diamonds of the Luxembourgeoise. It suited her, yet when it was time to dress her nerve failed and looking in the mirror she could only see herself as a gawky bird of ill omen, a tall, black-clad spectre about to haunt the feast with her unrequited love. In a sudden panic she tore it off and substituted a nondescript garment with puffed sleeves and a crossover neckline which she had worn many times before. It did little to improve her self-esteem and she lurked uneasily and with bent knees among the *biedermeier* and *art nouveau.*

The Grande Duchesse Charlotte arrived and the queue of those to be presented to Her Royal Highness assembled. Dr Kremer with a white gardenia in his buttonhole was the only one to make her smile at some brief and inaudible quip and watching yearningly from the doorway Cassie thought I bet she's in love with him, too. Her yearning increased as Josianne, the only other person she knew well, was removed from her side and tenderly escorted to the front row of crimson *fauteuils*.

The concert proceeded, and although she had been looking forward to it for so many weeks, she was conscious of a sense of anti-climax. And it was the same with the splendours of the ballroom which a while back she would have enjoyed describing in a letter to Emilia — *picture Eugene and me among all our fine-feathered friends, including royalty* . . . But for some reason she could no longer raise these old chirpy exaggerations; oppressed by a curious foreboding she could only sit staring down into her lap.

A rustle of expectancy greeted the return of the orchestra after the interval, and a spatter of applause for the first violin rapidly increased as Dr Kremer wound his way briskly through the music stands and reached the conductor's desk. They greeted him with enthusiasm, yet with the respect due to Luxembourg's leading composer. Smiling beneath the soft cloud of white hair he turned to them and bowed, and Cassie was blinded by a sudden rush of tears. Discreetly dabbing her eyes she thought I'd give anything not to be in love with him. Being in love's absolutely awful; no peace, no happiness, no self-confidence, but oh, God, if I thought I wasn't going to see him any more I'd die . . .

The music began, and all the familiar scraps and snippets of tunes now put together and made whole took her back through the past twelve months. Music, and the sound of the river at Entesmillen; music, and white ninon curtains billowing at the open window and reflected in the polished black lid of the Steinway in Luxembourg. Music and the taste of white wine and the little red cherries called mirabelles;

music echoing through empty rooms, spilling out through unshuttered windows into the park, the boulevard, the woods and the wild valleys; the *Berceuse pour Josianne*, the thunder of Beethoven and the little pattering feet of Scarlatti.

She loved him endlessly and for ever, but the frail hope that he loved her too was crumbling more and more. Finish the book and then there may be other plans to discuss, he had said, but the words had long ago been sucked dry and were now as arid as a row of pebbles.

When the music ended there were cries of '*Bravo!*' and Cassie applauded too, but as Dr Kremer returned to the platform to bow and smile his acknowledgement she realised that, after all the weeks of eager anticipation, his music had formed no more than a background to her thoughts. Sunk in self-pity, she had let it all slip through her fingers.

Following the rest of the audience to the supper-room she came to the conclusion that she could no longer endure the uncertainty of her position. She had to know, once and for all, precisely where she stood with him. Had he plans, or had he not? And if he had plans that concerned her, perhaps he would be kind enough to tell her what they were.

She accepted the first glass of champagne and it made even less impression than the music had done. It too was merely an accompaniment to her thoughts. Seeing the empty glass, a manservant politely removed it from her fingers and substituted a full one. She drank that one too, and the words ran smoothly through her mind: after all, Eugene, fond of you as I am, I have other things to consider. For one thing, there may be a second world war, in which case it would be my duty to return to my country to offer my services . . .

Edging towards the immense buffet table, she had her toe trodden on by an old chap in military uniform. When he apologised in German she nodded acceptance and said: '*Pas de tout, monsieur le colonel. Je sais bien que mes pieds sont trop grands.*'

'Aha,' he switched to French. 'But the mademoiselle is of admirable stature and the feet are merely in correct proportion.'

She studied the three rows of medals on his chest. Three rows seemed a little excessive. Too many ribbons (Ribbentrop, ha ha!) Thanking him for his courtesy she moved away, and began sipping a third glass of champagne.

Sitting alone in a corner she ate some foie gras and black truffles decorated with endive and red chicory while she watched Eugene twinkling with vivacity on the far side of the room. The Grande Duchesse was standing by Josianne's chair with her hand resting on her shoulder; Josianne looked pale and rather tired, then a group of people obscured the view. Oh, my darling, can't you sense me over here, beaming love at you like a great unwieldy lighthouse? Eugene, Eugene, oh, Eugene . . .

Someone else came over to speak to her, in halting English this time, and for a while it was comforting to exchange idle pleasantries; but the noise and the heat were increasing so she escaped and wandered out into the corridor bearing a fifth glass of champagne. A giant ormolu clock pointed to the time being ten minutes to midnight. Ten minutes more and then I must run from the ball and become Cinderella again. Although come to think of it, I've never been anything else. I haven't even had the pleasure of a smile from the Prince, let alone a waltz. The original wallflower, that's me. Unloved, unnoticed, God, I'd be better off in the dear old Rialto with Effie . . .

She wandered on a little unsteadily and found a small anteroom, its doors flung open, its walls lined with pleated silk. She sat down on a gilt and ebony sofa and after a moment's consideration slipped off her shoes. She felt rather tired, and thought how lovely it would be if she fell asleep and awoke to find him bending over her and about to restore her with a kiss.

If I was a character in a novel, she thought, that's how the author would write it.

* * *

She didn't go to sleep, and neither did Dr Kremer come to look for her in the anteroom.

Instead, she sat there in stockinged feet and melancholy boredom for about twenty minutes before putting her shoes on again and trailing back to the supper-room. Although the Grande Duchesse had departed, no one else seemed inclined to go home; they were still sipping and nibbling and chatting with unabated relish. What stamina, she thought, and made her way over to the group that enclosed Dr Kremer in its midst. It was not difficult to look down on him over their shoulders and catching sight of her he cheerily kissed his fingers to her.

'This is my dear, special friend,' he said in French. 'The friend of myself and the friend of my Josianne. Without her company we would be entirely desolated.'

They all turned to look at her with bright speculative eyes; eyes filled with worldly-wise experience, and with the very best champagne. Their gaze filled her with sudden anguish, with a red-faced, tongue-tied misery, and she bolted. Then, cursing her stupidity, sauntered carefully back again a few minutes later but the circle had broken up, dissolved into small isolated groups that no longer appeared to recognise her.

It was one thirty in the morning before they began to leave, and another half-hour had passed when she finally encountered Dr Kremer, alone, in the small cloakroom off the massive marble hall. He was washing his hands.

'Cuckoo!' The bright, comical expression that a child would love.

'Am I really your dear, special friend?' Parched and desperate, she loomed in the doorway.

'But of course — *naturellement* — why do you ask?'

'Because I love you. Because I'm *in* love with you. You must know I am.'

'Aah, Casseee.' He removed his hands from the water and began to dry them carefully. He looked at her with his head on one side. 'You have been drinking too much champagne, you foolish girl.'

'No, I haven't.' Having burned her boats and blurted the confession, the only thing she could do now was to appear calmly, lucidly matter-of-fact.

'Well, yes. I drank just enough to enable me to see the impossibility, the sheer impracticability of going on living under your roof under your patronage under false pretences. You may like to pretend that it's only friendship between us but you know perfectly well it's more than that. And I just want to know what's going to happen to us. Where we're going. I've very nearly finished the work on your book, and—'

'Oh, my poor dear.' He stopped drying his hands, those so loved little pale pink hands, and allowed them to rest motionless within the folds of the towel. 'Of course I want you to stay with us. I want you to make your home with us for the rest of our lives, but I hesitated to ask you in case you were discomposed—'

'Oh, my God, why ever should you think that? Oh, Eugene, you've absolutely no idea . . .' She choked, and feverishly rubbing her stinging eyes failed to notice that his expression had changed.

'But, my dear, it would be on the same terms as before. Dear friend and companion, assistant with my English work.'

'You mean—' Very slowly she removed her hands from her eyes. 'You mean, that would be all?'

He nodded.

She stood facing him for a moment in utter silence. Then she seemed to go mad. Rushing across the floor she clasped her arms round him and began showering kisses down on him; hungry, desperate kisses that exploded against his hair, his neck, his shoulders and his horrified face. His hands fought to free themselves from the towel and she seized them and tried to cram them into her mouth, kissing, biting, nibbling, chewing, all in a frantic effort to engulf and absorb him. He struggled, and protested furiously in German, then switched to French, but his voice was smothered in the front of her dress.

'Eugene, I love you I love you — I must say it and I don't care what happens any more now because I've burst out. I've burst out into the light — I can't go on living with it all pent up inside any longer — it's what Plato called living a lie of the soul . . . I've never been in love with anyone before, and I didn't know what it was like or what to expect, and it isn't just you — well, it *is*, but I love Josianne so much too, and your music and your whole life and everything that's connected with you — you give everything a special kind of *colour* — oh, my darling, my darling, just let me have the luxury of calling you darling out loud instead of only in secret—'

His feet left the floor. Tails swinging, he dangled in her grasp helpless as a marionette.

'You can do what you like. It doesn't matter now. You can kick me out, have me arrested for assault and battery, nothing you can do will ever make me change from how I feel—' She shook him. A coin fell out of his pocket and rolled noisily across the marble floor. The sound seemed to increase her madness and she clasped him even tighter.

'All right, I don't care if we don't get married! I'll just be your woman. Your squaw, your strumpet, your *cocotte* — I'll lie down on the floor and let you walk on me like a mat — use me, trample on me, do what you like. I know now what being in love means — it means being without shame or modesty or common sense, it means just wanting to *drown* yourself in the other person—'

He wrenched his fist free and hit her. The blow landed on the top of her head and made her stagger. She dropped him, and with the physical contact broken, she seemed to dwindle and die. With a last huge effort she reached the open doorway, and pushing through a handful of amazed spectators crept silently away.

* * *

It was a long while before she could bear to contemplate what had happened.

Wandering round the deserted city in the warm summer darkness she kept her mind carefully blank. No past, no present, no future. A woman with no identity traversing squares and tree-lined boulevards that had no name. I am nothing. Soon I will be less than nothing because I will be dead. She heard the faraway hoot of a car and told herself that if it came past she would walk out into the road in front of it. She was quite sincere. She wanted very much to die. But the car never came so she kept on walking, blank-eyed and dizzy with fatigue, until the first dawn streak silhouetted the trees in the park.

She reached the house expecting to find her suitcases already piled and waiting on the front steps. They were not, but lights were on in the porch and the door was standing open. She approached very slowly, too tired and too blank to react even when Eugene — Dr Kremer from now on — stepped out of the shadows and said: 'Josianne is ill. I am waiting for the doctor.'

Silently she went into the house and up to Josianne's room where a shaded lamp was paling in the strengthening daylight. The girl was lying on her back in bed and she appeared to be asleep, although her eyelids twitched restlessly as if she were dreaming. Her hair was still bound round her head in a thick plait, and the pink and violet dress lay discarded over a chair.

'Josianne . . .' Cassie took her hand and held it gently, uselessly. It felt very limp. After a moment or two she replaced it on the coverlet, and Dr Kremer came quietly into the room.

Without looking at Cassie he said: 'Romain drove her home after supper because she had a bad headache. She now appears to be worse, although she sleeps.'

'If only I'd known.'

If only I'd known I'd have come home with her. And then what happened wouldn't have happened . . .

'I'll be leaving tomorrow,' she said dully. 'Today, I mean.'

'As you wish.'

She left the room and went to pack her bags. But she didn't return to England because after the doctor had spent a long time with Josianne he called for a second opinion and the combined diagnosis was that of meningitis.

The household seemed immediately to change into another gear. The servants moved silently and reverently about their duties, two nuns belonging to a nursing order took possession of the sickroom, one for the daytime and one for the night-time vigils, and tanned bark was spread across the boulevard in front of the house to deaden the sound of traffic.

The house itself lapsed into silence; no music, no laughter, no click of footsteps across the polished floors. The life of the place seemed to remain suspended in sympathy with that of the girl who lay restless and moaning in the cool shadows of her room.

The news soon spread that the composer's daughter was seriously ill, and bouquets of flowers were left at the rear entrance; devout wishes for a speedy recovery were scribbled across visiting cards by people who had never even met her, and a Mass was said for her which Cassie yearned to attend but decided not to.

For in spite of the doctors and nurses, the hovering priest and the tiptoeing servants, she and Eugene Kremer were alone at the very heart of the situation. By tacit agreement they visited the sickroom separately and, although they had no knowledge of her real official position in the household, the nuns withdrew from the bedside when Cassie approached as they did for the arrival of Dr Kremer. It was eerily like the old, foolish sensation of mother, father and child.

Yet they were unable to comfort one another, or to share their grief. That terrible and bizarre encounter in the marble cloakroom had sealed them off from one another like a dense fall of rock. Neither could forget it, and neither could speak of it. At the end of one long and exceptionally miserable day Cassie scribbled the words 'Please forgive me' on a piece of paper and laid it on his pillow, then ten minutes later darted back and hastily retrieved it. She wasn't sure whether she wanted his forgiveness; whether in fact there was anything to forgive. She had behaved like a fool, like a silly love-tormented adolescent, but whose fault was that? He must have known, must have realised what was happening, and had probably enjoyed watching her hopes rise in vain. It was impossible to analyse the true state of her feelings, however, because they were now all centred on Josianne.

By the fourth day the girl appeared to be in a coma; the restless twitching and tossing of her head had ceased and she lay motionless and without pillows, her closed eyes like huge bruises on a surface of parched white. Cassie sat holding her hand while the nun laid ice compresses on her forehead, but whatever they did she seemed beyond their reach. That evening they cut off her hair, slicing away at the pale thick ropes of it like people determined to jettison the last of the cargo from a sinking ship.

In the music-room Dr Kremer sat at the closed piano, staring blindly in front of him. He too looked shockingly different; ivory white instead of ebullient pink, and with deep tortured lines which began at each nostril and dragged down the corners of his mouth.

'You ought to rest. I'll call you if anything changes.'

He made an impatient little movement with his hands. 'I cannot rest.'

She moved across to the window and looked out through the ninon curtains. White shutters and grey walls; summer window boxes blazing with colour and cars slowing down respectfully before the wide strip of tanned bark.

Nothing more had been said about her departure. That, like everything else, seemed to be a matter of mutual indifference and she was living out of her suitcases like a person of no fixed abode.

'Here comes the doctor again.'

'The maid will show him in.'

'Perhaps he'll have better news this time.' I'm whistling in the dark, she thought. Whistling to keep his spirits up, as well as mine.

But when the change in Josianne's condition finally came it was in the early hours of the morning. Sleeping lightly and restlessly Cassie heard the patter of slippers along the corridor, the soft urgent tapping on Dr Kremer's door.

Pulling on her dressing-gown she hurried towards him as he came stumbling out of his own room, breathing heavily. The nun had already hurried back to the sickroom and in the wan light Cassie saw him beckon to her.

'Come.'

She followed him, her heart thumping, and was first of all aware of the nun moving about the room with a new swiftness. Intoning quietly she seemed to be rearranging a number of small objects on the white-draped table, but whether they were of a religious or of a medical nature there was no time to decide. Dr Kremer had already sunk to his knees by the bedside and was holding his daughter's hand as Cassie apprehensively drew near.

'Oh, Casseee,' Josianne murmured, her eyes wide open. 'How nice . . .'

* * *

But it would take a very considerable time, the doctors warned, before she recovered. Due to her normally delicate health the inflammation of the meninges had lowered her general constitution to a dangerous level and there must be no risk of exposure to infection of any kind. Even the merest chill could prove a disastrous setback to recovery.

So she continued to remain in bed, although now permitted to lie with a bank of big square pillows at her back and the shutters raised to let in the sunlight. She looked very different with her hair cut short and curling thick as lambswool — like a fourteenth-century *putto,* her father said — and she accepted the change, when she discovered it, with passivity. She appeared passive about most things, content to remain in a quiet and dreamlike state through the long summer days, and only showed signs of mutiny when it was hinted that Cassie was on the point of returning to England.

'I do not want her to go. Therefore she cannot.'

How like the patrician simplicity of her father's statements; I propose to you that you remain with us. We both need you (and whether our requirements are the same as yours is neither here nor there) . . .

'But I have work to do in England, Josianne. I belong there, I have a little home of my own and I haven't seen it for well over a year.'

'This is your home. You belong here with Papa and me.'

'Not really . . .'

Soft opening chords from the Steinway drifting up the staircase and in through the open door. *Berceuse pour Josianne* played with a yearning wistful quality that touched the heart. What was he yearning for? Josianne's mother? Her real mother, and the early sunlit days of marriage and parenthood . . .

'You will stay, Casseee.' Josianne took her hand and lovingly examined it. The strong fingers and healthy rounded nails. She turned it over and scrutinised the palm.

'Ah, Casseee, I read the fate. I am soothsayer, you know? And I read that your future is here in Luxembourg close with us where you will become a stout and happy Luxembourgeoise with a little dachshund on a string and every afternoon we will go to the Place d'Armes and eat cream cake and we will both look after Papa and manage his affairs—'

'Stop torturing me, you hideous girl—' She was laughing, but the torture was real. 'Drink your tisane-thing and then I'll read to you for half an hour before dinner.'

So Cassie lingered on, still refusing to unpack her belongings properly as the languid summer days slid by and Josianne was allowed to sit in a chair by the window, and then finally to dress and be carried downstairs to a *chaise-longue* in the conservatory. She looked unbelievably frail, and the joy with which she seized her two sticks and tried to walk a few steps caused one of the watching maids to burst into tears.

'We will go to Entesmillen at the end of August,' Dr Kremer said. 'Where country air and good country food will complete the convalescence.'

'Yes. I think a change would do her the world of good.'

The wall of silence had been crumbling between them since the first hint of Josianne's recovery, and although the old sense of ease had gone, they were able to converse with reasonable lack of restraint. But many things were left unsaid and hung on the air like the faint invalid scent that still pervaded Josianne's room; it was as if the relationship between Cassie and Dr Kremer was also in a state of convalescence, and brighter things could be expected for the future.

But recovery brought for Cassie a reawakening of love. No longer wild, uncontrolled and tearful, it seemed to have matured into a seasoned and philosophical calm; she saw that, out of the three of them, she was the only one to recognise that what we want and what we get do not necessarily coincide. Now largely resigned to the impossibility of any future with Eugene Kremer save that of secretary-cum-daughter's-companion the sadness occasionally overwhelmed her, yet the ensuing tears brought genuine relief, and tranquillity followed. She wondered, a trifle dubiously, whether she was developing an inclination towards religion.

And so they drifted, and once again the servants began to make their annual preparations for closing the house. The curtains were taken down, the silver was packed and the dust sheets reappeared. In all the big houses the shutters had long ago rattled down over windows dulled by city dust and heat and the parks had become empty of small children and their uniformed nurses. It was now time to join them. Time to say goodbye.

On the last evening when Josianne had gone to bed, Cassie and Dr Kremer sat in rattan chairs in the conservatory, sipping after-dinner coffee. The fountain had been switched off and the pool drained of water. Through the open glass doors the trees of the park stood motionless.

'I remember us sitting here drinking coffee on the evening I arrived.'

'I remember, too.'

'I hope the book will be a success. Will you send me a copy?'

'But *of course.*' He looked at her with some of the old impish humour, the cloud of white hair turned to silver by the lamplight, the pink cheeks puffed and shining. In another moment he would suddenly cry *Cuckoo!*

But they lapsed into silence; an easy, companionable quiescence that they had never achieved before. Perhaps it was only ever achieved between people who knew one another very well; or at least, when one of them knew the other one very well.

'On that first evening,' Dr Kremer said eventually, 'I believe I spoke of my wife.'

'Yes. You told me that she was Viennese and very attractive.'

'Which was true. Very, very attractive and beautiful.'

'But I've never seen any portraits or photographs of her.'

'I only have one.'

He left his chair and walked through the room where Cassie and Josianne had sat during their first meeting. He returned carrying a small silver photo frame and from it gazed a delicate-looking woman with large luminous eyes under a heavy crown of upswept curls. Cassie studied it intently.

'Yes. She was very beautiful indeed.'

Another long silence, during the course of which Dr Kremer drained his coffee cup and set it down.

'She died of a muscular wasting disease, the same one from which my Josianne suffers. It runs in her family.'

Cassie closed her eyes.

'Eventually, too, Josianne will die.'

'So couldn't I — why couldn't I—' She fought to remain calm, to fight down the absurd eleventh-hour hope. 'I mean, would it be any help if I stayed after all?'

'No, my dear.' He looked at her with such wistful affection that for a moment it almost destroyed her. 'At first I thought ah yes, here is someone interesting and kind and *bien élevée* who will instruct and amuse my poor child and who will perhaps be persuaded to stay for as long as necessary. But once the heart becomes involved it is no longer practical to consider such things. The pain would be too great, and I have nothing to offer you in recompense.'

A few weeks ago she would have cried out in protest; would have argued vehemently that the pain was her own affair; might have sobbed, made a scene. But now, after staring hard into her coffee cup she was finally able to acknowledge that he had a wisdom far greater than her own. She even managed a precarious little smile.

'But we'll keep in touch, won't we?'

'Of *course*,' he said. 'Of course' was one of his favourite expressions.

She left early on the following morning, Romain driving her to the station before returning to play his part in the migration to Entesmillen.

Josianne wept when they said goodbye and gave her a little gold crucifix.

'Come back, Casseee — come back one day . . .'

'I'll be back,' Cassie lied. 'And in the meantime, I won't be all that far away.'

Her suitcases were stowed in the yellow Panhard and Romain was standing to attention with the rear door held open for her.

'Goodbye, Dr Kremer.' Smiling down at him, she held out her hand.

'Adieu, my dear Casseee.' He took her hand and touched it with his lips. Then looked up at her with a comical little grimace. 'My Gott, you seem to have grown even taller!'

'Not really. I've just stopped walking with my knees bent.'

'Is that an old English custom?'

'Sort of.'

She went down the steps and out to the car, moved by the tears in his eyes and proud because her own had managed to remain dry.

CHAPTER TWENTY-TWO

There were three hours to wait for the boat to Ostend so she put her luggage in a *consigne* and went to look round the town. She wandered past the quayside fish stalls and then had a meal and a glass of red wine in a small café where they were listening to the blare of news on the wireless and arguing about *la guerre*.

In the narrow streets opposite the sea a number of shopkeepers were already nailing the shutters in place over their windows, and she lingered outside a small antique shop admiring an oil painting in a heavily carved frame. It was a seascape, the setting sun lighting a serene golden pathway through quiet waves. There were no ships, no birds, nothing but a calm sense of certainty underlying the visual beauty, and it made her think of Hoylake for the first time for weeks. On impulse she enquired the price and, although it was more expensive than she had envisaged, she had sufficient Belgian currency left with which to buy it.

It was quite a big picture, and fairly heavy, but the dealer took endless trouble to pack it securely, and when the transaction was completed she shook his hand and wished him *bonne chance*.

'We will all need it,' he replied.

She lugged the picture back to the port, visualising Emilia's pleasure when she received it. I know I haven't kept in touch as much as I should have done — perhaps one day I'll be able to bring myself to tell you *why* — but in the meantime, Emilia dear, I want you to accept this not only as a token of my very real affection, but also as a sort of tribute to Wilfred . . .

The ferry was crowded with British holidaymakers hastening home; most of them seemed gloomily resigned to whatever lay ahead, and eavesdropping on conversations Cassie was surprised by how well informed they were about the latest developments in the crisis. It made her realise to what extent the past year had held her cocooned and protected against the unpleasant world outside; she couldn't even remember anyone in Luxembourg polluting the atmosphere with a mention of fascism.

Lime Street station: no one to meet her and, apart from the prospect of giving Emilia the picture, no sense of gladness at returning. Only a dull sense of surprise at seeing sandbags piled outside the North Western Hotel, and a twinge of irritation with a man in army uniform who bumped into her, cursed under his breath and then scurried away as if the war had already begun and he was in sole charge.

She took a taxi to Falkner Square and the caretaker slip-slapped up the basement steps and cried, 'Ay, love, we thought he'd got yer!'

'Who?'

'Adolf!'

'Oh — Hitler, you mean.' Cassie gave a wan smile and unlocked her door.

She was quite prepared for the flat to look dusty and unwelcoming, but its initial impact was far worse than she had envisaged. She had never realised before how small and tawdry it was.

She unpacked, made up the bed, opened the windows and then listlessly sorted through the accumulation of letters piled behind the door. Considering that she had been away for so long there was nothing of great interest. Bills, a few invitations to parties, a reminder that her library ticket had expired and, near the top, an official communication telling her where to collect her gas mask. She sat there for a long while with the letters in her lap, staring out of the window and thinking I must forget about Luxembourg. I mustn't be homesick for what was never a home.

So she pulled herself together and went out shopping. Granby Street looked much the same only grubbier, and Effie's ironmonger's was now a sweet shop with the upper windows bare of curtains. She went into a phone box to acquaint Emilia with the news that she was back and had a present for her, but there was no reply.

Sitting in the gloom because she had no blackout curtains, the loneliness that evening was awful, the sense of alienation acute. In desperation she walked round to Rodney Street in the glimmering streetlight to apologise to Godfrey Gibson-Rose for not keeping in touch, but a To Let sign hung outside his flat. So she walked home again, and towards dawn dreamed that she was eating crisp little mirabelles down by the river at Entesmillen.

The next day was Saturday, and again she telephoned Emilia. No reply. Peeved, she realised that she must be away on holiday. She then telephoned The Mount, and a maid's voice informed her that Mr Marlow and madam would be in Torquay for a further week. God damn everybody, she thought, and went down to one of the big stores to buy blackout material.

The evacuation of Liverpool's children was almost complete, but she passed one of the last contingents marching bravely towards Lime Street:

Whistle while you wairk!
Mussolini bought a shairt,
Hitler wore it, Chamberlain tore it
And rolled him in the dairt!

Their high little voices rose above the sound of traffic. Moved, she smiled and waved, and they waved back.

The weather was hot, but she didn't feel like staying at home so she walked on down into the city with the vague idea of going to the Pier Head and perhaps taking a ferry to New Brighton, or somewhere. Instead, years of habit guided her footsteps in the direction of Hockenhall Street.

And there it was, the same as ever. The tall sooty building with the grim facade that concealed the wandering basements, the gloomy hall and the splendid staircase that led to Emilia's sanctum. She stood outside, visualising the classrooms, the rows of typewriters with their keys covered to encourage the art of touch-typing, and although the place would be closed until the new term she went up the steps.

The front door was ajar and she heard the sound of voices. She went inside, and in the thunderous light which came from the big stained-glass window saw to her surprise that Miss Sturgeon and Miss Killigrew were standing at the foot of the staircase. Astonishment was mutual.

'Cassica!'

'Miss Sturgeon — Pauline!'

At last she had found people who seemed really pleased to see her. They hurried forward with outstretched hands and Pauline Killigrew kissed her cheek.

'How was Luxembourg? Why didn't you write, you mouldy old thing? Are you planning to follow tradition and marry the chap?'

Luxembourg was fine, she told them. Sorry I didn't write, and no, I'm not planning to marry anyone at the moment. But she could say it cheerfully, smilingly, because seeing them was so much more of a pleasure than she would have imagined.

'How's everything here? How's Emilia, and what are you both doing here in the hols?'

Their expressions changed. The smiles disappeared. 'You don't know, then?' Miss Killigrew said finally. 'No, if you've only just got back I don't suppose you do.'

'Miss Gathercole's dead,' Miss Sturgeon said. 'She died two weeks ago.'

* * *

She couldn't say much; just stand there and stare at them.

'So what's — going to . . .'

'We don't really know. But Miss Sturgeon had a key and we just came round to see if we could do anything. A bit silly I suppose, but . . .'

'What did she die of?' Suddenly she couldn't tolerate the thought of Emilia dying; she wanted to shout it's not true — it's not *true*! Yet, she needed to hear everything.

'The coroner said it was death from natural causes — there had to be a coroner's inquest because she was apparently found dead in the garden. Sitting in a chair, poor old dear, and the postman said he thought she was just sitting there staring out to sea. He went over to speak to her, then he realised that she must have been out there all night . . . she was wet with dew . . .'

Staring out to sea. The sea in which Wilfred had died. Swallowing hard, Cassie whispered: 'She died all alone. Oh, God, how dreadful.'

'But they seem to think it was in her sleep,' Miss Killigrew said. 'I don't think she suffered.'

'But she must have been so lonely . . .'

She turned and began to walk blindly across the hall. She went out to the little door that led to the garden and unlocked it. The leaves of the fig tree were turning to autumn gold. She sat down on the old bench. I can't believe it, I can't believe it. Not *Emilia.* Emilia wouldn't just go and die like *that* . . .

She sat staring helplessly at the toes of her shoes and after a little while Miss Sturgeon and Miss Killigrew came out and sat beside her. Aware that Cassie had been far closer to Miss Gathercole than the rest of the staff, they maintained a tactful silence.

'It's so quiet here,' Cassie said, finally rousing herself. 'Where are the pillbox girls? I thought they always worked until midday on Saturdays.'

'Closed down. They were all given a week's paid holiday and told not to come back.'

'They'd been on short time for ages. I suppose nobody wants pillboxes any more . . .'

'I suppose we'll be closing down, too?' Oh, Emilia, my dear old Emilia, did you die hating me for being so neglectful? Or perhaps I'm flattering myself; perhaps you'd forgotten me as I'd forgotten you.

'Autumn term's due to start on the eleventh.'

'I can't believe there mightn't be a Gathercoles anymore,' Miss Sturgeon said tearfully. 'It's part of Liverpool, somehow.'

'Who knows if there'll be a Liverpool left? Once the war starts, anything could happen.'

'Perhaps it won't start. Don't jump to conclusions.'

'Listen,' Pauline Killigrew said, 'Hitler's already bombed Poland, it said so on the news. Any minute now Chamberlain's going to issue an ultimatum to him, but it's only a formality as everyone knows. I mean, he's not going to stop now, just because we tell him to, is he?'

Listening in silence, Cassie watched a beetle meandering between the cracks of the paving. (Emilia, did you ever sit here with Wilfred? Holding hands and feeling you loved him so much that nothing else was real?)

'My friend told me that if anything happens she wants to join the army as a driver.'

'They don't have women in the army, do they?'

'No, but they *will* have. When the balloon goes up they'll be free to order everyone about as they please.'

'Oh well, human beings can get used to anything,' Miss Sturgeon said. 'My father always said that that's the secret of our superiority over things on four legs.'

'Did she seem any different at the end of term?' Cassie asked, still thinking of Emilia. 'Tired, I mean, or not very well?'

They looked at one another, their nice, open faces constricting with the effort to remember.

'No, I don't think so . . .'

'She got jolly ratty with me about bad results in a typing test and ticked a pupil off for coming to the academy without stockings.'

'In other words, she was much the same as usual,' Cassie said, trying to sound light-hearted. But went on thinking, Emilia *dead.* I could believe in the heavens falling, but not that.

'I'm not going to like the war,' Pauline Killigrew said. 'I hate the blackout, and everywhere seems so quiet and unnatural now all the kiddies have gone.'

'It said in last night's paper that all members of the Formby Golf Club have been asked to clear their lockers in preparation for hostilities.'

'Come on,' Cassie said, with an effort, 'I think it's time we went to find a bite of lunch somewhere.'

Banging the heavy front door of Gathercoles behind them, they wondered whether they could really be leaving for the last time.

And on the following morning at 11.15 people all over Britain who had access to a wireless set listened to the sad old-gentleman voice of Neville Chamberlain as he explained slowly and patiently about the ultimatum having expired without any undertaking on the part of Herr Hitler to withdraw his troops from Polish territory. Consequently, we were now in a state of war with Germany.

Barrage balloons floated in the serene sky over Liverpool, and in Falkner Square, Cassie's caretaker rushed out and grabbed her cat off the railings and hurried it indoors to safety. No one knew what to expect, what to do, but there was no rejoicing as there had been in 1914; merely a dull acceptance of the inevitable, and Cassie spent the rest of the day sewing her blackout curtains. And as she sewed she thought about Emilia. I let her down . . . far worse even than I let Mona down . . .

On the following day an affable man in a linen jacket called in order to issue her with a national registration card — When I called before they told me you were abroad. Anywhere interesting? And then on the following morning, Tuesday 5 September, she received a letter from a firm of solicitors in Dale Street asking her to call. She did so and learned that as sole beneficiary under the last will and testament of the late Miss Emilia Charlotte Gathercole she had inherited not only a dwelling-house and all its contents in Hoylake, but also the premises and business establishment in Hockenhall Street known as the Gathercole Commercial Academy.

* * *

It took her twenty-four hours to believe it, and on Thursday she went back to the solicitor and said thank you very much but I can't accept it.

'*It,* Miss Marlow?' He looked at her with a questioning smile.

'Any of it,' Cassie said. 'I can't accept the house or anything that's in it, and neither can I accept the academy. Least of all the academy.'

'You would be throwing away quite a fortune—'

'I don't care!' she cried with mounting agitation. 'I just don't want to have anything to do with it!'

'Now don't upset yourself, Miss Marlow,' he replied.

He had seen it all before. In his opinion legatees were seldom satisfied with their lot and always complained that they had been bequeathed either too little or else all the wrong things. It was more unusual that a sole legatee should quibble about the inheritance of an entire estate, but that too had been known before. So he patted her shoulder with a fatherly hand and told her to go home and think about the matter very carefully. Hasty decisions were always regretted, and she must remember that she would be making one that would affect not only the rest of her life but also the lives of others.

'I suppose you know Gathercoles?' she said.

'My own dear Miss Booth received her training there, and over the years has proved herself a pearl beyond price.'

Suppressing a shudder Cassie mumbled something appropriate and, promising to get in touch with him again tomorrow, made a beeline for the door. She went back to the flat and locked herself in.

I don't want it. God help me, I don't. I loved Emilia, I realise that now, but I've spent most of my life trying to get away from Gathercoles and I'm sick to death of training office girl fodder. I'm sick of the pettiness and the primness — undies worn twice are not quite nice and if your employer tries to fondle your knees you must discourage him politely and make sure that your skirts are of an appropriate length. Hems can always be lengthened with the aid of bias binding . . .

She went out to the kitchen to make a pot of tea.

I'm biased. I'm biased against the rattle of typewriters and the niggling boredom of shorthand which girls get fobbed off with instead of being vicars or sailors or racehorse trainers. When I was young, I won a place at university where I was really going to achieve something, but it was taken away from me. Be a secretary, they said. A training in shorthand and typing always gives girls something to fall back on. I should have told them that I didn't want to fall back; that I wanted to stand upright and proud, and march boldly out into the unknown instead of meekly churning out Dear Sirs all day . . .

Opening the kitchen cupboard to find the tea caddy her eye fell upon a bottle of gin which must have been there since before she went away. It was still almost half full. Removing the kettle from the gas stove she searched for a glass. Gin and water, it would have to be. The first sip made her facial muscles contort.

I suppose I'm lucky I haven't had to churn out Dear Sirs all day, but on the other hand it's pretty reprehensible to spend your life teaching people to do what you don't believe in. I wonder how much Emilia believed in it? Oh, Emilia, you dear, strange and complicated old woman, why did you have to choose me? I've been nothing but a pain in the arse to you all these years. You must have known other people you liked better, and who would have been more worthy. What about Miss Sturgeon, for instance? An honest, stout-hearted old spinster, steady as a rock and in love with her motorcar . . .

She wandered through to the living-room, glass in hand. She looked at Emilia's picture, still in its wrappings, propped against the wall, and at the jug of marigolds that were dropping their petals. She stood contemplating herself in the mirror that hung over the fireplace.

And your petals are dropping too, dear. Trembling on the brink of forty and silver threads among the dark brown. Life, and certainly love, have almost passed you by so go out and do something different. Tell them to stuff Gathercoles and all that goes with it — or better still, give it to charity and then go out and join the war. Be a land girl and learn how to milk a cow.

Someone was knocking on the door. She decided not to answer. They knocked again, more authoritatively, so swallowing the last of the gin she went to open it.

'Hullo, chicken.'

'No . . .' A moment of utter disbelief, then she peered closer. 'Oh, my God, Effie — it really *is* you, is it?'

'Of course it's me, you daft thing!'

Apart from the glimpse of joyous red hair, the change in her appearance was sensational. Despite the warmth of the day she was wearing a full-length mink coat, very high-heeled black patent leather shoes, a large black hat with a spotted eye-veil and enough diamonds to sink a small boat,

'Effie Morris — where on earth have you been?'

Effie laughed, disclosing the gold filling in one of her teeth. She kicked her shoes off and embraced Cassie, and it was like being enveloped by a large strong cat.

'D'yer like me fair coat then, petal? An' I got four more; there's me sable fair jacket, me chinchilla fair coat, me full-length ocelot, me—'

'So far as I know you've still got some poor lonely old bit of fur awaiting collection in Swears & Wells, except they've probably lost it by now — but oh, *Effie*!' They embraced again.

'I don't cur if they have lost it,' Effie said, straightening her hat. 'I've gorrall the fairs I'm likely to want, but ooh I've been dyin' to get back home—'

She followed Cassie out to the kitchen, and once again Cassie went through the preliminary motions of making tea then poured two gins instead.

'D'you mind it with water?'

'Try me.'

'Come on now, Effie, tell all. We'd made our minds up that you'd been kidnapped by white slavers—'

'So I had. Well, I wasn't exactly carried off kickin' an' screamin' like, but that's what it amounted to. Lopez told me all about this hotel place in B.A. where they paid a lot of money to dance with girls with red hur, and although I didn't really believe it I thought I'd give it a go, like.'

'But why didn't you even say goodbye, you rotten thing?'

'I didn't make me mind up until the last minute, and I didn't want anyone unmaking it for me.'

'So go on, what was it like?' They sat down opposite one another with their feet tucked up, Effie still wearing her hat and coat.

'It was a house.'

'You mean a brothel? So all the rumours were really true about girls being . . .' Cassie stared at her in awed fascination. 'What was it like? What did you have to do?'

'Oh, this and that, depending on the client.'

'But, Effie, how ghastly! And did they keep you locked up and everything, and make you walk about in your knickers?'

'In that place,' Effie said with a raucous guffaw, 'knickers were rarer than balls on a maiden aunt. No, I didn't cur for it much to start with, but having got meself out there it was up to me to do something about it. So I started giving a hand with the accounts, and when they found I was the only one who could type they made me manageress and I only helped out upstairs when there was a rush on. To cut a long story short, I've now got three houses of me own.'

'What — *brothels*?'

'Don't keep sayin' that word, chicken. Then when I haird the war was comin' I thought it's high time I got back to Liverpool. I think everybody wants to be back where they belong when there's a war . . .'

She sighed complacently, and Cassie sat gazing at her with ever mounting incredulity.

'So all in all, you must be about the most dazzlingly successful pupil Gathercoles ever turned out—' She began to laugh, and still laughing went out to the kitchen to refill their glasses.

'If ever I had a daughter — an' I suppose I've left it a bit late now — I'd see she lairned shorthand and typing. I mean, apart from ju-jitsu, it's the best means of defence she could have, isn't it?'

Still laughing, Cassie groped for her handkerchief and wiped her eyes.

'By the way,' continued Effie, ignoring her, 'have you seen Arnold? He's come back too, and he was asking about you.'

'Oh?'

'He an' his wife have parted and someone said she'd gone off to Russia, which is why he can't get divorced.'

'Gerraway!' Cassie's laughter, now semi-hysterical, bubbled up again.

'An' he says he's given up party politics for the duration. As I say, he was lookin' for you but somebody told him you'd gone away.'

'So I had. I was in Luxembourg.' Funny how the word 'Luxembourg' extinguished her laughter.

'Ooh, where's that? Was it nice?'

'Yes. Very nice. I was with a Dr Kremer.' It was the first time she had mentioned his name aloud since her return, and it was like putting a finger on a raw nerve. 'I was sent there by Miss Gathercole.'

'The Gathercole Commercial Academy,' said Effie in a posh voice. She took a large swig from her refilled glass and then leaned back voluptuously. Her hat slid down over her nose. 'Tell me, my deah, how is the effing old place?'

'Fine,' said Cassie. 'And I've just discovered it's mine.'

* * *

Effie's reappearance had a complicated effect on her; surprise, delight, amusement, all those things and more, and they promised to meet again within a day or two. (I'm livin' at the Adelphi, chicken, given me a ring any time . . .) After she left, Cassie wandered out into the square, deep in thought.

It was now mid-afternoon, and the warmth of early September covered the soot-streaked buildings with a soft amber light. Sparrows and pigeons pecked at the gritty dust and some of the leaves were already crisping at the edges.

Without hat or coat she walked down into Grove Street. The old brown trams had now given way to more streamlined models in green and cream, but their sweet melancholy cry was much the same. She went on down Upper Parliament Street, past the flat where Mona had died and past the Rialto. The drone of an aircraft made passers-by look up, but it wasn't a Gerry. Not yet. Liverpool lay basking and strangely tranquil and, sharing the same mood, Cassie watched gangs of workmen erecting static water tanks and building street shelters against what was to come.

'Nice to see 'em with summat to do at last,' remarked an old lady waiting to cross St James Road. She was wearing carpet slippers and a brown felt hat. 'Daresay they're gettin' paid for it an' all!' The idea seemed to please her very much.

In Rodney Street the To Let notice still hung outside Godfrey's flat, and already it had been joined by several others on either side. Rats leaving a sinking ship, Cassie thought. Except that Liverpool will never sink. It's far too tough and far too cussed for that, and I almost think I've grown to love it.

Across in Mount Pleasant the two white urns tastefully arranged with wax flowers still stood on display in the windows of Hoskins's Funeral Parlour, and from behind the premises came the sound of vigorous sawing and the tapping of masons' hammers. A new crop of marble angels was arising, a new stack of coffins mounting in the workshops, presumably for those who didn't make it to the air raid shelters in time. A gruesome thought, but the Emergency Control Committee was now in operation as instructed by the Home Office, and Liverpool's Lord Mayor, her aldermen and the Town Clerk had publicly declared themselves ready for anything. Yet in the mellow sunlight it was ridiculous to take it all too seriously. Tomorrow would be time enough.

Lime Street, Ranalagh Street . . . and in the big stores they were already doing a brisk trade in ladies' siren suits ready for the winter. Walking through to the cafeteria in search of an ice cream Cassie suddenly paused by the haberdashery counter. She recognised the woman who was winding velvet ribbon on her fingers; older now, and with her hair dyed black to match her frock.

'Excuse me.' Cassie hovered. 'How are Ciss and Norah? Are they still here?'

'Well, we don't really know.' The woman slid the ribbon from her fingers, and, after a quick glance to make sure that authority's back was turned, leaned across the counter. 'After years and years of arguing they finally went away on holiday, but they haven't come back.'

A quick vision of Ciss and Norah playing truant among the dubious pleasures of Blackpool made Cassie grin.

'Where did they go to?'

'Austria,' said the woman. 'They *said* they wanted to see the wild flowers, but Miss Shepherd over on hosiery says she thinks there's something very funny about them.' She lowered her voice even more. 'I wouldn't go so far as to mention the word *spies,* but everyone agrees there was something very funny — very funny *indeed* — about them . . .'

'Oh, I can't possibly imagine—'

'Perhaps not,' said the woman, looking mysterious. 'But there's no smoke without fire, is there?'

In the cafeteria Cassie sat eating an ice cream among the portly Liverpool matrons; not as portly or as matronly as the ones in Luxembourg (oh shut up, shut up about Luxembourg, it never really happened . . .) and on the way out she bought herself a new torch with a little circle of black paper inside so that it complied with the blackout regulations.

It was almost half past four now, and there were no children coming out of school. They had all gone to their places of safety, as it said in the paper that the Crown Jewels had been buried in a field somewhere. We were doing our best to hide or protect or build scaffolding around all our most precious things, but a lot of them would just have to take their chance. No one really knew what was going to happen, but Liverpool would survive. Liverpool, like Effing Effie, would survive anything.

She walked on down to the solicitor's office in Dale Street.

* * *

Ten minutes to nine on the first morning of September term at the Gathercole Commercial Academy in Hockenhall Street.

The smell of chalk and paper and newly oiled typewriters, and up on the top floor of the imposing yet ramshackle old building the rhythmic stamp-stamp of machinery. The pillbox girls were back and rumoured to be making government issue containers for VD ointment to be issued to the troops. The back basement had been hastily converted into a shelter against enemy action, and red buckets filled with sand stood outside each classroom.

Miss Sturgeon in her dark blue smock clapped her hands in the doorway of the cloakroom and asked the seventy-odd short-skirted, red-lipsticked young ladies to accompany her upstairs. They did so and stood jostling and fidgeting in the dark green hall illuminated by the stained-glass window.

'Oh heck, are we going to have prayers?'

'Don't be daft — people don't pray in offices . . .'

They waited, while upstairs Cassie was saying defiantly: 'It's no use expecting me to go on with all that stuff about being proud to be secretaries. If it happens to make them feel proud, well, bully for them.'

'I must admit that I don't feel totally at ease, either.'

She and Arnold sat facing one another, Cassie behind Emilia's large and imposing desk while Arnold crouched untidily behind the smaller one that had once belonged to Wilfred. He looked even thinner, and his ears still stuck out.

'But it's better than footling about with politics. Nothing could be worse or more boring than that.'

'Politics are in abeyance until after the war, by which time there'll be a huge and natural swing back to Labour, you mark my words—'

'Now then, Arnold, for God's sake don't start—'

'In the meantime, I'm still hoping they'll accept me in the fire service.'

'With flat feet and bad eyesight I fear you must reconcile yourself to a civilian role,' she said repressively. 'Come on, it's time to go down and face them.'

She rose from the desk, then gave a convulsive little choke as her glance encountered the two gold-framed portraits hanging opposite.

'It's no use, Arnold, I can't. She was so *good* at it. She had such wisdom, and such love . . .'

'And so have you.' He came across and put his arm round her shoulders, easily, comfortably, because they were both the same height. 'Don't worry, you'll make a marvellous success of it.'

'Success,' she said. 'That's all I used to think about, at one time.'

The girls in the hall stopped fidgeting as a very tall, dark-haired woman slowly descended the ornate staircase. She paused, four steps from the bottom, and surveyed them all with a grave smile.

'Good morning.'

'Good morning,' they all replied.

'The name is Marlow,' Cassie said graciously. 'I am Miss Marlow, and my first duty is to welcome you to the Gathercole Commercial Academy . . .'

THE END

THE JOFFE BOOKS STORY

We began in 2014 when Jasper agreed to publish his mum's much-rejected romance novel and it became a bestseller.

Since then we've grown into the largest independent publisher in the UK. We're extremely proud to publish some of the very best writers in the world, including Joy Ellis, Faith Martin, Caro Ramsay, Helen Forrester, Simon Brett and Robert Goddard. Everyone at Joffe Books loves reading and we never forget that it all begins with the magic of an author telling a story.

We are proud to publish talented first-time authors, as well as established writers whose books we love introducing to a new generation of readers.

We have been shortlisted for Independent Publisher of the Year at the British Book Awards three times, in 2020, 2021 and 2022, and for the Diversity and Inclusivity Award at the Independent Publishing Awards in 2022.

We built this company with your help, and we love to hear from you, so please email us about absolutely anything bookish at: feedback@joffebooks.com.

If you want to receive free books every Friday and hear about all our new releases, join our mailing list: www.joffebooks.com/contact

And when you tell your friends about us, just remember: it's pronounced Joffe as in coffee or toffee!

ALSO BY JUDY GARDINER

STANDALONES

MY LOVE, MY LAND

WHO WAS SYLVIA?

THE ROSE BOWL

ECHOES AND SHADOWS

MISS GATHERCOLE'S GIRLS

Printed in Great Britain
by Amazon

24751604R00229